EVErYTHING IS ILLUMINATED

EVERYTHING IS ILLUMINATED

a novel

JONATHAN SAFRAN FOER

HAMISH HAMILTON
an imprint of
PENGUIN BOOKS

HAMISH HAMILTON

Published by the Penguin Group
Penguin Books Ltd, 80 Strand, London WC2R ORL, England
Penguin Putnam Inc., 375 Hudson Street, New York, New York 10014, USA
Penguin Books Australia Ltd, 250 Camberwell Road,
Camberwell, Victoria 3124, Australia
Penguin Books Canada Ltd, 10 Alcorn Avenue, Toronto, Ontario, Canada M4V 3B2
Penguin Books India (P) Ltd, 11 Community Centre,
Panchsheel Park, New Delhi - 110 017, India
Penguin Books (NZ) Ltd, Cnr Rosedale and Airborne Roads,
Albany, Auckland, New Zealand
Penguin Books (South Africa) (Pty) Ltd, 24 Sturdee Avenue,
Rosebank 2196, South Africa

Penguin Books Ltd, Registered Offices: 80 Strand, London WC2R ORL, England

www.penguin.com

First published by Houghton Mifflin Company 2002
Published by Hamish Hamilton 2002
5

A portion of this book previously appeared in the *New Yorker*

This is a work of fiction. Names, characters and incidents are the product of
the author's imagination, except in the case of historical figures and events,
which are used fictitiously, and, of course, in the case of JSF himself

Visit the author's website: www.theprojectmuseum.com

This book is set in Janson Text and Filosophia
Printed in Great Britain by Clays Ltd, St Ives plc

A CIP catalogue record for this book is available from the British Library

HARDBACK ISBN 0-241-14166-4
TRADE PAPERBACK ISBN 0-241-14183-4

ACKNOWLEDGEMENTS
At least once every day since I met her, I have felt blessed to know Nicole Aragi.
She inspires me not only to try to write more ambitiously, but to smile more widely
and to have a fuller, better heart. I am so, so grateful. (*Atyab lee itha entee toukleha.*)
And it has been my pleasure becoming close – from afar – with the wonderful people at
Hamish Hamilton. Andrew Kidd, in particular, has a unique gift for making things feel
special, and for making them special. Thanks, also, to Abner Stein, not only for putting
this book in the hands of the ideal publisher, but for treating me like an old friend.
And, finally, to Paul Marsh, whose office is full of good work and good feelings.

Simply and impossibly:

FOR MY FAMILY

An overture to the commencement of a very RIGID journey

MY LEGAL NAME is Alexander Perchov. But all of my many friends dub me Alex, because that is a more flaccid-to-utter version of my legal name. Mother dubs me Alexi-stop-spleening-me!, because I am always spleening her. If you want to know why I am always spleening her, it is because I am always elsewhere with friends, and disseminating so much currency, and performing so many things that can spleen a mother. Father used to dub me Shapka, for the fur hat I would don even in the summer month. He ceased dubbing me that because I ordered him to cease dubbing me that. It sounded boyish to me, and I have always thought of myself as very potent and generative. I have many many girls, believe me, and they all have a different name for me. One dubs me Baby, not because I am a baby, but because she attends to me. Another dubs me All Night. Do you want to know why? I have a girl who dubs me Currency, because I disseminate so much currency around her. She licks my chops for it. I have a miniature brother who dubs me Alli. I do not dig this name very much, but I dig him very much, so OK, I permit him to dub me Alli. As for his name, it is Little Igor, but Father dubs him Clumsy One, because he is always promenading into things. It was only four days previous that he made his eye blue from a mismanagement with a brick wall. If you're wondering what my bitch's name is, it is Sammy Davis, Junior, Junior. She has this name because Sammy Davis, Junior was Grandfather's beloved singer, and the bitch is his, not mine, because I am not the one who thinks he is blind.

As for me, I was sired in 1977, the same year as the hero of this story. In truth, my life has been very ordinary. As I mentioned before, I do many good things with myself and others, but they are ordinary things. I dig American movies. I dig Negroes, particularly Michael Jackson. I dig to disseminate very much currency at famous nightclubs in Odessa. Lamborghini Countaches are excellent, and so are cappuccinos. Many girls want to be carnal with me in many good arrangements, notwithstanding the Inebriated Kangaroo, the Gorky Tickle, and the Unyielding Zookeeper. If you want to know why so many girls want to be with me, it is because I am a very premium person to be with. I am homely, and also severely funny, and these are winning things. But nonetheless, I know many people who dig rapid cars and famous discotheques. There are so many who perform the Sputnik Bosom Dalliance—which is always terminated with a slimy underface—that I cannot tally them on all of my hands. There are even many people named Alex. (Three in my house alone!) That is why I was so effervescent to go to Lutsk and translate for Jonathan Safran Foer. It would be unordinary.

I had performed recklessly well in my second year of English at university. This was a very majestic thing I did because my instructor was having shit between his brains. Mother was so proud of me, she said, "Alexi-stop-spleening-me! You have made me so proud of you." I inquired her to purchase me leather pants, but she said no. "Shorts?" "No." Father was also so proud. He said, "Shapka," and I said, "Do not dub me that," and he said, "Alex, you have made Mother so proud."

Mother is a humble woman. Very, very humble. She toils at a small café one hour distance from our home. She presents food and drink to customers there, and says to me, "I mount the autobus for an hour to work all day doing things I hate. You want to know why? It is for you, Alexi-stop-spleening-me! One day you will do things for me that you hate. That is what it means to be a family." What she does not clutch is that I already do things for her that I hate. I listen to her when she talks to me. I resist complaining about my pygmy allowance. And did I mention that I do not spleen her nearly so much as I desire to? But I do not do these things because we are a family. I do them because they are common decencies. That is an idiom that the hero taught me. I do them because I am not a big fucking asshole. That is another idiom that the hero taught me.

Father toils for a travel agency, denominated Heritage Touring. It is for Jewish people, like the hero, who have cravings to leave that ennobled country America and visit humble towns in Poland and Ukraine. Father's agency scores a translator, guide, and driver for the Jews, who try to unearth places where their families once existed. OK, I had never met a Jewish person until the voyage. But this was their fault, not mine, as I had always been willing, and one might even write lukewarm, to meet one. I will be truthful again and mention that before the voyage I had the opinion that Jewish people were having shit between their brains. This is because all I knew of Jewish people was that they paid Father very much currency in order to make vacations *from* America *to* Ukraine. But then I met Jonathan Safran Foer, and I will tell you, he is not having shit between his brains. He is an ingenious Jew.

So as for the Clumsy One, who I never ever dub the Clumsy One but always Little Igor, he is a first-rate boy. It is now evident to me that he will become a very potent and generative man, and that his brain will have many muscles. We do not speak in volumes, because he is such a silent person, but I am certain that we are friends, and I do not think I would be lying if I wrote that we are paramount friends. I have tutored Little Igor to be a man of this world. For an example, I exhibited him a smutty magazine three days yore, so that he should be appraised of the many positions in which I am carnal. "This is the sixty-nine," I told him, presenting the magazine in front of him. I put my fingers — two of them — on the action, so that he would not overlook it. "Why is it dubbed sixty-nine?" he asked, because he is a person hot on fire with curiosity. "It was invented in 1969. My friend Gregory knows a friend of the nephew of the inventor." "What did people do before 1969?" "Merely blowjobs and masticating box, but never in chorus." He will be made a VIP if I have a thing to do with it.

This is where the story begins.

But first I am burdened to recite my good appearance. I am unequivocally tall. I do not know any women who are taller than me. The women I know who are taller than me are lesbians, for whom 1969 was a very momentous year. I have handsome hairs, which are split in the middle. This is because Mother used to split them on the side when I was a boy, and to spleen her I split them in the middle. "Alexi-stop-spleening-me!," she said, "you appear mentally unbalanced with your hairs split like that." She did not intend it, I know. Very often Mother utters things that I know she does not intend. I have an aristocratic smile and like to punch people. My stomach is very strong, although it presently lacks muscles. Father is a fat man, and Mother is also. This does not disquiet me, because my stomach is very strong, even if it appears very fat. I will describe my eyes and then begin the story. My eyes are blue and resplendent. Now I will begin the story.

Father obtained a telephone call from the American office of Heritage Touring. They required a driver, guide, and translator for a young man who would be in Lutsk at the dawn of the month of July. This was a troublesome supplication, because at the dawn of July, Ukraine was to celebrate the first birthday of its ultramodern constitution, which makes us feel very nationalistic, and so many people would be on vacation in foreign places. It was an impossible situation, like the 1984 Olympics. But Father is an overawing man who always obtains what he desires. "Shapka," he said on the phone to me, who was at home enjoying the greatest of all documentary movies, *The Making of "Thriller,"* "what was the language you studied this year at school?" "Do not dub me Shapka," I said. "Alex," he said, "what was the language you studied this year at school?" "The language of English," I told him. "Are you good and fine at it?" he asked me. "I am fluid," I told him, hoping I might make him proud enough to buy me the zebra-skin seat coverings of my dreams. "Excellent, Shapka," he said. "Do not dub me that," I said. "Excellent, Alex. Excellent. You must nullify any plans you possess for the first week of the month of July." "I do not possess any plans," I said to him. "Yes you do," he said.

Now is a befitting time to mention Grandfather, who is also fat, but yet more fat than my parents. OK, I will mention him. He has gold teeth and cultivates ample hairs on his face to comb by the dusk of every day. He toiled for fifty years at many employments, primarily farming, and later machine manipulating. His final employment was at Heritage Touring, where he commenced to toil in the 1950s and persevered until of late. But now he is retarded and lives on our street. My grandmother died two years yore of a cancer in her brain, and Grandfather became very melancholy, and also, he says, blind. Father does not believe him, but purchased Sammy Davis, Junior, Junior for him nonetheless, because a Seeing Eye bitch is not only for blind people but for people who pine for the negative of loneliness. (I should not have used "purchased," because in truth Father did not purchase Sammy Davis, Junior, Junior, but only received her from the home for forgetful dogs. Because of this, she is not a real Seeing Eye bitch, and is also mentally deranged.) Grandfather disperses most of the day at our house, viewing television. He yells at me often. "Sasha!" he yells. "Sasha, do not be so lazy! Do not be so worthless! Do something! Do something worthy!" I never rejoinder him, and never spleen him with intentions, and never understand what worthy means. He did not have the unappetizing habit of yelling at Little Igor and me before Grandmother died. That is how we are certain that he does not intend it, and that is why we can forgive him. I discovered him crying once, in front of the television. (Jonathan, this part about Grandfather must remain amid you and me, yes?) The weather report was exhibiting, so I was certain that it was not something melancholy on the television that made him cry. I never mentioned it, because it was a common decency to not mention it.

Grandfather's name is also Alexander. Supplementally is Father's. We are all the primogenitory children in our families, which brings us tremendous honor, on the scale of the sport of baseball, which was invented in Ukraine. I will dub my first child Alexander. If you want to know what will occur if my first child is a girl, I will tell you. He will not be a girl. Grandfather was sired in Odessa in 1918. He has never departed Ukraine. The remotest he ever traveled was Kiev, and that was for when my uncle wedded The Cow. When I was a boy, Grandfather would tutor that Odessa is the most beautiful city in the world, because the vodka is cheap, and so are the women. He would manufacture funnies with Grandmother before she died about how he was in love with other women who were not her. She knew it was only funnies because she would laugh in volumes. "Anna," he would say, "I am going to marry that one with the pink hat." And she would say, "To whom are you going to marry her?" And he would say, "To me." I would laugh very much in the back seat, and she would say to him, "But you are no priest." And he would say, "I am today." And she would say, "Today you believe in God?" And he would say, "Today I believe in love." Father commanded me never to mention Grandmother to Grandfather. "It will make him melancholy, Shapka," Father said. "Do not dub me that," I said. "It will make him melancholy, Alex, and it will make him think he is more blind. Let him forget." So I never mention her, because unless I do not want to, I do what Father tells me to do. Also, he is a first-rate puncher.

After telephoning me, Father telephoned Grandfather to inform him that he would be the driver of our journey. If you want to know who would be the guide, the answer is there would be no guide. Father said that a guide was not an indispensable thing, because Grandfather knew a beefy amount from all of his years at Heritage Touring. Father dubbed him an expert. (At the time when he said this, it seemed like a very reasonable thing to say. But how does this make you feel, Jonathan, in the luminescence of everything that occurred?)

When the three of us, the three men named Alex, gathered in Father's house that night to converse the journey, Grandfather said, "I do not want to do it. I am retarded, and I did not become a retarded person in order to have to perform shit such as this. I am done with it." "I do not care what you want," Father told him. Grandfather punched the table with much violence and shouted, "Do not forget who is who!" I thought that that would be the end of the conversation. But Father said something queer. "Please." And then he said something even queerer. He said, "Father." I must confess that there is so much I do not understand. Grandfather returned to his chair and said, "This is the final one. I will never do it again."

So we made schemes to procure the hero at the Lvov train station on 2 July, at 1500 of the afternoon. Then we would be for two days in the area of Lutsk. "Lutsk?" Grandfather said. "You did not say it was Lutsk." "It is Lutsk," Father said. Grandfather became in thought. "He is looking for the town his grandfather came from," Father said, "and someone, Augustine he calls her, who salvaged his grandfather from the war. He desires to write a book about his grandfather's village." "Oh," I said, "so he is intelligent?" "No," Father corrected. "He has low-grade brains.

The American office informs me that he telephones them every day and manufactures numerous half-witted queries about finding suitable food." "There will certainly be sausage," I said. "Of course," Father said. "He is only half-witted." Here I will repeat that the hero is a very ingenious Jew. "Where is the town?" I asked. "The name of the town is Trachimbrod." "Trachimbrod?" Grandfather asked. "It is near 50 kilometers from Lutsk," Father said. "He possesses a map and is sanguine of the coordinates. It should be simple."

Grandfather and I viewed television for several hours after Father reposed. We are both people who remain conscious very tardy. (I was near-at-hand to writing that we both relish to remain conscious tardy, but that is not faithful.) We viewed an American television program that had the words in Russian at the bottom of the screen. It was about a Chinaman who was resourceful with a bazooka. We also viewed the weather report. The weatherman said that the weather would be very abnormal the next day, but that the next day after that would be normal. Amid Grandfather and I was a silence you could cut with a scimitar. The only time that either of us spoke was when he rotated to me during an advertisement for McDonald's McPorkburgers and said, "I do not want to drive ten hours to an ugly city to attend to a very spoiled Jew."

IT WAS March 18, 1791, when Trachim B's double-axle wagon either did or did not pin him against the bottom of the Brod River. The young W twins were the first to see the curious flotsam rising to the surface: wandering snakes of white string, a crushed-velvet glove with outstretched fingers, barren spools, schmootzy pince-nez, rasp- and boysenberries, feces, frillwork, the shards of a shattered atomizer, the bleeding red-ink script of a resolution: *I will... I will...*

Hannah wailed. Chana waded into the cold water, pulling up above her knees the yarn ties at the ends of her britches, sweeping the rising life-debris to her sides as she waded farther. *What are you doing over there!* the disgraced usurer Yankel D called, kicking up shoreline mud as he hobbled toward the girls. He extended one hand to Chana and held the other, as always, over the incriminating abacus bead he was forced by shtetl proclamation to wear on a string around his neck. *Stay back from the water! You will get hurt!*

The good gefiltefishmonger Bitzl Bitzl R watched the commotion from his paddleboat, which was fastened with twine to one of his traps. *What's going on over there?* he shouted to shore. *Is that you, Yankel? Is there some sort of trouble?*

It's the Well-Regarded Rabbi's twins, Yankel called back. *They're playing in the water and I'm afraid someone will get hurt!*

It's turning up the most unusual things! Chana laughed, splashing at the mass that grew like a garden around her. She picked up the hands of a baby doll, and those of a grandfather clock. Umbrella ribs. A skeleton key. The articles rose on the crowns of bubbles that burst when they reached the surface. The slightly younger and less cautious twin raked her fingers through the water and each time came up with something new: a yellow pinwheel, a muddy hand mirror, the petals of some sunken forget-me-not, silt and cracked black pepper, a packet of seeds...

But her slightly older and more cautious sister, Hannah—identical in every way save the hairs connecting her eyebrows—watched from shore and cried. The disgraced usurer Yankel D took her into his arms, pressed her head against his chest, murmured, *Here...here...*, and called to Bitzl Bitzl: *Row to the Well-Regarded Rabbi's and bring him back with you. Also bring Menasha the physician and Isaac the man of law. Quickly!*

The mad squire Sofiowka N, whose name the shtetl would later take for maps and Mormon census records, emerged from behind a tree. *I have seen everything that happened,* he said hysterically. *I witnessed it all. The wagon was moving too fast for this dirt road — the only thing worse than to be late to your own wedding is to be late to the wedding of the girl who should have been your wife — and it suddenly flipped itself, and if that's not exactly the truth, then the wagon didn't flip itself, but was itself flipped by a wind from Kiev or Odessa or wherever, and if that doesn't seem quite correct, then what happened was — and I would swear on my lily-white name to this — an angel with grave-stone-feathered wings descended from heaven to take Trachim back with him, for Trachim was too good for this world. Of course, who isn't? We are all too good for each other.*

Trachim? Yankel asked, allowing Hannah to finger the incriminating bead. *Wasn't Trachim the shoemaker from Lutsk who died half a year ago of pneumonia?*

Look at this! Chana called, giggling, holding above her head the jack of cunnilingus from a dirty deck of cards.

No, Sofiowka said. *That man's name was Trachum with a* u. *This is with an* i. *And that Trachum died in the Night of the Longest Night. No, wait. No, wait. He died from being an artist.*

And this! Chana shrieked with joy, holding up a faded map of the universe.

Get out of the water! Yankel hollered at her, raising his voice louder than he would have wished at the Well-Regarded Rabbi's daughter, or any young girl. *You will get hurt!*

Chana ran to shore. The deep green water obscured the zodiac as the star chart sank to the river's bottom, coming to rest, like a veil, on the horse's face.

The shutters of the shtetl's windows were opening to the commotion (curiosity being the only thing the citizens shared). The accident had happened by the small falls—the part of shore that marked the current division of the shtetl into its two sections, the Jewish Quarter and the Human Three-Quarters. All so-called sacred activities—religious studies, kosher butchering, bargaining, etc.—were contained within the Jewish Quarter. Those activities concerned with the humdrum of daily existence—secular studies, communal justice, buying and selling, etc.— took place in the Human Three-Quarters. Straddling the two was the Upright Synagogue. (The ark itself was built along the Jewish/Human fault line, such that one of the two Torah scrolls would exist in each zone.) As the ratio of sacred to secular shifted—usually no more than a hair in this or that direction, save for that exceptional hour in 1764, immediately following the Pogrom of Beaten Chests, when the shtetl was completely secular—so did the fault line, drawn in chalk from Radziwell Forest to the river. And so was the synagogue lifted and moved. It was in 1783 that wheels were attached, making the shtetl's ever-changing negotiation of Jewishness and Humanness less of a schlep.

I understand there has been an accident, panted Shloim W, the humble antiques salesman who survived off charity, unable to part with any of his candelabras, figurines, or hourglasses since his wife's untimely death.

How did you know? Yankel asked.

Bitzl Bitzl yelled to me from his boat on his way to the Well-Regarded Rabbi's. I knocked on as many doors as I could on my way here.

Good, Yankel said. *We'll need a shtetl proclamation.*

Are we sure he's dead? someone asked.

Quite, Sofiowka assured. *Dead as he was before his parents met. Or deader, maybe, for then he was at least a bullet in his father's cock and an emptiness in his mother's belly.*

Did you try to save him? Yankel asked.

No.

Cover their eyes, Shloim told Yankel, gesturing at the girls. He quickly undressed himself—revealing a belly larger than most, and a back matted with ringlets of thick black hair—and dove into the water. Feathers washed over him on the wings of water swells. Unstrung pearls and ungummed teeth. Blood clots, Merlot, and splintered chandelier crystal. The rising wreckage became increasingly dense, until he couldn't see his hands in front of him. *Where? Where?*

Did you find him? the man of law Isaac M asked when Shloim finally surfaced. *Is it clear how long he's been down there?*

Was he alone or with a wife? asked grieving Shanda T, widow of the deceased philosopher Pinchas T, who, in his only notable paper, "To the Dust: From Man You Came and to Man You Shall Return," argued it would be possible, in theory, for life and art to be reversed.

A powerful wind swept through the shtetl, making it whistle. Those studying obscure texts in dimly lit rooms looked up. Lovers making amends and promises, amendments and excuses, fell silent. The lonely candle dipper, Mordechai C, submerged his hands in a vat of warm blue wax.

He did have a wife, Sofiowka inserted, his left hand diving deep into his trouser pocket. *I remember her well. She had a set of such voluptuous tits. God, she had great tits. Who could forget those? They were, oh God, they were great. I'd trade all of the words I've since learned to be young again, oh yes, yes, getting a good suck on those titties. Yes I would! Yes I would!*

How do you know these things? someone asked.

I went to Rovno once, as a child, on an errand for my father. It was to this Trachim's house. His surname escapes my tongue, but I remember quite well that he was Trachim with an i, that he had a young wife with a great set of tits, a small apartment with many knickknacks, and a scar from his eye to his mouth, or his mouth to his eye. One or the other.

YOU WERE ABLE TO SEE HIS FACE AS HE WAGONED BY? the Well-Regarded Rabbi asked in a holler as his girls ran to hide under opposite ends of his prayer shawl. *THE SCAR?*

And then, ay yay yay, I saw him again when I was a young man applying myself in Lvov. Trachim was making a delivery of peaches, if I remember, or perhaps plums, to a house of schoolgirls across the street. Or was he a postman? Yes, it was love letters.

Of course he couldn't be alive anymore, said Menasha the physician, opening his medical bag. He removed several pages of death certificates, which were picked up by another breeze and sent into the trees. Some would fall with the leaves that September. Some would fall with the trees generations later.

And even if he were alive, we couldn't free him, said Shloim, drying himself behind a large rock. *It won't be possible to get to the wagon until all of its contents have risen.*

WE MUST MAKE A SHTETL PROCLAMATION, proclaimed the Well-Regarded Rabbi, mustering a more authoritative holler.

Now what was his name, exactly? Menasha asked, touching quill to tongue.

Can we say for sure that he had a wife? grieving Shanda asked, touching hand to heart.

Did the girls see anything? asked Avrum R, the lapidary, who wore no rings himself (although the Well-Regarded Rabbi had promised he knew of a young woman in Lodz who could make him happy [forever]).

The girls saw nothing, Sofiowka said. *I saw that they saw nothing.*

And the twins, this time both of them, began to cry.

But we can't leave the matter entirely to his word, Shloim said, gesturing at Sofiowka, who returned the favor with a gesture of his own.

Do not ask the girls, Yankel said. *Leave them alone. They've been through enough.*

By now, almost all of the shtetl's three hundred–odd citizens had gathered to debate that about which they knew nothing. The less a citizen knew, the more adamantly he or she argued. There was nothing new in this. A month before there had been the question of whether it might send a better message to the children to plug, finally, the bagel's hole. Two months before there had been the cruel and comic debate over the question of typesetting, and before that the question of Polish identity, which moved many to tears, and many to laughter, and all to more questions. And still to come would be other questions to debate, and others after that. Questions from the beginning of time—whenever that was—to whenever would be the end. From *ashes?* to *ashes?*

PERHAPS, the Well-Regarded Rabbi said, raising his hands even higher, his voice even louder, *WE DO NOT HAVE TO SETTLE THE MATTER AT ALL. WHAT IF WE NEVER FILL OUT A DEATH CERTIFICATE? WHAT IF WE GIVE THE BODY A PROPER BURIAL, BURN ANYTHING THAT WASHES ASHORE, AND ALLOW LIFE TO GO ON IN THE FACE OF THIS DEATH?*

But we need a proclamation, said Froida Y, the candy maker.

Not if the shtetl proclaims otherwise, corrected Isaac.

Perhaps we should try to contact his wife, said grieving Shanda.

Perhaps we should begin to gather the remains, said Eliezar Z, the dentist.

And in the braid of argument, young Hannah's voice almost went unnoticed as she peeked her head from beneath the fringed wing of her father's prayer shawl.

I see something.

WHAT? her father asked, quieting the others. *WHAT DO YOU SEE?*

Over there, pointing to the frothing water.

In the middle of the string and feathers, surrounded by candles and soaked matches, prawns, pawns, and silk tassels that curtsied like jellyfish, was a baby girl, still mucus-glazed, still pink as the inside of a plum.

The twins hid their bodies under their father's tallis, like ghosts. The horse at the bottom of the river, shrouded by the sunken night sky, closed its heavy eyes. The prehistoric ant in Yankel's ring, which had lain motionless in the honey-colored amber since long before Noah hammered the first plank, hid its head between its many legs, in shame.

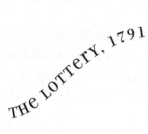

THE LOTTERY, 1791

BITZL BITZL R was able to recover the wagon a few days later with the help of a group of strong men from Kolki, and his traps saw more action than ever. But sifting through the remains, they didn't find a body. For the next one hundred fifty years, the shtetl would host an annual contest to "find" Trachim, although a shtetl proclamation withdrew the reward in 1793 — on Menasha's counsel that any ordinary corpse would begin to break apart after two years in water, so searching not only would be pointless but could result in rather offensive findings, or even worse, multiple rewards — and the contest became more of a festival, for which the line of short-tempered bakers P would create particular pastry treats, and the girls of the shtetl would dress as the twins dressed on that fateful day: in wool britches with yarn ties, and canvas blouses with blue-fringed butterfly collars. Men came from great distances to dive for the cotton sacks that the Float Queen would throw into the Brod, all but one of which, the golden sack, were filled with earth.

There were those who thought that Trachim would never be found, that the current brushed enough loose sediment over him to properly bury his body. These people laid stones on the shoreside when they made their monthly cemetery rounds, and said things like:

Poor Trachim, I didn't know him well, but I sure could have.

or

I miss you, Trachim. Without having ever met you, I do.

or

Rest, Trachim, rest. And make safe our flour mill.

There were those who suspected that he was not pinned under his wagon but swept out to sea, with the secrets of his life kept forever inside him, like a love note in a bottle, to be found one morning by an unsuspecting couple on a romantic beach stroll. It's possible that he, or some part of him, washed up on the sands of the Black Sea, or in Rio, or that he made it all the way to Ellis Island.

Or perhaps a widow found him and took him in: bought him an easy chair, changed his sweater every morning, shaved his face until the hair stopped growing, took him faithfully to bed with her every night, whispered sweet nothings into what was left of his ear, laughed with him over black coffee, cried with him over yellowing pictures, talked greenly about having kids of her own, began to miss him before she became sick, left him everything in her will, thought of only him as she died, always knew he was a fiction but believed in him anyway.

Some argued that there was never a body at all. Trachim wanted to be dead without being dead, the con artist. He packed a wagon with all of his possessions, rode it into the nondescript, nameless shtetl—which was soon to be known across eastern Poland for its yearly festival, Trachimday, and to carry his name like an orphan baby (except for maps and Mormon census records, for which it would go by Sofiowka)—patted his nameless horse its last pat, and spurred it into the undertow. Was he escaping debt? An unfavorable arranged marriage? Lies that had caught up with him? Was his death an essential stage in the continuation of his life?

Of course there are those who pointed to Sofiowka's madness, how he would sit naked in the fountain of the prostrate mermaid, caressing her scaly tuches like a newborn's fontanel, caressing his own better half as if there were nothing in the world wrong with beating one's boner, wherever, whenever. Or how he was once found on the Well-Regarded Rabbi's front lawn, bound in white string, and said he tied one around his index finger to remember something terribly important, and fearing he would forget the index finger, he tied a string around his pinky, and then one from waist to neck, and fearing he would forget this one, he tied a string from ear to tooth to scrotum to heel, and used his body to remember his body, but in the end could remember only the string. Is this someone to trust for a story?

And the baby? My great-great-great-great-great-grandmother? This is a more difficult problem, for it's relatively easy to reason how a life could be lost in a river, but for one to arise from it?

Harry V, the shtetl's master logician and resident pervert—who had been working for as many years and with as little success as one could imagine on his magnum opus, "The Host of Hoists," which, he promised, contained the tightest of tight logical proofs that God indiscriminatingly loves the indiscriminate lover—put forth a lengthy argument concerning the presence of another on the ill-starred wagon: Trachim's wife. Perhaps, Harry argued, her water broke while the two were munching deviled eggs in a meadow between shtetls, and perhaps Trachim urged the wagon to dangerous speeds in order to get her to a doctor before the baby squirmed out like a flapping flounder from a fisherman's grip. As the waves of her tidal contractions began to break over her head, Trachim turned to his wife, perhaps put his callused hand on her soft face, perhaps took his eyes off the riddled road, and perhaps inadvertently steered into the river. Perhaps the wagon flipped, the bodies plunged under its weight, and perhaps, sometime between her mother's last breath and her father's final attempt to free himself, the baby was born. Perhaps. But not even Harry could explain the absence of an umbilical cord.

The Wisps of Ardisht—that clan of artisan smokers in Rovno who smoked so much they smoked even when they were not smoking, and were condemned by shtetl proclamation to a life of rooftops as shingle layers and chimney sweeps—believed that my great-great-great-great-great-grandmother was Trachim reborn. In his moment of afterworldly judgment, as his softening body was presented before the Keeper of those glorious and barbed Gates, something went wrong. There was unfinished business. The soul was not ready to transcend, but was sent back, given a chance to right a previous generation's wrong. This, of course, doesn't make any sense. But what does?

More concerned with the baby's future than its past, the Well-Regarded Rabbi offered no official interpretation of her origins for either the shtetl or *The Book of Antecedents*, but took her in as his own responsibility until her final home should be decided. He brought her to the Upright Synagogue—for not even a baby, he swore, should set foot in the Slouching Synagogue (wherever it happened to be on that given day)—and tucked her makeshift crib in the ark while the men in long black suits hollered prayers at the top of their lungs. *HOLY, HOLY, HOLY IS THE LORD OF HOSTS! THE WHOLE WORLD IS FILLED WITH HIS GLORY!*

The goers of the Upright Synagogue had been screaming for more than two hundred years, since the Venerable Rabbi enlightened that we are always drowning, and our prayers are nothing less than pleas for rescue from deep under the spiritual waters. *AND IF OUR PLIGHT IS SO DESPERATE,* he said (always starting his sentences with "and," as if what he verbalized were some logical continuation of his innermost thoughts), *SHOULD WE NOT ACT LIKE IT? AND SHOULD WE NOT SOUND LIKE DESPERATE PEOPLE?* So they screamed, and had been screaming for the two hundred years since.

And they screamed now, never allowing the baby a moment of rest, and hung—with one hand on prayer book and one on rope—from the pulleys that clipped to their belts, and kept the crowns of their black hats brushing against the ceiling. *AND IF WE ASPIRE TO BE CLOSER TO GOD,* the Venerable Rabbi had enlightened, *SHOULD WE NOT ACT LIKE IT? AND SHOULD WE NOT MAKE OURSELVES CLOSER?* Which made enough sense. It was on the eve of Yom Kippur, the holiest of holy days, that a fly flew under the door of the synagogue and began to pester the hanging congregants. It flew from face to face, buzzing, landing on long noses, going in and out of hairy ears. *AND IF THIS IS A TEST,* the Venerable Rabbi enlightened, trying to keep his congregation together, *SHOULD WE NOT RISE TO ITS CHALLENGE? AND I URGE YOU: CRASH TO THE GROUND BEFORE YOU RELEASE THE GREAT BOOK!*

But how pestering that fly was, tickling some of the most ticklish places. *AND AS GOD ASKED ABRAHAM TO SHOW ISAAC THE KNIFE'S POINT, SO IS HE ASKING US NOT TO SCRATCH OUR ASSES! AND IF WE MUST, BY ALL MEANS WITH THE LEFT HAND!* Half did as the Venerable Rabbi enlightened, and released the rope before the Great Book. These were the ancestors of the Upright

Synagogue's congregants, who continued for two hundred years to walk with an affected limp to remind themselves—or, more importantly, to remind others—of their response to The Test: that the Holy Word prevailed. (*EXCUSE ME, RABBI, BUT JUST WHICH WORD IS IT EXACTLY?* The Venerable Rabbi knocked his disciple with the business end of a Torah pointer: *AND IF YOU HAVE TO ASK!*...) Some Uprighters went so far as to refuse to walk at all, signifying an even more dramatic fall. Which meant they couldn't get to synagogue, of course. *WE PRAY BY NOT PRAYING*, they said. *WE FULFILL THE LAW BY TRANSGRESSING IT.*

Those who dropped the prayer book rather than fall were the ancestors of the Slouching Synagogue's congregants—so named by the Uprighters. They twiddled with the fringes sewn to the ends of their shirtsleeves, which they put there to remind themselves—or, more importantly, to remind others—of their response to The Test: that the strings are carried around with you, that the *spirit* of the Holy Word should always prevail. (*Excuse me, but does anyone know what that thing about the Holy Word means?* The others shrugged and went back to their argument about how best to divide thirteen knishes among forty-three people.) It was the Slouchers' customs that changed: the pulleys were traded in for pillows, the Hebrew prayer book for a more understandable Yiddish one, and the Rabbi for a group-led service and discussion, followed, but more often interrupted, by food, drink, and gossip. The Upright congregants looked down on the Slouchers, who seemed willing to sacrifice any Jewish law for the sake of what they feebly termed *the great and necessary reconciliation of religion with life.* The Uprighters called them names and promised them an eternity of agony in the next world for their eagerness to be comfortable in this one. But like Shmul S, the intestine-tied milkman, the Slouchers couldn't give a shit. Save for those rare occasions when Uprighters and Slouchers pushed at the synagogue from opposite sides, trying to make the shtetl more sacred or secular, they learned to ignore each other.

For six days the citizens of the shtetl, Uprighters and Slouchers alike, stood in lines outside the Upright Synagogue to get their chance to view my very-great-grandmother. Many returned many times. Men could examine the baby, touch it, talk to it, even hold it. Women were not allowed inside the Upright Synagogue, of course, for as the Venerable Rabbi so long ago enlightened, *AND HOW CAN WE BE EXPECTED TO KEEP OUR MINDS AND HEARTS WITH GOD WHEN THAT OTHER PART IS POINTING US TOWARD IMPURE THOUGHTS OF YOU KNOW WHAT?*

What seemed like a reasonable compromise was reached when, in 1763, the women were allowed to pray in a dank and cramped room beneath a specially installed glass floor. But it wasn't long before the dangling men took their eyes from the Great Book to partake in the chorus of cleavages below. Black pants became form-fitting, there was more bumping and swaying than ever as those *other parts* protruded in fantasies of *you know what*, and an extra hole was unknowingly inserted in the holiest of prayers: *HOLY, HOLY, HOLY,* HOLEY *IS THE LORD OF HOSTS! THE WHOLE WORLD IS FILLED WITH HIS GLORY!*

The Venerable Rabbi addressed the disconcerting matter in one of his many midafternoon sermons. *AND WE MUST ALL BE FAMILIAR WITH THAT MOST PORTENTOUS OF BIBLICAL PARABLES, THE PERFECTION OF HEAVEN AND HELL. AND AS WE ALL DO OR SHOULD KNOW, IT WAS ON THE SECOND DAY THAT THE LORD OUR GOD CREATED THE OPPOSING REGIONS OF HEAVEN AND HELL, TO WHICH WE AND THE SLOUCHERS, MAY THEY PACK ONLY SWEATERS, WILL BE SENT, RESPECTIVELY. AND BUT WE MUST NOT FORGET THAT THIRD AND NEXT DAY, WHEN GOD SAW THAT HEAVEN WAS NOT AS MUCH LIKE HEAVEN AS HE WOULD HAVE PRAYED, AND HELL NOT AS MUCH LIKE HELL. AND SO, THE LESSER AND HARDER-TO-FIND TEXTS TELL US, HE, FATHER OF FATHER OF FATHERS, RAISED THE SHADE BETWEEN THE OPPOSING REGIONS, ALLOWING THE BLESSED AND THE CONDEMNED TO SEE ONE ANOTHER. AND AS WAS HIS HOPE, THE BLESSED REJOICED IN THE PAIN OF THE CONDEMNED, AND THEIR JOY BECAME THAT MUCH GREATER IN THE FACE OF SORROW. AND THE CONDEMNED SAW THE BLESSED, SAW THEIR LOBSTER TAILS AND PROSCIUTTO, SAW WHAT THEY PUT IN THE TUCHESES OF MENSTRUATING SHIK-*

SAS, AND FELT THAT MUCH WORSE FOR THEMSELVES. AND GOD SAW THAT IT WAS GOODER. AND BUT THE APPEAL OF THE WINDOW BECAME TOO STRONG. AND RATHER THAN ENJOY THE KINGDOM OF HEAVEN, THE BLESSED WERE FASCINATED BY THE CRUELTIES OF HELL. AND RATHER THAN SUFFER THOSE CRUELTIES, THE CONDEMNED ENJOYED THE VICARIOUS PLEASURES OF HEAVEN. AND OVER TIME, THE TWO REACHED AN EQUILIBRIUM, STARING AT THE OTHER, STARING AT THEMSELVES. AND THE WINDOW BECAME A MIRROR, FROM WHICH NEITHER THE BLESSED NOR THE CONDEMNED COULD, OR WOULD, LEAVE. AND SO GOD DROPPED THE SHADE, FOREVER CLOSING OFF THE PORTAL BETWEEN KINGDOMS, AND SO MUST WE, IN THE FACE OF OUR TOO TEMPTING WINDOW, DROP THE SHADE BETWEEN THE KINGDOMS OF MAN AND WOMAN.

The cellar was filled with runoff from the Brod, and an egg-sized hole was cut out of the synagogue's back wall, through which one woman at a time could see only the ark and the feet of the dangling men, some of which, to add insult to insult, were caked with shit.

It was through this hole that the women of the shtetl took turns viewing my great-great-great-great-great-grandmother. Many were convinced, perhaps because of the new baby's perfectly adult features, that she was of an evil nature—a sign from the devil himself. But more likely their mixed feelings were inspired by the hole. From such a distance—palms pressed against the partition, an eye in an absent egg—they couldn't satisfy any of their mothering instincts. The hole wasn't even large enough to show all of the baby at once, and they had to piece together mental collages of her from each of the fragmented views—the fingers connected to the palm, which was attached to the wrist, which was at the end of the arm, which fit into the shoulder socket...They learned to hate her unknowability, her untouchability, the collage of her.

On the seventh day, the Well-Regarded Rabbi paid four quarter-chickens and a handful of blue cat's-eye marbles for the following announcement to be printed in Shimon T's weekly newsletter: that without precise knowledge of the cause, a baby was delivered to the shtetl, that it was quite beautiful, well behaved, and not at all stinky, and that he was resolved, out of consideration for the baby and himself, to give it to any righteous man who would be willing to call it daughter.

The next morning, he found fifty-two notes fanned like a peacock's plumage under the Upright Synagogue's front door.

From the maker of copper-wire knickknacks Peshel S, who had lost a wife of only two months in the Pogrom of Torn Garments: *If not for the girl, then for me. I am a righteous person, and there are things that I deserve.*

From the lonely candle dipper Mordechai C, whose hands were encased in gloves of wax that could never be washed off: *I am so alone in my workshop all day. There will be no candle dippers after me. Doesn't it make a kind of sense?*

From the unemployed Sloucher Lumpl W, who reclined on Passover not because it was religious custom but because why should that night be different from all others?: *I'm not the greatest person that ever lived, but I would be a good father, and you know it.*

From the deceased philosopher Pinchas T, who was struck on the head by a falling beam at the flour mill: *Put her back in the water and let her be with me.*

The Well-Regarded Rabbi was exceedingly knowledgeable about the large, extra-large, and extra-extra-large matters of the Jewish faith, and was able to draw upon the most obscure and indecipherable texts to reason seemingly impossible religious quandaries, but he knew hardly anything about life itself, and for this reason, because the baby's birth had no textual precedents, because he couldn't ask for anyone's advice — because how would it look for the very source of all advice to be an advice seeker? — because the baby was about life, and was life, he found himself to be quite stuck. *THEY'RE ALL DECENT MEN*, he thought. *ALL A LITTLE BELOW AVERAGE, PERHAPS, BUT TOLERABLE AT HEART. WHO IS LEAST UNDESERVING?*

THE BEST DECISION IS NO DECISION, he decided, and put the letters in her crib, vowing to give my great-great-great-great-great-grandmother — and, in a certain sense, me — to the author of the first note she grabbed for. But she didn't grab for any of them. She paid them no notice at all. For two days she didn't move a muscle, never crying or opening her mouth for food. The black-hatted men continued to holler prayers from their pulleys (*HOLY, HOLY, HOLY*…), continued to sway above the transplanted Brod, continued to hold more tightly to the Great Book than the rope, praying that someone was listening to their prayers, until in the middle of one early late-evening service, the good gefiltefishmonger Bitzl Bitzl R hollered what every man in the congregation had been thinking: *THE SMELL IS INTOLERABLE! HOW CAN I ACT CLOSE TO GOD WHEN I FEEL SO CLOSE TO THE SHITTER!*

The Well-Regarded Rabbi, who didn't disagree, put a halt to the prayers. He lowered himself to the glass floor and opened the ark. A most terrible stench poured forth, an all-encompassing, impossible to overlook, inhuman and inexcusable stink of supreme repugnance. It flooded from the ark, swept through the synagogue, streamed down every street, every alleyway of the shtetl, flowed under every pillow in every bedroom—entering the nostrils of the sleeping for long enough to misdirect their dreams before exiting with the next snore—and drained, finally, into the Brod.

The baby was still perfectly silent and unmoving. The Well-Regarded Rabbi placed the crib on the floor, removed a single sopping slip of paper, and hollered, *IT APPEARS THAT THE BABY HAS CHOSEN YANKEL AS HER FATHER!*

We were to be in good hands.

Dear Jonathan,

I hanker for this letter to be good. Like you know, I am not first rate with English. In Russian my ideas are asserted abnormally well, but my second tongue is not so premium. I undertaked to input the things you counseled me to, and I fatigued the thesaurus you presented me, as you counseled me to, when my words appeared too petite, or not befitting. If you are not happy with what I have performed, I command you to return it back to me. I will persevere to toil on it until you are appeased.

I have girdled in the envelope the items you inquired, not withholding postcards of Lutsk, the census ledgers of the six villages from before the war, and the photographs you had me keep for cautious purposes. It was a very, very, very good thing, no? I must eat a slice of humble pie for what occurred to you on the train. I know how momentous the box was for you, for both of us, and how its ingredients were not exchangeable. Stealing is an ignomin-ious thing, but a thing that occurs very repeatedly to people on the train from Ukraine. Since you do not have at the tips of your finger the name of the guard who stole the box, it will be impossible to have it recouped, so you must confess that it is lost to you forever. But please do not let your experience in Ukraine injure the way you perceive Ukraine, which must be as a totally awesome former Soviet republic.

This is my occasion to utter thank you for being so long-suffering and stoical with me on our voyage. You were perhaps accounting upon a transla-tor with more faculties, but I am certain that I did a mediocre job. I must eat a slice of humble pie for not finding Augustine, but you clutch how rigid it was. Perhaps if we had more days we could have discovered her. We could have investigated the six villages and interrogated many people. We could have lifted every boulder. But we have uttered all of these things so many times.

Thank you for the reproduction of the photograph of Augustine with her family. I have thought without end of what you said about falling in love with her. In truth, I never fathomed it when you uttered it in Ukraine. But I am certain that I fathom it now. I examine her once when it is morning, and once before I manufacture Z's, and on every instance I see something new, some manner in which her hairs produce shadows, or her lips summarize angles.

I am so so happy because you were appeased by the first division that I posted to you. You must know that I have performed the corrections you demanded. I apologize for the last line, about how you are a very spoiled Jew. It has been changed, and is now written, "I do not want to drive ten hours to an ugly city to attend to a spoiled Jew." I made more protracted the first part about me, and jettisoned out the word "Negroes," as you ordered me to, even though it is true that I am so fond of them. It makes me happy that you relished the sentence "One day you will do things for me that you hate. That is what it means to be a family." I must inquire you, however, what is a truism?

I have ruminated what you told me about making the part about my grandmother more protracted. Because you felt with so much gravity about this, I thought OK to include the parts that you posted me. I cannot say that I brooded those things, but I can say that I would covet to be the variety of person to have brooded those things. They were very beautiful, Jonathan, and I felt them as true.

And thank you, I feel indebted to utter, for not mentioning the not-truth about how I am tall. I thought it might appear superior if I was tall.

I strived to perform the next section as you ordered me, placing primary in my thoughts all that you tutored. I also attempted to be not obvious, or unduly subtle, as you demonstrated. Per the currency that you sent along, you must be informed that I would write this even in the absence of it. It is a mammoth honor for me to write for a writer, especially when he is an American writer, like Ernest Hemingway or you.

And mentioning your writing, "The Beginning of the World Often Comes" was a very exalted beginning. There were parts that I did not understand, but I conjecture that this is because they were very Jewish, and only a Jewish person could understand something so Jewish. Is this why you think you are chosen by God, because only you can understand the funnies that you make about yourself? I have one small query about this section, which is do you know that many of the names you exploit are not truthful names for Ukraine? Yankel is a name I have heard of, and so is Hannah, but the rest are very strange. Did you invent them? There were many mishaps like this, I will inform you. Are you being a humorous writer here, or an uninformed one?

I do not have any additional luminous remarks, because I must possess more of the novel in order to lumin. For present, be aware that I am ravished. I will counsel you that even after you have presented me more, I may not possess many intelligent things to utter, but I could be perhaps of some nonetheless use. Perhaps if I think something is very half-witted, I could tell you, and you could make it whole-witted. You have informed me so much about it that I am certain I will love very much to read the remnants, and think loftier of you, if that is a possibility. Oh yes, what is cunnilingus?

And now for a little private business. (You may decide not to read this part, if it makes you a boring person. I would understand, although please do not inform me.) Grandfather has not been healthful. He has altered to our residence for permanent. He reposed on Little Igor's bed with Sammy Davis, Junior, Junior, and Little Igor reposed on the sofa. This does not spleen Little Igor, because he is such a good boy, who understands many more things than anyone thinks he does. I have the opinion that the melancholy is what makes Grandfather unhealthful, and it is what makes him blind, although he is not truly blind, of course. It has become tremendously worse since we returned from Lutsk. As you know, he was very defeated about Augustine, more than even you or I were defeated. It is rigid not to talk about Grandfather's melancholy with Father, because we have both encountered him crying. Last night we were roosting at the table in the kitchen. We were eating black bread and conversing about athletics. There was a sound from above us. Little Igor's room is above us. I was certain that it was the crying of Grandfa-

ther, and Father was also certain of this. There was also a quiet rapping against the ceiling. *(Of normal, rapping is excellent, like the Dnipropetrovsk Crew, who are totally deaf, but this kind I was not amorous of.)* We tried so rigidly to neglect it. The sound moved Little Igor from his repose, and he came into the kitchen. "Hello, Clumsy One," Father said, because Little Igor had fallen again, and made his eye blue again, this time his left eye. "I would also like to eat black bread," Little Igor said, not looking at Father. Even though he is only thirteen almost fourteen, he is very smart. *(You are the only person I have remarked this to. Please do not remark it to any other person.)*

I hope that you are happy, and that your family is healthful and prosperous. We became like friends while you were in Ukraine, yes? In a different world, we could have been real friends. I will be in suspense for your next letter, and I will also be in suspense for the coming division of your novel. I feel oblongated to again eat a slice of humble pie *(my stomach is becoming chock-full)* for the new section that I am bestowing you, but understand that I tried bestly, and did the best I could, which was the best that I could do. It is so rigid for me. Please be truthful, but also please be benevolent, please.

Guilelessly,
Alexander

An Overture to Encountering the Hero, and Then Encountering the Hero

How I ANTICIPATED, it made my girls very sad that I should not be with them for the celebration of the first birthday of the new constitution. "All Night," one of my girls said to me, "how am I expected to pleasure myself in your void?" I had a notion. "Baby," another one of my girls said to me, "it is not good." I told them all, "If possible, I would be here with only you, forever. But I am a man who toils, and I must go where I must. We need currency for famous nightclubs, yes? I am doing something I hate for you. This is what it means to be in love. So do not spleen me." But to be truthful, I was not even the smallest portion sad to go to Lutsk to translate for Jonathan Safran Foer. As I mentioned before, my life is ordinary. But I had never been to Lutsk, or any of the multitudinous petite villages that still endure after the war. I desired to see new things. I desired to experience volumes. And I would be electrical to meet an American.

"You will need to bring along with you food for your drive, Shapka," Father said to me. "Do not dub me that," I said. "And also drink and maps," he said. "It is near ten hours to Lvov, where you will pick up the Jew at the train station." "How much currency will I receive for my toils?" I inquired, because that query had very much gravity on me. "Less than you think you deserve," he said, "and more than you deserve." This spleened me very much and I told Father, "Then maybe I do not want to do it." "I do not care what you want," he said, and extended to put his hand on my shoulder. In my family, Father is the world champion at ending conversations.

It was agreed that Grandfather and I would go forth at midnight of

1 July. This would present us with fifteen hours. It was agreed, by everyone except for Grandfather and I, that we should travel to the Lvov train station as soon as we entered the city of Lvov. It was agreed by Father that Grandfather should loiter with patience in the car, while I loitered on the tracks for the train of the hero. I did not know what his appearance would be, and he did not know how tall and aristocratic I would be. This was something we made much repartee about after. He was very nervous, he said. He said he made shit of a brick. I said to him that I also made shit of a brick, but if you want to know why, it was not that I would not recognize him. An American in Ukraine is so flaccid to recognize. I made shit of a brick because he was an American, and I desired to show him that I too could be an American.

I have given abnormally many thoughts to altering residences to America when I am more aged. They have many superior schools for accounting, I know. I know this because a friend of mine, Gregory, who is sociable with a friend of the nephew of the person who invented the sixty-nine, told me that they have many superior schools for accounting in America, and he knows everything. My friends are appeased to stay in Odessa for their entire lives. They are appeased to age like their parents, and become parents like their parents. They do not desire anything more than everything they have known. OK, but this is not for me, and it will not be for Little Igor.

A few days before the hero was to arrive, I inquired Father if I could go forth to America when I made to graduate from university. "No," he said. "But I want to," I informed him. "I do not care what you want," he said, and that is usually the end of the conversation, but it was not this time. "Why?" I asked. "Because what you want is not important to me, Shapka." "No," I said, "why is it that I cannot go forth to America after I graduate?" "If you want to know why you cannot go forth to America," he said, unclosing the refrigerator, investigating for food, "it is because Great-Grandfather was from Odessa, and Grandfather was from Odessa, and Father, me, was from Odessa, and your boys will be from Odessa. Also, you are going to toil at Heritage Touring when you are graduated. It is a necessary employment, premium enough for Grandfather, premium enough for me, and premium enough for you." "But what if that is not what I desire?" I said. "What if I do not want to toil at Heritage Touring, but instead toil someplace where I can do something unordinary, and make very much currency instead of just a petite amount? What if I do not want my boys to grow up here, but instead to grow up someplace superior, with superior things, and more things? What if I have girls?" Father removed three pieces of ice from the refrigerator, closed the refrigerator, and punched me. "Put these on your face," he said, giving the ice to me, "so you do not look terrible and manufacture a disaster in Lvov." This was the end of the conversation. I should have been smarter.

And I still haven't mentioned that Grandfather demanded to bring Sammy Davis, Junior, Junior along. That was another thing. "You are being a fool," Father informed him. "I need her to help me see the road," Grandfather said, pointing his finger at his eyes. "I am blind." "You are not blind, and you are not bringing the bitch." "I am blind, and the bitch is coming with us." "No," Father said. "It is not professional for the bitch to go along." I would have uttered something on the half of Grandfather, but I did not want to be stupid again. "It is either I go with the bitch or I do not go." Father was in a position. Not like the Latvian Home Stretch, but like amid a rock and a rigid place, which is, in truth, somewhat similar to the Latvian Home Stretch. There was fire amid them. I had seen this before, and nothing in the world frightened me more. Finally my father yielded, although it was agreed that Sammy Davis, Junior, Junior must don a special shirt that Father would have fabricated, which would say: OFFICIOUS SEEING-EYE BITCH OF HERITAGE TOURING. This was so she would appear professional.

Notwithstanding that we had a deranged bitch in the car, who made a proclivity of throwing her body against the windows, the drive was also difficult because the car is so much shit that it would not travel any faster than as fast as I could run, which is sixty kilometers per the hour. Many cars passed us, which made me feel second rate, especially when the cars were heavy with families, and when they were bicycles. Grandfather and I did not utter words pending the drive, which is not abnormal, because we have never uttered multitudinous words. I made efforts not to spleen him, but nonetheless did. For one example, I forgot to examine the map, and we missed our entrance to the superway. "Please do not punch me," I said, "but I made a miniature error with the map." Grandfather kicked the stop pedal, and my face gave a high-five to the front window. He did not say anything for the majority of a minute. "Did I ask you to drive the car?" he asked. "I do not have a license to drive the car," I said. (Keep this as a secret, Jonathan.) "Did I ask you to prepare me breakfast while you roost there?" he asked. "No," I said. "Did I ask you to invent a new kind of wheel?" he asked. "No," I said, "I would not have been very good at that." "How many things did I ask you to do?" he asked. "Only one," I said, and I knew that he was pissing off, pissing everywhere, and that he would yell at me for some durable time, and perhaps even violence me, which I deserved, nothing is new. But he did not. (So you are aware, Jonathan, he has never violenced me or Little Igor.) If you want to know what he did, he rotated the car around, and we drove back to where I fashioned the error. Twenty minutes it captured. When we arrived at the location, I informed him that we were there. "Are you cocksure?" he asked. I told him I was cocksure. He moved the car to the side of the road. "We will stop here and eat breakfast," he said. "Here?" I asked, because it was an unimpressive location, with only a few meters of dirt amid the road and a concrete wall separating the road and farmlands. "I think this is a premium location," he said, and I knew it would be a common decency not to argue. We roosted on the grass and ate, while Sammy Davis, Junior, Junior attempted to lick the yellow lines off of the superway. "If you blunder again," Grandfather said while he masticated a sausage, "I will stop the car and you will get out with a foot in the backside. It will be my foot. It will be your backside. Is this a thing you understand?"

We arrived in Lvov in only eleven hours, but yet traveled at once to the train station as Father ordered. It was rigid to find, and we became lost people many times. This gave Grandfather anger. "I hate Lvov!" he said. We had been there for ten minutes. Lvov is big and impressive, but not like Odessa. Odessa is very beautiful, with many famous beaches where girls are lying on their backs and exhibiting their first-rate bosoms. Lvov is a city like New York City in America. New York City, in truth, was designed on the model of Lvov. It has very tall buildings (with as many as six levels) and comprehensive streets (with enough room for as many as three cars) and many cellular phones. There are many statues in Lvov, and many places where statues used to be located. I have never witnessed a place fashioned of so much concrete. Everything was concrete, everywhere, and I will tell you that even the sky, which was gray, appeared like concrete. This is something that the hero and I would speak about later, when we were having an absence of words. "Do you remember all the concrete in Lvov?" he asked. "Yes," I said. "Me too," he said. Lvov is a very important city in the history of Ukraine. If you want to know why, I do not know why, but I am certain that my friend Gregory does.

Lvov is not very impressive from inside the train station. This is where I loitered for the hero for more than four hours. His train was dilatory, so it was five hours. I was spleened to have to loiter there with nothing to do, without even a hi-fi, but I was very good-humored to not have to be in the car with Grandfather, who was likely becoming a deranged person, and Sammy Davis, Junior, Junior, who was already deranged. The station was not ordinary, because there were blue and yellow papers from the ceiling. They were there for the first birthday of the new constitution. This did not make me so proud, but I was appeased that the hero should view them when disembarking the train from Prague. He would obtain an excellent picture of our country. Perhaps he would think that the yellow and blue papers were for him, because I know that they are the Jewish colors.

When his train finally arrived, both of my legs were needles and nails from being an upright person for such a duration. I would have roosted, but the floor was very dirty, and I wore my peerless blue jeans to oppress the hero. I knew which car he would be disembarking from, because Father told me, and I tried to walk to it when the train arrived, but it was very difficult with two legs that were all needles and nails. I held a sign with his name in front of me, and fell many times on my legs, and looked into the eyes of every person that walked past.

When we found each other, I was very flabbergasted by his appearance. This is an American? I thought. And also, This is a Jew? He was severely short. He wore spectacles and had diminutive hairs which were not split anywhere, but rested on his head like a Shapka. (If I were like Father, I might even have dubbed him Shapka.) He did not appear like either the Americans I had witnessed in magazines, with yellow hairs and muscles, or the Jews from history books, with no hairs and prominent bones. He was wearing nor blue jeans nor the uniform. In truth, he did not look like anything special at all. I was underwhelmed to the maximum.

He must have witnessed the sign I was holding, because he punched me on the shoulder and said, "Alex?" I told him yes. "You're my translator, right?" I asked him to be slow, because I could not understand him. In truth I was manufacturing a brick wall of shits. I attempted to be sedate. "Lesson one. Hello. How are you doing this day?" "What?" "Lesson two. OK, isn't the weather full of delight?" "You're my translator," he said, manufacturing movements, "yes?" "Yes," I said, presenting him my hand. "I am Alexander Perchov. I am your humble translator." "It would not be nice to beat you," he said. "What?" I said. "I said," he said, "it would not be nice to beat you." "Oh yes," I laughed, "it would not be nice to beat you also. I implore you to forgive my speaking of English. I am not so premium with it." "Jonathan Safran Foer," he said, and presented me his hand. "What?" "I'm Jonathan Safran Foer." "Jon-fen?" "Safran Foer." "I am Alex," I said. "I know," he said. "Did someone hit you?" he inquired, witnessing my right eye. "It was nice for Father to beat me," I said. I took his bags from him and we went forth to the car.

"Your train ride appeased you?" I asked. "Oh, God," he said, "twenty-six hours, fucking unbelievable." This girl Unbelievable must be very majestic, I thought. "You were able to Z Z Z Z Z?" I asked. "What?" "Did you manufacture any Z's?" "I don't understand." "Repose." "What?" "Did you repose?" "Oh. No," he said, "didn't repose at all." "What?" "I...did...not...repose...at...all." "And the guards at the border?" "It was nothing," he said. "I've heard so much about them, that they would, you know, give me a hard time. But they came in, checked my passport, and didn't bother me at all." "What?" "I had heard it might be a problem, but it wasn't a problem." "You had heard about them?" "Oh yeah, I heard they were big fucking assholes." Big fucking assholes. I wrote this on my brain.

In truth, I was flabbergasted that the hero did not have any legal hearings and tribulations with the border guards. They have an unsavory habit for taking things without asking from people on the train. Father went to Prague once, as part of his toiling for Heritage Touring, and while he reposed the guards removed many premium things from his bag, which is terrible because he does not have many premium things. (It is so queer to think of someone injuring Father. I more usually think of the roles as unmovable.) I have also been informed stories of travelers who must present currency to the guards in order to receive their documents in return. For Americans it can be either best or worst. It is best if the guard is in love with America and wants to overawe the American by being a premium guard. This kind of guard thinks that he will encounter the American again one day in America, and that the American will offer to take him to a Chicago Bulls game, and buy him blue jeans and white bread and delicate toilet paper. This guard dreams of speaking English without an accent and obtaining a wife with an unmalleable bosom. This guard will confess that he does not love where he lives.

The other kind of guard is also in love with America, but he will hate the American for being an American. This is worst. This guard knows he will never go to America, and knows that he will never meet the American again. He will steal from the American, and terror the American, only to teach that he can. This is the only occasion in his life to have his Ukraine be more than America, and to have himself be more than the American. Father told me this, and I am certain that he is certain that it is faithful.

When we arrived at the car, Grandfather was loitering with patience as Father ordered him to. He was very patient. He was snoring. He was snoring with such volume that the hero and I could hear him even though the windows were elevated, and it sounded as if the car was operating. "This is our driver," I said. "He is an expert at driving." I observed distress in the smile of our hero. This was the second time. It had been four minutes. "Is he OK?" he asked. "What?" I said. "I do not make to understand. Speak more slower, please." I may have appeared noncompetent to the hero. "Is...the...dri...ver...heal...thy?" "With certainty," I said. "But I must tell you, I am very familiar with this driver. He is my grandfather." At this moment, Sammy Davis, Junior, Junior made herself evident, because she jumped up from the back seat and barked in volumes. "Oh Jesus Christ!" the hero said with terror, and he moved distant from the car. "Do not be distressed," I informed him as Sammy Davis, Junior, Junior punched her head against the window. "That is only the driver's Seeing Eye bitch." I pointed to the shirt that she was donning, but she had masticated the major of it, so that it only said: OF-FICIOUS BITCH. "She is deranged," I said, "but so so playful."

"Grandfather," I said, moving his arm to arouse him. "Grandfather, he is here." Grandfather rotated his head from this to that. "He is always reposing," I told the hero, hoping that might make him less distressed. "That must come to hands," the hero said. "What?" I asked. "I said that must come to hands." "What does it mean come to hands?" "To be useful. You know, to be helpful. What about that dog, though?" I use this American idiom very often now. I told a girl at a famous nightclub, "My eyes come to hands when I observe your peerless bosom." I could perceive that she perceived that I was a premium person. Later we became very carnal, and she smelled her knees, and also my knees.

I was able to move Grandfather from his repose. If you want to know how, I fastened his nose with my fingers so that he could not breathe. He did not know where he was. "Anna?" he asked. That was the name of my grandmother who died two years yore. "No, Grandfather," I said, "it is me. Sasha." He was very shamed. I could perceive this because he rotated his face away from me. "I acquired Jon-fen," I said. "Um, that's Jon-a-than," the hero said, who was observing Sammy Davis, Junior, Junior as she licked the windows. "I acquired him. His train arrived." "Oh," Grandfather said, and I perceived that he was still departing from a dream. "We should go forth to Lutsk," I suggested, "as Father ordered." "What?" the hero inquired. "I told him that we should go forth to Lutsk." "Yes, Lutsk. That's where I was told we would go. And from there to Trachimbrod." "What?" I inquired. "Lutsk, then Trachimbrod." "Correct," I said. Grandfather put his hands on the wheel. He looked in front of him for a protracted time. He was breathing very large breaths, and his hands were shaking. "Yes?" I inquired him. "Shut up," he informed me. "Where's the dog going to be?" the hero inquired. "What?"

"Where's…the…dog…going…to…be?" "I do not understand." "I'm afraid of dogs," he said. "I've had some pretty bad experiences with them." I told this to Grandfather, who was still half of himself in dream. "No one is afraid of dogs," he said. "Grandfather informs me that no one is afraid of dogs." The hero moved his shirt up to exhibit me the remains of a wound. "That's from a dog bite," he said. "What is?" "That." "What?" "This thing." "What thing?" "Here. It looks like two intersecting lines." "I don't see it." "Here," he said. "Where?" "Right here," he said, and I said, "Oh yes," although in truth I still could not witness a thing. "My mother is afraid of dogs." "So?" "So I'm afraid of dogs. I can't help it." I clutched the situation now. "Sammy Davis, Junior, Junior must roost in the front with us," I told Grandfather. "Get in the fucking car," he said, having misplaced all of the patience that he had while snoring. "The bitch and the Jew will share the back seat. It is vast enough for both of them." I did not mention how the back seat was not vast enough for even one of them. "What are we going to do?" the hero asked, afraid to become close to the car, while in the back seat Sammy Davis, Junior, Junior had made her mouth with blood from masticating her own tail.

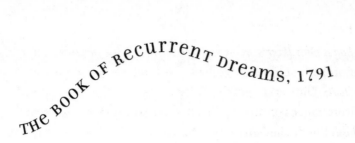

THE BOOK OF RECURRENT DREAMS, 1791

THE NEWS of his good fortune reached Yankel D as the Slouchers were concluding their weekly service.

It is most important that we remember, the narcoleptic potato farmer Didl S said to the congregation, which was reclining on pillows around his living room. (The Sloucher congregation was a wandering one, calling home a different congregant's house each Shabbos.)

Remember what? the schoolteacher Tzadik P asked, expelling yellow chalk with each syllable.

The what, Didl said, *is not so important, but that we should remember. It is the act of remembering, the process of remembrance, the recognition of our past ... Memories are small prayers to God, if we believed in that sort of thing ... For it says somewhere something about just this, or something just like this ... I had my finger on it a few minutes ago ... I swear, it was right here. Has anyone seen* The Book of Antecedents *around? I had an early volume here just a second ago ... Crap! ... Can somebody tell me where I was? Now I'm totally confused, and embarrassed, and I always screw it up when it's at my house —*

Memory, grieving Shanda assisted, but Didl had fallen uncontrollably asleep. She woke him up and whispered, *Memory.*

— There we go, he said, not missing a beat as he riffled through a stack of papers on his pulpit, which was really a chicken coop. *Memory. Memory and reproduction. And dreams, of course. What is being awake if not interpreting our dreams, or dreaming if not interpreting our wake? Circle of circles! Dreams, yes? No? Yes. Yes, it is the first Shabbos. First of the month. And it being the first Shabbos of the month, we must make our additions to* The Book of Recurrent Dreams. *Yes? Someone tell me if I'm fucking this up.*

I've had a most interesting dream for the past two weeks, said Lilla F, descendant of the first Sloucher to drop the Great Book.

Excellent, Didl said, pulling Volume IV of *The Book of Recurrent Dreams* from the makeshift ark, which was really his wood-burning oven.

As did I, Shloim added. *Several of them.*

I, too, had a recurrent dream, Yankel said.

Excellent, Didl said. *Most excellent. It won't be long before another volume is complete!*

But first, Shanda whispered, *we must review last month's entries.*

But first, Didl said, assuming the authority of a rabbi, *we must review last month's entries. We must go backward in order to go forward.*

But don't take too long, Shloim said, *or I'll forget. It's amazing I've been able to remember it this long.*

He'll take exactly as long as it takes, Lilla said.

I'll take exactly as long as it takes, Didl said, and blackened his hand with the ash that had collected on the cover of the heavy leather-bound book. He opened it to a page near the end, picked up the silver pointer, which was really a tin knife, and began to chant, following the slice of the blade through the heart of Sloucher dream life:

> 4:512—*The dream of sex without pain.* I dreamt four nights ago of clock hands descending from the universe like rain, of the moon as a green eye, of mirrors and insects, of a love that never withdrew. It was not the feeling of completeness that I so needed, but the feeling of not being empty. This dream ended when I felt my husband enter me. 4:513—*The dream of angels dreaming of men.* It was during an afternoon nap that I dreamt of a ladder. Angels were sleepwalking up and down the rungs, their eyes closed, their breath heavy and dull, their wings hanging limp at the sides. I bumped into an old angel as I passed him, waking and startling him.

He looked like my grandfather did before he passed away last year, when he would pray each night to die in his sleep. Oh, the angel said to me, I was just dreaming of you. 4:514 — *The dream of, as silly as it sounds, flight.* 4:515 — *The dream of the waltz of feast, famine, and feast.* 4:516 — *The dream of disembodied birds (46).* I'm not sure if you would consider this a dream or a memory, because it actually happened, but when I fall asleep I see the room in which I mourned the death of my son. For those of you who were there, you will remember how we sat without speaking, eating only as much as we had to. You will remember when a bird crashed through the window and fell to the floor. You will remember, those of you who were there, how it jerked its wings before dying, and left a spot of blood on the floor after it was removed. But who among you was first to notice the negative bird it left in the window? Who first saw the shadow that the bird left behind, the shadow that drew blood from any finger that dared to trace it, the shadow that was better proof of the bird's existence than the bird ever was? Who was with me when I mourned the death of my son, when I excused my-self to bury that bird with my own hands? 4:517 — *The dream of falling in love, mar-riage, death, love.* This dream seems as if it lasts for hours, although it always takes place in the five minutes between my re-turning from the field and being woken for dinner. I dream of when I met my wife, fifty years ago, and it's exactly as it happened. I dream of our marriage, and I can even see my father's tears of pride. It's all there, just as it was. But then I dream of my own death, which I have heard is impossible to do, but you must believe me. I dream of my wife telling me on my deathbed that she loves me, and even though she thinks I can't hear her, I can, and she says she wouldn't have changed anything. It feels like a moment I've lived a thousand times before, as if everything is familiar, right up to the moment of my death, that it will happen again an infinite number of times, that we will meet, marry, have our children, succeed in the ways we have, fail in the ways we have, all exactly the same, always unable to change a thing. I am again at the bottom of an unstoppable wheel, and when I feel my eyes close for death, as they have and will a thousand times, I awake. 4:518 — *The dream of perpetual motion.* 4:519 — *The dream of low windows.* 4:520 — *The dream of safety and peace.* I dreamt that I was born from a stranger's body. She gave birth to me in a secret dwelling, far away from everything that I would grow to know. Immediately after I was born, she handed me to my mother, for the sake of appearances, and my mother said, Thank you. You have given me a son, the gift of life. And for this reason, because I was of a stranger's body, I did not fear the body of my mother, and I could embrace it without shame, with only love. Because I was not from my mother's body, my desire to go home never led back to her, and I was free to say Mother, and mean only Mother. 4:521 — *The dream of disembodied birds (47)*. It's dusk in this dream that I have every night, and I'm making love to my wife, my real wife, I mean, to whom I've been married for thirty years, and you all know how I love her, I love her so much. I massage her thighs in my hands, and I move my hands up her waist and belly, and touch her breasts. My wife is such a beautiful woman, you all know that, and in the dream she's the same, just as beautiful. I look down at my hands on her breasts—callused, worn things, a man's hands, veiny, shaky, fluttering— and I remember, I don't know why, but it's this way every night, I remember two white birds that my mother brought back for me from Warsaw when I was only a child. We let them fly around the house and perch wherever they wanted to. I re- member seeing my mother's back as she cooked eggs for me, and I remember the birds perching on her shoulders, with their beaks up next to her ears, as if they were about to tell her a secret. She reached her right hand up into the cup- board, searching without looking for some spice on a high shelf, grasping at something elusive, fluttering, not letting my food burn. 4:522 — *The dream of meet- ing your younger self.* 4:523 — *The dream of animals, two by two.* 4:524 — *The dream of I won't be ashamed.* 4:525 — *The dream that we are our fathers.* I walked to the Brod, without knowing why, and looked into my reflection in the water. I couldn't look away. What was the image that pulled me in after it? What was it that I loved? And then I recognized it. So simple. In the water I saw my father's face, and that face saw the face of its father, and so on, and so on, reflecting backward to the beginning of time, to the face of God, in whose image we were created. We burned with love for ourselves, all of us, starters of the fire we suffered—our love was the affliction for which only our love was the cure...

The chanting was interrupted by a pounding at the door. Two men in black hats limped in before any of the congregants had time to get up.

WE ARE HERE ON BEHALF OF THE UPRIGHT CONGREGATION! hollered the taller of the two.

THE UPRIGHT CONGREGATION! echoed the short and squat one.

Shush! Shanda said.

IS YANKEL PRESENT? hollered the taller of the two, as if in response to her request.

YEAH, IS YANKEL PRESENT? echoed the short, squat one.

Here. I am here, Yankel said, rising from his pillow. He assumed the Well-Regarded Rabbi was requesting his financial services, as had happened so many times in the past, piety being as expensive as it was those days. *What can I do for you?*

YOU WILL BE THE FATHER OF THE BABY FROM THE RIVER! hollered the taller.

YOU WILL BE THE FATHER! echoed the short, squat one.

Excellent! Didl said, closing Volume IV of *The Book of Recurrent Dreams*, which released a cloud of dust as the covers clapped. *This is most excellent! Yankel will be the father!*

Mazel tov! the congregants began to sing. *Mazel tov!*

Suddenly Yankel was overcome with a fear of dying, stronger than he felt when his parents passed of natural causes, stronger than when his only brother was killed in the flour mill or when his children died, stronger even than when he was a child and it first occurred to him that he must try to understand what it could mean not to be alive—to be not in darkness, not in unfeeling—to be not being, not to be.

Slouchers congratulated him, failing to notice as they patted him on the back that he was crying. *Thank you,* he said, and said again, without once wondering just whom he was thanking. *Thank you so much.* He had been given a baby, and I a great-great-great-great-great-great-grandfather.

FALLING IN LOVE, 1791–1796

THE DISGRACED USURER Yankel D took the baby girl home that evening. *Here we go*, he said, *up the front step. Here we are. This is your door. And here, this is your doorknob I am opening. And here, this is where we put the shoes when we come in. And here is where we hang the jackets.* He spoke to her as if she could understand him, never in a high pitch or in monosyllables, and never in nonsense words. *This is milk that I am feeding you. It comes from Mordechai the milkman, whom you will meet one day. He gets the milk from a cow, which is a very strange and troubling thing if you think about it, so don't think about it...This is my hand that is petting your face. Some people are left-handed and some are right-handed. We don't know which you are yet, because you just sit there and let me do the handling...This is a kiss. It is what happens when lips are puckered and pressed against something, sometimes other lips, sometimes a cheek, sometimes something else. It depends...This is my heart. You are touching it with your left hand, not because you are left-handed, although you might be, but because I am holding it against my heart. What you are feeling is the beating of my heart. It is what keeps me alive.*

He made a bed of crumpled newspaper in a deep baking pan and gently tucked it in the oven, so that she wouldn't be disturbed by the noise of the small falls outside. He left the oven door open, and would sit for hours and watch her, as one might watch a loaf of bread rise. He watched her chest rise and fall in rapid succession as her fingers made fists and released, and her eyes squinted for no apparent reason. *Could she be dreaming?* he wondered. *And if so, what would a baby dream of? She must be dreaming of the before-life, just as I dream of the afterlife.* When he pulled her out to feed or just hold her, her body was tattooed with the newsprint. TIME OF DYED HANDS IS FINALLY OVER! MOUSE WILL

HANG! Or, SOFIOWKA ACCUSED OF RAPE, PLEADS POSSESSED BY PENIS PERSUASION, BECAME "OUT OF HAND." Or, AVRUM R KILLED IN FLOUR MILL MISHAP, LEAVES BEHIND A LOST SIAMESE CAT OF FORTY-EIGHT YEARS, TAWNY, CHUBBY, BUT NOT FAT, PERSONABLE, MAYBE A LITTLE FAT, ANSWERS TO "METHUSELAH," OK, FAT AS SHIT. IF FOUND, FREE TO KEEP. Sometimes he would rock her to sleep in his arms, and read her left to right, and know everything he needed to know about the world. If it wasn't written on her, it wasn't important to him.

Yankel had lost two babies, one to fever and the other to the industrial flour mill, which had taken a shtetl member's life every year since it first opened. He had also lost a wife, not to death but to another man. He had returned from an afternoon at the library to find a note covering the SHALOM! of their home's welcome mat: *I had to do it for myself.*

Lilla F fingered the soil around one of her daisies. Bitzl Bitzl stood by his kitchen window, pretending to scrub the counter clean. Shloim W peered through the upper bulb of one of the hourglasses with which he could no longer bring himself to part. No one said anything as Yankel read the note, and no one ever said anything afterward, as if the disappearance of his wife weren't the slightest bit unusual, or as if they hadn't noticed that he had been married at all.

Why couldn't she have slid it under the door? he wondered. *Why couldn't she have folded it?* It looked just like any other note she would leave him, like, *Could you try to fix the broken knocker?* or *I'll be back soon, don't worry.* It was so strange to him that such a different kind of note — *I had to do it for myself* — could look exactly the same: trivial, mundane, nothing. He could have hated her for leaving it there in plain sight, and he could have hated her for the plainness of it, a message without adornment, without any small clue to indicate that yes, this is important, yes, this is the most painful note I've ever written, yes, I would sooner die than have to write this again. Where were the dried teardrops? Where was the tremor in the script?

But his wife was his first and only love, and it was the nature of those from the tiny shtetl to forgive their first and only loves, so he forced himself to understand, or pretend to understand. He never once blamed her for fleeing to Kiev with the traveling and mustachioed bureaucrat who was called in to help mediate the messy proceedings of Yankel's shameful trial; the bureaucrat could promise to provide for her future, could take her away from everything, move her to someplace quieter, without thinking, without confessions or plea-bargaining. No, that's not it. Without Yankel. She wanted to be without Yankel.

He spent the next weeks blocking scenes of the bureaucrat fucking his wife. On the floor with cooking ingredients. Standing, with socks still on. In the grass of the yard of their new and immense house. He imagined her making noises she never made for him and feeling pleasures he could never provide because the bureaucrat was a man, and he was not a man. *Does she suck his penis?* he wondered. *I know this is a silly thought, a thought that will only bring me pain, but I can't free myself of it. And when she sucks his penis, because she must, what is he doing? Is he pulling her hair back to watch? Is he touching her chest? Is he thinking of someone else? I'll kill him if he is.*

With the shtetl still watching—Lilla still fingering, Bitzl Bitzl still scrubbing, Shloim still pretending to measure time with sand—he folded the note into a teardrop shape, slid it into his lapel, and went inside. *I don't know what to do*, he thought. *I should probably kill myself.*

He couldn't bear to live, but he couldn't bear to die. He couldn't bear the thought of her making love to someone else, but neither could he bear the absence of the thought. And as for the note, he couldn't bear to keep it, but he couldn't bear to destroy it either. So he tried to lose it. He left it by the wax-weeping candle holders, placed it between matzos every Passover, dropped it without regard among rumpled papers on his cluttered desk, hoping it wouldn't be there when he returned. But it was always there. He tried to massage it out of his pocket while sitting on the bench in front of the fountain of the prostrate mermaid, but when he inserted his hand for his hanky, it was there. He hid it like a bookmark in one of the novels he most hated, but the note would appear several days later between the pages of one of the Western books that he alone in the shtetl read, one of the books that the note had now spoiled for him forever. But like his life, he couldn't for the life of him lose the note. It kept returning to him. It stayed with him, like a part of him, like a birthmark, like a limb, it was on him, in him, him, his hymn: *I had to do it for myself.*

He had lost so many slips of paper over time, and keys, pens, shirts, glasses, watches, silverware. He had lost a shoe, his favorite opal cufflinks (the Sloucher fringes of his sleeves bloomed unruly), three years away from Trachimbrod, millions of ideas he intended to write down (some of them wholly original, some of them deeply meaningful), his hair, his posture, two parents, two babies, a wife, a fortune in pocket change, more chances than could be counted. He had even lost a name: he was Safran before he fled the shtetl, Safran from birth to his first death. There seemed to be nothing he couldn't lose. But that slip of paper wouldn't disappear, ever, and neither would the image of his prostrate wife, and neither would the thought that if he could, it might greatly improve his life to end it.

Before the trial, Yankel-then-Safran was unconditionally admired. He was the president (and treasurer and secretary and only member) of the Committee for the Good and Fine Arts, and the founder, multiterm chairman, and only teacher of the School for Loftier Learning, which met in his house and whose classes were attended by Yankel himself. It was not unusual for a family to host a multicourse dinner in his name (if not in his presence), or for one of the more wealthy community members to commission a traveling artist to paint a portrait of him. And the portraits were always flattering. He was someone whom everyone admired and liked but whom nobody knew. He was like a book that you could feel good holding, that you could talk about without ever having read, that you could recommend.

On the advice of his lawyer, Isaac M, who gestured quotation marks in the air with every syllable of every word he spoke, Yankel pleaded guilty to all charges of unfit practice, with the hope that it might lighten his punishment. In the end, he lost his usurer's license. And more than his license. He lost his good name, which is, as they say, the only thing worse than losing your good health. Passersby sneered at him or muttered under their breath names like scoundrel, cheat, cur, fucker. He wouldn't have been so hated if he hadn't been so loved before. But along with the Garden-Variety Rabbi and Sofiowka, he was one of the vertices of the community—the invisible one—and with his shame came a sense of imbalance, a void.

Safran moved through the neighboring villages, finding work as a teacher of harpsichord theory and performance, a perfume consultant (feigning deafness and blindness to grant himself some legitimacy in the absence of references), and even an ill-starred stint as the world's worst fortuneteller—*I'm not going to lie and tell you that the future is full of promise*...He awoke each morning with the desire to do right, to be a good and meaningful person, to be, as simple as it sounded and as impossible as it actually was, happy. And during the course of each day his heart would descend from his chest into his stomach. By early afternoon he was overcome by the feeling that nothing was right, or nothing was right for him, and by the desire to be alone. By evening he was fulfilled: alone in the magnitude of his grief, alone in his aimless guilt, alone even in his loneliness. *I am not sad*, he would repeat to himself over and over, *I am not sad*. As if he might one day convince himself. Or fool himself. Or convince others—the only thing worse than being sad is for others to know that you are sad. *I am not sad. I am not sad.* Because his life had unlimited potential for happiness, insofar as it was an empty white room. He would fall asleep with his heart at the foot of his bed, like some domesticated animal that was no part of him at all. And each morning he would wake with it again in the cupboard of his rib cage, having become a little heavier, a little weaker, but still pumping. And by midafternoon he was again overcome with the desire to be somewhere else, someone else, someone else somewhere else. *I am not sad.*

After three years he returned to the shtetl—I am the final piece of proof that all citizens who leave eventually return—and lived a quiet life like a Sloucher fringe, sewn to the sleeve of Trachimbrod, forced to wear that horrible bead around his neck as a mark of his shame. He changed his name to Yankel, the name of the bureaucrat who ran away with his wife, and asked that no one ever call him Safran again (although he thought he heard that name every now and then, muttered behind his back). Many of his old clients returned to him, and while they refused to pay the rates of his heyday, he was nevertheless able to reestablish himself in the shtetl of his birth—as all who are exiled eventually try to do.

When the black-hatted men gave him the baby, he felt that he too was only a baby, with a chance to live without shame, without need of consolation for a life lived wrong, a chance to be again innocent, simply and impossibly happy. He named her Brod, after the river of her curious birth, and gave her a string necklace of her own, with a tiny abacus bead of her own, so she would never feel out of place in what would be her family.

As my great-great-great-great-great-grandmother grew, she remembered, of course, nothing, and was told nothing. Yankel made up a story about her mother's early death—*painless, in childbirth*—and answered the many questions that arose in the way he felt would cause her the least pain. It was her mother who gave her those beautiful big ears. It was her mother's sense of humor that all of the boys admired so much in her. He told Brod of vacations he and his wife had taken (when she pulled a splinter from his heel in Venice, when he sketched a red-pencil portrait of her in front of a tall fountain in Paris), showed her love letters they had sent each other (writing with his left hand those from Brod's mother), and put her to bed with stories of their romance.

Was it love at first sight, Yankel?

I loved your mother even before seeing her—it was her smell!

Tell me about what she looked like again.

She looked like you. She was beautiful, with those mismatched eyes, like you. One blue, one brown, like yours. She had your strong cheekbones and also your soft skin.

What was her favorite book?

Genesis, of course.

Did she believe in God?

She would never tell me.

How long were her fingers?

This long.

And her legs?

Like this.

Tell me again about how she would blow on your face before she kissed you.

Well that's just it, she would blow on my lips before she kissed me, like I was some very hot food and she was going to eat me!

Was she funny? Funnier than me?

She was the funniest person in the world. Exactly like you.

She was beautiful?

It was inevitable: Yankel fell in love with his never-wife. He would wake from sleep to miss the weight that never depressed the bed next to him, remember in earnest the weight of gestures she never made, long for the un-weight of her un-arm slung over his too real chest, making his widower's remembrances that much more convincing and his pain that much more real. He felt that he had lost her. He *had* lost her. At night he would reread the letters that she had never written him.

Dearest Yankel,

I'll be home to you soon, so there's no need for you to carry on with your missing me so much, however sweet it may be. You're so silly. Do you know that? Do you know how silly you are? Maybe that's why I love you so much, because I'm also silly.

Things are wonderful here. It's very beautiful, just as you promised it would be. The people have been kind, and I'm eating well, which I only mention because I know that you're always worried about me taking good enough care of myself. Well I am, so don't worry.

I really miss you. It's just about unbearable. Every moment of every day I think about your absence, and it almost kills me. But of course I'll be back with you soon, and will not have to miss you, and will not have to know that something, everything, is missing, that what is here is only what is not here. I kiss my pillow before I go to sleep and imagine it's you. It sounds like something you might do, I know. That's probably why I do it.

It almost worked. He had repeated the details so many times that it was nearly impossible to distinguish them from the facts. But the real note kept returning to him, and that, he was sure, was what kept him from that most simple and impossible thing: happiness. *I had to do it for myself.* Brod discovered it one day when she was only a few years old. It had found its way into her right pocket, as if the note had a mind of its own, as if those seven scribbled words were capable of wanting to inflict reality. *I had to do it for myself.* She either sensed the immense importance of it or deemed it entirely unimportant, because she never mentioned it to Yankel, but put it on his bedside table, where he would find it that night after rereading another letter that was not from her mother, not from his wife. *I had to do it for myself.*

I am not sad.

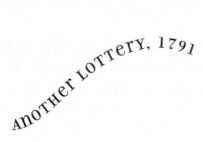

ANOTHER LOTTERY, 1791

THE WELL-REGARDED RABBI paid half a baker's dozen of eggs and a handful of blueberries for the following announcement to be printed in Shimon T's weekly newsletter: that an irascible magistrate in Lvov had demanded a name for the nameless shtetl, that the name would be used for new maps and census records, that it should not offend the refined sensibilities of either the Ukrainian or the Polish gentry, or be too hard to pronounce, and that it must be decided upon by week's end.

A VOTE! the Well-Regarded Rabbi proclaimed. *WE SHALL TAKE IT TO A VOTE.* For as the Venerable Rabbi once enlightened, *AND IF WE BELIEVE THAT EVERY SANE, STRICTLY MORAL, ABOVE-AVERAGE, PROPERTY-HOLDING, OBSERVANT ADULT JEWISH MALE IS BORN WITH A VOICE THAT MUST BE HEARD, SHALL WE NOT HEAR THEM ALL?*

The next morning a polling box was placed outside the Upright Synagogue, and the qualifying citizens queued up along the Jewish/Human fault line. Bitzl Bitzl R voted for "Gefilteville"; the deceased philosopher Pinchas T for "Time Capsule of Dust and String." The Well-Regarded Rabbi cast his ballot for *"SHTETL OF THE PIOUS UPRIGHTERS AND THE UNMENTIONABLE SLOUCHERS WITH WHOM NO RESPECTABLE JEW SHOULD HAVE ANYTHING TO DO UNLESS THE HOT SPOT IS HIS IDEA OF A VACATION."*

The mad squire Sofiowka N, having so much time and so little to do, took it upon himself to guard the box all afternoon and then deliver it to the magistrate's office in Lvov that evening. By morning it was official: resting twenty-three kilometers southeast of Lvov, four north of Kolki, and straddling the Polish-Ukrainian border like a twig alighted on a fence was the shtetl of Sofiowka. The new name was, much to the dismay of those who had to bear it, official and irrevocable. It would be with the shtetl until its death.

Of course, no one in Sofiowka called it Sofiowka. Until it had such a disagreeable official name, no one felt the need to call it anything. But now that there was an offense — that the shtetl should be that shithead's namesake — the citizens had a name *not* to go by. Some even called the shtetl Not-Sofiowka, and would continue to even after a new name was chosen.

The Well-Regarded Rabbi called for another vote. *THE OFFICIAL NAME CANNOT BE CHANGED*, he said, *BUT WE MUST HAVE A REASONABLE NAME FOR OUR OWN PURPOSES*. While no one was quite sure what was meant by purposes — *Did we have purposes before? What, exactly, is my purpose among our purposes?* — the second vote seemed unquestionably necessary. The polling box was placed outside the Upright Synagogue, and it was the Well-Regarded Rabbi's twins, this time, who guarded it.

The arthritic locksmith Yitzhak W voted for "Borderland." The man of law Isaac M for "Shtetlprudence." Lilla F, descendant of the first Sloucher to drop the book, persuaded the twins to let her sneak in a ballot, on which was written "Pinchas." (The twins also voted: Hannah for "Chana," and Chana for "Hannah.")

The Well-Regarded Rabbi counted the ballots that evening. It was a tie; every name got one vote: Lutsk Minor, *UPRIGHTLAND*, New Promise, Fault Line, Joshua, Lock-and-Key...Figuring that the fiasco had gone on long enough, he decided, reasoning that this is what God would do in such a situation, to pick a slip of paper randomly from the box and name the shtetl whatever it should say.

He nodded as he read what had become familiar script. *YANKEL HAS WON AGAIN*, he said. *YANKEL HAS NAMED US TRACHIM-BROD.*

Dear Jonathan,

It made me a tickled-pink person to receive your letter, and to know that you are reinstated at university for your conclusive year. As for me, I still have two years of studies among the remnants. I do not know what I will perform after that. Many of the things you informed me in July are still momentous to me, like what you uttered about searching for dreams, and how if you have a good and meaningful dream you are oblongated to search for it. This may be cinchier for you, I must say.

I did not yearn to mention this, but I will. Soon I will possess enough currency to purchase a plane voucher to America. Father does not know this. He thinks I disseminate everything I possess at famous discotheques, but as proxy for I often go to the beach and roost for many hours, so I do not have to disseminate currency. When I roost at the beach I think about how lucky you are.

It was Little Igor's fourteen birthday yesterday. He made his arm broken the day yore, because he fell again, this time from a fence he was hiking on, if you can believe it. We all tried very inflexibly to make him a happy person, and Mother prepared a premium cake that had many ceilings, and we even had a small festival. Grandfather was present, of course. He inquired how you are, and I told him that you would be reverting to university in September, which is now. I did not inform him about how the guard stole Augustine's box, because I knew that he would feel ashamed, and it made him happy to hear of you, and he is never happy. He wanted for me to inquire if it would be a possible thing for you to post another reproduction of the photograph of Augustine. He said that he would present you currency for any ex-

penses. I am very distressed about him, as I informed you in the last letter. His health is being defeated. He does not possess the energy to get spleened often, and is usually in silence. In truth, I would favor it if he yelled at me, and even if he punched me.

Father purchased a new bicycle for Little Igor for his birthday, which is a superior present, because I know Father does not possess enough currency for presents such as bicycles. "The poor Clumsy One," he said, extending to put his hand on Little Igor's shoulder, "he should be happy on his birthday." I have girdled a picture of the bicycle in the envelope. Tell me if it is awesome. Please, be truthful. I will not be angry if you tell me that it is not awesome.

I resolved not to go anywhere famous last night. Instead I roosted on the beach. But I was not in my normal solitude, because I took the photograph of Augustine with me. I must confess to you that I examine it very recurrently, and persevere to think about what you said about falling in love with her. She is beautiful. You are correct.

Enough of my miniature talking. I am making you a very boring person. I will now speak about the business of the story. I perceived that you were not as appeased by the second division. I eat another slice for this. But your corrections were so easy. Thank you for informing me that it is "shit a brick," and "shitting bricks," and also "to come in handy." It is very useful for me to know the correct idioms. It is necessary. I know that you asked me not to alter the mistakes because they sound humorous, and humorous is the only truthful way to tell a sad story, but I think I will alter them. Please do not hate me.

I did fashion all of the other corrections you commanded. I inserted what you ordered me to in the part about when I first encountered you. (Do you in truth think that we are comparable?) As you commanded, I removed the sentence "He was severely short," and inserted in its place, "Like me, he was not tall." And after the sentence " 'Oh,' Grandfather said, and I perceived that he was still departing from a dream," I added, as you commanded, "About Grandmother?"

With these changes, I am confident that the second part of the story is perfect. I was unable to ignore observing that you again posted me currency.

For this I again thank you. But I parrot what I uttered before: if you are not appeased by what I post to you, and would like to have your currency posted back, I will post it back immediately. I could not feel proud in any other manner.

I toiled very hard on this next section. It was the most rigid yet. I attempted to guess some of the things you would have me alter, and I altered them myself. For example, I did not utilize the word "spleen" with such habituality, because I could perceive that it made you on nerves by the sentence in your letter when you said, "Stop using the word 'spleen.' It's getting on my nerves." I also invented things that I thought would appease you, funny things and sad things. I am certain that you will inform me when I have traveled too far.

Concerned about your writing, you sent me many pages, but I must tell you that I read every one of them. The Book of Recurrent Dreams *was a very beautiful thing, and I must say that the dream that we are our fathers made me melancholy. This is what you intended, yes? Of course I am not Father, so perhaps I am the rare bird to your novel. When I look in the reflection, what I view is not Father, but the negative of Father.*

Yankel. He is a good man, yes? Why do you think he made to swindle that man so many years ago? Perhaps he needed the currency very severely. I know what this is like, although I would never swindle any person. I found it stimulating that you made another lottery, this time to dub the shtetl. It made me think about what I would dub Odessa if I was given the power. I think that I might dub it Alex, because then everyone would know that I am Alex, and that the name of the city is Alex, so I must be a very premium person. I also might name it Little Igor, because people would think that my brother is a premium person, which he is, but it would be good for people to think so. (It is a queer thing how I wish everything for my brother that I wish for myself, only more rigidly.) Perhaps I would name it Trachimbrod, because then Trachimbrod could exist, and also, everyone here would purchase your book, and you could become famous.

I am regretted to end this letter. It is as proximal a thing as we have to talking. I hope you are appeased by the third division, and as always, I ask for your forgiveness. I attempted to be truthful and beautiful, as you told me to.

Oh, yes. There is one additional item. I did not amputate Sammy Davis, Junior, Junior from the story, even though you counseled that I should amputate her. You uttered that the story would be more "refined" with her absence, and I know that refined is like cultivated, polished, and well bred, but I will inform you that Sammy Davis, Junior, Junior is a very distinguished character, one with variegated appetites and seats of passion. Let us view her evolution and then resolve.

Guilelessly,
Alexander

GOING FORTH TO LUTSK

SAMMY DAVIS, JUNIOR, JUNIOR converted her attention from masticating her tail to trying to lick clean the hero's spectacles, which I will tell you were in need of cleaning. I write that she was trying because the hero was not being sociable. "Can you please get this dog away from me," he said, making his body into a ball. "Please. I really don't like dogs." "She is only making games with you," I told him when she put her body on top of his and kicked him with her back legs. "It signifies that she likes you." "Please," he said, attempting to remove her. She was now jumping up and also down on his face. "I really don't like her. I don't feel like games. She's going to break my glasses."

I will now mention that Sammy Davis, Junior, Junior is very often sociable with her new friends, but I had never witnessed a thing like this. I reasoned that she was in love with the hero. "Are you donning cologne?" I asked. "What?" "Are you donning any cologne?" He rotated his body so that his face was in the seat, away from Sammy Davis, Junior, Junior. "Maybe a little," he said, defending the back of his head with his hands. "Because she loves cologne. It makes her sexually stimulated." "Jesus." "She is trying to make sex to you. This is a good sign. It signifies that she will not bite." "Help!" he said as Sammy Davis, Junior, Junior rotated to do a sixty-nine. Pending all of this, Grandfather was still returning from his repose. "He does not like her," I told him. "Yes he does," Grandfather said, and that was all. "Sammy Davis, Junior, Junior!" I called. "Sit!" And do you know what? She sat. On the hero. In the sixty-nine position. "Sammy Davis, Junior, Junior! Sit on your side of the back seat! Get off the hero!" I think that she understood me, because she removed herself from the hero and returned to punching her face against the window on the other side. Or perhaps she had licked off all of the hero's cologne and was no longer interested in him sexually, but only as friends. "Do you smell something really awful?" the hero inquired, moving the wetness off of the back of his neck. "No," I said. A befitting not-truth. "Something smells just awful. It smells like someone died in this car. What is that?" "I do not know," I said, although I had a notion.

I do not cogitate that there was a person in the car that was surprised when we became lost amid the Lvov train station and the superway to Lutsk. "I hate Lvov," Grandfather rotated to tell the hero. "What's he saying?" the hero asked me. "He said it will not be long," I told him, another befitting not-truth. "Long until what?" the hero asked. I said to Grandfather, "You do not have to be kind to me, but do not blunder with the Jew." He said, "I can say anything I want to him. He will not understand." I rotated my head vertically to benefit the hero. "He says it will not be long until we get to the superway to Lutsk." "And from there?" the hero asked. "How long from there to Lutsk?" He affixed his attention to Sammy Davis, Junior, Junior, who was still punching her head against the window. (But I will mention that she was being a good bitch, because she punched her head against only her window, and when you are in a car, bitch or no bitch, you can do anything you desire as long as you remain on your side. Also, she was not farting very much.) "Tell him to shut his mouth," Grandfather said. "I cannot drive if he is going to talk." "Our driver says there are many buildings in Lutsk," I told the hero. "We are being paid tremendously to listen to him talk," I told Grandfather. "I am not," he said. "Neither am I," I said, "but someone is." "What?" "He says from the superway it is not more than two hours to Lutsk, where we will find a terrible hotel for the night." "What do you mean when you say terrible?" "What?" "I said, what...do...you...mean...when...you...say...the...hotel...will...be...terrible?" "Tell him to shut his mouth." "Grandfather says that you should look out of your window if you want to see anything." "What about the terrible hotel?" "Oh, I implore you to forget I said that." "I hate Lvov. I hate Lutsk. I hate the Jew in the back seat of this car that I hate." "You do not make this any cinchier." "I am blind. I am supposed to be retarded." "What are you saying up there? And what the hell is that smell?" "What?" "Tell him to shut his mouth or I will drive us off the road." "What...are...you...say...ing...up...there?" "The Jew must be silenced. I will kill us." "We were saying that the trip will perhaps be longer than we were desiring."

It captured five very long hours. If you want to know why, it is because Grandfather is Grandfather first and a driver second. He made us lost often and became on his nerves. I had to translate his anger into useful information for the hero. "Fuck," Grandfather said. I said, "He says if you look at the statues, you can see that some no longer endure. Those are where Communist statues used to be." "Fucking fuck, fuck!" Grandfather shouted. "Oh," I said, "he wants you to know that that building, that building, and that building are all important." "Why?" the hero inquired. "Fuck!" Grandfather said. "He cannot remember," I said.

"Could you turn on some air conditioning?" the hero commanded. I was humiliated to the maximum. "This car does not have air conditioning," I said. "I am eating humble pie." "Well, can we roll down the windows? It's really hot in here, and it smells like something died." "Sammy Davis, Junior, Junior will jump out." "Who?" "The bitch. Her name is Sammy Davis, Junior, Junior." "Is that a joke?" "No, she will truly go forth from the car." "His name, though." "*Her* name," I rectified him, because I am first rate with pronouns. "Tell him to Velcro his lip together," Grandfather said. "He says that the bitch was named for his favorite singer, who was Sammy Davis, Junior." "A Jew," the hero said. "What?" "Sammy Davis, Junior was a Jew." "This is not possible," I said. "A convert. He found the Jewish God. Funny." I told this to Grandfather. "Sammy Davis, Junior was not a Jew!" he hollered. "He was the Negro of the Rat Pack!" "The Jew is certain of it." "The Music Man? A Jew? This is not a possible thing!" "This is what he informs me." "Dean Martin, Junior!" he hollered to the back seat. "Get up here! Come on, girl!" "Can we please roll down the window?" the hero said. "I can't live with that smell." With this I licked the last crumb of humble pie from the plate. "It is only Sammy Davis, Junior, Junior. She gets terrible farting in the car because it has nor shock absorbers nor struts, but if we roll down the window she will jump out, and we need her because she is the Seeing Eye bitch for our blind driver, who is also my grandfather. What do you not understand?"

It was pending this five-hour car drive from the Lvov train station to Lutsk that the hero explained to me why he came to Ukraine. He excavated several items from his side bag. First he exhibited me a photograph. It was yellow and folded and had many pieces of fixative affixing it together. "See this?" he said. "This here is my grandfather Safran." He pointed to a young man who I will say appeared very much like the hero, and could have been the hero. "This was taken during the war." "From who?" "No, not taken like that. The photograph was made." "I understand." "These people he is with are the family that saved him from the Nazis." "What?" "They...saved...him...from...the...Na...zis." "In Trachimbrod?" "No, somewhere outside of Trachimbrod. He escaped the Nazi raid on Trachimbrod. Everyone else was killed. He lost a wife and a baby." "He lost?" "They were killed by the Nazis." "But if it was not Trachimbrod, why do we go to Trachimbrod? And how will we find this family?" He explained to me that we were not looking for the family, but for this girl. She would be the only one still alive.

He moved his finger along the face of the girl in the photograph as he mentioned her. She was standing down and right to his grandfather in the picture. A man who I am certain was her father was next to her, and a woman who I am certain was her mother was behind her. Her parents appeared very Russian, but she did not. She appeared American. She was a youthful girl, perhaps fifteen. But it is possible that she had more age. She could have been so old as the hero and me, as could have been the hero's grandfather. I looked at the girl for many minutes. She was so so beautiful. Her hair was brown, and rested only on her shoulders. Her eyes appeared sad, and full of intelligence.

"I want to see Trachimbrod," the hero said. "To see what it's like, how my grandfather grew up, where I would be now if it weren't for the war." "You would be Ukrainian." "That's right." "Like me." "I guess." "Only not like me because you would be a farmer in an unimpressive town, and I live in Odessa, which is very much like Miami." "And I want to see what it's like now. I don't think there are any Jews left, but maybe there are. And the shtetls weren't only Jews, so there should be others to talk to." "The whats?" "Shtetls. A shtetl is like a village." "Why don't you merely dub it a village?" "It's a Jewish word." "A Jewish word?" "Yiddish. Like schmuck." "What does it mean schmuck?" "Someone who does something that you don't agree with is a schmuck." "Teach me another." "Putz." "What does that mean?" "It's like schmuck." "Teach me another." "Schmendrik." "What does that mean?" "It's also like schmuck." "Do you know any words that are not like schmuck?" He pondered for a moment. "Shalom," he said, "which is actually three words, but that's Hebrew, not Yiddish. Everything I can think of is basically schmuck. The Eskimos have four hundred words for snow, and the Jews have four hundred for schmuck." I wondered, What is an Eskimo?

"So, we will sightsee the shtetl?" I asked the hero. "I figured it would be a good place to begin our search." "Search?" "For Augustine." "Who is Augustine?" "The girl in the photograph. She's the only one who would still be alive." "Ah. We will search for Augustine, who you think saved your grandfather from the Nazis." "Yes." It was very silent for a moment. "I would like to find her," I said. I perceived that this appeased the hero, but I did not say it to appease him. I said it because it was faithful. "And then," I said, "if we find her?" The hero was a pensive person. "I don't know what then. I suppose I'd thank her." "For saving your grandfather." "Yes." "That will be very queer, yes?" "What?" "When we find her." "If we find her." "We will find her." "Probably not," he said. "Then why do we search?" I queried, but before he could answer, I interrupted myself with another query. "And how do you know that her name is Augustine?" "I guess I don't, really. On the back, see, here, are written a few words, in my grandfather's writing, I think. Maybe not. It's in Yiddish. It says: 'This is me with Augustine, February 21, 1943.'" "It's very difficult to read." "Yes." "Why do you think he remarks only about Augustine and not the other two people in the photograph?" "I don't know." "It is queer, yes? It is queer that he remarks only her. Do you think he loved her?" "What?" "Because he remarks only her." "So?" "So perhaps he loved her." "It's funny that you should think that. We must think alike." (Thank you, Jonathan.) "I've actually thought a lot about it, without having any good reason to. He was eighteen, and she was, what,

60

about fifteen? He had just lost a wife and daughter when the Nazis raided his shtetl." "Trachimbrod?" "Right. For all I know the writing doesn't have anything to do with the picture. It could be that he used this for scrap paper." "Scrap?" "Paper that's unimportant. Just something to write on." "Oh." "So I don't really have any idea. It seems so improbable that he could have loved her. But isn't there something strange about the picture, the closeness between them, even though they're not looking at each other? The *way* that they aren't looking at each other. The distance. It's very powerful, don't you think? And his words on the back." "Yes." "And that we should both think about the possibility of his loving her is also strange." "Yes," I said. "Part of me wants him to have loved her, and part of me hates to think it." "What is the part of you that hates it if he loved her?" "Well, it's nice to think of some things as irreplaceable." "I do not understand. He married your present grandmother, so something must have been replaced." "But that's different." "Why?" "Because she's my grandmother." "Augustine could have been your grandmother." "No, she could have been someone else's grandmother. For all I know she is. Maybe he had children with her." "Do not say this about your grandfather." "Well, I know he had other children before, so why would that be so different?" "What if we reveal a brother of yours?" "We won't." "And how did you obtain this photograph?" I asked, holding it to the window. "My grandmother gave it to my mother two years ago, and she said that this was the family that saved my grandfather from the Nazis." "Why merely two years?" "What do you mean?" "Why was it so newly that she gave it to your mother?" "Oh, I see what you're asking. She has her reasons." "What are these reasons?" "I don't know." "Did you inquire her about the writing on the back?" "No. We couldn't ask her anything about it." "Why not?" "She held on to the photograph for fifty years. If she had wanted to tell us anything about it, she would have." "Now I understand what you are saying." "I couldn't even tell her I was coming to the Ukraine. She thinks I'm still in Prague." "Why is this?" "Her memories of the Ukraine aren't good. Her shtetl, Kolki, is only a few kilometers from Trachimbrod. I figure we'd go there too. But all of her family was killed, everyone, mother, father, sisters, grandparents." "Did a Ukrainian save her?" "No, she fled before the war. She was young, and left her family behind." She left her family behind. I wrote this on my brain. "It surprises me that no one saved her family," I said. "It shouldn't be surprising. The Ukrainians, back then, were terrible to the Jews. They were almost as bad as the Nazis. It was a different world. At the beginning of the war, a lot of Jews wanted to go to the Nazis to be protected from the Ukrainians." "This is not true." "It is." "I cannot believe what you are saying." "Look it up in the history books." "It does not say this in the history books." "Well, that's the way it was. Ukrainians were known for being terrible to the Jews. So were the Poles. Listen, I don't mean to offend you. It's got nothing to do with you. We're talking about fifty years ago." "I think you are mistaken," I told the hero. "I don't know what to say." "Say that you are mistaken." "I can't." "You must."

"Here are my maps," he said, excavating a few pieces of paper from his bag. He pointed to one that was wet from Sammy Davis, Junior, Junior. Her tongue, I hoped. "This is Trachimbrod," he said. "It's also called Sofiowka on certain maps. This is Lutsk. This is Kolki. It's an old map. Most of the places we're looking for aren't on new maps. Here," he said, and presented it to me. "You can see where we have to go. This is all I have, these maps and the photograph. It's not much." "I can promise you that we will find this Augustine," I said. I could perceive that this made the hero appeased. It also made me appeased. "Grandfather," I said, rotating to the front again. I explained everything that the hero had just uttered to me. I informed him about Augustine, and the maps, and the hero's grandmother. "Kolki?" he asked. "Kolki," I said. I made certain to involve every detail, and I also invented several new details, so that Grandfather would understand the story more. I could perceive that this story made Grandfather very melancholy. "Augustine," he said, and pushed Sammy Davis, Junior, Junior onto me. He scrutinized at the photograph while I fastened the wheel. He put it close to his face, like he wanted to smell it, or touch it with his eyes. "Augustine." "She is the one we are looking for," I said. He moved his head this and that. "We will find her," he said. "I know," I said. But I did not know, and nor did Grandfather.

When we reached the hotel, it was already commencing darkness.

"You must remain in the car," I told the hero, because the proprietor of the hotel would know that the hero is American, and Father told me that they charge Americans in surplus. "Why?" he asked. I told him why. "How will they know I am American?" "Tell him to remain in the car," Grandfather said, "or they will charge him twice." "I am making efforts," I told him. "I'd like to go in with you," the hero said, "to check the place out." "Why?" "Just to check things out. See what it's like." "You can see what it is like after I get the rooms." "I'd prefer to do it now," he said, and I must confess that he was beginning to be on my nerves. "What the fucking hell is he still talking about?" Grandfather asked. "He wants to go in with me." "Why?" "Because he is an American." "Is it OK if I go in?" he asked again. Grandfather turned to him, and said to me, "He is paying. If he wants to pay surplus, let him pay surplus." So I took him with me when I entered the hotel to pay for two rooms. If you want to know why two rooms, one was for Grandfather and me, and one was for the hero. Father said it should be this manner.

When we entered the hotel, I told the hero not to speak. "Do not speak," I said. "Why?" he asked. "Do not speak," I said without much volume. "Why?" he asked. "I will tutor you later. Shhh." But he kept inquiring why he should not speak, and as I was certain, he was heard by the owner of the hotel. "I will need to view your documents," the owner said. "He needs to view your documents," I said to the hero. "Why?" "Give them to me." "Why?" "If we are going to have a room, he needs to view your documents." "I don't understand." "There is nothing to understand." "Is there a problem?" the owner inquired me. "Because this is the only hotel in Lutsk that is still possessing rooms at this time of the night. Do you desire to attempt your luck on the street?"

I was finally able to prevail on the hero to give his documents. He stored them in a thing on his belt. Later he told me that this is called a fanny pack, and that fanny packs are not cool in America, and that he was only donning a fanny pack because a guidebook said he should don one to keep his documents close to his middle section. As I was certain, the owner of the hotel charged the hero a special foreigner tariff. I did not enlighten the hero this, because I knew he would have manufactured queries until he had to pay four times, and not only two, or until we received no room for the night at all, and had to repose in the car, as Grandfather had made an addiction of doing.

When we returned to the car, Sammy Davis, Junior, Junior was masticating her tail in the back seat, and Grandfather was again manufacturing Z's. "Grandfather," I said, adjusting his arm, "we obtained a room." I had to move him with very much violence in order to wake him. When he unclosed his eyes, he did not know where he was. "Anna?" he asked. "No, Grandfather," I said, "it is me, Sasha." He was very shamed, and hid his face from me. "We obtained a room," I said. "Is he feeling OK?" the hero asked me. "Yes, he is fatigued." "Will he be OK for tomorrow?" "Of course." But in truth Grandfather was not his normal self. Or maybe he was his normal self. I did not know what his normal self was. I remembered a thing that Father told me. When I was a boy, Grandfather said I looked like a combination of Father, Mother, Brezhnev, and myself. I had always thought that story was very funny until at that moment at the car in front of the hotel in Lutsk.

I told the hero not to leave any of his bags in the car. It is a bad and popular habit for people in Ukraine to take things without asking. I have read that New York City is very dangerous, but I must say that Ukraine is more dangerous. If you want to know who protects you from the people that take without asking, it is the police. If you want to know who protects you from the police, it is the people who take without asking. And very often they are the same people.

"Let us eat," Grandfather said, and commenced to drive. "You are hungry?" I asked the hero, who was again the sexual object of Sammy Davis, Junior, Junior. "Get it off of me," he said. "Are you hungry?" I repeated. "Please!" he implored. I called to her, and when she did not respond I punched her in the face. She moved to her side of the back seat, because now she understanded what it means to be stupid with the wrong person, and commenced to cry. Did I feel awful? "I'm famished," the hero said, lifting his head from his knees. "What?" "Yes, I'm hungry." "You are hungry, then." "Yes." "Good. Our driver—" "You can call him your grandfather. It doesn't bother me." "He is not your brother." "*Bother*, I said. Bother." "What does it mean to bother me?" "To upset." "What does it mean to upset?" "To distress." "I understand to distress." "So you can call him your grandfather, is what I'm saying."

We became very busy talking. When I rotated back to Grandfather, I saw that he was examining Augustine again. There was a sadness amid him and the photograph, and nothing in the world frightened me more. "We will eat," I told him. "Good," he said, holding the photograph very near to his face. Sammy Davis, Junior, Junior was persisting to cry. "One thing, though," the hero said. "What?" "You should know…" "Yes?" "I am a…how to say this…" "What?" "I'm a…" "You are very hungry, yes?" "I'm a vegetarian." "I do not understand." "I don't eat meat." "Why not?" "I just don't." "How can you not eat meat?" "I just don't." "He does not eat meat," I told Grandfather. "Yes he does," he informed me. "Yes you do," I likewise informed the hero. "No. I don't." "Why not?" I inquired him again. "I just don't. No meat." "Pork?" "No." "Meat?" "No meat." "Steak?" "Nope." "Chickens?" "No." "Do you eat veal?" "Oh, God. Absolutely no veal." "What about sausage?" "No sausage either." I told Grandfather this, and he presented me a very bothered look. "What is wrong with him?" he asked. "What is wrong with you?" I asked him. "It's just the way I am," he said. "Hamburger?" "No." "Tongue?" "What did he say is wrong with him?" Grandfather asked. "It is just the way he is." "Does he eat sausage?" "No." "No sausage!" "No. He says he does not eat sausage." "In truth?" "That is what he says." "But sausage…" "I know." "In truth you do not eat any sausage?" "No sausage." "No sausage," I told Grandfather. He closed his eyes and tried to put his arms around his stomach, but there was not room because of the wheel. It appeared like he was becoming sick because the hero would not eat sausage. "Well, let him deduce what he is going to eat. We will go to the most proximal restaurant." "You are a schmuck," I informed the hero. "You're not using the word correctly," he said. "Yes I am," I said.

"What do you mean he does not eat meat?" the waitress asked, and Grandfather put his head in his hands. "What is wrong with him?" she asked. "Which? The one who does not eat meat, the one with his head in his hands, or the bitch who is masticating her tail?" "The one who does not eat meat." "It is only the way that he is." The hero asked what we were talking about. "They do not have anything without meat," I informed him. "He does not eat any meat at all?" she inquired me again. "It is merely the way he is," I told her. "Sausage?" "No sausage," Grandfather answered to the waitress, rotating his head from here to there. "Maybe you could eat some meat," I suggested to the hero, "because they do not have anything that is not meat." "Don't they have potatoes or something?" he asked. "Do you have potatoes?" I asked the waitress. "Or something?" "You only receive a potato with the meat," she said. I told the hero. "Couldn't I just get a plate of potatoes?" "What?" "Couldn't I get two or three potatoes, without meat?" I asked the waitress, and she said she would go to the chef and inquire him. "Ask him if he eats liver," Grandfather said.

The waitress returned and said, "Here is what I have to say. We can make concessions to give him two potatoes, but they are served with a piece of meat on the plate. The chef says that this cannot be negotiated. He will have to eat it." "Two potatoes is fine?" I asked the hero. "Oh, that would be great." Grandfather and I both ordered the pork steak, and ordered one for Sammy Davis, Junior, Junior as well, who was becoming sociable with the hero's leg.

When the food arrived, the hero asked for me to remove the meat off of his plate. "I'd prefer not to touch it," he said. This was on my nerves to the maximum. If you want to know why, it is because I perceived that the hero perceived he was too good for our food. I took the meat off his plate, because I knew that is what Father would have desired me to do, and I did not utter a thing. "Tell him we will commence very early in the morning tomorrow," Grandfather said. "Early?" "So we can have as much of the day for searching as possible. It will be rigid at night." "We will commence very early in the morning tomorrow," I said to the hero. "That's good," he said, kicking his leg. I was very flabbergasted that Grandfather would desire to go forth early in the morning. He hated to not repose tardy. He hated to not repose ever. He also hated Lutsk, and the car, and the hero, and, of late, me. Leaving early in the morning would provide him with more of the day aroused with all of us. "Let me inspect at his maps," he said. I asked the hero for the maps. As he was reaching into his fanny pack, he again kicked his leg, which made Sammy Davis, Junior, Junior become sociable with the table, and also made the plates move. One of the hero's potatoes descended to the floor. When it hit the floor it made a sound. PLOMP. It rolled over, and then was inert. Grandfather and I examined each other. I did not know what to do. "A terrible thing has occurred," Grandfather said. The hero continued to view the potato on the floor. It was a dirty floor. It was one of his two potatoes. "This is awful," Grandfather said silently, and moved his plate to the side. "Awful." He was correct.

The waitress returned to our table with the colas we ordered. "Here are—" she began, but then she witnessed the potato on the floor and walked away with warp speed. The hero was still witnessing the potato on the floor. I do not know for certain, but I imagine he was imagining that he could pick it up, put it back on his plate, and eat it, or he could leave it on the floor, delude the mishap never happened, eat his one potato, and counterfeit to be happy, or he could push it with his foot to Sammy Davis, Junior, Junior, who was aristocratic enough not to eat it as it laid on that dirty floor, or he could tell the waitress for another, which would mean he would have to get another piece of meat for me to remove from his plate because for him meat is disgusting, or he could just eat the piece of meat I removed from his plate before, as I would hope for him to. But what he did was not any of these things. If you want to know what he did, he did not do anything. We remained silent, witnessing the potato. Grandfather inserted his fork in the potato, picked it up from the floor, and put it on his plate. He cut it into four pieces and gave one to Sammy Davis, Junior, Junior under the table, one to me, and one to the hero. He cut off a piece from his piece and ate it. Then he looked at me. I did not want to, but I knew that I had to. To say that it was not delicious would be an overstatement. Then we looked at the hero. He looked at the floor, and then at his plate. He cut off a piece from his piece and looked at it. "Welcome to Ukraine," Grandfather said to him, and punched me on the back, which was a thing I relished very much. Then Grandfather started laughing. "Welcome to Ukraine," I translated. Then I started laughing. Then the hero started laughing. We laughed with much violence for a long time. We obtained the attention of every person in the restaurant. We laughed with violence, and then more violence. I witnessed that each of us was manufacturing tears at his eyes. It was not until very much in the posterior that I understood that each of us was laughing for a different reason, for our own reason, and that not one of those reasons had a thing to do with the potato.

There is something that I did not mention before, which it would now be befitting to mention. (Please, Jonathan, I implore you never to exhibit this to one soul. I do not know why I am writing this here.) I returned home from a famous nightclub one night and desired to view television. I was surprised when I heard that the television was already on, because it was so tardy. I cogitated that it was Grandfather. As I illuminated before, he would very often come to our house when he could not repose. This was before he came to live with us. What would occur is that he would commence to repose while viewing television, but then rise a few hours later and return to his house. Unless I could not repose, and because I could not repose would hear Grandfather viewing television, I would not know the next day if he had been in the house the night previous. He might have been there every night. Because I never knew, I thought of him as a ghost.

I would never say hello to Grandfather when he was viewing television, because I did not want to meddle with him. So I walked slowly that night, and without noise. I was already on the four stair when I heard something queer. It was not crying, exactly. It was something a little less than crying. I submerged the four stairs with slowness. I walked on toes through the kitchen and observed from around the corner, amid the kitchen and the television room. First I witnessed the television. It was exhibiting a football game. (I do not remember who was competing, but I am confident that we were winning.) I witnessed a hand on the chair that Grandfather likes to view television in. But it was not Grandfather's hand. I tried to see more, and I almost fell over. I know that I should have recognized the sound that was a little less than crying. It was Little Igor. (I am such a stupid fool.)

This made me a suffering person. I will tell you why. I knew why he was a little less than crying. I knew very well, and I wanted to go to him and tell him that I had a little less than cried too, just like him, and that no matter how much it seemed like he would never grow up to be a premium person like me, with many girls and so many famous places to go, he would. He would be exactly like me. And look at me, Little Igor, the bruises go away, and so does how you hate, and so does the feeling that everything you receive in life is something you have earned.

But I could not tell him any of these things. I roosted on the floor of the kitchen, only several meters distance from him, and I commenced to laugh. I did not know why I was laughing, but I could not stop. I pressed my hand against my mouth so that I would not manufacture any noise. My laughing got more and more, until my stomach pained. I attempted to rise, so that I could walk to my room, but I was afraid that it would be too difficult to control my laughing. I remained there for many, many minutes. My brother persevered to a little less than cry, which made my silent laughing even more. I am able to understand now that it was the same laugh that I had in the restaurant in Lutsk, the laugh that had the same darkness as Grandfather's laugh and the hero's laugh. (I ask leniency for writing this. Perhaps I will remove it before I post this part to you. I am sorry.) As for Sammy Davis, Junior, Junior, she did not eat her piece of the potato.

The hero and I spoke very much at dinner, mostly about America. "Tell me about things that you have in America," I said. "What do you want to know about?" "My friend Gregory informs me that there are many good schools for accounting in America. Is this true?" "I guess. I don't really know. I could find out for you when I get back." "Thank you," I said, because now I had a connection in America, and was not alone, and then, "What do you want to make?" "What do I want to make?" "Yes. What will you become?" "I don't know." "Surely you know." "This and that." "What does it mean this and that?" "I'm just not sure yet." "Father informs me that you are writing a book about this trip." "I like to write." I punched his back. "You are a writer!" "Shhhh." "But it is a good career, yes?" "What?" "Writing. It is very noble." "Noble? I don't know." "Do you have any books published?" "No, but I'm still very young." "You have stories published?" "No. Well, one or two." "What are they dubbed?" "Forget it." "This is a first-rate title." "No. I mean, forget it." "I would love very much to read your stories." "You probably won't like them." "Why do you say that?" "*I* don't even like them." "Oh." "They're apprentice pieces." "What does it mean apprentice pieces?" "They're not real stories. I was just learning how to write." "But one day you will have learned how to write." "That's the hope." "Like becoming an accountant." "Maybe." "Why do you want to write?" "I don't know. I used to think it was what I was born to do. No, I

69

never really thought that. It's just something people say." "No, it is not. I truly feel that I was born to be an accountant." "You're lucky." "Perhaps you were born to write?" "I don't know. Maybe. It sounds terrible to say. Cheap." "It sounds nor terrible nor cheap." "It's so hard to express yourself." "I understand this." "I want to express myself." "The same is true for me." "I'm looking for my voice." "It is in your mouth." "I want to do something I'm not ashamed of." "Something you are proud of, yes?" "Not even. I just don't want to be ashamed." "There are many premium Russian writers, yes?" "Oh, of course. Tons." "Tolstoy, yes? He wrote *War*, and also *Peace*, which are premium books, and he also earned the Noble Peace Prize for writing, if I am not so wrong." "Tolstoy. Bely. Turgenev." "A question." "Yes?" "Do you write because you have a thing to say?" "No." "And if I may partake in a different theme: how much currency would an accountant receive in America?" "I'm not sure. A lot, I imagine, if he or she is good." "She!" "Or he." "Are there Negro accountants?" "There are African-American accountants. You don't want to use that word, though, Alex." "And homosexual accountants?" "There are homosexual everythings. There are homosexual garbage men." "How much currency would a Negro homosexual accountant receive?" "You shouldn't use that word." "Which word?" "The one before homosexual." "What?" "The n-word. Well, it's not *the* n-word, but—" "Negro?" "Shhh." "I dig Negroes." "You really shouldn't say that." "But I dig them all the way. They are premium people." "It's that word, though. It's not a nice thing to say." "Negro?" "Please." "What's wrong with Negroes?" "Shhh." "How much does a cup of coffee cost in America?" "Oh, it depends. Maybe one dollar." "One dollar! This is for free! In Ukraine one cup of coffee is five dollars!" "Oh, well, I didn't mention cappuccinos. They can be as much as five or six dollars." "Cappuccinos," I said, elevating my hands above my head, "there is no maximum!" "Do you have lattes in the Ukraine?" "What is latte?" "Oh, because they're very cool in America. Really, they're basically everywhere." "Do you have mochas in America?" "Of course, but only children drink them. They're not very cool in America." "Yes, it is very much the same here. We have also mochaccinos." "Yeah, of course. We have those in America. They might be seven dollars." "Are they much-loved things?" "Mochaccinos?" "Yes."

"I think they're for people who want to drink a coffee drink but also really like hot chocolate." "I understand this. What about the girls in America?" "What about them?" "They are very informal with their boxes, yes?" "You hear about them, but nobody I know has ever met one of them." "Are you carnal very often?" "Are you?" "I inquired you. Are you?" "Are you?" "I inquired headmost. Are you?" "Not really." "What do you intend by not really?" "I'm not a priest, but I'm not John Holmes either." "I know of this John Holmes." I lifted my hands to my sides. "With the premium penis." "That's the one," he said, and laughed. I made him laugh with my funny. "In Ukraine everyone has a penis like that." He laughed again. "Even the women?" he asked. "You made a funny?" I asked. "Yes," he said. So I laughed. "Have you ever had a girlfriend?" I asked the hero. "Have you?" "I am inquiring you." "I sort of have," he said. "What do you signify with sort of?" "Nothing formal, really. Not a girlfriend girlfriend, really. I've dated, I guess, once or twice. I don't want to be formal." "It is the same state of affairs with me," I said. "I also do not want to be formal. I do not want to be handcuffed to only one girl." "Exactly," he said. "I mean, I've fooled around with girls." "Of course." "Blowjobs." "Yes, of course." "But once you get a girlfriend, well, you know." "I know very well."

"A question," I said. "Do you think the women in Ukraine are first rate?" "I haven't seen many since I've been here." "Do you have women like this in America?" "There's at least one of everything in America." "I have heard this. Do you have many motorcycles in America?" "Of course." "And fax machines?" "Everywhere." "You have a fax machine?" "No. They're very passé." "What does it mean passé?" "They're out-of-date. Paper is so tedious." "Tedious?" "Tiresome." "I understand what you are telling me, and I harmonize. I would not ever use paper. It makes me a sleeping person." "It's so messy." "Yes, it is true, it makes a mess, and you are asleep." "Another question. Do most young people have impressive cars in America? Lotus Esprit V8 Twin Turbos?" "Not really. I don't. I have a real piece-of-shit Toyota." "It is brown?" "No, it's an expression." "How can your car be an expression?" "I have a car that is like a piece of shit. You know, it stinks like shit and looks shitty like shit." "And if you are a good accountant, you could buy an impressive car?"

"Absolutely. You could probably buy most anything you want." "What kind of wife would a good accountant have?" "Who knows." "Would she have rigid tits?" "I couldn't say for sure." "Probably, although?" "I guess." "I dig this. I dig rigid tits." "But there are also accountants, even very good ones, who have ugly wives. That's just the way it works." "If John Holmes was a first-rate accountant, he could have any woman he would like for his wife, yes?" "Probably." "My penis is very big." "OK."

After dinner at the restaurant, we drove back to the hotel. As I knew, it was an unimpressive hotel. There was no area for swimming and no famous discotheque. When we unclosed the door to the hero's room, I could perceive that he was distressed. "It's nice," he said, because he could perceive that I could perceive that he was distressed. "Really, it's just for sleeping." "You do not have hotels like this in America!" I made a funny. "No," he said, and he was laughing. We were like friends. For the first time that I could remember, I felt entirely good. "Make sure you secure the door after we go to our room," I told him. "I do not want to make you a petrified person, but there are many dangerous people who want to take things without asking from Americans, and also kidnap them. Good night." The hero laughed again, but he laughed because he did not know that I was not making a funny. "Come on, Sammy Davis, Junior, Junior," Grandfather called to the bitch, but she would not leave the door. "Come on." Nothing. "Come on!" he bellowed, but she would not dislodge. I tried to sing to her, which she relishes, especially when I sing "Billie Jean," by Michael Jackson. "She's just a girl who claims that I am the one." But nothing. She only pushed her head against the door to the hero's room. Grandfather attempted to remove her with force, but she commenced to cry. I knocked on the door, and the hero had a teethbrush in his mouth. "Sammy Davis, Junior, Junior will manufacture Z's with you this evening," I told him, although I knew that would not be successful. "No," he said, and that was all. "She will not depart from your door," I told him. "Then let her sleep in the hall." "It would be benevolent of you." "Not interested." "Only for one night." "One too many. She'll kill me." "It is so unlikely." "She's crazy." "Yes, I cannot dispute that she is crazy. But she is also compassionate." I knew that I would not prevail. "Listen," the hero said, "if she wants to sleep in the room, I'd be happy to sleep in the hall. But if I'm in the room, I'm alone in the room." "Perhaps you could both sleep in the hall," I suggested.

After we left the hero and the bitch to repose—hero in room, bitch in hall—Grandfather and I went downstairs to the hotel bar for drinks of vodka. It was Grandfather's notion. In truth, I was a petite amount terrified of being alone with him. "He is a good boy," Grandfather said. I could not perceive if he was inquiring me or tutoring me. "He seems good," I said. Grandfather moved his hand over his face, which had become covered with hairs during the day. It was only then that I noticed that his hands were still shaking, that they had been shaking all day. "We should try very inflexibly to help him." "We should," I said. "I would like very much to find Augustine," he said. "So would I."

That was all the talking for the night. We had three vodkas each and watched the weather report that was on the television behind the bar. It said that the weather for the next day would be normal. I was appeased that the weather would be normal. It would make our search cinchier. After the vodka, we went up to our room, which flanked the room of the hero. "I will repose on the bed, and you will repose on the floor," Grandfather said. "Of course," I said. "I will make my alarm for six in the morning." "Six?" I inquired. If you want to know why I inquired, it is because six is not very early in the morning for me, it is tardy in the night. "Six," he said, and I knew that it was the end of the conversation.

While Grandfather washed his teeth, I went to make certain that everything was acceptable with the hero's room. I listened at the door to detect if he was able to manufacture Z's, and I could not hear anything abnormal, only the wind penetrating the windows and the sound of insects. Good, I said to my brain, he reposes well. He will not be fatigued in the morning. I tried to unclose the door, to make sure it was secured. It opened a percentage, and Sammy Davis, Junior, Junior, who was still conscious, walked in. I watched her lay herself next to the bed, where the hero reposed in peace. This is acceptable, I thought, and closed the door with silence. I walked back to the room of Grandfather and I. The lights were already off, but I could perceive that he was not yet reposing. His body rotated over and over. The bed sheets moved, and the pillow made noises as he rotated over and over, over and then again over. I heard his large breathing. I heard his body move. It was like this all night. I knew why he could not repose. It was the same reason that I would not be able to repose. We were both regarding the same question: what did he do during the war?

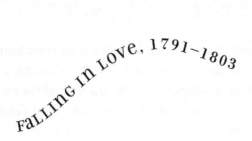

Falling in Love, 1791–1803

TRACHIMBROD was somehow different from the nameless shtetl that used to exist in the same place. Business went on as usual. The Uprighters still hollered, hung, and limped, and still looked down on the Slouchers, who still twiddled the fringes at the ends of their shirtsleeves, and still ate cookies and knishes after, but more often during, services. Grieving Shanda still grieved for her deceased philosopher husband, Pinchas, who still played an active role in shtetl politics. Yankel still tried to do right, still told himself again and again that he wasn't sad, and still always ended up sad. The synagogue still rolled, still trying to land itself on the shtetl's wandering Jewish/Human fault line. Sofiowka was as mad as ever, still masturbating a handful, still binding himself in string, using his body to remember his body, and still remembering only the string. But with the name came a new self-consciousness, which often revealed itself in shameful ways.

The women of the shtetl raised their impressive noses to my great-great-great-great-great-grandmother. They called her *dirty river girl* and *waterbaby* under their breath. While they were too superstitious ever to reveal to her the truth of her history, they saw to it that she had no friends her own age (telling their children that she was not as much fun as the fun she had, or as kind as her kind deeds), and that she associated only with Yankel and any man of the shtetl who was brave enough to risk being seen by his wife. Of which there were quite a few. Even the surest gentleman stumbled over himself in her presence. After only ten years of life, she was already the most desired creature in the shtetl, and her reputation had spread like rivulets into the neighboring villages.

I've imagined her many times. She's a bit short, even for her age—not short in the endearing, childish way, but as a malnourished child might be short. The same is true for how skinny she is. Every night before putting her to sleep, Yankel counts her ribs, as if one might have disappeared in the course of the day and become the seed and soil for some new companion to steal her away from him. She eats well enough and is healthy, insofar as she's never sick, but her body looks like that of a chronically sick girl, a girl squeezed in some biological vise, or a starving girl, a skin-and-bones girl, a girl who is not entirely free. Her hair is thick and black, her lips are thin and bright and white. How else could it be?

Much to Yankel's dismay, Brod insisted on cutting that thick black hair herself.

It's not ladylike, he said. *You look like a little boy when it's so short.*

Don't be a fool, she told him.

But doesn't it bother you?

Of course it bothers me when you're a fool.

Your hair, he said.

I think it's very pretty.

Can it be pretty if no one thinks it's pretty?

I think it's pretty.

If you're the only one?

That's pretty pretty.

And what about the boys? Don't you want them to think you're pretty?

I wouldn't want a boy to think I was pretty unless he was the kind of boy who thought I was pretty.

I think it's pretty, he said. *I think it's very beautiful.*

Say it again and I'll grow it long.

I know, he laughed, kissing her forehead as he pinched her ears between his fingers.

Her learning to sew (from a book Yankel brought back from Lvov) coincided with her refusal to wear any clothes that she did not make for herself, and when he bought her a book about animal physiology, she held the pictures to his face and said, *Don't you think it's strange, Yankel, how we eat them?*

I've never eaten a picture.

The animals. Don't you find that strange? I can't believe I never found it strange before. It's like your name, how you don't notice it for so long, but when you finally do, you can't help but say it over and over, and wonder why you never thought it was strange that you should have that name, and that everyone has been calling you that name for your whole life.

Yankel. Yankel. Yankel. Nothing so strange for me.

I won't eat them, at least not until it doesn't seem strange to me.

Brod resisted everything, gave in to no one, would not be challenged or not challenged.

I don't think you're stubborn, Yankel told her one afternoon when she refused to eat dinner before dessert.

Well I am!

And she was loved for it. Loved by everyone, even those who hated her. The curious circumstances of her creation lit the men's intrigue, but it was her clever manipulations, her coy gestures and pivots of phrase, her refusal to acknowledge or ignore their existence that made them follow her through the streets, gaze at her from their windows, dream of her — not their wives, not even themselves — at night.

Yes, Yoske. The men in the flour mill are so strong and brave.

Yes, Feivel. Yes, I am a good girl.

Yes, Saul. Yes, yes, I love sweets.

Yes, oh yes, Itzik. Oh yes.

Yankel didn't have the heart to tell her that he was not her father, that she was the Float Queen of Trachimday not only because she was, without question, the most loved young girl in the shtetl, but because it was her real father at the bottom of the river with her name, her papa the hardy men dove for. So he created more stories — wild stories, with undomesticated imagery and flamboyant characters. He invented stories so fantastic that she had to believe. Of course, she was only a child, still removing the dust from her first death. What else could she do? And he was already accumulating the dust of his second death. What else could *he* do?

With the help of the shtetl's desirous men and hateful women, my very-great-grandmother grew into herself, cultivating private interests:

weaving, gardening, reading anything she could get her hands on—which was just about anything in Yankel's prodigious library, a room filled from floor to ceiling with books, which would one day serve as Trachimbrod's first public library. Not only was she the smartest citizen in Trachimbrod, called upon to solve difficult problems of mathematics or logic—*THE HOLY WORD*, the Well-Regarded Rabbi once asked her in the dark, *WHICH IS IT, BROD?*—she was also the most lonely and sad. She was a genius of sadness, immersing herself in it, separating its numerous strands, appreciating its subtle nuances. She was a prism through which sadness could be divided into its infinite spectrum.

Are you sad, Yankel? she asked one morning over breakfast.

Of course, he said, feeding melon slices into her mouth with a shaking spoon.

Why?

Because you are talking instead of eating your breakfast.

Were you sad before that?

Of course.

Why?

Because you were eating then, instead of talking, and I become sad when I don't hear your voice.

When you watch people dance, does that make you sad?

Of course.

It also makes me sad. Why do you think it does that?

He kissed her on the forehead, put his hand under her chin. *You really must eat*, he said. *It's getting late.*

Do you think Bitzl Bitzl is a particularly sad person?

I don't know.

What about grieving Shanda?

Oh yes, she's particularly sad.

That's an obvious one, isn't it? Is Shloim sad?

Who knows?

The twins?

Maybe. It's none of our business.

Is God sad?

He would have to exist to be sad, wouldn't He?

I know, she said, giving his shoulder a little slap. *That's why I was asking, so I might finally know if you believed!*

Well, let me leave it at this: if God does exist, He would have a great deal to be sad about. And if He doesn't exist, then that too would make Him quite sad, I imagine. So to answer your question, God must be sad.

Yankel! She wrapped her arms around his neck, as if trying to pull herself into him, or him into her.

Brod discovered 613 sadnesses, each perfectly unique, each a singular emotion, no more similar to any other sadness than to anger, ecstasy, guilt, or frustration. Mirror Sadness. Sadness of Domesticated Birds. Sadness of Being Sad in Front of One's Parent. Humor Sadness. Sadness of Love Without Release.

She was like a drowning person, flailing, reaching for anything that might save her. Her life was an urgent, desperate struggle to justify her life. She learned impossibly difficult songs on her violin, songs outside of what she thought she could know, and would each time come crying to Yankel, *I have learned to play this one too! It's so terrible! I must write something that not even I can play!* She spent evenings with the art books Yankel had bought for her in Lutsk, and each morning sulked over breakfast, *They were good and fine, but not beautiful. No, not if I'm being honest with myself. They are only the best of what exists.* She spent an afternoon staring at their front door.

Waiting for someone? Yankel asked.

What color is this?

He stood very close to the door, letting the end of his nose touch the peephole. He licked the wood and joked, *It certainly tastes like red.*

Yes, it is red, isn't it?

Seems so.

She buried her head in her hands. *But couldn't it be just a bit more red?*

Brod's life was a slow realization that the world was not for her, and that for whatever reason, she would never be happy and honest at the same time. She felt as if she were brimming, always producing and hoarding more love inside her. But there was no release. Table, ivory elephant charm, rainbow, onion, hairdo, mollusk, Shabbos, violence, cuticle, melodrama, ditch, honey, doily...None of it moved her. She addressed her world honestly, searching for something deserving of the volumes of love she knew she had within her, but to each she would have to say, *I don't love you.* Bark-brown fence post: *I don't love you.* Poem too long: *I don't love you.* Lunch in a bowl: *I don't love you.* Physics, the idea of you, the laws of you: *I don't love you.* Nothing felt like anything more than what it actually was. Everything was just a thing, mired completely in its thingness.

If we were to open to a random page in her journal—which she must have kept and kept with her at all times, not fearing that it would be lost, or discovered and read, but that she would one day stumble upon that thing which was finally worth writing about and remembering, only to find that she had no place to write it—we would find some rendering of the following sentiment: *I am not in love.*

So she had to satisfy herself with the *idea* of love—loving the loving of things whose existence she didn't care at all about. Love itself became the object of her love. She loved herself in love, she loved loving love, as love loves loving, and was able, in that way, to reconcile herself with a world that fell so short of what she would have hoped for. It was not the world that was the great and saving lie, but her willingness to make it beautiful and fair, to live a once-removed life, in a world once-removed from the one in which everyone else seemed to exist.

The boys, young men, men, and elderly of the shtetl would sit vigil outside her window at all hours of the day and night, asking if they could assist her with her studies (with which she needed no help, of course, with which they couldn't possibly help her even if she let them try), or in the garden (which grew as if charmed, which bloomed red tulips and roses, orange and restless impatiens), or if perhaps Brod would like to go for a stroll to the river (to which she was perfectly able to stroll on her own, thank you). She never said no and never said yes, but pulled, slackened, pulled her strings of control.

Pull: *What would be nicest*, she would say, *is if I had a tall glass of iced tea.* What happened next: the men raced to get one for her. The first to return might get a peck on the forehead (slacken), or (pull) a promised walk (to be granted at a later date), or (slacken) a simple *Thank you, good-bye.* She maintained a careful balance by her window, never allowing the men to come too close, never allowing them to stray too far. She needed them desperately, not only for the favors, not only for the things that they could get for Yankel and her that Yankel couldn't afford, but because they were a few more fingers to plug the dike that held back what she knew to be true: she didn't love life. There was no convincing reason to live.

Yankel was already seventy-two years old when the wagon went into the river, his house more ready for a funeral than a birth. Brod read under the muted canary light of oil lamps covered with lace shawls, and bathed in a tub lined with sandpaper to prevent slipping. He tutored her in literature and simple mathematics until she had far surpassed his knowledge, laughed with her even when there was nothing funny, read to her before watching her fall asleep, and was the only person she could consider a friend. She acquired his uneven walk, spoke with his old man's inflections, even rubbed at a five-o'clock shadow that was never, at any time of any day of her life, there.

I bought you some books in Lutsk, he told her, shutting the door on the early evening and the rest of the world.

We can't afford these, she said, taking the heavy bag. *I'll have to return them tomorrow.*

But we can't afford not to have them. Which can we not afford more, having them or not having them? As I see it, we lose either way. My way, we lose with the books.

You're ridiculous, Yankel.

I know, he said, *because I also bought you a compass from my architect friend and several books of French poetry.*

But I don't speak French.

What could be a better occasion to learn?

Having a French language textbook.

Ah yes, I knew there was a reason I bought this! he said, removing a thick brown book from the bottom of the bag.

You're impossible, Yankel!

I'm possibly possible.

Thank you, she said, and kissed him on the forehead, which was the only place she had ever kissed or been kissed, and would have been, if not for all the novels she had read, the only place she thought people ever kissed.

She had to secretly return so many of the things that Yankel bought for her. He never noticed, because he couldn't remember ever having bought them. It was Brod's idea to make their personal library a public one, and to charge a small fee to take out books. It was with this money, along with what she was able to secure from the men who loved her, that they were able to survive.

Yankel made every effort to prevent Brod from feeling like a stranger, from being aware of their age difference, their genders. He would leave the door open when he urinated (always sitting down, always wiping himself after), and would sometimes spill water on his pants and say, *Look, it also happens to me*, unaware that it was Brod who spilled water on her pants to comfort him. When Brod fell from the swing in the park, Yankel scraped his own knees against the sandpaper floor of his bathtub and said, *I too have fallen.* When she started to grow breasts, he pulled up his shirt to reveal his old, dropped chest and said, *It's not only you.*

This was the world in which she grew and he aged. They made for themselves a sanctuary from Trachimbrod, a habitat completely unlike the rest of the world. No hateful words were ever spoken, and no hands raised. More than that, no angry words were ever spoken, and nothing was denied. But more than that, no unloving words were ever spoken, and everything was held up as another small piece of proof that it can be this way, it doesn't have to be that way; if there is no love in the world, we will make a new world, and we will give it heavy walls, and we will furnish it with soft red interiors, from the inside out, and give it a knocker that resonates like a diamond falling to a jeweler's felt so that we should never hear it. Love me, because love doesn't exist, and I have tried everything that does.

But my very-great-and-lonely-grandmother didn't love Yankel, not in the simple and impossible sense of the word. In reality she hardly knew him. And he hardly knew her. They knew intimately the aspects of themselves in the other, but never the other. Could Yankel have guessed what Brod dreamed of? Could Brod have guessed, could she have cared to guess, where Yankel traveled at night? They were strangers, like my grandmother and me.

But...

But each was the closest thing to a deserving recipient of love that the other would find. So they gave each other all of it. He scraped his knee and said, *I too have fallen.* She spilled water on her pants so he wouldn't feel alone. He gave her that bead. She wore it. And when Yankel said he would die for Brod, he certainly meant it, but that thing he would die for was not Brod, exactly, but his love for her. And when she said, *Father, I love you,* she was neither naïve nor dishonest, but the opposite: she was wise and truthful enough to lie. They reciprocated the great and saving lie — that our love for things is greater than our love for our love for things — willfully playing the parts they wrote for themselves, willfully creating and believing fictions necessary for life.

She was twelve, and he was at least eighty-four. Even if he were to live to ninety, he reasoned, she would be only eighteen. And he knew he would not live to ninety. He was secretly weak, and secretly in pain. Who would take care of her when he died? Who would sing to her and continue to tickle her back, in the particular way she liked, long after she'd fallen asleep? How would she learn of her real father? How could he be sure that she would be safe from daily violence, unintentional and intentional violence? How could he be sure that she would never change?

He did everything he could to impede his rapid deterioration. He tried to eat a good meal even when he wasn't hungry, and drink a bit of vodka between meals even when he felt it would tie his stomach into a knot. He took long walks each afternoon, knowing that the pain in his legs was a good pain, and chopped one piece of wood every morning, knowing that it was not in sickness that his arms ached, but health.

Fearing his frequent deficiencies of memory, he began writing fragments of his life story on his bedroom ceiling with one of Brod's lipsticks that he found wrapped in a sock in her desk drawer. This way, his life would be the first thing he would see when he awoke each morning, and the last thing before going to sleep each night. *You used to be married, but she left you,* above his bureau. *You hate green vegetables,* at the far end of the ceiling. *You are a Sloucher,* where the ceiling met the door. *You don't believe in an afterlife,* written in a circle around the hanging lamp. He never wanted Brod to know how much like a sheet of glass his mind had become, how it would steam with confusion, how thoughts skated off it, how he couldn't understand so many of the things she told him, how he often forgot his name, and, like a small part of him dying, even hers.

4:812 — *The dream of living forever with Brod.* I have this dream every night. Even when I can't remember it the next morning, I know it was there, like the depression a lover's head leaves on the pillow next to you after she's left. I dream not of growing old with her, but of never growing old, either of us. She never leaves me, and I never leave her. It's true, I am afraid of dying. I am afraid of the world moving forward without me, of my absence going unnoticed, or worse, being some natural force propelling life on. Is it selfish? Am I such a bad person for dreaming of a world that ends when I do? I don't mean the world ending with respect to me, but every set of eyes closing with mine. Sometimes my dream of living forever with Brod is the dream of our dying together. I know there is no afterlife. I'm no fool. And I know there is no God. It's not her company I need, but to know that she won't need mine, or that she won't not need it. I imagine scenes of her without me, and I become so jealous. She will marry and have children and touch what I could never approach—all things that should make me happy. I cannot tell her this dream, of course, but I want to so desperately. She is the only thing that matters.

He read her a story in bed and listened to her interpretations, never interrupting her, not even to tell her how proud he was, how smart and beautiful she was. After kissing her good night and blessing her, he went to the kitchen, drank the few sips of vodka his stomach could handle, and blew out the lamp. He wandered down the dark hallway, following the warm glow from beneath his bedroom door. He stumbled once over a stack of Brod's books on the floor outside her room, and again over her bag. Entering his own room, he imagined that he would die in his bed that night. He imagined how Brod would find him in the morning. He imagined the position he would be in, the expression on his face. He imagined how he would feel, or not feel. *It's late,* he thought, *and I must wake up early in the morning to cook for Brod before her classes.* He lowered himself to the floor, did the three push-ups he could summon, and picked himself back up. *It's late,* he thought, *and I must be thankful for everything I have, and reconciled with everything I have lost and not lost. I tried very hard to be a good person today, to do things as God would have wanted, had He existed. Thank you for the gifts of life and Brod,* he thought, *and thank you, Brod, for giving me a reason to live. I am not sad.* He slid under the red woolen sheets and looked directly above his head: *You are Yankel. You love Brod.*

Recurrent Secrets, 1791–1943

IT WAS A SECRET when Yankel shrouded the clock in black cloth. It was a secret when the Well-Regarded Rabbi awoke one morning with these words on his tongue: *BUT WHAT IF?* And when the most outspoken Sloucher, Rachel F, awoke wondering, *But what if?* It was not a secret when Brod didn't think to tell Yankel that she found spots of red in her underpants, and that she was sure she was dying, and how poetic that she should die like this. But it was a secret when she did think to tell him and then didn't. They were secrets at least some of the times Sofiowka masturbated, which made him the greatest keeper of secrets in Trachimbrod, and perhaps anywhere, ever. It was a secret when grieving Shanda didn't grieve. And it was a secret when the Rabbi's twins implied that they saw nothing and knew nothing of what happened that day, March 18, 1791, when Trachim B's wagon either did or did not pin him against the bottom of the Brod River.

Yankel goes through the house with black sheets. He drapes the standing clock in black cloth and wraps his silver pocket watch in a swatch of black linen. He stops observing Shabbos, unwilling to mark the end of another week, and he avoids the sun because shadows, too, are clocks. *I am tempted, on occasion, to strike Brod*, he thinks to himself, *not because she does wrong, but because I love her so much*. Which is also a secret. He covers the window of his bedroom with black cloth. He wraps the calendar in black paper, as if it were a gift. He reads Brod's diary while she bathes, which is a secret, which is a terrible thing, he knows, but there are some terrible things to which a father is entitled, even a counterfeit father.

March 18, 1803
. . . I'm feeling overwhelmed. Before tomorrow I have to finish reading the first volume of the biography of Copernicus, since it has to be returned to the man from whom Yankel purchased it. Then there are the Greek and Roman heroes to be sorted out, and the Bible stories to try to find meaning in, and then — as if there were enough hours in the day — there is math. I bring it upon myself . . .

June 20, 1803
. . . "Deep down, the young are lonelier than the old." I read that in a book somewhere and it's stuck in my head. Maybe it's true. Maybe it's not true. More likely, the young and old are lonely in different ways, in their own ways . . .

September 23, 1803
. . . It occurred to me this afternoon that there is nothing in the world I like so much as writing in my diary. It never misunderstands me and I never misunderstand it. We are like perfect lovers, like one person. Sometimes I take it to bed with me and hold it as I fall asleep. Sometimes I kiss its pages, one after another. For now, at least, it will have to do . . .

Which is also a secret, of course, because Brod keeps her own life a secret from herself. Like Yankel, she repeats things until they are true, or until she can't tell whether they are true or not. She has become an expert at confusing *what is* with *what was* with *what should be* with *what could be*. She avoids mirrors, and lifts a powerful telescope to find herself. She aims it into the sky, and can see, or so she thinks, past the blue, past the black, even past the stars, and back into a different black, and a different blue—an arc that begins with her eye and ends with a narrow house. She studies the façade, notices where the wood of the door frame has warped and faded, where rainpipe drainage has left white tracks, and then looks through the windows, one at a time. Through the lower-left window she can see a woman scrubbing a plate with a rag. It looks as if the woman is singing to herself, and Brod imagines the song to be the very song with which her mother would have sung her to sleep had she not died, painless, in childbirth, as Yankel promised. The woman looks for her reflection in the plate and then puts it down atop a stack. She brushes her hair away from her face for Brod to see, or so Brod thinks. The woman has too much skin for her bones and too many wrinkles for her years, as if her face were some animal of its own, slowly descending the skull each day, until one day it would cling to her jaw, and one day fall off completely, landing in the woman's hands for her to look at and say, *This is the face I've worn my whole life.* There is nothing in the lower-right window save a broad bureau cluttered with books, papers, and pictures—pictures of a man and a woman, of children and the children's children. *What wonderful portraits,* she thinks, *so small, so accurate!* She focuses in on one particular photograph. It is of a girl holding her mother's hand. They are on a beach, or so it seems from such a great distance. The girl, the perfect little girl, is looking off in another direction, as if someone were making faces to get her to smile, and the mother—assuming she is the girl's mother—is looking at the girl. Brod focuses in even more, this time on the eyes of the mother. They are green, she assumes, and deep, not unlike the river of her name. *Is she crying?* Brod wonders, leaning her chin against the windowsill. *Or was the artist just trying to make her look more beautifu?* Because she was beautiful to Brod. She looked exactly like what Brod had imagined of her own mother.

Up…up…

She looks into an upstairs bedroom and sees an empty bed. The pillow is a perfect rectangle. The sheets are as smooth as water. *It may be that no one has ever slept in this bed,* Brod thinks. *Or maybe it was the scene of something improper, and in the haste to be rid of the evidence, new evidence was created. Even if Lady Macbeth could have removed that damned spot, wouldn't her hands have been red from all of the scrubbing?* There is a cup of water on the bedside table, and Brod thinks she sees a ripple.

Left…left…

She looks into another room. A study? A children's playroom? It's impossible to tell. She turns away and turns back, as if in that moment she might have acquired some new perspective, but the room remains a puzzle to her. She tries to piece it together: A half-smoked cigarette balancing itself on an ashtray's lip. A damp washcloth on the sill. A scrap of paper on the desk, with handwriting that looks like hers: *This is me with Augustine, February 21, 1943.*

88

Up and up...

But there's no window to the attic. So she looks through the wall, which is not terribly hard because the walls are thin and her telescope is a powerful one. A boy and a girl are lying on the floor facing the slant of the roof. She focuses in on the young boy, who looks, from this distance, to be her age. And even from such a distance she can see that it is a copy of *The Book of Antecedents* from which he is reading to her.

Oh, she thinks. *It's Trachimbrod I'm seeing!*

His mouth, her ears. His eyes, his mouth, her ears. The hand of the scribe, the boy's eyes, his mouth, the girl's ears. She traces the causal string back, to the face of the scribe's inspiration, and the lips of the lover and palms of the parents of the scribe's inspiration, and their lovers' lips and parents' palms and neighbors' knees and enemies, and the lovers of their lovers, parents of their parents, neighbors of their neighbors, enemies of their enemies, until she convinces herself that it is not only the boy who is reading to the girl in that attic, but everyone reading to her, everyone who ever lived. She reads along as they read:

THE FIRST RAPE OF BROD D

The first rape of Brod D occurred amid the celebrations following the thirteenth Trachimday festival, March 18, 1804. Brod was walking home from the blue-flowered float—on which she had stood in such austere beauty for so many hours on end, waving her mermaid's tail only when appropriate, throwing deep into the river of her name those heavy sacks only when the Rabbi gave her the necessary nod— when she was approached by the mad squire Sofiowka N, whose name our shtetl now uses for maps and Mormon

The boy falls asleep, and the girl puts her head on his chest. Brod wants to read more—to scream, *READ TO ME! I NEED TO KNOW!*—but they can't hear her from where she is, and from where she is, she can't turn the page. From where she is, the page—her paper-thin future—is infinitely heavy.

A Parade, a Death, a Proposition, 1804–1969

BY HER TWELFTH BIRTHDAY, my great-great-great-great-great-grandmother had received at least one proposal of marriage from every citizen of Trachimbrod: from men who already had wives, from broken old men who argued on stoops about things that might or might not have happened decades before, from boys without armpit hair, from women with armpit hair, and from the deceased philosopher Pinchas T, who, in his only notable paper, "To the Dust: From Man You Came and to Man You Shall Return," argued it would be possible, in theory, for life and art to be reversed. She forced a blush, batted her long eyelashes, and said to each, *Perhaps no. Yankel says I am still too young. But the offer is such a tempting one.*

They are so silly, turning back to Yankel.

Wait until I pass, closing his book. *Then you can have your choice of them. But not while I'm still alive.*

I would not have any one of them, kissing his forehead. *They are not for me. And besides,* laughing, *I already have the most handsome man in all of Trachimbrod.*

Who is it? pulling her onto his lap. *I'll kill him.*

Flicking his nose with her pinky. *It's you, fool.*

Oh no, are you telling me I have to kill myself?

I suppose I am.

Couldn't I be a bit less handsome? If it means sparing my life from my own hand? Couldn't I be a bit ugly?

OK, laughing, *I suppose your nose is a bit crooked. And on close examination, that smile of yours is a good bit less than handsome.*

Now you're killing me, laughing.

Better than killing yourself.

I suppose that's right. This way I don't have to feel guilty afterward.

I'm doing you a great service.

Thank you, then, dear. How can I ever repay you?

You're dead. You can't do anything.

I'll come back for this one favor. Just name it.

Well, I suppose I'd have to ask you to kill me, then. Spare me the guilt.

Consider it done.

Aren't we so terribly lucky to have one another?

It was after Bitzl Bitzl's son's son's proposal—*I'm so sorry, but Yankel thinks it best that I wait*—that she put on her Float Queen costume for the thirteenth annual Trachimday festival. Yankel had heard the women speak of his daughter (he was not deaf), and he had seen the men grope at her (he was not blind), but helping her pull up her mermaid suit, having to tie the straps around her bony shoulders, made everything else seem easy (he was only human).

You don't have to get dressed up if you don't want to, he said, easing her slim arms into the long sleeves of the mermaid suit, which she had re-designed each of the last eight years. *You don't have to be the Float Queen, you know.*

But of course I do, she said. *I am the most beautiful girl in Trachimbrod.*

I thought you didn't want to be beautiful.

I don't, she said, pulling her bead necklace over the neckline of the suit. *It's such a burden. But what can I do about it? I'm cursed.*

But you don't have to do this, he said, putting the bead back under. *They could choose another girl this year. You could give someone else a chance.*

That doesn't sound like me.

But you could do it anyway.

Nope.

But we agreed that ceremony and ritual are so foolish.

But we also agreed that they are foolish only to those on the outside. I'm the center of this one.

I order you not to go, he said, knowing that would never work.

I order you not to order me, she said.

My order takes precedence.

Why?

Because I'm older.

That's a foolish person talking.

Then because I ordered first.

That's the same person talking.

But you don't even like it, he said. *You always complain after.*

I know, she said, adjusting the tail, which was scaled with blue se-
quins.

Then why?

Do you like thinking about Mom?

No.

Does it hurt after?

Yes.

Then why do you continue to do it? she asked. And why, she wondered,
remembering the description of her rape, do we pursue it?

Yankel lost himself in thought, trying many times to start a sentence.

When you think of an acceptable answer, I'll relinquish my throne. She
kissed him on the forehead and headed out of the house for the river with
her name.

He stood by the window and waited.

Canopies of thin white string spanned the narrow dirt arteries of
Trachimbrod that afternoon, spring, 1804, as they had every Trachimday
for thirteen years. It was Bitzl Bitzl's idea, to commemorate the first of
the wagon's refuse to surface. One end of white string tied around the
half-empty bottle of old vermouth on the floor of the drunkard Omeler
S's tipsy shanty, the other around a tarnished silver candle holder on the
dining room table of the Tolerable Rabbi's four-bedroom brick house
across muddy Shelister Street; thin white string like a clothesline from a
third-floor harlot's back-left bedpost to the cool copper doorknob of an
ice closet in the Gentile Kerman K's basement embalming shop; white
string connecting butcher to matchmaker over the tranquil (and breath-
less with anticipation) palm of the Brod River; white string from carpen-
ter to wax modeler to midwife, in a scalene triangle above the fountain
with the prostrate mermaid, in the middle of the shtetl square.

The handsome men assembled along the shoreline as the parade of floats made its way from the small falls to the toy and pastry stands set up by the plaque marking where the wagon did or didn't flip and sink:

THIS PLAQUE MARKS THE SPOT

(OR A SPOT CLOSE TO THE SPOT)

WHERE THE WAGON OF ONE

TRACHIM B

(WE THINK)

WENT IN.

Shtetl Proclamation, 1791

The first to pass the Tolerable Rabbi's window, from which he gave the necessary nod of approval, was the float from Kolki. It was adorned with thousands of orange and red butterflies, which flocked to the float because of the specific combination of animal carcasses strapped to its underside. A red-headed boy dressed in orange slacks and dress shirt stood as still as a statue on the wooden podium. Above him was a sign that read, THE PEOPLE OF KOLKI CELEBRATE WITH THEIR TRA-CHIMBROD NEIGHBORS! He would be the subject of many paintings one day, when the children then watching grew old and sat with water-colors on their crumbling stoops. But he didn't know that then, and neither did they, just as none of them knew that I would one day write this.

Next came Rovno's float, which was covered from end to end in green butterflies. Then the floats from Lutsk, Sarny, Kivertsy, Soke-retchy, and Kovel. They were each covered with color, thousands of butterflies drawn to bloody carcasses: brown butterflies, purple butter-flies, yellow butterflies, pink butterflies, white. The crowd lining the pa-rade route hollered with so much excitement and so little humanity that an impenetrable wall of noise was erected, a common wail so pervasive and constant that it could be mistaken for a common silence.

The Trachimbrod float was covered in blue butterflies. Brod sat on a raised platform in the middle, surrounded by the young float princesses of the shtetl, dressed in blue lace, waving their arms about like waves. A quartet of fiddlers played Polish national songs from a stand in the front of the float while a different quartet played Ukrainian traditionals from the back, and the interference between the two produced a third, dissonant song, heard only by the float princesses and Brod. Yankel watched from his window, fingering the bead that seemed to have gained all the weight he had lost in the last sixty years.

When the Trachimbrod float reached the toy and pastry stands, Brod was given the signal by the Tolerable Rabbi to throw the sacks into the water. *Up, up...*The arc of the collective gaze—from Brod's palm to the river's—was the only thing in the universe that existed at that moment: a single indelible rainbow. *Down, down...* It was not until the Tolerable Rabbi was relatively sure that the sacks had reached the river's bottom that the men were given permission—another of his dramatic nods—to dive after them.

It was impossible to see what was going on in the water with all of the splashing. Women and children cheered furiously while men stroked furiously, grabbing and tugging at one another's limbs to gain advantage. They surfaced in waves, sometimes with bags in their mouths or hands, and then plunged back down with all the vigor they could summon. The water leapt, the trees swayed in expectation, the sky slowly pulled up its blue dress to reveal night.

And then:

I've got it! a man shouted from the far end of the river. *I've got it!* The other divers sighed in disappointment and backstroked to the river's bank or floated in place while they cursed the winner's good fortune. My great-great-great-great-great-grandfather swam back to shore, pumping the golden sack above his head. A large crowd was waiting for him when he fell to his knees and poured the contents onto the mud. Eighteen gold coins. Half a year's salary.

WHAT'S YOUR NAME? the Tolerable Rabbi asked.

I am Shalom, he said. *I am from Kolki.*

THE KOLKER HAS WON THE DAY! the Rabbi proclaimed, losing his yarmulke in all the excitement.

As the hum of crickets summoned the darkness, Brod remained on the float to watch the beginning of the festival without the pestering of men. The paraders and shtetl folk were already drunk—arms around one another, hands on one another, fingers probing, thighs accommodating, all thinking only of her. The strings were beginning to sag (birds landed, depressing the middles; winds blew, swinging them side to side like waves), and the princesses had run to the shore to see the gold and lean against the visiting men.

Mist came first, then rain, so slow that the drops could be followed as they fell. The men and women continued their groping dance as the klezmer bands poured their music through the streets. Young girls captured fireflies in cheesecloth nets. They peeled open the bulbs and painted their eyelids with the phosphorescence. Boys squashed ants between fingers, not knowing why.

The rain intensified, and paraders drank themselves sick on homemade vodka and beer. People made wild, urgent love in the dark corners where houses met and under the hanging canopies of weeping willows. Couples cut their backs on the shells, twigs, and pebbles of the Brod's shallow waters. They pulled at one another in the grass: brassy young men driven with lust, jaded women less wet than breath on glass, virgin boys moving like blind boys, widows lifting their veils, spreading their legs, pleading—to whom?

From space, astronauts can see people making love as a tiny speck of light. Not light, exactly, but a glow that could be mistaken for light—a coital radiance that takes generations to pour like honey through the darkness to the astronaut's eyes.

In about one and a half centuries—after the lovers who made the glow will have long since been laid permanently on their backs—metropolises will be seen from space. They will glow all year. Smaller cities will also be seen, but with great difficulty. Shtetls will be virtually impossible to spot. Individual couples, invisible.

The glow is born from the sum of thousands of loves: newlyweds and teenagers who spark like lighters out of butane, pairs of men who burn fast and bright, pairs of women who illuminate for hours with soft multiple glows, orgies like rock and flint toys sold at festivals, couples trying unsuccessfully to have children who burn their frustrated image on the continent like the bloom a bright light leaves on the eye after you turn away from it.

Some nights, some places are a little brighter. It's difficult to stare at

New York City on Valentine's Day, or Dublin on St. Patrick's. The old walled city of Jerusalem lights up like a candle on each of Chanukah's eight nights. Trachimday is the only time all year when the tiny village of Trachimbrod can be seen from space, when enough copulative voltage is generated to sex the Polish-Ukrainian skies electric. *We're here*, the glow of 1804 will say in one and a half centuries. *We're here, and we're alive.*

But Brod was not a point of this special kind of light, not adding her current to the collective voltage. She climbed down from the float, pools of rainwater collected in the channels between her ribs, and walked the Jewish/Human fault line back toward her house, where the noise and revelry could be observed from a distance. Women sneered at her, and men used their drunkenness as an excuse to bump into her, to brush against her and stick their faces close enough to her face to smell her or kiss her cheek.

> *Brod, you are a dirty river girl!*
> *Wouldn't you like to hold my hand, Brod?*
> *Your father is a shameful man, Brod.*
> *Come on, you can do it. One little shout out of pleasure.*

She ignored them all. Ignored them when they spat at her feet or pinched her backside. Ignored them when they cursed and kissed her, and cursed her with their kisses. Ignored them even when they made a woman out of her, ignored them as she had learned to ignore everything in the world that was not once-removed.

Yankel! she said, opening the door. *Yankel, I'm home. Let's watch the dancing from the roof and eat pineapple with our hands!*

She walked through the den with the hobble of a man six times her age, and through the kitchen pulling off her mermaid suit, and through the bedroom searching for her father. The house was filled with the odor of wetness and decay, as if a window had been left open as an invitation for all the ghosts of eastern Europe. But it was the water that had seeped through the spaces between shingles, like breath between the teeth of a closed mouth. And the odor of death.

Yankel! she called, pulling her skinny legs from the mermaid's tail, revealing her tightly wound pubic hair, which was still new enough to trace out a sharp triangle.

Outside: Lips locked lips on hay in barns and fingers met thighs met lips met ears met undersides of knees on quilts on lawns of strangers, all thinking of Brod, everyone thinking only of Brod.

Yankel? Are you home? she called, walking naked from room to room, her nipples hard and purple from the cold, her skin pale and goose-bumped, her eyelashes holding pearls of rainwater at their ends.

Outside: Breasts were kneaded in callused hands. Many buttons were undone. Sentences became words became sighs became groans became grunts became light.

Yankel? You said we could watch from the roof.

She found him in the library. But he was not asleep in his favorite chair, as she suspected he might be, with the wings of a half-finished book spread across his chest. He was on the floor, fetal, clutching a balled-up slip of paper. Otherwise the room was in perfect order. He had tried not to make a mess when he felt the first flash of heat across his scalp. He was embarrassed when his legs gave out beneath him, ashamed when he realized he would die on the floor, alone in the magnitude of his grief when he understood that he would die before he could tell Brod how beautiful she was that day, and that she had a good heart (which was worth more than a good brain), and that he was not her real father but wished with every blessing, every day and night of his life, that he was; before he could tell her of his dream of eternal life with her, of dying with her, or never dying. He died with the crumpled slip of paper clutched in one hand and the abacus bead in the other.

The water seeped through the shingles as if the house were a cavern. Yankel's lipstick autobiography came flaking off his bedroom ceiling, falling gently like blood-stained snow to his bed and floor. *You are Yankel ...You love Brod...You are a Sloucher...You were once married, but she left you...You don't believe in an afterlife...* Brod was afraid any tears of her own would cause the walls of the old house to give way, so she sand-bagged them behind her eyes, exiled them to someplace deeper, safer.

She took the paper from Yankel's hand, which was damp with rain, and fear of death, and death. Scrawled in a child's writing: *Everything for Brod.*

A wink of lightning illuminated the Kolker at the window. He was strong, with a heavy brow protruding over his maple-bark eyes. Brod had seen him when he surfaced with the coins, when he spilt them onto the shore like golden vomit from the sack, but took little notice.

Go away! she cried, covering her bare chest with her arms and turning back toward Yankel, protecting their bodies from the Kolker's gaze. But he did not leave.

Go away!

I won't go without you, he called to her through the window.

Go away! Go away!

The rain dripped from his upper lip. *Not without you.*

I'll kill myself! she hollered.

Then I'll take your body with me, he said, palms against the glass.

Go away!

I won't!

Yankel jerked in rigor mortis, knocking over the oil lamp, which blew itself out on its way to the floor, leaving the room completely dark. His cheeks pulled into a tight smile, revealing, to the banished shadows, a contentedness. Brod let her arms brush down her skin to her sides and turned to face my great-great-great-great-great-grandfather.

Then you must do something for me, she said.

Her belly lit up like a firefly's bulb—brighter than a hundred thousand virgins making love for the first time.

⌒

Get en heyar! my grandmother calls to my mother. *Hurry!* My mother is twenty-one. My age as I write these words. She lives at home, goes to school at night, has three jobs, wants to find and marry my father, wants to create and love and sing to and die many times every day for me. *Look et diz,* my grandmother says into the television's glow. *Look.* She puts her hand on my mother's hand and feels her own blood flow through the veins, and the blood of my grandfather (who died only five weeks after coming to the States, just half a year after my mother was born), and my mother's blood, and my blood, and the blood of my children and grandchildren. A crackling: *That's one small step for man...* They stare at a blue marble floating in the void—a homecoming from so far away. My

98

grandmother, trying to control her voice, says, *Yer fadder vood hef luffed ta see diz.* The blue marble is replaced with an anchorman, who has removed his glasses and is rubbing his eyes. *Ladies and gentlemen, America has put a man on the moon tonight.* My grandmother struggles to her feet —old, even then—and says, with many different kinds of tears in her eyes, *Etz vunderful!* She kisses my mother, hides her hands in my mother's hair, and says, *Etz vunderrful!* My mother is also crying, each tear unique. They cry together, cheek to cheek. And neither of them hears the astronaut whisper, *I see something,* while gazing over the lunar horizon at the tiny village of Trachimbrod. *There's definitely something out there.*

Dear Jonathan,

I luxuriated the receipt of your letter. You are always so rapid to write to me. This will be a lucrative thing for when you are a real writer and not an apprentice. Mazel tov!

Grandfather ordered me to thank you for the duplicate photograph. It was benevolent of you to post it and not to demand him for any currency. In truth, he does not possess very much. I was certain that Father did not disperse him any for the voyage, because Grandfather often mentions that he has no currency, and I know Father well around manners like this. This made me very wrathful (not spleened or on nerves, as you have informed me that these are not befitting words how often I use them), and I went to Father. He hollered at me, "I ATTEMPTED TO DISPERSE GRANDFATHER CURRENCY, BUT HE WOULD NOT RECEIVE IT." I told him that I did not believe him, and he pushed me and ordered that I should interrogate Grandfather on the matter, but of course I cannot do that. When I was on the floor, he told me that I do not know everything, as I think I do. (But I will tell you, Jonathan, I do not think I know everything.) This made me feel like a schmendrik for receiving the currency. But I was constrained to receive it, because as I have informed you, I have a dream of one day changing residences to America. Grandfather does not have any dreams like this, and so does not need currency. Then I became very biled at Grandfather, because why was it impossible for him to receive the currency from Father and present it to me?

Do not inform one soul, but I keep all of my reserves of currency in a cookie box in the kitchen. It is a place that nobody investigates, because it has been ten years since Mother manufactured a cookie. I reason that when the cookie box is full, I will have a sufficient quantity to change residences to America. I am being a cautious person, because I desire to be cocksure that I have enough for a luxurious apartment in Times Square, vast enough for both me and Little Igor. We will have a large-screen television to watch basketball, a jacuzzi, and a hi-fi to write home about, although we will already be home. Little Igor must go forth with me, of course, whatever occurs.

It appeared that you did not have very many arguments with the previous division. I ask leniency if it angered you in any manner, but I wanted to be truthful and humorous, as you counseled. Do you think that I am a humorous person? I signify humorous with intentions, not humorous because I do foolish things. Mother once said that I was humorous, but that was when I asked her to purchase a Ferrari Testarossa on my behalf. Not desiring to be laughed upon in the wrong way, I revised my offer to hubcaps.

I fashioned the very sparse changes that you posted to me. I altered the division about the hotel in Lutsk. Now you only pay once. "I will not be treated like a second-class citizen!" you apprise to the hotel owner, and while I am obligated (thank you, Jonathan) to inform you that you are not a second-, third-, or fourth-class citizen, it does sound very potent. The owner says, "You win. You win. I tried to pull a fast one" (what does it mean to pull a fast one?), "but you win. OK. You will pay only once." This is now an excellent scene. I have considered making you speak Ukrainian, so that you could have more scenes like this, but that would make me a useless person, because if you spoke Ukrainian, you would still have need for a driver, but not for a translator. I ruminated exterminating Grandfather from the story, so that I would be the driver, but if he ever ascertained this, I am certain that he would be injured, and nor of us desire that, yes? Also, I do not possess a license.

Finally, I altered the division about Sammy Davis, Junior, Junior's fondness for you. I will iterate again, I do not think that the befitting settlement is to amputate her from the story, or to have her "killed in a tragicomic accident while crossing the road to the hotel," as you counsel. To appease you, I modified the scene so that the two of you appear more as friends and less as lovers or nemesises. For one example, she no longer rotates to do a sixty-nine with you. It is now merely a blowjob.

It is very difficult for me to write about Grandfather, just as you said it is very difficult for you to write about your grandmother. I desire to know more about her, if it would not distress you. It might make it less rigid for me to speak about Grandfather. You have not enlightened her about our voyage, have you? I am certain that you would have told me if you had. You know my thinkings on this matter.

As for Grandfather, he is always becoming worse. When I think he is worstest, he becomes worse. Something must occur. He does not conceal his melancholy with mastery anymore. I have witnessed him crying three times this week, each very tardy at night when I was returning from roosting at the beach. I will tell you (because you are the only person I have to tell) that I occasionally KGB on him from behind the corner amid the kitchen and the television room. The first night I witnessed him crying he was investigating an aged leather bag, brimmed with many photographs and pieces of paper, like one of Augustine's boxes. The photographs were yellow, and so were the papers. I am certain that he was having memories for when he was only a boy, and not an old man. The second night he was crying he had the photograph of Augustine in his hands. The weather program was on, but it was so late that they only presented a map of planet Earth, without any weather on it. "Augustine," I could hear him say. "Augustine." The third night he was crying he had a photograph of you in his hands. It is only possible that he secured it from my desk where I keep all of the photographs that you posted me. Again he was saying "Augustine," although I do not understand why.

Little Igor wanted me to utter hello to you from him. He does not know you, of course, but I have informed him very much about you. I informed him about how you are so funny, and so intelligent, and also how we can speak about momentous matters as well as farts. I even informed him about how you made bags of dirt when we were in Trachimbrod. Everything I could remember about you I informed him, because I want him to know you, and because it makes it feel that you are yet near, that you did not go away. You will laugh, but I presented him with one of the photographs of us that you posted. He is a very good boy, better even than me, and he still has a chance to be a very good man. I am certain that you would be appeased by him.

Father and Mother are the same as always, but more humble. Mother has stopped cooking dinner for Father to punish him because he never comes *home for dinner. She wanted to bile him, but he does not give shit (yes? give shit?), because he never comes home for dinner. He eats with his friends very often at restaurants, and also drinks vodka at clubs, but not famous clubs. I am sure that Father possesses more friends than the rest of my family summed. He knocks many things over when he comes home late at night. It is Little Igor and I who clean and return things to their proper locations. (I keep Little Igor with me at these occasions.) The lamp belongs here. The hanging picture belongs here. The plate belongs here. The telephone belongs here. (When Little Igor and I have our apartment, we will keep everything exclusively clean. Not even one piece of dust.) To be truthful, I do not miss Father when he is out so much. He could exist every night with his friends and I would be content. I will inform you that he awoke Little Igor last night when he returned from vodka with his friends. It is my fault, because I did not insist that Little Igor should manufacture Z's in my room with me, as he now does. Was I supposed to counterfeit sleep? Was Mother? I was in my bed at the time, and it is a cosmic thing, because at the moment I was reading the section about Yankel's death. "Everything for Brod," he writes, and I thought, "Everything for Little Igor."*

Per your novel, I have been very dispirited for Brod. She is a good person in a bad world. Everyone is lying to her. Even her father who is not her true father. They are both keeping secrets from each other. I thought about this when you said that Brod "would never be happy and honest at the same time." Do you feel this way?

I understand what you write when you write that Brod does not love Yankel. It does not signify that she does not feel volumes for him, or that she will not be melancholy when he expires. It is something else. Love, in your writing, is the immovability of truth. Brod is not truthful with anything. Not Yankel and not herself. Everything is one world in distance from the real world. Does this manufacture sense? If I am sounding like a thinker, this is an homage to your writing.

This ultimate part that you gave me, about Trachimday, was certainly the most ultimate. I am remaining with nothing to utter about it. When Brod asks Yankel why he thinks about her mom even though it hurts, and he says he does not know why, that is a momentous query. Why do we do that?

Why are the painful things always electromagnets? With concerns about the part with the sex light, I must tell you that I have seen this before. Once I was carnal with a girl, and I saw petite lightning between her backsides. I could clutch how it would require many to be perceived from outer space. At the ultimate part, I have a suggestion that perhaps you should make it a Russian cosmonaut instead of Mr. Armstrong. Try Yuri Alekseyevich Gagarin, who in 1961 became the first human being to make an orbital space flight.

Ultimately, if you possess any magazines or articles that you enjoy, I would be very happy if you could post them to me. I will imburse for any expenses, clear-cuttedly. I intend articles about America, you know. Articles about American sports, or American movies, or American girls, of course, or American accounting schools. I will utter no more of this. I do not know how much more of your novel exists at this moment, but I demand to see it. I am so wanting to know what happens to Brod and the Kolker. Will she love him? Say yes. I hope that you say yes. It will prove a thing to me. Also, perhaps I can continue to aid you as you write more. But not be distressed. I will not require that my name is on the cover. You may pretend that it is only yours.

Please say hello to your family from me, except your grandmother, of course, because she is not aware that I exist. If you would desire to inform me any things about your family, I would be very good-humored to listen. For one example, inform me more about your miniature brother, who I know you love like I love Little Igor. For another example, inform me about your parents. Mother asked about you yesterday. She said, "And what about the troublemaking Jew?" I informed her that you are not troublemaking, but a good person, and that you are not a Jew with a large-size letter J, but a jew, like Albert Einstein or Jerry Seinfeld.

I anticipate with bumps on my skin your consequent letter and the consequent division of your novel. In the pending time, I hope you are loving this next division of mine. Please be pleased, please.

Guilelessly,
Alexander

THE VERY RIGID SEARCH

THE ALARM made a noise at 6:00 of the morning, but it was not a consequential noise, because Grandfather and I had not manufactured even one Z among us. "Go get the Jew," Grandfather said. "I will loiter downstairs." "Breakfast?" I asked. "Oh," he said. "Let us descend to the restaurant and eat breakfast. Then you will get the Jew." "What about his breakfast?" "They will not have anything without meat, so we should not make him an uncomfortable person." "You are smart," I told him.

We were very circumspect when we departed our room so that we would not manufacture any noise. We did not want the hero to be aware that we were eating. When we roosted at the restaurant Grandfather said, "Eat very much. It will be a long day, and who could be certain when we will eat next?" For this reason we ordered three breakfasts for the two of us, and ate very much sausage, which is a delicious food. When we finished, we purchased chewing gum from the waitress so that the hero would not uncover breakfast from our mouths. "Get the Jew," Grandfather said. "I will loiter with patience in the car."

I am certain that the hero was not reposing, because before I could punch for the second time, he unclosed the door. He was already in clothing, and I could see that he was donning his fanny pack. "Sammy Davis, Junior, Junior ate all of my documents." "This is not possible," I said, although in truth I knew that it was possible. "I put them on the bedside table when I went to sleep, and when I woke up this morning she was chewing them. This is all I was able to wrestle free." He exhibited a half-masticated passport and several pieces of maps. "The photograph!" I said. "It's OK. I've got lots of copies. She only got through a couple before I stopped her." "I am so ashamed." "What troubles me," he said, "is that she wasn't in the room when I went to sleep and closed the door." "She is such a smart bitch." "She must be," he said, using his x-ray vision with me. "It is because she is Jewish that she is so smart." "Well, I'm just glad that she didn't eat my glasses." "She would not eat your glasses." "She ate my driver's license. She ate my student ID, my credit card, a bunch of cigarettes, some of my money..." "But she would not eat your glasses. She is not an animal."

"Listen," he said, "what do you say we have a little breakfast?" "What?" "Breakfast," he said, putting his hands on his stomach. "No," I said, "I think it is superior if we commence the search. We want to search as much as possible while light still exists." "But it's only 6:30." "Yes, but it will not be 6:30 forever. Look," I said, and pointed to my watch, which is a Rolex from Bulgaria, "it is already 6:31. We are misplacing time." "Maybe a little something?" he said. "What?" "Just a cracker. I'm really hungry." "This cannot be negotiated. I think it is best—" "We have a minute or two. What's that on your breath?" "You will have one mochaccino in the restaurant downstairs, and that will be the end of the conversation. You must try to pull a fast one." He began to say something, and I put my fingers on my lips. This signified: SHUT UP!

"Back for more breakfast?" the waitress asked. "She says, Good morning, would you like a mochaccino?" "Oh," he said. "Tell her yes. And maybe some bread or something." "He is an American," I said. "I know," she said, "I can see." "But he does not eat meat, so just give him a mochaccino." "He does not eat meat!" "Rapid bowel proceedings," I said, because I did not want to embarrass him. "What are you telling her?" "I told her not to make it too watery." "Good. I hate it when it's watery." "So just one mochaccino will be adequate," I told the waitress, who was a very beautiful girl with the most breasts I had ever seen. "We do not have any." "What is she saying?" "Then give him a cappuccino." "We do not have any cappuccino." "What is she saying?" "She says mochaccinos are special today, because they are coffee." "What?" "Would you like to do the Electric Slide with me at a famous discotheque tonight?" I asked the waitress. "Will you bring the American?" she asked. Oh, did this piss all over me! "He is a Jew," I said, and I know that I should not have uttered that, but I was beginning to feel very awful about myself. The problem is that I felt more awful after uttering it. "Oh," she said. "I have never seen a Jew before. Can I see his horns?" (It is possible that you will think she did not inquire this, Jonathan, but she did. Without a doubt, you do not have horns, so I told her to attend to her own affairs and merely bring a coffee for the Jew and two orders of sausage for the bitch, because who could be certain when she would eat again.)

When the coffee arrived, the hero drank only a small amount. "This tastes terrible," he said. It is one thing for him to not eat meat, and it is another thing for him to make Grandfather loiter in the car asleep, but it is another thing for him to slander our coffee. "YOU WILL DRINK THE COFFEE UNTIL I CAN SEE MY FACE IN THE BOTTOM OF THE CUP!" I did not mean to roar. "But it's a clay cup." "I DO NOT CARE!" He finished the coffee. "You did not have to finish it," I said, because I could perceive that he was rebuilding the Great Wall of China with shit bricks. "It's OK," he said, and put the cup down on the table. "It was really good coffee. Delicious. I'm stuffed." "What?" "We can go whenever you want." A simpleton, I thought. Two tons.

It captured several minutes to recover Grandfather from his sleep. He had locked himself in the car, and all of the windows were sealed. I had to punch the glass with very much violence in order to make him not sleep. I was surprised that the glass did not fracture. When Grandfather finally opened his eyes, he did not know where he was. "Anna?" "No, Grandfather," I said through the window, "it is me, Sasha." He closed his hands and also his eyes. "I thought you were someone else." He touched the wheel with his head. "We are primed to go," I said through the window. "Grandfather?" He made a large breath and opened the doors.

"How do we get there?" Grandfather inquired me, who was in the front seat, because when I am in a car I always sit in the front seat, unless the car is a motorcycle, because I do not know how to operate a motorcycle, although I will very soon. The hero was in the back seat with Sammy Davis, Junior, Junior, and they were attending to their own affairs: the hero masticated the nails of his fingers, and the bitch masticated her tail. "I do not know," I said. "Inquire the Jew," he ordered, so I did. "I don't know," he said. "He does not know." "What do you mean he does not know?" said Grandfather. "We are in the car. We are primed to go forth on our voyage. How can he not know?" His voice was now with volume, and it frightened Sammy Davis, Junior, Junior, making her bark. BARK. I asked the hero, "What do you mean you do not know?" "I told you everything I know. I thought one of you was supposed to be the trained and certified Heritage guide. I paid for a certified guide, you know." Grandfather punched the car's horn, and it made a sound. HONK. "Grandfather is certified!" I informed him, BARK, which was faithfully faithful, although he was certified to operate an automobile, not find lost history. HONK. "Please!" I said at Grandfather. BARK. HONK. "Please! You are making this impossible!" HONK! BARK! "Shut up," he said, "and shut the bitch up and shut the Jew up!" BARK! "Please!" HONK! "You're sure he's certified?" "Of course," I said. HONK! "I would not deceive." BARK! "Do something," I told Grandfather. HONK! "Not that!" I said with volume. BARK! He commenced to drive the automobile that he was fully certified to drive. "Where are we going?" The hero and I manufactured this query at the same time. "SHUT UP!" he said, and I did not have to translate that for the hero.

He drove us to a petrol store that we passed on the way to the hotel the night yore. We arrested in front of the petrol machine. A man came to the window. He was very svelte, and had petrol in his eyes. "Yes?" the man asked. "We are looking for Trachimbrod," Grandfather said. "We do not have any," the man said. "It is a place. We are trying to find it." The man turned to a group of men standing in front of the store. "Do we have anything called trachimbrod?" They all elevated their shoulders and continued to talk to themselves. "Apologies," he said, "we do not have any." "No," I said, "it is the name of a place we are searching for. We are trying to find the girl who saved his grandfather from the Nazis." I pointed to the hero. "What?" the man asked. "What?" the hero asked. "Shut up," Grandfather told me. "We have a map," I told the man. "Present me the map," I ordered the hero. He investigated his bag. "Sammy Davis, Junior, Junior ate it." "It is not possible," I said, although again I knew that it was possible. "Mention him some of the other names of the towns and perhaps one will sound informal." The petrol man leaned his head in the car. "Kovel," the hero said, "Kivertsy, Sokeretchy." "Kolki," Grandfather said. "Yes, yes," the petrol man said, "I have heard of all of these towns." "And you could direct us to them?" I asked. "Of course. They are very proximal. Maybe thirty kilometers distant. No more. Merely travel north on the superway, and then east through the farmlands." "But you have never heard of Trachimbrod?" "Say it again to me." "Trachimbrod." "No, but many of the towns have new names." "Jon-fen," I said, turning back, "what was the other name for Trachimbrod?" "Sofiowka." "Do you know of Sofiowka?" I asked the man. "No," he said, "but it sounds like something that is more similar to something I have heard of. There are many villages in that area. Perhaps there are nine or even more. Once you become proximal, you could inquire anyone and they would be able to inform you where to find what you are investigating for." (Jonathan, this man spoke not so good Ukrainian, but I have made it sound abnormally good in my translation for the story. If it would appease you, I could counterfeit his substandard utterances.) The man fashioned a map on a piece of paper that Grandfather excavated from the drawer for gloves, where I will keep lubricated extra-large condoms when I have the car of my dreams. (They will not be ribbed for her pleasure, because there is no need, if you understand what I mean.) They made conversation about the map for many minutes. "Here," the hero said. He was holding a package of Marlboro cigarettes at the petrol man. "What the hell is he doing?" Grandfather inquired. "What the hell is he doing?" the petrol man inquired. "What the hell are you doing?" I inquired. "For his help," he said. "I read in my guidebook that it's hard to get Marlboro cigarettes here, and that you should bring several packs with you wherever you go, and give them as tips." "What is a tip?" "It's something you give someone in exchange for help." "So OK, you are informed that you will be paying for this trip with currency, yes?" "No, not like that," he said. "Tips are for small things, like directions, or for the valet." "Valet?" "He does not eat meat," Grandfather told the petrol man. "Oh." "Valet," the hero said, "the guy who parks your car." America is always proving itself greater than I thought.

It was already 7:10 when we were driving again. It captured only several minutes for us to find the superway. I must confess that it was a beautiful day, with much light of the sun. "It is beautiful, yes?" I said to the hero. "What?" "The day. It is a beautiful day." He put down the glass of his window, which was acceptable because Sammy Davis, Junior, Junior was sleeping, and he put his head outside of the car. "Yes," he said. "It's absolutely beautiful." This made me proud, and I told Grandfather, and he smiled, and I could perceive that he also became a very proud person. "Inform him about Odessa," Grandfather said. "Inform him how beautiful it is there." "In Odessa," I rotated to the hero and said, "it is more beautiful than even this. You have never witnessed a thing similar to it." "I'd like to hear about it," he said, and opened his diary. "He wants to hear about Odessa," I told Grandfather, because I wanted for him to like the hero. "Inform him that the sand on the beaches is more soft than a woman's hairs, and that the water is like the inside of a woman's mouth." "The sand on the beaches is like a woman's mouth." "Inform him," Grandfather said, "that Odessa is the most wonderful place to become in love, and also to make a family." So I informed the hero. "Odessa," I said, "is the most wonderful place to become in love, and also to make a family." "Have you ever fallen in love?" he inquired me, which seemed like such a queer inquiry, so I returned it to him. "Have you?" "I don't know," he said. "Nor I," I said. "I've been close to love." "Yes." "Really close, like almost there." "Almost." "But never, I don't think." "No." "Maybe I should go to Odessa," he said. "I could fall in love. It sounds like that would make more sense than Trachimbrod." We both laughed. "What is he saying?" Grandfather inquired. I told him, and he also laughed. All of this felt so wonderful. "Show me the map," Grandfather said. He examined it while he drove, making his blindness even less trustworthy, I must confess.

We made an exit from the superway. Grandfather returned me the map. "We will drive for approximately twenty kilometers, and then we will inquire someone about Trachimbrod." "That is reasonable," I said. It sounded like a queer thing to say, but I have never known what to say to Grandfather without it sounding queer. "I know it is reasonable," he said. "Of course it is reasonable." "May I view Augustine again?" I asked the hero. (Here I must confess that I had been desiring to view her since the hero first exhibited her to me. But I was ashamed to make this known.) "Of course," he said, and excavated his fanny pack. He had many duplicates, and removed one like a playing card. "Here you go."

I observed the photograph while he observed the beautiful day. Augustine had such pretty hairs. They were thin hairs. I did not need to touch them to be certain. Her eyes were blue. Even though the photograph lacked color, I was certain that her eyes were blue. "Look at those fields," the hero said with his finger outside of the car. "They're so green." I told Grandfather what the hero said. "Tell him that the land is premium for farming." "Grandfather desires me to tell you that the land is very premium for farming." "And tell him that much of this land was destroyed when the Nazis came, but before it was yet more beautiful. They bombed with airplanes and then advanced through it in tanks." "But it does not appear like this." "They made it all again after the war. Before it was different." "You were here before the war?" "Look at those people working in their underwear in the fields," the hero said from the back seat. I inquired Grandfather about this. "This is not abnormal," he said. "It is very hot in the morning. Too hot to be anxious about clothing." I told the hero. He was covering many pages in his diary. I wanted Grandfather to continue the before conversation, and to tell me when he was in the area, but I could perceive that the conversation had been finished. "They're such old people working," the hero said. "Some of those women must be sixty or seventy." I inquired Grandfather about this, because I also did not find it canny. "It is canny," he said. "In the fields, you toil until you are not able to toil. Your great-grandfather died in the fields." "Did Great-Grandmother work in the fields?" "She was working with him when he died." "What is he saying?" the hero inquired, and again he prohibited Grandfather from continuing, and again when I viewed Grandfather I could perceive that it was the end of the conversation.

It was the first occasion that I had ever heard Grandfather speak of his parents, and I wanted to know very much more of them. What did they do during the war? Who did they save? But I felt that it was a common decency for me to be quiet on the matter. He would speak when he needed to speak, and until that moment I would persevere silence. So I did what the hero did, which is look out the window. I do not know how much time tumbled, but a lot of time tumbled. "It is beautiful, yes?" I said to him without rotating around. "Yes." For the next minutes, we used no words, but only witnessed the farmlands. "It would be a reasonable time to inquire someone how to get to Trachimbrod," Grandfather said. "I do not think that we are more than ten kilometers distant."

We moved the car to the side of the road, although it was very difficult to perceive where the road terminated and the side commenced. "Go inquire someone," Grandfather said. "And bring the Jew with you." "Will you come?" I asked. "No," he said. "Please." "No." "Come," I informed the hero. "Where?" I pointed at a herd of men in the field who were smoking. "You want me to go with you?" "Of course," I said, because I desired the hero to feel that he was involved in every aspect of the voyage. But in truth, I was also afraid of the men in the field. I had never talked to people like that, poor farming people, and similar to most people from Odessa, I speak a fusion of Russian and Ukrainian, and they spoke only Ukrainian, and while Russian and Ukrainian sound so so similar, people who speak only Ukrainian sometimes hate people who speak a fusion of Russian and Ukrainian, because very often people who speak a fusion of Russian and Ukrainian come from the cities and think they are superior to people who speak only Ukrainian, who often come from the fields. We think this because we are superior, but that is for another story.

I commanded the hero not to speak, because at times people who speak Ukrainian who hate people who speak a fusion of Russian and Ukrainian also hate people who speak English. It is for the selfsame reason that I brought Sammy Davis, Junior, Junior with us, although she speaks nor Ukrainian nor a fusion of Russian and Ukrainian nor English. BARK. "Why?" the hero inquired. "Why what?" "Why can't I talk?" "It distresses some people greatly to hear English. We will have a more easy time procuring assistance if you keep your lips together." "What?" "Shut up." "No, what was that word you said?" "Which?" "With the *p*." I felt very proud because I knew a word of English that the hero, who was American, did not know. "Procure. It is like to obtain, get, acquire, secure, and gain. Now shut up, putz."

"I have never heard of it," said one of the men, with his cigarette at the side of his mouth. "Nor have I," said another, and they exhibited their backs. "Thank you," I said. The hero punched my side with the bend in his arm. He was trying to say something to me without words. "What?" I whispered. "Sofiowka," he said without volume, although in truth it did not matter. It did not matter because the men were not giving any attention to us. "Oh yes," I said to the men. They did not rotate to glance at me. "It is also called Sofiowka. Do you know of this town?" "We have never heard of it," one of them said without discussing the matter with the others. He cast his cigarette to the ground. I rotated my head from this to that to inform the hero that they did not know. "Maybe you've seen this woman," the hero said, taking a duplicate of the photograph of Augustine out of his fanny pack. "Put that back!" I said. "What are you intending here?" one of the men inquired, and also cast his cigarette to the ground. "What did he say?" the hero asked. "We are searching for the town Trachimbrod," I informed them, and I could perceive that I was not selling like pancakes. "I told you, there is no place Trachimbrod." "So stop bothering us," one of the other men said. "Do you want a Marlboro cigarette?" I proposed, because I could not think of anything else. "Get out of here," one of the men said. "Go back to Kiev." "I am from Odessa," I said, and this made them laugh with very much violence. "Then go back to Odessa." "Can they help us?" the hero inquired. "Do they know anything?" "Come," I said, and I took his hand and we walked back to the car. I was humbled to the maximum. "Come on Sammy Davis, Junior, Junior!" But she would not come, even though the smoking men harassed her. There was only one option remaining. "Billie Jean is not my lover. She's just a girl who claims that I am the one." The maximum of humbling was made maximumer.

"What in hell were you doing uttering English!" I said. "I commanded you not to speak English! You understanded me, yes?" "Yes." "Then why did you speak English?" "I don't know." "You don't know! Did I ask you to prepare breakfast?" "What?" "Did I ask you to invent a new kind of wheel?" "I don't—" "No, I asked you to do one thing, and you made a disaster of it! You were so stupid!" "I just thought it would be helpful." "But it was not helpful. You made those men very angry!" "Because of my English?" "I commanded you not to speak and you did. You may have contaminated everything." "Sorry, I just thought, the picture." "I will do the thinking. You will do the silence!" "I'm sorry." "I am the one who is sorry! I am sorry that I brought you with me on this voyage!"

I was very shamed by the manner in which the men spoke to me, and I did not want to inform Grandfather of what occurred, because I knew that it would shame him also. But when we returned to the car, I realized that I did not have to inform him a thing. If you want to know why, it is because I first had to move him from his sleep. "Grandfather," I said, touching his arm. "Grandfather. It is me, Sasha." "I was dreaming," he said, and this surprised me very much. It is so weird to imagine one of your parents or grandparents dreaming. If they dream, then they think of things when you are not there, and they think of things that are not you. Also, if they dream, then they must have dreams, which is one more thing to think about. "They did not know where Trachimbrod is." "Well, enter the car," he said. He moved his hands over his eyes. "We will persevere to drive, and search for another person to inquire."

We discovered many other people to inquire, but in truth, every person regarded us in the same manner. "Go away," an old man uttered. "Why now?" a woman in a yellow dress inquired. Not one of them knew where Trachimbrod was, and not one of them had ever heard of it, but all of them became angry or silent when I inquired. I wished that Grandfather would help me, but he refused to exit the car. We persevered to drive, now unto subordinate roads lacking any markings. The houses were less near to one another, and it was an abnormal thing to see anyone at all. "I have lived here my whole life," one old man said without removing himself from his seat under a tree, "and I can inform you that there is no place called Trachimbrod." Another old man, who was escorting a cow across the dirt road, said, "You should stop searching now. I can promise you that you will not find anything." I did not tell this to the hero. Perhaps this is because I am a good person. Perhaps it is because I am a bad one. As proxy for the truth, I told him that each person told us to drive more, and that if we drove more we would discover some person who knew where Trachimbrod was. We would drive until we found Trachimbrod, and drive until we found Augustine. So we drove more, because we were severely lost, and because we did not know what else to do. It was very difficult for the car to travel on some of the roads because there were so many rocks and holes. "Do not be distressed," I told the hero. "We will find something. If we continue to drive, I am certain that we will find Trachimbrod, and then Augustine. Everything is in harmony with design."

It was already after the center of the day. "What are we going to do?" I inquired Grandfather. "We have been driving for many hours, and we are no more proximal than many hours yore." "I do not know," he said. "Are you fatigued?" I inquired him. "No." "Are you hungry?" "No." We drove more, farther and farther in the same circles. The car became fixed in the ground many times, and the hero and I had to get out to impel it unencumbered. "It's not easy," the hero said. "No, it is not," I yielded. "But I guess we should keep driving. Don't you think? If that's what people have been telling us to do." I saw that he kept filling his diary. The less we saw, the more he wrote. We drove beyond many of the towns that the hero named to the petrol man. Kovel. Sokeretchy. Kivertsy. But there were no people anywhere, and when there was a person, the person could not help us. "Go away." "There is no Trachimbrod here." "I do not know what you are speaking of." "You are lost." It was seeming as if we were in the wrong country, or the wrong century, or as if Trachimbrod had disappeared, and so had the memory of it.

We followed roads that we had already followed, we witnessed parts of the land that we had already witnessed, and both Grandfather and I were desiring that the hero was not aware of this. I remembered when I was a boy and Father would punch me, and after he would say, "It does not hurt. It does not hurt." And the more he would utter it, the more it was faithful. I believed him, in some measure because he was Father, and in some measure because I too did not want it to hurt. This is how I felt with the hero as we persevered to drive. It was as if I was uttering to him, "We will find her. We will find her." I was deceiving him, and I am certain that he desired to be deceived. So we painted more circles into the dirt roads.

"There," Grandfather said, pointing his finger at a person roosting on the steps of a very diminutive house. It was the first person that we had viewed in many minutes. Had we witnessed this person before? Had we already inquired with no fruit? He stopped the car. "Go." "Will you come?" I asked. "Go." Because I did not know what else to say, I said, "OK," and because I did not know what else to do, I amputated myself from the car. "Come," I said to the hero. There was no rejoinder. "Come," I said, and rotated. The hero was manufacturing Z's, as still was Sammy Davis, Junior, Junior. There is no necessity for me to move them from sleep, I said to my brain. I took with me the duplicate photograph of Augustine, and was careful not to disturb them as I closed the car's door.

The house was white wood that was falling off of itself. There were four windows, and one of them was broken. As I walked more proximal, I could perceive that it was a woman roosting on the steps. She was very aged and peeling the skin off of corn. Many clothes were lying across her yard. I am certain that they were drying after a cleaning, but they were in abnormal arrangements, and they appeared like the clothes of unvisible dead bodies. I reasoned that there were many people in the white house, because there were men's clothes and women's clothes and clothes for children and even babies. "Leniency," I said while I was still some amount distant. I said this so that I would not make her a terrified person. "I have a query for you." She was donning a white shirt and a white dress, but they were covered with dirt and places where liquids had dried. I could perceive that she was a poor woman. All of the people in the small towns are poor, but she was more poor. This was clear-cut because of how svelte she was, and how broken all of her belongings were. It must be expensive, I thought, to care for so many people as she did. I decided then that when I become a rich person in America, I would give some currency to this woman.

She smiled as I became proximal to her, and I could see that she did not have any teeth. Her hairs were white, her skin had brown marks, and her eyes were blue. She was not so much of a woman, and what I signify here is that she was very fragile, and appeared as if she could be obliterated with one finger. I could hear, as I approached, that she was humming. (This is called humming, yes?) "Leniency," I said. "I do not want to pester you." "How could anything pester me on such a beautiful day?" "Yes, it is beautiful." "Yes," she said. "Where are you from?" she asked. This shamed me. I rotated over in my head what to say, and ended with the truth. "Odessa." She put down one piece of corn and picked up another. "I have never been to Odessa," she said, and moved hairs that were in front of her face to behind her ear. It was not until this moment that I perceived how her hairs were as long as her. "You must go there," I said. "I know. I know I must. I am sure there are many things that I must do." "And many things that you must not do also." I was trying to make her a sedate person, and I did. She laughed. "You are a sweet boy." "Have you ever heard of a town dubbed Trachimbrod?" I inquired. "I was informed that someone proximal to here would know of it." She put her corn on her lap and looked inquiring. "I do not want to pester you," I said, "but have you ever heard of a town dubbed Trachimbrod?" "No," she said, picking up her corn and removing its skin. "Have you ever heard of a town dubbed Sofiowka?" "I have never heard of that either." "I am sorry to have stolen your time," I said. "Have a good day." She presented me with a sad smile, which was like when the ant in Yankel's ring made to conceal its face—I knew it was a symbol, but I did not know what it was a symbol for.

I could hear her humming as I commenced to walk away. What would I inform the hero when he was no longer manufacturing Z's? What would I inform Grandfather? For how long could we fail until we surrendered? I felt as if all of the weight was residing on me. As with Father, there are only so many times that you can utter "It does not hurt" before it begins to hurt even more than the hurt. You become enlightened of the feeling of feeling hurt, which is worse, I am certain, than the existent hurt. Not-truths hung in front of me like fruit. Which could I pick for the hero? Which could I pick for Grandfather? Which for myself? Which for Little Igor? Then I remembered that I had taken the photograph of Augustine, and although I do not know what it was that coerced me to feel that I should, I rotated back around and displayed the photograph to the woman.

"Have you ever witnessed anyone in this photograph?"

She examined it for several moments. "No."

I do not know why, but I inquired again.

"Have you ever witnessed anyone in this photograph?"

"No," she said again, although this second no did not seem like a parrot, but like a different variety of no.

"Have you ever witnessed anyone in this photograph?" I inquired, and this time I held it very proximal to her face, like Grandfather held it to his face.

"No," she said again, and this seemed like a third variety of no.

I put the photograph in her hands.

"Have you ever witnessed anyone in the photograph?"

"No," she said, but in her no I was certain that I could hear, Please persevere. Inquire me again. So I did.

"Have you ever witnessed anyone in the photograph?"

She moved her thumbs over the faces, as if she were attempting to erase them. "No."

"Have you ever witnessed anyone in the photograph?"

"No," she said, and she put the photograph on her lap.

"Have you ever witnessed anyone in the photograph?" I inquired.

"No," she said, still examining it, but only from the angles of her eyes.

"Have you ever witnessed anyone in the photograph?"

"No." She was humming again, with more volume.

"Have you ever witnessed anyone in the photograph?"

"No," she said. "No." I saw a tear descend to her white dress. It too would dry and leave a mark.

"Have you ever witnessed anyone in the photograph?" I inquired, and I felt cruel, I felt like an awful person, but I was certain that I was performing the right thing.

"No," she said, "I have not. They all look like strangers."

I periled everything.

"Has anyone in this photograph ever witnessed you?"

Another tear descended.

"I have been waiting for you for so long."

I pointed to the car. "We are searching for Trachimbrod."

"Oh," she said, and she released a river of tears. "You are here. I am it."

THE DIAL, 1941–1804–1941

SHE USED HER THUMBS to pull the lace panties from her waist, allowing her engorged genitalia the teasing satisfaction of the humid summer updrafts, which brought with them the smells of burdock, birch, burning rubber, and beef broth, and would now pass on her particular animal scent to northward noses, like a message transmitted through a line of schoolchildren in a childish game, so that the final one to smell might lift his head and say, *Borsht?* She eased them off her ankles with extraordinary deliberateness, as if that action alone could have justified her birth, every hour of her parents' labors, and the oxygen she consumed with every breath. As if it could have justified the tears that her children would have shed at her proper death, had she not died in the water with the rest of the shtetl — too young, like the rest of the shtetl — before having children. She folded the panties over themselves six times into a teardrop shape and slid them into the pocket of his black nuptial suit, halfway under the lapel, blossoming in petal folds at the top like a good kerchief should.

This is so you will think about me, she said, *until —*

I don't need reminders, he said, kissing the moist divot above her upper lip.

Hurry, she giggled, straightening his tie with one hand and the rope between his legs with the other. *You'll be late. Now run to the Dial.*

She silenced with a kiss whatever he was about to say, and pushed him to go.

It was summer already. The ivy that clung to the synagogue's crumbling portico was darkening at the lobes. The soil had recovered its rich coffee blush, and was again soft enough for tomatoes and mint. The lilac bushes had flirted halfway up the veranda railings, the railings were beginning to splinter, and the splinters were chipping off into the summer breezes. The shtetl men were already crowded around the Dial when my grandfather arrived, panting and damp with sweat.

Safran is here! the Upright Rabbi announced, to the cheers of those packed in the square. *The bridegroom has arrived!* A septet of violins began the traditional Dial Waltz, with the elders of the shtetl clapping their hands on every downbeat and the children whistling every *ta-ta*.

THE CHORUS OF THE DIAL WALTZ SONG
FOR SOON-TO-BE-MARRIED MEN

Ohhhhhhh, gather group, [insert groom's name]'s here,
Well groomed he'd better be, his wedding's near.
One great hand he's been dealt,
[insert bride's name]'s a girl to make you loosen your belt.
Sooooooo kiss his lips, smell his knees,
Beg please for prolific birds and bees.
May you be happily
Wed, then off to bed, for ohhhhhhh...

[Repeat from beginning, indefinitely]

My grandfather regained his composure, felt to make sure the zipper of his slacks was indeed zippered, and marched into the Dial's long shadow. He was to fulfill the sacred ritual that had been fulfilled by every married man in Trachimbrod since his great-great-great-grandfather's tragic flour mill accident. He was about to throw his bachelorhood and, in theory, his sexual exploits to the wind. But what struck him as he approached the Dial (with long, deliberate steps) was not the beauty of ceremony, or the inherent insincerity of organized rites of passage, or even how much he wished the Gypsy girl could be with him now so his true love could experience his wedding with him, but that he was no longer a boy. He was growing older, had begun to look like his great-great-great-grandfather: the furrowed brow shadowing his delicate, softly feminine eyes, the similar protrusion at the bridge of his nose, the way his lips met in a sideways U at one end and in a V at the other. Safety and profound sadness: he was growing into his place in the family; he looked unmistakably like his father's father's father's father's father, and because of that, because his cleft chin spoke of the same mongrel gene-stew (stirred by the chefs of war, disease, opportunity, love, and false love), he was granted a place in a long line—certain assurances of being and permanence, but also a burdensome restriction of movement. He was not altogether free.

He was also aware of his place among married men, all of whom had given their vows of fidelity with their knees planted on the same ground on which his now were. Each had prayed for the blessings of sound mind, good health, handsome sons, inflated wages, and deflated libido. Each had been told a thousand times the story of the Dial, the tragic circumstances of its creation and the magnitude of its power. Each knew of how his great-great-great-grandmother Brod had said *Don't go* to her new husband, too familiar with the flour mill's curse of taking without warning the lives of its young workers. *Please, find another job or don't work at all. But promise me you won't go.*

And each knew of how the Kolker had responded, *Don't be silly, Brod,* patting her belly, which after seven months could still be concealed under a baggy dress. *It's a very good job, and I'll be very careful, and that'll be all.*

And each bridegroom knew of how Brod had wept, and hid his work clothes the previous night, and shook him from sleep every few minutes so that he would be too exhausted to leave the house the next day, and refused to make his coffee in the morning, and even tried ordering him.

This is love, she thought, *isn't it? When you notice someone's absence and hate that absence more than anything? More, even, than you love his presence?* Each knew of how she had waited for the Kolker by the window every day, how she became acquainted with its surface, learned where it had melted slightly, where it was slightly discolored, where it was opaque. She felt its tiny wrinkles and bubbles. Like a blind woman learning language, she moved her fingers over the window, and like a blind woman learning language, she felt liberated. The frame of the window was the walls of the prison that set her free. She loved what it felt like to wait for the Kolker, to be entirely dependent on him for her happiness, to be, as ridiculous as she had always thought it sounded, someone's wife. She loved her new vocabulary of simply loving something more than she loved her love for that thing, and the vulnerability that went along with living in the primary world. *Finally*, she thought, *finally. I only wish Yankel could know how happy I am.*

When she woke up crying from one of her nightmares, the Kolker would stay with her, brush her hair with his hands, collect her tears in thimbles for her to drink the next morning (*The only way to overcome sadness is to consume it*, he said), and more than that: once her eyes closed and she fell back asleep, he was left to bear the insomnia. There was a complete transfer, like a speeding billiard ball colliding with a resting one. Should Brod feel depressed—she was always depressed—the Kolker would sit with her until he could convince her that it's OK. It is. Really. And when she would move on with her day, he would stay behind, paralyzed with a grief he couldn't name and that wasn't his. Should Brod become sick, it was the Kolker who would be bedridden by week's end. Should Brod feel bored, knowing too many languages, too many facts, with too much knowledge to be happy, the Kolker would stay up all night studying her books, studying the pictures, so the next day he could try to make the kind of small talk that would please his young wife.

Brod, isn't it strange how some mathematical phrases can have a lot on one side and just a little on the other? Isn't that fascinating! And what does it say about life!...Brod, you're making that face again, the one like the man who plays that musical instrument that is all wound up in a big coil...Brod, he would say, pointing to Castor as they lay on their backs on the tin-shingled roof of their small house, *that, over there, is a star. So is that one*, pointing to Pollux. *I'm sure of it. Those are as well. Yes, those are very familiar stars. The rest I can't be one hundred percent sure of. I'm not familiar with them.*

She always saw through him, as if he were just another window. She always felt that she knew everything about him that could be known—not that he was simple, but that he was knowable, like a list of errands, like an encyclopedia. He had a birthmark on the third toe of his left foot. He wasn't able to urinate if someone could hear him. He thought cucumbers were good enough, but pickles were delicious — so absolutely delicious, in fact, that he questioned whether they were, indeed, made from cucumbers, which were only good enough. He hadn't heard of Shakespeare, but Hamlet sounded familiar. He liked making love from behind. That, he thought, was about as nice as it gets. He had never kissed anyone besides his mother and her. He had dived for the golden sack only because he wanted to impress her. He sometimes looked in the mirror for hours at a time, making faces, tensing muscles, winking, smiling, puckering. He had never seen another man naked, and so had no idea if his body was normal. The word "butterfly" made him blush, although he didn't know why. He had never been out of the Ukraine. He once thought that the earth was the center of the universe, but learned better. He admired magicians more after learning the secrets of their tricks.

You are such a sweet husband, she told him when he brought her gifts.

I just want to be good to you.

I know, she said, *and you are.*

But there are so many things I can't give you.

But there are so many things you can.

I'm not a smart man —

Stop, she said, *just stop.* Smart was the last thing she ever wanted the Kolker to be. That, she knew, would ruin everything. She wanted nothing more than someone to miss, to touch, with whom to speak like a child, with whom to be a child. He was very good for that. And she was in love.

I'm the one who isn't smart, she said.

That's the dumbest thing I've ever heard, Brod.

Exactly, she said, putting his arm around her and nestling her face in his chest.

Brod, I'm trying to have a serious talk with you. Sometimes I just feel like everything I want to say will come out wrong.

So what do you do?

I don't say it.

Well, that's smart of you, she said, playing with the loose skin under his chin.

Brod, backing away, *you're not taking me seriously.* She nestled deeper into him and closed her eyes like a cat. *I've kept a list, you know,* he said, taking back his arms.

That's wonderful, honey.

Aren't you going to ask what kind of list?

I figured you'd have told me if you wanted me to know. When you didn't, I just assumed it was none of my business. Do you want me to ask you?

Ask me.

OK. What kind of list have you been keeping so secretly?

I've kept a list of the number of conversations we've had since we've been married. Would you like to guess how many?

Is this really necessary?

We've only had six conversations, Brod. Six in almost three years.

Are you counting this one?

You never take me seriously.

Of course I do.

No, you always joke, or cut our talking short before we ever say anything.

I'm sorry if I do that. I never noticed. But do we really need to do this right now? We talk all the time.

I don't mean talking, Brod. I mean conversing. Things that last more than five minutes.

Let me get this straight. You're not talking about talking? You want us to converse about conversing? Is that right?

We've had six conversations. It's pathetic, I know, but I've counted them. Otherwise it's all worthless words. We talk about cucumbers and how I like pickles more. We talk about how I blush when I hear that word. We talk about grieving Shanda and Pinchas, about how bruises sometimes don't show up for a day or two. Talk talk talk. We talk about nothing. Cucumbers, butterflies, bruises. It's nothing.

What's something, then? You want to talk about war a bit? Maybe we could talk about literature. Just tell me what something is, and we'll talk about it. God? We could talk about Him.

You're doing it again.

What am I doing?

You're not taking me seriously.

It's a privilege you have to earn.

I'm trying.

Try a bit harder, she said, and unbuttoned his slacks. She licked him from the base of his neck to his chin, pulled his shirt from his pants, his pants from his waist, and nipped their seventh conversation in the bud. All she wanted from him was cuddling and high voices. Whispers. Assurances. Promises of fidelity and truth she made him swear to again and again: that he would never kiss another woman, that he would never even think of another woman, that he would never leave her alone.

Say it again.

I won't leave you alone.

Say it again.

I won't leave you alone.

Again.

I won't.

Won't what?

Leave you alone.

It was halfway into his second month at work when two men from the flour mill knocked on her door. She didn't have to ask why they came, but collapsed immediately to the floor.

Go away! she screamed, running her hands up and down the carpet as if it were a new language to learn, another window.

He felt no pain, they told her. *He felt nothing, really.* Which made her cry more, and harder. Death is the only thing in life that you absolutely have to be aware of as it's happening.

A disk-saw blade from the chaff splitter had spun off its bearings and raced through the mill, caroming off walls and scaffold beams while men jumped for cover. The Kolker was eating a cheese sandwich on a makeshift stool of stacked flour sacks, lost in thought about something Brod had said about something, oblivious to the chaos around him, when the blade hopped off an iron rod (left carelessly on the ground by a mill worker who was later struck by lightning) and embedded itself, perfectly vertical, in the middle of his skull. He looked up, dropped his sandwich to the floor—witnesses swore the slices of bread switched places in midair—and closed his eyes.

Leave me! she hollered at the men, who were still standing mute in her doorway. *Leave!*

But we were told —

Go! she said, beating her chest. *Go!*

Our boss said —

You bastards! she shouted. *Leave the griever to grieve!*

Oh, he's not dead, the fatter of the men corrected.

What?

He's not dead.

He's not dead? she asked, picking her head up off the floor.

No, the other said. *He's in the doctor's care, but it seems that there's little permanent damage. You can see him if you like. He is in no way repulsive looking. Well, maybe a little, but there was hardly any blood, except for the blood from his nose and ears, and the blade seems to be holding everything in its good and right place, more or less.*

Crying more now than when she heard the news of her new husband's supposed death, Brod hugged both men and then punched them both in the nose with all of the might her skinny fifteen-year-old arm could summon.

In fact, the Kolker was barely hurt at all. He had regained consciousness in only a few minutes and been able to walk himself, parade himself, through the maze of muddy capillaries to the office of Dr. (and caterer without clients) Abraham M.

What's your name? measuring the circular blade with calipers.

The Kolker.

Very good, lightly touching his finger to one of the blade's teeth. *Now, can you remember the name of your wife?*

Brod, of course. Her name is Brod.

Very good. Now, what seems to have happened to you?

A disk-saw blade stuck in my head.

Very good, examining the blade from all sides. It looked to the doctor like a five-o'clock summer sun, setting over the horizon of the Kolker's head, which reminded him that it was almost time for dinner, one of his favorite meals of the day. *Do you feel any pain?*

I feel different. It's not pain, really. It's almost a homesickness.

Very good. Homesickness. Now, can you follow my finger with your eyes? No, no. This finger... Very good. Can you walk across the room for me?... Very good.

And then, without provocation, the Kolker slammed his fist against the examining table and hollered, *You are a fat fuckhead!*

Excuse me? What?

What just happened?

You called me a fuckhead.

Did I?

You did.

I'm sorry. You're not a fuckhead. I'm very sorry.

You're probably just —

But it's true! the Kolker shouted. *You are an insolent fuckhead! And a fat one too, if I didn't mention that before.*

I'm afraid I don't under —

Did I say something? the Kolker asked, frantically looking around the room.

You said I was an insolent fuckhead.

You've got to believe me . . . Your tuches is huge! . . . I'm sorry, this is not me . . . I'm so sorry, you fat-tuchesed fuckhead, I —

Did you call my tuches fat?

No! . . . Yes!

Is it these slacks? They're cut rather tight around the —

Fat ass!

Fat ass?

Fat ass!

Who do you think you are?

No! . . . Yes!

Get out of my office!

No! . . . Yes!

Well, disk saw or not! the doctor said, and with a huff, he slammed shut his folder and stormed out of his own office, pounding the floor loudly with each of his heavy steps.

The doctor-caterer was the first victim of the Kolker's malicious eruptions—the only symptom of the blade that would remain embedded in his skull, perfectly perpendicular to the horizon, for the rest of his life.

The marriage was able to return to a kind of normality, after the removal of the headboard from their bed and the birth of the first of their three sons, but the Kolker was undeniably different. The man who had kneaded Brod's prematurely old legs at night when they were all pins and needles, who had rubbed milk into her burns when there was nothing else, who had counted her toes because she liked the way it felt, would now, on occasion, curse her. It began with comments made under his breath about the temperature of the brisket, or the soap residue under his collar. Brod was able to overlook it, could even find it endearing.

Brod, where are my fucking socks? You misplaced them again.

I know, she would say, smiling inwardly at the joys of being unappreciated and bullied around. *You're right. It won't happen again.*

Why the hell can't I remember the name of that coiled instrument!

Because of me. It's my fault.

With time he became worse. Dirty dirt became grounds for a tirade. Wet water in the bathtub and he might yell at her until the neighbors had to close their shutters (the desire for a little peace and quiet being the only thing the citizens of the shtetl shared). It was less than a year after the accident before he started hitting her. But, she reasoned, it was such a small fraction of the time. Once or twice a week. Never more. And when he was not in a "mood," he was more kind to her than any husband to his wife. His moods were not him. They were the other Kolker, born of the metal teeth in his brain. And she was in love, which gave her a reason to live.

Whore poison bitch! the other Kolker would howl at her with raised arms, and then the Kolker would take her into those arms, as he did the night they first met.

Filthy water monster! with a backhanded slap across the cheek, and then he would tenderly lead her, or she him, to the bedroom.

In the middle of lovemaking he might damn her, or hit her, or push her off the bed onto the floor. She would climb back up, remount, and begin again where they left off. Neither of them knew what he might do next.

They saw every doctor in the six villages—the Kolker broke the nose of the confident young physician in Lutsk who suggested the couple sleep in separate beds—and all agreed that the only possible cure for his disposition would be to remove the blade from his head, which would certainly kill him.

The women of the shtetl were happy to see Brod suffer. Even after sixteen years, they still thought of her as a product of that terrible hole, because of which they could never see her all at once, because of which they could never know and mother her, because of which they hated her. Rumors spread that the Kolker beat her because she was cold in bed (only two children to show after three years of marriage!) and couldn't manage a household with any competency.

I would expect black eyes if I pranced around like her!
Have you seen the mess their yard has become? What a pigsty!
It proves, again, that there is some justice in this world!

The Kolker hated himself, or his other self, for it. He would pace the bedroom at night, arguing savagely with his other self at the top of the two lungs they shared, often beating the chest that housed those lungs, or boxing their face. After badly injuring Brod in several night incidents, he decided (against her will) that the doctor with the broken nose was right: they must sleep apart.

I won't.

There's nothing to be said.

Then leave me. I'd rather that than this. Or kill me. That would be even better than your leaving.

You're being ridiculous, Brod. I'm only going to sleep in a different room.

But love is a room, she said. *That's what it is.*

This is what we have to do.

This is not what we have to do.

It is.

It worked for a few months. They were able to assume a regular daily life with only the occasional outburst of brutality, and would part in the evening to undress and go to bed alone. They would explain their dreams to each other over bread and coffee the next morning and describe the positions of their restlessness. It was an opportunity that their hurried marriage had never allowed for: coyness, slowness, discovering one another from a distance. They had their seventh, eighth, and ninth conversations. The Kolker tried to articulate what he wanted to say, and it always came out wrong. Brod was in love and had a reason to live.

His condition worsened. In time, Brod could expect a sound beating every morning before the Kolker went to work—where he was able, to the bafflement of all doctors, to refrain entirely from outbursts—and every late afternoon before dinner. He beat her in the kitchen in front of the pots and pans, in the living room in front of their two children, and in the pantry in front of the mirror in which they both watched. She never ran from his fists, but took them, went to them, certain that her bruises were not marks of violence, but violent love. The Kolker was trapped in his body—like a love note in an unbreakable bottle, whose script never fades or smudges, and is never read by the eyes of the intended lover—forced to hurt the one with whom he wanted most to be gentle.

Even toward the end, the Kolker had periods of clarity, lasting as long as several days at a time.

I have something for you, he said, leading Brod by the hand through the kitchen and out into the garden.

What is it? she asked, making no effort to keep a safe distance. (There was no such thing as a safe distance, then. Everything was either too close or too far.)

For your birthday. I got you a gift.

It's my birthday?

It's your birthday.

I must be seventeen.

Eighteen.

What's the surprise?

That would ruin the surprise.

I hate surprises, she said.

But I like them.

Whom is this gift for? You or me?

The gift is for you, he said. *The surprise is for me.*

What if I surprised you and told you to keep the gift? Then the surprise would be for me, and the gift for you.

But you hate surprises.

I know. So give me the gift already.

He handed her a small package. It was wrapped in blue vellum, with a light blue ribbon tied around it.

What is this? she asked.

We've gone over this, he said. *It's your surprise gift. Open it.*

No, she said, gesturing to the wrapping, *this.*

What do you mean? That's just wrapping.

She put down the package and began to cry. He had never seen her cry.

What is it, Brod? What? It was supposed to make you happy.

She shook her head. Crying was new to her.

What, Brod. What happened?

She hadn't cried since that Trachimday five years before, when on the way home from the float she was stopped by the mad squire Sofiowka N, who made a woman of her.

I don't love you, she said.

What?

I don't love you, pushing him away. *I'm sorry.*

Brod, putting his hand on her shoulder.

Get off me! she hollered, pulling herself away from him. *Don't touch me! I don't want you touching me ever again!* She turned her head to the side and vomited onto the grass.

She ran. He chased her. She ran around the house many times, past the front door, the winding walk, the gate at the back, the pigsty of a yard, the side garden, and back to the front door again. The Kolker kept close behind, and although he was much faster, he decided never to catch up, never to turn around and wait for her lap to bring her to him. So they went around and around: front door, winding walk, pigsty of a yard, side garden, front door, winding walk, pigsty of a yard, side garden. Finally, as the afternoon put on its early-evening dress, Brod collapsed from fatigue in the garden.

I'm tired, she said.

The Kolker sat beside her. *Did you ever love me?*

She turned her head from him. *No. Never.*

I've always loved you, he told her.

I'm sorry for you.

You're a terrible person.

I know, she said.

I just wanted you to know that I know that.

Well, know that I do.

He ran the back of his hand up her cheek, with the pretense of wiping away sweat. *Do you think you could ever love me?*

I don't think so.

Because I'm not good enough.

It's not like that.

Because I'm not smart.

No.

Because you couldn't love me.

Because I couldn't love you.

He walked inside.

Brod, my great-great-great-great-great-grandmother, was left alone in the garden. The wind revealed the undersides of the leaves and made waves of the grass. It rushed across her face, drying the sweat, urging more tears. She opened the package, which she realized she had never put down. Blue ribbon, blue vellum, box. A bottle of perfume. He must have bought it in Lutsk last week. What a sweet gesture. She sprayed a bit on her wrist. It was subtle. Not too pristine. *What?* she said once to herself, and then once aloud, *What?* She felt a total displacement, like a spinning globe brought to a sudden halt by the light touch of a finger. How did she end up here, like this? How could there have been so much —so many moments, so many people and things, so many razors and pillows, timepieces and subtle coffins—without her being aware? How did her life live itself without her?

She put the atomizer back in the box, along with the blue vellum and light blue ribbon, and went inside. The Kolker had made a mess of the kitchen. Spices were scattered on the floor. Bent silverware on scratched countertops. Unhinged cabinets, dirt, and broken glass. There were so many things to attend to—so much gathering and throwing away; and after gathering and throwing away, saving what was salvageable; and after saving what was salvageable, cleaning; and after cleaning, washing down with soapy water; and after washing down with soapy water, dusting; and after dusting, something else; and after something else, something else. So many little things to do. Hundreds of millions of them. Everything in the universe felt like something to do. She cleared a spot on the floor, laid herself down, and tried to make a mental list.

It was almost dark when the sound of crickets awoke her. She lit the Shabbos candles, observed the shadows against her hands, covered her eyes and said the blessing, and went up to the Kolker's bed. His face was badly bruised and swollen.

Brod, he said, but she silenced him. She brought up a small block of ice from the cellar and held it against his eye until his face couldn't feel anything, and her hand couldn't feel anything.

I love you, she said. *I do.*

No you don't, he said.

But I do, she said, touching his hair.

No. It's OK. I know you're much smarter than me, Brod, and that I'm not good enough for you. I was always waiting for you to figure it out. Every day. I felt like the czar's food taster, waiting for the night when the dinner would be poisoned.

Stop, she said. *It's not true. I do love you.*

You stop.

But I love you.

It's OK. I'm OK. She touched the puffy blackness around his left eye. The down, which the saw blade had released from the pillow, clung to the tears on their cheeks. *Listen*, he said, *I'll be dead soon.*

Stop.

We both know it.

Stop.

There's no use in avoiding it.

Stop.

And I wonder if you could just pretend for a while, if we could pretend to love each other. Until I'm gone.

Silence.

She felt it again, the same as that night when she met him, when he was illuminated at her window, when she let her arms brush down her skin to her sides and turned to face him.

We can do that, she said.

She cut a small hole in the wall to allow him to speak to her from the adjoining bedroom to which he had exiled himself, and a one-way flap was built into the door through which food could be passed. That's how it was for the last year of their marriage. She pushed her bed against the wall so she could hear him mutter his passionate profanity and feel the wiggle of his extended index finger, which could neither hurt nor caress in such a position. When she was brave enough, she would stick one of her own fingers through the hole (like tempting a lion in his cage) and summon her love to the pine divide.

What are you doing? he whispered.

I'm talking to you.

He put his eye to the hole. *You look very beautiful.*

Thank you, she said. *Can I look at you?*

He moved away from the hole so she would be able to see at least some of him.

Will you take off your shirt? she asked.

I feel shy. He laughed and took off his shirt. *Can you take off yours, so I don't feel so strange standing here?*

That would make you feel less strange? She laughed. But she did it, and made sure that she was far enough from the hole so that he could go to it and look at her.

Will you also take off your socks? she asked. *And your pants?*

Will you take off yours?

I also feel shy, she said, which, in spite of the fact that they had seen each other's naked body hundreds, and probably thousands, of times, was true. They had never seen one another from afar. They had never known the deepest intimacy, that closeness attainable only with distance. She went to the hole and looked at him for several silent minutes. Then she backed away from the hole. He went to it and looked at her for several more silent minutes. In the silence they attained another intimacy, that of words without talking.

Now will you take off your underwear? she asked.

Will you take off yours?

If you'll take off yours.

You will?

Yes.

Do you promise?

They removed their underwear and took turns gazing through the hole, experiencing the sudden and profound joy of discovering each other's body, and the pain of not being able to discover each other at the same time.

Touch yourself as if your hands were mine, she said.

Brod —

Please.

He did it, even though he was embarrassed, even though he was a body's length from the hole. And even though he couldn't see anything more than her eye — a blue marble in the black expanse — she did as he did, used her hands to remember his hands. She leaned back, and with her right forefinger she fingered the hole in the pine divide, and with her left she pressed circles over her greatest secret, which was also a hole, also a negative space, and when is enough proof enough?

Will you come to me? she asked.

I will.

Yes?

I will.

They made love through the hole. The three lovers pressed against one another, but never fully touched. The Kolker kissed the wall, and Brod kissed the wall, but the selfish wall never kissed either back. The Kolker pressed his palms against the wall, and Brod, who turned her back to the wall to accommodate love, pressed the backs of her thighs against the wall, but the wall remained indifferent, never acknowledging what they were trying so hard to do.

They lived with the hole. The absence that defined it became a presence that defined them. Life was a small negative space cut out of the eternal solidity, and for the first time, it felt precious — not like all of the words that had come to mean nothing, but like the last breath of a drowning victim.

Without being able to examine the Kolker's body, the doctor offered a diagnosis of consumption — little more than a guess for the sake of some dotted line. Brod watched through the hole in the black wall as her still-young husband withered away. The strong, treelike man who had been illuminated by a wink of lightning that night of Yankel's death, who had explained to her the nature of her first period, who had awoken early and returned late only to provide for her, who wouldn't lay a finger on her but would too often impart the might of his fist, now looked eighty. His hair had grayed around the ears and fallen out on top. Pulsing veins had risen to the surface of his prematurely wrinkled hands. His stomach had dropped. His breasts were larger than her own, which is to say little of their size, but volumes of how much it hurt Brod to see them.

She persuaded him to change his name for the second time. Perhaps this would confuse the Angel of Death when He came to take the Kolker away. (The inevitable is, after all, inevitable.) Perhaps He could be tricked into thinking the Kolker was someone he was not, just as the Kolker himself was tricked. So Brod named him Safran, after a lipstick passage she remembered with longing from her father's ceiling. (And it was this Safran for whom my grandfather, the kneeling groom, was named.) But it didn't work. Shalom-then-Kolker-now-Safran's condition worsened, the years continued to pass in days, and his grief left him too weak even to rub his wrist with enough strength over the blade in his head to end his own life.

Not long after their exile to the rooftops, the Wisps of Ardisht realized that they would soon run out of matches to light their beloved cigarettes. They kept a chalk-line count on the side of the tallest chimney. Five hundred. The next day three hundred. The next day one hundred. They rationed them, burned them down to the striker's fingers, trying to light at least thirty cigarettes with each. When they were down to twenty matches, lighting became a ceremony. By ten, the women were crying. Nine. Eight. The clan leader dropped the seventh off the roof by accident, and proceeded to throw his own body after it in shame. Six. Five. It was inevitable. The fourth match was blown out by a breeze — a gross oversight by the new clan leader, who also plunged to his death, although his nosedive was not of his own choosing. Three: *We will die without them.* Two: *It's too painful to go on.* And then, in the moment of deepest desperation, a grand idea emerged, devised by a child, no less: simply make sure that there is always someone smoking. Each cigarette can be lit from the previous one. As long as there is a lit cigarette, there is the promise of another. The glowing ash end is the seed of continuity! Schedules were drawn up: dawn duty, morning smoke, lunchtime puffer, midafternoon and late-afternoon assignments, crepuscular puller, lonely midnight sentinel. The sky was always lit with at least one cigarette, the candle of hope.

So it was with Brod, who knew that the Kolker's days were numbered, and so began her grieving long before he died. She wore rent black clothes and sat close to the ground on a wooden stool. She even recited the Mourner's Kaddish loud enough for Safran to hear. There are only weeks left, she thought. Days. Although she never cried tears, she wailed and wailed in dry heaves. (Which could not have been good for my great-great-great-great-grandfather—conceived through the hole —who was eight months heavy in her stomach.) And then, in one of his moments of mental clarity, Shalom-then-Kolker-now-Safran called to her through the wall: *I'm still here, you know. You promised you'd pretend to love me until I died, and instead you're pretending I'm dead.*

It's true, Brod thought. *I'm breaking my promise.*

So they strung their minutes like pearls on an hour-string. Neither slept. They stood vigil with their cheeks against the pine divide, passing notes through the hole like schoolchildren, passing vulgarities, blown kisses, blasphemous hollers and songs.

Weep not, my love,
Weep not, my love,
Your heart is close to me.
You fucking bitch,
Ungrateful cunt,
Your heart is close to me.
Oh, do not fear,
I'm nearer than near,
Your heart is close to me.
I'll gouge out your eyes
And pound in your fucking head,
You fucking bitch whore,
Your heart is close to me.

Their final conversations (ninety-eight, ninety-nine, and one hundred) consisted of exchanged vows, which took the form of sonnets Brod would read from one of Yankel's favorite books—a loose scrap descended to the floor: *I had to do it for myself*—and of Shalom-then-Kolker-now-Safran's most loathsome obscenities, which didn't mean what they said, but spoke in harmonics that could be heard only by his wife: *I'm sorry that this has been your life. Thank you for pretending with me.*

You are dying, Brod said, because it was the truth, the all-consuming and unacknowledged truth, and she was tired of saying things that weren't the truth.

I am, he said.

What does it feel like?

I don't know, through the hole. *I'm scared.*

You don't have to be scared, she said. *It's going to be OK.*

How is it going to be OK?

It's not going to hurt.

I don't think that's what I'm afraid of.

What are you afraid of?

I'm afraid of not being alive.

You don't have to be afraid, she said again.

Silence.

He put his forefinger through the hole.

I have to tell you something, Brod.

What?

This is something I've wanted to tell you since I met you, and I should have told you this so long ago, but the longer I waited, the more impossible it became. I don't want you to hate me.

I couldn't hate you, she said, and held his finger.

This is all completely wrong. It's not how I meant for it to be. You have to know that.

Shhh...shhh...

I owe you so much more than this.

You don't owe me anything. Shhh...

I'm a bad person.

You're a good person.

I have to tell you something.

It's OK.

He pressed his lips to the hole. *Yankel was not your real father.*

The minutes were unstrung. They fell to the floor and rolled through the house, losing themselves.

I love you, she said, and for the first time in her life, the words had meaning.

After eighteen days, the baby—who had, with its ear pressed against Brod's bellybutton, heard everything—was born. In postlabor exhaustion, Brod had finally slept. Only minutes later, or perhaps at the exact moment of the birth—the house was so consumed with new life that no one was aware of new death—Shalom-then-Kolker-now-Safran died, never having seen his third child. Brod later regretted not knowing precisely when her husband passed away. If it had been before the birth of her child, she would have named him Shalom, or Kolker, or Safran. But Jewish custom forbade the naming of a child after a living relative. It was said to be bad luck. So instead she named him Yankel, like her other two children.

She cut around the hole that had separated her from the Kolker for those last months, and put the pine loop on her necklace, next to the abacus bead that Yankel had given her so long ago. This new bead would remind her of the second man she had lost in her eighteen years, and of the hole that she was learning is not the exception in life, but the rule. The hole is no void; the void exists around it.

The men at the flour mill, who wanted so desperately to do something kind for Brod, something that might make her love them as they loved her, chipped in to have the Kolker's body bronzed, and they petitioned the governing council to stand the statue in the center of the shtetl square as a symbol of strength and vigilance, which, because of the perfectly perpendicular saw blade, could also be used to tell more or less accurate time by the sun.

But rather than of strength and vigilance, he soon became a symbol of luck's power. It was luck, after all, that had given him the golden sack that Trachimday, and luck that had brought him to Brod as Yankel left her. It was luck that had put that blade in his head, and luck that had kept it there, and luck that had timed his passing to coincide with the birth of his child.

Men and women journeyed from distant shtetls to rub his nose, which was worn to the flesh in only a month's time and had to be rebronzed. Babies were brought before him—always at noon when he cast no shadow at all—to be protected from lightning, the evil eye, and stray partisan fire. The old folks told him their secrets, hoping he might be amused, take pity on them, grant a few more years. Unmarried women kissed his lips, praying for love, so many kisses that the lips became indented, became negative kisses, and also had to be rebronzed. So many visitors came to rub and kiss different parts of him for the fulfillment of their various wishes that his entire body had to be rebronzed every month. He was a changing god, destroyed and recreated by his believers, destroyed and recreated by their belief.

His dimensions changed slightly with each rebronzing. Over time, his arms lifted, inch by inch, from down at his sides to high above his head. The sickly forearms of the end of his life became thick and virile. His face had been polished down so many times by so many beseeching hands, and rebuilt as many times by as many others, that it no longer resembled that of the god to whom those first few prayed. For each recasting, the craftsmen modeled the Dial's face after the faces of his male descendants—reverse heredity. (So when my grandfather thought he saw that he was growing to look like his great-great-great-grandfather, what he really saw was that his great-great-great-grandfather was growing to look like him. His revelation was just how much like himself he looked.) Those who prayed came to believe less and less in the god of their creation and more and more in their belief. The unmarried women kissed the Dial's battered lips, although they were not faithful to their god, but to the kiss: they were kissing themselves. And when the bridegrooms knelt, it was not the god they believed in, it was the kneel; not the god's bronzed knees, but their own bruised ones.

So my young grandfather knelt—a perfectly unique link in a perfectly uniform chain—almost one hundred fifty years after his great-great-great-grandmother Brod saw the Kolker illuminated at her window. With the hand of his functional left arm, he removed his panty-hanky and wiped the sweat from his brow, then from above his upper lip.

Great-great-great-grandfather, he sighed, *don't let me hate who I become.*

When he felt ready to continue—with the ceremony, with the afternoon, with his life—he rose to his feet and was again met with the cheers of the shtetl's men.

Hoorah! The groom!

Yoidle-doidle!

To the synagogue!

They paraded him through the streets on their shoulders. Long white banners hung from the high windows, and the cobblestones had been caked white—if they had only known—with flour. The fiddles continued to play from the front of the parade, this time faster klezmer melodies to which the men sang along in unison:

Biddle biddle biddle biddle

bop

biddle bop...

Because my grandfather and his bride were Slouchers, the ceremony under the chuppah was extremely short. The recitation of the seven blessings was officiated by the Innocuous Rabbi, and at the proper moment my grandfather lifted the veil of his new wife—who gave a quick, enticing wink when the Rabbi was turned to face the ark—and then smashed the crystal, which was not really crystal but glass, under his foot.

Dear Jonathan,

Humph. I feel as if I have so many things to inform you. Beginning is very rigid, yes? I will begin with the less rigid matter, which is the writing. I could not perceive if you were appeased by the last section. I do not understand, to where did it move you? I am glad that you were good-humored about the part I invented about commanding you to drink the coffee until I could see my face in the cup, and how you said it was a clay cup. I am a very funny person, I think, although Little Igor says that I merely look funny. My other inventions were also first rate, yes? I ask because you did not utter anything about them in your letter. Oh yes, I of course am eating humble pie for the section I invented about the word "procure," and how you did not know what it signified. It has been removed, and so has my effrontery. Even Alf is not humorous at times. I have made efforts to make you appear as a person with less anxiety, as you have commanded me to do on so many occasions. This is difficult to achieve, because in truth you are a person with very much anxiety. Perhaps you should be a drug user.

As for your story, I will tell you that I was at first a very perplexed person. Who is this new Safran, and Dial, and who is becoming married? Primarily I thought it was the wedding of Brod and Kolker, but when I learned that it was not, I thought, Why did their story not continue? You will be happy to know that I proceeded, suspending my temptation to cast off your writing into the garbage, and it all became illuminated. I am very happy that you returned to Brod and Kolker, although I am not happy that he became the person that he became because of the saw (I do not think that there were these kinds of saws at that time, but I trust that you have a good purpose for your ignorance), although I am happy that they were able to discover a kind of love, although I am not happy because it really was not love, was it? One could learn very much from the marriage of Brod and Kolker. I do not know what, but I am certain that it has to do with love. And also, why do you term him "the Kolker"? It is similar to how you term it "the Ukraine," which also makes no sense to me.

If I could utter a proposal, please allow Brod to be happy. Please. Is this such an impossible thing? Perhaps she could still exist, and be proximal with your grandfather Safran. Or, here is a majestic idea: perhaps Brod could be Augustine. Do you comprehend what I signify? You would have to alter your story very much, and she would be very aged, of course, but might it be wonderful in this manner?

Those things that you wrote in your letter about your grandmother made me remember how you told me on Augustine's steps about when you would sit under her dress, and how that presented you safety and peace. I must confess that I became melancholy then, and still am melancholy. I was also very moved — is this how you use it? — by what you wrote about how impossible it must have been for your grandmother to be a mother without a husband. It is amazing, yes, how your grandfather survived so much only to die when he came to America? It is as if after surviving so much, there was no longer a reason to survive. When you wrote about the early death of your grandfather, it helped me to understand, in some manners, the melancholy that Grandfather has felt since Grandmother died, and not only because they both died from cancer. I do not know your mother, of course, but I know you, and I can tell you that your grandfather would have been so so proud. It is my hope that I will be a person that Grandmother would have been so so proud of.

And now, to concern informing your grandmother of our voyage, there could not be a question that you must do it, even if it will make her to cry. In truth, it is something abnormal to witness your grandparent cry. I have told you about when I have witnessed Grandfather cry, and I implore myself to say that I desire to never witness him cry again. If this signifies that I must do things for him so that he will not cry, then I will do those things. If this signifies that I must not look when he cries, then I will not look. You are very different from me in this manner. I think that you need to see your grandmother cry, and if this means doing things to make her cry, then you must do them, and if this means looking at her when she cries, then you must look.

Your grandmother will find some manner to be content with what you did when you went to Ukraine. I am certain that she will forgive you if you inform her. But if you never inform her, she will never be able to forgive you. And this is what you desire, yes? For her to forgive you? Is not that why you did everything? One part of your letter made me most melancholy. It was the part when you said that you do not know anybody, and how that encompasses even you. I understand very much what you are saying. Do you remember the division that I wrote about how Grandfather said I looked like a combination of Father, Mother, Brezhnev, and myself? I made to remember that when I read what you wrote. (With our writing, we are reminding each other of things. We are making one story, yes?) I must inform you something now. This is a thing I have never informed anyone, and you must promise that you will not inform it to one soul. I have never been carnal with a girl. I know. I know. You cannot believe it, but all of the stories that I told you about my girls who dub me All Night, Baby, and Currency were all not-truths, and they were not befitting not-truths. I think I manufacture these not-truths because it makes me feel like a premium person. Father asks me very often about girls, and which girls I am being carnal with, and in what arrangements we are carnal. He likes to laugh with me about it, especially late at night when he is full of vodka. I know that it would disappoint him very much if he knew what I am really like.

But more, I manufacture not-truths for Little Igor. I desire him to feel as if he has a cool brother, and a brother whose life he would desire to impersonate one day. I want Little Igor to be able to boast to his friends about his brother, and to want to be viewed in public places with him. I think that this is why I relish writing for you so much. It makes it possible for me to be not like I am, but as I desire for Little Igor to see me. I can be funny, because I have time to meditate about how to be funny, and I can repair my mistakes when I perform mistakes, and I can be a melancholy person in manners that are interesting, not only melancholy. With writing, we have second chances. You mentioned to me that first evening of our voyage that you thought you might have been born to be a writer. What a terrible thing, I think. But I must tell you, I do not think that you understood the meaning of what you said when you said that. You were making suggestions of how you like to write, and how it is an interesting thing for you to imagine worlds that are not exactly like this one, or worlds that are exactly like this one. It is true, I am certain, that you will write very many more books than I will, but it is me, not you, who was born to be the writer.

Grandfather interrogates me about you every day. He desires to know if you forgive him for the things he told you about the war, and about Herschel. (You could alter it, Jonathan. For him, not for me. Your novel is now verging on the war. It is possible.) He is not a bad person. He is a good person, alive in a bad time. Do you remember when he said this? It makes him so melancholy to remember his life. I discover him crying almost every night, but must counterfeit that I am reposing. Little Igor also discovers him crying, and so does Father, and even though Father could never inform me, I am certain that it makes him melancholy to see his father crying.

Everything is the way it is because everything was the way it was. Sometimes I feel ensnared in this, as if no matter what I do, what will come has already been fixed. For me, OK, but there are things that I want for Little Igor. There is so much violence around him, and I mean more than merely the kind that occurs with fists. I do not want him to feel violence anymore, but also I do not want him to one day make others feel violence.

Father is never home because then he would witness Grandfather crying. This is my notion. "His stomach," he said to me last week when we heard Grandfather in the television room. "His stomach." But it is not his stomach, I understand, and Father understands this also. (This is why I forgive Father. I do not love him. I hate him. But I forgive him for everything.) I parrot: Grandfather is not a bad person, Jonathan. Everyone performs bad actions. I do. Father does. Even you do. A bad person is someone who does not lament his bad actions. Grandfather is now dying because of his. I beseech you to forgive us, and to make us better than we are. Make us good.

Guilelessly,
Alexander

Falling in Love

"JON-FEN," I said, "Jon-fen, arouse! Look who I have!" "Huh?" "Look,"
I said, and pointed to Augustine. "How long have I been asleep?" he
asked. "Where are we?" "Trachimbrod! We are in Trachimbrod!" I was
so proud. "Grandfather," I uttered, and moved Grandfather with much
violence. "What?" "Look, Grandfather! Look who I have found!" He
moved his hands across his eyes. "Augustine?" he asked, and it appeared
as if he could not be certain if he was still in dreams. "Sammy Davis, Junior, Junior!" I said, shaking her. "We are here!" "Who are these people?" Augustine asked, and she was persevering to cry. She dried her
tears with her dress, which signified lifting it enough to exhibit her legs.
But she was not ashamed. "Augustine?" the hero asked. "Let us roost," I
said, "and we will illuminate everything." The hero and the bitch removed themselves from the car. I was not certain if Grandfather would
come, but he did. "Are you hungry?" Augustine asked. The hero must
have been acquiring some Ukrainian, because he put his hand on his
stomach. I moved my head to say, Yes, some of us are very hungry people. "Come," Augustine said, and I detected that she was not melancholy
at all, but happy without controls. She took my hand. "Come inside. I
will arrange lunch, and we will eat." We walked up the wood stairs that I
first witnessed her roosting on and went into her house. Sammy Davis,
Junior, Junior loitered outside, smelling the clothes on the ground.

First, I must describe that Augustine had a very unusual walk, which
went from here to there with heaviness. She could not move any faster
than slow. It looked like she had a leg that was damaged goods. (If we
knew then, Jonathan, would we have still gone in?) Second, I must de-

scribe her house. It was not similar to any house that I have seen, and I do not think that I would dub it a house. If you want to know what I would dub it, I would dub it two rooms. One of the rooms had a bed, and a small desk, a bureau, and many things from the floor to the ceiling, including piles of more clothes and hundreds of shoes of different sizes and fashions. I could not see the wall through all of the photographs. They appeared as if they came from many different families, although I did recognize that a few of the people were in more than one or two. All of the clothing and shoes and pictures made me to reason that there must have been at least one hundred people living in that room. The other room was also very populous. There were many boxes, which were overflowing with items. These had writing on their sides. A white cloth was overwhelming from the box marked WEDDINGS AND OTHER CELEBRATIONS. The box marked PRIVATES: JOURNALS/DIARIES/ SKETCHBOOKS/UNDERWEAR was so overfilled that it appeared prepared to rupture. There was another box, marked SILVER/PERFUME/ PINWHEELS, and one marked WATCHES/WINTER, and one marked HYGIENE/SPOOLS/CANDLES, and one marked FIGURINES/SPECTA- CLES. If I had been a smart person, I would have recorded all of the names on a piece of paper, as the hero did in his diary, but I was not a smart person, and have since forgotten many of them. Some of the names I could not reason, like the box marked DARKNESS, or the one with DEATH OF THE FIRSTBORN written in pencil on its front. I noticed that there was a box on the top of one of these skyscrapers of boxes that was marked DUST.

There was a petite stove in this room, a shelf with vegetables and potatoes, and a wooden table. It was at this wooden table that we sat. It was hard to remove the chairs because there was almost no room for them with all of the boxes. "Allow me to cook you a little something," she said, giving all of her words and glances to me. "Please, do not make any efforts," Grandfather said. "It is nothing," she said, "but I must tell you that I do not have so much currency, and for that reason I have no meat." Grandfather looked at me and closed one of his eyes. "Do you like potatoes and cabbage?" she asked. "This is a perfect thing," Grandfather said. He was smiling so so much, and I am not lying if I tell you that I had never seen him smile so much since Grandmother was alive. I saw that when she rotated to excavate a cabbage from a wooden box on the floor, Grandfather arranged his hairs with a comb from his pocket.

"Tell her I'm so glad to meet her," the hero said. "We are all so glad to meet you," I said, and on accident I punched the PILLOWCASES box with my elbow. "It would be impossible for you to comprehend how long we have been searching for you." She made a fire on the stove and began to cook the food. "Ask her to tell us everything," the hero said. "I want to hear about how she met my grandfather, and why she decided to save him, and what happened to her family, and if she ever talked to my grandfather after the war. Find out," he said quietly, as if she might have comprehended, "if they were in love." "Slowness," I said, because I did not want Augustine to shit a brick. "You are being very kind," Grandfather said to her, "to take us into your home, and to cook for us your food. You are very kind." "You are kinder," she said, and then she performed a thing that surprised me. She looked at her face in the reflection of the window above the stove, and I think that she desired to see how she appeared. This is only my notion, but I am certain that it is a true one.

We watched her, as if the whole world and its future were because of her. When she cut a cabbage into little pieces, the hero moved his head this and that with the knife. When she put those pieces in a pan, Grandfather smiled and held one of his hands with the other. As for me, I could not retrieve my eyes from her. She had thin fingers and high bones. Her hairs, as I mentioned, were white and long. The ends of them moved against the floor, taking the dust and dirt with them. It was rigid to examine her eyes because they were so far back in her face, but I could see when she looked at me that they were blue and resplendent. It was her eyes that let me understand that she was, without a query, the Augustine from the picture. And I was certain, looking at her eyes, that she had saved the hero's grandfather, and probably many others. I could imagine in my brain how the days connected the girl in the photograph to the woman who was in the room with us. Each day was like another photograph. Her life was a book of photographs. One was with the hero's grandfather, and now one was with us.

When the food was ready, after many minutes of cooking, she transported it to the table on plates, one for each of us, and not one for her. One of the potatoes descended to the floor, PLOMP, which made us laugh for reasons that a subtle writer does not have to illuminate. But Augustine did not laugh. She must have been very shamed, because she hid her face for a long time before being able to view us again. "Are you OK?" Grandfather asked. She did not answer. "Are you OK?" And suddenly she returned to us. "You must be very fatigued from all of your traveling," she said. "Yes," he said, and he rotated his head, like he was embarrassed, but I do not know what he would be embarrassed about. "I could walk to the market and purchase some cold drinks," she said, "if you like cola, or something else." "No," Grandfather said with urgency, as if she might leave us and never return. "That is not necessary. You are being so generous. Please, sit." He removed one of the wooden chairs from the table, and on accident gave a small punch to the box marked MENORAHS/INK/KEYS. "Thank you," she said, and lowered her head. "You are very beautiful," Grandfather said, and I did not anticipate him to say that, and I do not think that he anticipated to say that. There was silence for a moment. "Thank you," she said, and she moved her eyes from him. "You are the one who is generous." "But you are beautiful," he said. "No," she said, "no, I am not." "I think you are beautiful," I said, and while I was not anticipating to say that, I do not lament saying it. She was so beautiful, like someone who you will never meet, but always dream of meeting, like someone who is too good for you. She was also very timid, I could perceive. It was rigid for her to view us, and she stored her hands in the pockets of her dress. I will tell you that when she did confer us a look, it was never to us, but always to me.

"What are you talking about?" the hero asked. "Has she mentioned my grandfather?" "He does not speak Ukrainian?" she asked. "No," I said. "Where is he from?" "America." "Is that in Poland?" I could not believe this thing, that she did not know of America, and I must tell you that it made her even more beautiful to me. "No, it is far away. He came on an airplane." "A what?" "An airplane," I said, "in the sky." I moved my hand in the air like an airplane, and on accident I gave a small punch to the box with FILLINGS written across it. I made the sound of an airplane with my lips. This made her distressed. "No more," she said. "What?"

"Please," she said. "From the war?" Grandfather asked. She did not say a thing. "He came to see you," I said. "He came from America for you." "I thought it was you," she said to me. "I thought you were the one." This made me laugh, and also made Grandfather laugh. "No," I said, "it is him." I placed my hand on the head of the hero. "He is the one who voyaged over the world to find you." This incited her to cry again, which I did not intend to do, but I must say that it seemed befitting. "You came for me?" she said to the hero. "She wants to know if you came for her." "Yes," the hero said, "tell her yes." "Yes," I said, "everything is for you." "Why?" she asked. "Why?" I asked the hero. "Because if it weren't for her, I couldn't be here to find her. She made the search possible." "Because you created him," I said. "By saving his grandfather, you allowed him to be born." Her breaths became brief. "I would like to give her something," the hero said. He excavated an envelope from his fanny pack. "Tell her it has money. I know it isn't enough. There couldn't be enough. It's just some money from my parents to make her life easier. Give it to her." I secured the envelope. It was brimming. There must have been many thousands of dollars in it. "Augustine," Grandfather said, "would you return with us? To Odessa?" She did not answer. "We could care for you. Do you have family here? We could take them into our house also. This is not a way to live," he said, pointing to the chaos. "We will give you a new life." I told the hero what Grandfather said. I saw that his eyes were impending tears. "Augustine," Grandfather said, "we can save you from all of this." He pointed to her house again, and he pointed to all of the boxes: HAIR/HAND MIRRORS, POETRY/NAILS/PISCES, CHESS/RELICS/BLACK MAGIC, STARS/MUSIC BOXES, SLEEP/SLEEP/SLEEP, STOCKINGS/KIDDUSH CUPS, WATER INTO BLOOD.

"Who is Augustine?" she asked.

"What?" I asked. "Who is Augustine?" "Augustine?" "What's she saying?" "The photograph," Grandfather said to me. "We do not know what the writing is on the back. It might not be her name." I exhibited her the photograph again. Again she made to cry. "This is you," Grandfather said, putting his finger under her face in the photograph. "Here. You are the girl." Augustine moved her head to say, No, this is not me, I am not her. "It is a very aged photograph," Grandfather said to me, "and she has forgotten." But I had already secured into my heart what Grandfather would not allow in. I returned the currency back to the hero. "You know this man," Grandfather said and did not inquire, putting his finger on the hero's grandfather. "Yes," she said, "that is Safran." "Yes," he said, looking at me, then looking at her. "Yes. And he is with you." "No," she said, "I do not know who those others are. They are not from Trachimbrod." "You saved him." "No," she said, "I did not." "Augustine?" he asked. "No," she said, and she exited from the table. "You saved him," he said. She put her hands on her face. "She is not Augustine," I told the hero. "What?" "She is not Augustine." "I don't understand." "Yes," Grandfather said. "No," she said. "She is not Augustine," I told the hero. "I thought that she was, but she is not." "Augustine," Grandfather said, but she was in the other room. "She is timid," Grandfather said. "We surprised her very much." "Perhaps we should go forth," I said. "We are not going anywhere. We must help her to remember. Many people try so rigidly to forget after the war that they can no longer remember." "This is not the situation," I said. "What are you saying?" the hero asked. "Grandfather thinks she is Augustine," I told him. "Even though she says she isn't?" "Yes," I said. "He is not being reasonable."

She returned with a box from the other room. The word REMAINS was written on it. She put it on the table and dislodged the top. It was brimmed with many photographs, and many pieces of paper, and many ribbons, and cloths, and queer things like combs, rings, and flowers that had become more paper. She removed each item, one at a time, and exhibited it to each of us, although I will say that it still seemed that she gave her attention only to me. "This is a photograph of Baruch in front of the old library. He used to sit there all day long and you know he could not even read! He said he liked to think about the books, think about them without reading them. He would always walk around with a book under his arm, and he took out more books from the library than anyone in the shtetl. What nonsense! This one," she said, and excavated another photograph out of the box, "is Yosef and his brother Tzvi. I used to play with them when they came home from school. I always had a little thing in my heart for Tzvi, but I never told him. I planned on telling him, but

I never did. I was such a funny girl, always having little things in my heart. It would drive Leah crazy when I would tell her about them, she would say, 'All of those little things, you are not going to have room for any blood!'" This made her laugh at herself, and then she became silent.

"Augustine?" Grandfather asked, but she must not have heard him, because she did not rotate to him, but only moved her hands through the things in the box, like the things were water. Now she did not give her eyes to any of us but me. Grandfather and the hero did not exist to her anymore.

"Here is Rivka's wedding ring," she said, and put it on her finger. "She hid it in a jar that she put in the ground. I knew this because she told me. She said, 'Just in case.' Many people did this. The ground is still filled with rings, and money, and pictures, and Jewish things. I was only able to find a few of them, but they fill the earth." The hero did not ask me once what she was saying, and he never did ask me. I am not certain if he knew what she was saying, or if he knew not to inquire.

"Here is Herschel," she said, holding a photograph up to the light of the window. "We will go," Grandfather said. "Tell him we are leaving." "Do not go," she said. "Shut up," he told her, and even if she was not Augustine, he still should not have uttered this to her. "I am sorry," I told her, "please continue." "He lived in Kolki, which was a shtetl near to Trachimbrod. Herschel and Eli were best friends, and Eli had to shoot Herschel, because if he did not, they would shoot him." "Shut up," he said again, and this time he also punched the table. But she did not shut up. "Eli did not want to, but he did it." "You are lying about it all." "He does not intend this," I told her, and I could not clutch why he was doing what he was doing. "Grandfather—" "You can keep your not-truths for yourself," he said. "I heard this story," she said, "and I believe it is a truth." I could perceive that he was making her to cry.

"Here is a clip," she said, "that Miriam would keep in her hair so that it would not be in her face. She was always running from here to there. It would kill her to sit down, you know, because she was always loving to do things. I found this under her pillow. It's true. Why was her clip under her pillow, you must want to know. The secret is that she would hold it all night so that she would not suck on her thumb! That was a bad thing she did for so long, even when she was twelve years old already! Only I know that. She would kill me if she knew I was talking about her thumb, but I'll tell you, if you witnessed close enough, if you gave it attention, you could see that it was always red. She was always ashamed about it." She restored the clip back into REMAINS and excavated another photograph.

"Here, oh, I remember this, this is Kalman and Izzy, they were such jokers." Grandfather did not view at anything except for Augustine. "See how Kalman is holding Izzy's nose! What a joker! They would make so much joking all day, Father called them the clowns of Trachimbrod. He would say, 'They are such clowns that not even a circus would have them!' " "You are from Trachimbrod?" I asked. "She is not from Trachimbrod," Grandfather said, and rotated his head away from her. "I am," she said. "I am the only one remaining." "What do you signify?" I asked, because I just did not know. "They were all killed," she said, and here I commenced to translate for the hero what she was saying, "except for the one or two who were able to escape." "You were the lucky ones," I told her. "We were the not-lucky ones," she said. "It is not true," Grandfather said, although I do not know what part he was saying was not true. "It is. You should never have to be the one remaining." "You should have died with the others," he said. (I will never allow that to remain in the story.)

"Ask her if she knew my grandfather." "Did you know the man in the photograph? He was the boy's grandfather." I presented her the photograph again. "Of course," she said, and again disbursed her eyes to me. "That was Safran. He was the first boy I ever kissed. I am such an old lady that I am too old to be shy anymore. I kissed him when I was only a girl, and he was only a boy. Tell him," she said to me, and she took my hand into her own hand. "Tell him that he was the first boy I ever kissed." "She says that your grandfather was the first boy she ever kissed." "We were very good friends. He lost a wife and two babies, you know, in the war. Does he know that?" "Two babies?" I asked. "Yes," she said. "He knows," I said. She inspected REMAINS, excavating photographs and putting them on the table. "How can you do this?" Grandfather asked her.

"Here," she said after a long search. "This is a photograph of Safran and me." I observed that the hero had small rivers descending his face, and I wanted to put my hand on his face, to be architecture for him. "This is his house we are in front of," she said. "I remember the day very much. My mother made this photograph. She was so fond for Safran. I think she wanted me to marry him, and even told the Rabbi." "Then you would be his grandmother," I told her. She laughed, and this made me feel good. "My mother liked him so much because he was a very polite boy, and very shy, and he would tell her that she was pretty even when she was not pretty." "What was her name?" I asked, and I was attempting to be kind, but the woman rotated her head to tell me, No, I will not ever utter her name. And then I remembered that I did not know this woman's name. I persevered to think of her as Augustine, because like Grandfather, I could not stop desiring that she was Augustine. "I know I have another," she said, and again investigated REMAINS. Grandfather would not look at her. "Yes," she said, excavating another yellow photograph, "here is one of Safran and his wife in front of their house after they became married."

I gave the hero each picture as she gave it to me, and he could only with difficulty hold it in his hands that were doing so much shaking. It appeared that a part of him wanted to write everything, every word of what occurred, into his diary. And a part of him refused to write even one word. He opened the diary and closed it, opened it and closed it, and it looked as if it wanted to fly away from his hands. "Tell him I was at the wedding. Tell him." "She was at the wedding of your grandfather and his first wife," I said. "Ask her what it was like," he said. "It was beautiful," she said. "My brother held one of the chuppah poles, I remember. It was a spring day. Zosha was such a pretty girl." "It was so beautiful," I told the hero. "There was white, and flowers, and many children, and the bride in a long dress. Zosha was a beautiful girl, and all of the other men were jealous people." "Ask her if we could see this house," he said, pointing to the photograph. "Could you exhibit us this house?" I asked. "There is nothing," she said. "I already told you. Nothing. It used to be four kilometers distance from here, but everything that still exists from Trachimbrod is in this house." "You say it is four kilometers from here?" "There is no Trachimbrod anymore. It ended fifty years ago." "Take us there," Grandfather said. "There is nothing to see. It is only a field. I could exhibit you any field and it would be the same as exhibiting you Trachimbrod." "We have come to see Trachimbrod," Grandfather said, "and you will take us to Trachimbrod."

She looked at me, and she put her hand on my face. "Tell him I think about it every day. Tell him." "Think about what?" I asked. "Tell him." "She thinks about it every day," I told the hero. "I think about Trachim-. brod, and when we were all so young. We used to run in the streets naked, can you believe it? We were just children, yes. That was how it was. Tell him." "They used to run in the streets naked. They were just children." "I remember Safran so well. He kissed me behind the synagogue, which was a thing to get us murdered, you know. I can still remember just how I felt. It was a little like flying. Tell it to him." "She remembers when your grandfather kissed her. She flew a little." "I also remember Rosh Hashanah, when we would go to the river and throw breadcrumbs in it so our sins would float away from us. Tell him." "She remembers the river and breadcrumbs and her sins." "The Brod?" the hero asked. She moved her head to say, Yes, yes. "Tell him that his grandfather and I and all of the children would jump into the Brod when it was so hot, and our parents would sit on the side of the water and watch and play cards. Tell him." I told him. "Everyone had his own family, but it was something like we were all one big family. People would fight, yes, but it was nothing."

She retrieved her hands from me and put them on her knees. "I am so ashamed," she said. "You had to do anything. You could not allow anyone to see your face after." "You should be ashamed," Grandfather said. "Do not be ashamed," I told her. "Ask her how my grandfather escaped." "He would like to know how his grandfather escaped." "She does not know anything," Grandfather said. "She is a fool." "You do not have to utter anything that you do not want to utter," I told her, and she said, "Then I would never utter another word again." "You do not have to do anything that you do not want to do." "Then I would never do anything again." "She is a liar," Grandfather said, and I could not understand what was forcing him to behave this way.

"Could you please leave us to be in solitude," Augustine said to me, "for a few moments." "Let us go outside," I told Grandfather. "No," Augustine said, "him." "Him?" I asked. "Please leave us to be in solitude for a few moments." I looked to Grandfather so that he could give me a beacon of what to do, but I could see that his eyes were impending tears, and that he would not look at me. This was my beacon. "We must go outside," I told the hero. "Why?" "They are going to utter things in secrecy." "What kinds of things?" "We cannot be here."

We walked out and closed the door behind us. I yearned to be on the other side of the door, the side on which such momentous truths were being uttered. Or I yearned to press my ear to the door so that I could at minimum hear. But I knew that my side was on the outside with the hero. Part of me hated this, and part of me was grateful, because once you hear something, you can never return to the time before you heard it. "We can remove the skin from the corn for her," I said, and the hero harmonized. It was approximately four o'clock of the afternoon, and the temperature was commencing to become cold. The wind was making the first noises of night.

"I don't know what to do," the hero said.

"I do not know also."

After that there was a famine of words for a long time. We only removed the skin from corn. I was not concerned about what Augustine was saying. It was Grandfather's talking that I desired to hear. Why could he say things to this woman that he had never before encountered when he could not say things to me? Or perhaps he was not saying anything to her. Or perhaps he was lying. This is what I wanted, for him to present not-truths to her. She did not deserve the truth, not as I deserved the truth. Or we both deserved the truth, and the hero, too. All of us.

"What should we converse about?" I asked, because I knew that it was a common decency for us to speak. "I don't know." "There must be a thing." "Do you want to know anything else about America?" he asked. "I cannot think of anything at this moment." "Do you know about Times Square?" "Yes," I said, "Times Square in Manhattan on 42nd Street and Broadway Avenue." "Do you know about people who sit in front of slot machines all day and waste all of the money they have?" "Yes," I said. "Las Vegas, Nevada. I have read an article about this." "What about skyscrapers?" "Of course. World Trade Center. Empire State Building. Sears Tower." I do not comprehend why, but I was not proud of everything that I knew about America. I was ashamed. "What else?" he said. "Tell me more about your grandmother," I said. "My grandmother?" "Who you spoke of in the car. Your grandmother from Kolki." "You remember." "Yes." "What do you want to know?" "How old is she?" "She's about the age of your grandfather, I suppose, but she looks much older." "What does she look like?" "She's short. She calls herself a shrimp, which is funny. I don't know what color her hair really is, but she dyes it a kind of brown and yellow, sort of like the hairs on this corn. Her eyes are mismatched, one blue and one green. She has terrible varicose veins." "What does it mean varicose veins?" "The veins in her legs, where the blood goes through, they're above the level of her skin and they look kind of weird." "Yes," I said, "Grandfather has these also, because when he worked he would stand for all day, and so this happened to him." "My grandmother got them from the war, because she had to walk across Europe to escape. It was too much for her legs." "She walked across Europe?" "Remember, I told you she left Kolki before the Nazis." "Yes, I remember." He stopped for a moment. I decided to peril everything once again. "Tell me about you and her."

"What do you mean me and her?" "I only want to listen." "I don't know what to say." "Tell me about when you were young, and how it was with her then." He made a laugh. "When I was young?" "Tell me anything." "When I was young," he said, "I used to sit under her dress at family dinners. That's something I remember." "Tell me." "I haven't thought about this in a really long time." I did not utter a thing, so that he would persevere. This was so difficult at times, because there existed so much silence. But I ~~understanded~~ understood that the silence was necessary for him to talk. "I'd run my hands up and down her varicose veins. I don't know why, or how I started doing it. It was just something I did. I was a kid, and kids do things like that, I guess. I remembered that because I mentioned her legs." I refused to utter even one word. "It was like sucking your thumb. I did it, and it felt good, and that was it." Be silent, Alex. You do not have to speak. "I would watch the world through her dresses. I could see everything, but no one could see me. Like a fort, a hiding place under the covers. I was just a kid. Four. Five. I don't know." With my silence, I gave him a space to fill. "I felt safety and peace. You know, real safety and real peace. I felt it." "Safety and peace from what?" "I don't know. Safety and peace from not-safety and not-peace." "This is a nice story." "It's true. I'm not making it up." "Of course. I know that you are faithful." "It's just that sometimes we make things up, just to talk. But this really happened." "I know." "Really." "I believe you." There was a silence. This silence was so heavy, and so long, that I was coerced to speak. "When did you stop hiding under her dress?" "I don't know. Maybe I was five or six. Maybe a bit later. I just got too old for it, I guess. Someone must have told me it was no longer appropriate." "What else do you remember?" "What do you mean?" "About her. About you and her." "Why are you so curious?" "What are you so ashamed?" "I remember those veins of hers, and I remember the smell of my secret hiding place, that's how I used to think of it, I remember, like a secret, and I remember when my grandmother once told me that I'm lucky because I'm funny." "You are very funny, Jonathan." "No. That's the last thing I want to be." "Why? To be funny is a great thing." "No it's not." "Why is this?" "I used to think that humor was the only way to appreciate how wonderful and terrible the world is, to celebrate how big life is. You know what I mean?" "Yes, of course." "But now I think it's the opposite. Humor is a way of shrinking from that wonderful and terrible world." "Inform me more about when you were young, Jonathan." He made more laughing. "Why do you laugh?" He laughed again. "Inform me." "When I was a boy, I would spend Friday nights at my grandmother's house. Not every Friday, but most. On the way in, she would lift me from the ground with one of her wonderful terrifying hugs. And on the way out the next afternoon, I was again taken into the air with her love. I'm laughing because it wasn't until years later that I realized she was weighing me." "Weighing you?" "When she was our age, she was feeding from waste while walking across Europe barefoot. It was important to her—more important than that I had a good time—that I gained weight whenever I visited. I think she wanted the fattest grandchildren in the world." "Tell me more about these Fridays. Tell me about measuring and humor and hiding beneath her dress." "I think I'm done talking." "You must talk." Did you feel sorry for me? Is that why you persevered? "My grandmother and I used to scream words off her back porch at night, when I would stay over. That's something I remember. We screamed the longest words we could think of. 'Phantasmagoria!' I screamed." He laughed. "I remember that one. And then she would scream a Yiddish word I didn't understand. Then I would scream. 'Antediluvian!'" He screamed the word into the street, and this would have been an embarrassment except that there was no one in the street. "And then I would watch the veins in her neck bulge as she screamed some Yiddish word. We were both secretly in love with words, I guess." "And you were both secretly in love with each other." He laughed again. "What were the words that she would scream?" "I don't know. I never knew what they meant. I can still hear her." He screamed a Yiddish word into the street. "Why did you not ask her what the words meant?" "I was afraid." "Of what were you afraid?" "I don't know. I was just too afraid. I knew I wasn't supposed to ask, so I didn't." "Perhaps she desired for you to ask." "No." "Perhaps she needed you to ask, because if you didn't ask, she could not tell you." "No." "Perhaps she was shouting, Ask me! Ask me what I'm shouting!"

We peeled the corn. The silence was a mountain.

"Do you remember all of the concrete in Lvov?" he asked.

"Yes," I said.

"Me too."

More silence. We had nothing to talk about, nothing important. Nothing could have been important enough.

"What do you write in your diary?" "I take notes." "About what?" "For the book I'm working on. Little things that I want to remember." "About Trachimbrod?" "Right." "It is a good book?" "I've only written pieces. I wrote a few pages before I came this summer, a few on the plane to Prague, a few on the train to Lvov, a few last night." "Read to me from it." "It's embarrassing." "It is not like this. It is not embarrassing." "It is." "Not if you recount it for me. I will relish it, I promise you. I am very simple to enchant." "No," he said, so I did what I thought was the OK and even funny thing. I took his diary and opened it. He did not say that I could read it, but nor did he ask for it back. This is what I read:

He told his father that he could care for Mother and Little Igor. It took his saying it to make it true. Finally, he was ready. His father could not believe this thing. What? he asked. What? And Sasha told him again that he would take care of the family, that he would understand if his father had to leave and never return, and that it would not even make him less of a father. He told his father that he would forgive. Oh, his father became so angry, so full of wrath, and he told Sasha that he would kill him, and Sasha told his father that he would kill him, and they moved at each other with violence and his father said, Say it to my face, not to the floor, and Sasha said, You are not my father.

By the time Grandfather and Augustine descended from the house, we had finished a pile of corn, and left the skin as a pile on the other side of the stairs. I had read several pages in his diary. Some scenes were like this. Some were very different. Some happened early in history and some had not even happened yet. I understood what he was doing when he wrote like this. At first it made me angry, but then it made me sad, and then it made me so grateful, and then it made me angry again, and I went through these feelings hundreds of times, stopping on each for only a moment and then moving to the next.

"Thank you," Augustine said, and she was examining the piles, one of corn, one of skins. "That was a very kind thing that you did." "She is going to take us to Trachimbrod," Grandfather said. "We must not squander time. It is becoming late." I told this to the hero. "Tell her thank you for me." "Thank you," I told her. Grandfather said, "She knows."

The Wedding Reception Was So Extraordinary!
or
It All Goes Downhill After the Wedding, 1941

THERE IS A SENSE in which the bride's family had been preparing their house for her wedding since long before Zosha was born, but it wasn't until my grandfather reluctantly proposed—on both knees rather than one—that the renovations achieved their hysterical pace. The hardwood floors were covered in white canvas, and tables were set in a line stretching from the master bedroom to the kitchen, each feathered with precisely positioned name cards, whose placement had been agonized over for weeks. (Avra cannot sit next to Zosha, but should be near Yoske and Libby, but not if it means seating Libby near Anshel, or Anshel near Avra, or Avra anywhere near the centerpieces, because he's terribly allergic and will die. And by all means keep the Uprighters and Slouchers on opposite sides of the table.) New curtains were bought for the new windows, not because there was anything wrong with the old curtains on the old windows, but because Zosha was to be married, and that called for new curtains and windows. The new mirrors were cleaned spotless, their faux-antique frames meticulously dirtied. The proud parents, Menachem and Tova, saw to it that everything, down to the last and smallest detail, was made extraordinary.

The house was actually two houses, connected at the attic when Menachem's risky trout venture proved so remarkably lucrative. It was the largest house in Trachimbrod, but also the least convenient, as one might have to climb and descend the three flights and pass through twelve rooms in order to get from one room to another. It was divided by function: the bedrooms, children's playroom, and library in one half, the kitchen, dining room, and den in the other. The cellars—one of which housed the impressive wine racks, which, Menachem promised, would one day be filled with impressive wines, the other used as a quiet place for Tova's sewing—were separated by only a brick wall, but were, for all practical purposes, a four-minute walk apart.

The Double House revealed every aspect of its owners' new affluence. A veranda was half completed, jutting like broken glass off the back. Marble newels of idle spiral stairways connected floors to ceilings. The ceilings were raised on the lower floors, rendering the third-floor rooms livable only for children and midgets. Porcelain toilets were installed in the outhouse to replace the seatless brick stools on which everyone else in the shtetl took shits. The perfectly good garden was uprooted and replaced with a gravel walk, lined with azaleas that were cut too short to flower. But Menachem was most proud of the scaffolding: the symbol that things were always changing, always getting a little better. He loved the skeleton of makeshift beams and rafters more and more as construction progressed, loved them more than the house itself, and eventually persuaded the reluctant architect to draw them into the final plans. Workers, too, were drawn into the plans. Not workers, exactly, but local actors paid to look like workers, to walk the planks of the scaffolding, to hammer functionless nails into gratuitous walls, to pull those nails out, to examine blueprints. (The blueprints themselves were drawn into the blueprints, and in those blueprints were blueprints with blueprints with blueprints...) Menachem's problem was this: he had more money than there were things to buy. Menachem's solution was this: rather than buy more things, he would continue to buy the things he already owned, like a man on a desert island who retells and embellishes the only joke he can remember. His dream was for the Double House to be a kind of infinity, always a fraction of itself—suggestive of a bottomless money pit —always approaching but never reaching completion.

Gorgeous! Almost all of it, Tova! Gorgeous!

What a house! And you look like you've lost some weight in your face.

Marvelous! Everyone should be jealous of you.

The wedding—the reception—was the event of 1941, with enough attendees that, should the house have burned down or been swallowed by the earth, Trachimbrod's Jewish population would have completely disappeared. Reminders were sent out a few weeks before the invitation, which was sent out a week before the official arrangement. ,

DON'T FORGET:

THE WEDDING OF THE DAUGHTER OF

TOVA

AND HER HUSBAND*

JUNE 18, 1941

YOU KNOW THE HOUSE

* Menachem

And no one forgot. Only the various Trachimbroders who weren't, in Tova's estimation, worthy of an invitation were not at the reception, and hence not in the guest book, and hence not included in the last practical census of the shtetl before its destruction, and hence forgotten forever.

As the guests filtered in, unable to help but admire the stylized wainscoting, my grandfather excused himself and went down to the wine-rack cellar to change from his traditional marriage suit into a light cotton blazer, more suited to the wet heat.

Absolutely ravishing, Tova. Look at me, I'm ravished.

It looks like nothing else, ever.

You must have spent a fortune on those lovely centerpieces. Achoo!

So extraordinary!

A fissure of thunder resounded in the distance, and before there was time to close any of the new windows, or even their new curtains, a wind of haunting speed and strength breathed through the house, blowing over the floral centerpieces and tossing the place settings into the air. Pandemonium. The cat screeched, the water boiled, the elderly women held tight to the mesh hats that covered their balding heads. The gust left as soon as it entered, easing the place cards back on the table, not one card in its original place—Libby next to Kerman (who had said his attendance at the reception was dependent on a three-table separation between himself and that horrible cunt), Tova at the very end of the last table (a spot reserved for the fishmonger, whose name no one could remember, and whose invitation had been slid under his door at the last minute out of guilt for the recent loss of his wife to cancer), the Upright

Rabbi next to the outspoken Sloucher Shana P (who was as repulsed and turned on by him as he was by her), and my grandfather landing doggie-style on his bride's younger sister.

Zosha and her mother — red with embarrassment, pale with the sadness of an imperfect wedding — scurried about, trying in vain to reset everything that had been so deliberately arranged, picking up forks and knives, wiping the floors of spilled wine, recentering the centerpieces, replacing the names that had been scattered like a thrown deck of playing cards.

Let's hope it's not true, the father of the bride tried to joke over the shuffle, *that it all goes downhill after the wedding!*

The bride's younger sister was leaning against a shelf of empty wine racks when my grandfather entered the cellar.

Hello, Maya.

Hello, Safran.

I came to change.

Zosha will be so disappointed.

Why?

Because she thinks you're perfect. She told me so. And your wedding day is no time to change.

Not even into something more comfortable?

Your wedding day is no time to be comfortable.

Oh, sister, he said, and kissed her where her cheek became her lips. *A sense of humor to match your beauty.*

She slid her lace panties from under his lapel. *Finally,* pulling him into her arms, *any longer and I would have just burst.*

THE DUPE OF CHANCE, 1941–1924

As THEY MADE hurried love beneath the twelve-foot ceiling, which sounded as if it might collapse at any moment under the gunshots of so many heels—in the effort to clean up, nobody even noticed the groom's prolonged absence—my grandfather wondered if he was nothing more than a dupe of chance. Wasn't everything that had happened, from his first kiss to this, his first marital infidelity, the inevitable result of circumstances over which he had no control? How guilty could he be, really, when he never had any real choice? Could he have been with Zosha upstairs? Was that a possibility? Could his penis have been anywhere other than where it then was, and wasn't, and was, and wasn't, and was? Could he have been good?

His teeth. It's the first thing I notice whenever I examine his baby portrait. It's not my dandruff. It's not a smudge of gesso or white paint. Between my grandfather's thin lips, planted like albino pits in those plum-purple gums, is a full set of teeth. The physician must have shrugged, as physicians used to do when they couldn't explain a medical phenomenon, and comforted my great-grandmother with talk of good omens. But then there is the family portrait, painted three months later. Look, this time, at *her* lips, and you will see that she wasn't entirely comforted: my young great-grandmother was frowning.

It was my grandfather's teeth, so admired by his father for the virility they declared, that made his mother's nipples bloody and sore, that forced her to sleep on her side, and eventually made breastfeeding impossible. It was because of those teeth, those wee dinky molars, those cute bicuspids, that my great-grandparents stopped making love and had only one child. It's because of those teeth that my grandfather was pulled prematurely from his mother's well, and never received the nutrients his callow body needed.

His arm. It would be possible to look through all of the photographs many times and still miss what's so unusual. But it occurs too frequently to be explained as the photographer's choice of pose, or mere coincidence. My grandfather's right hand is never holding anything—not a briefcase, not any papers, not even his other hand. (And in the only picture taken of him in America—just two weeks after arriving, and three before he passed away—he holds my baby mother with his left arm.) Without proper calcium, his infant body had to allocate its resources judiciously, and his right arm drew the short straw. He watched helplessly as that red, swollen nipple got smaller and smaller, moving away from him forever. By the time he most needed to reach out for it, he couldn't.

So it was because of his teeth, I imagine, that he got no milk, and it was because he got no milk that his right arm died. It was because his arm died that he never worked in the menacing flour mill, but in the tannery just outside the shtetl, and that he was exempted from the draft that sent his schoolmates off to be killed in hopeless battles against the Nazis. His arm would save him again when it kept him from swimming back to Trachimbrod to save his only love (who died in the river with the rest of them), and again when it kept him from drowning himself. His arm saved him again when it caused Augustine to fall in love with him and save him, and it saved him once again, years later, when it prevented him from boarding the *New Ancestry* to Ellis Island, which would be turned back on orders of U.S. immigration officials, and whose passengers would all eventually perish in the Treblinka death camp.

And it was because of his arm, I'm sure—that flaccid hang of useless muscle—that he had the power to make any woman who crossed his path fall in hopeless love with him, that he had slept with more than forty women in Trachimbrod, and at least twice as many from the neighboring villages, and was now making standing, hurried love with his new bride's younger sister.

The first was the widow Rose W, who lived in one of the old wooden ramblers along the Brod. She thought it was pity that she felt for the crippled boy who had come on behalf of the Sloucher congregation to help clean the house, pity that moved her to bring him a plate of mandelbread and a glass of milk (the very sight of which turned his stomach), pity that moved her to ask how old he was and to tell him her own age, something not even her husband ever knew. It was pity she thought she felt when she removed her layers of mascara to show him the only part of her body that no one, not even her husband, had seen in more than sixty years. And it was pity, or so she thought, when she led him to the bedroom to show him her husband's love letters, sent from a naval ship in the Black Sea during the First World War.

In this one, she said, taking his lifeless hand, *he enclosed pieces of string that he used to measure out his body — his head, thigh, forearm, finger, neck, everything. He wanted me to sleep with them under my pillow. He said that when he came back, we would remeasure his body against the string as proof that he hadn't changed... Oh, I remember this one,* she said, fingering a sheet of yellowed paper, running her hand—aware, or not aware, of what she was doing—up and down my grandfather's dead arm. *In this one he wrote about the house he was going to build for us. He even drew a little picture of it, although he was such a bad artist. It was going to have a small pond, not a pond really, but a little thing, so we could have fish. And there would be a glass window over the bed so we could talk about the constellations before going to sleep ...And here,* she said, guiding his arm under the hem of her skirt, *is the letter in which he pledged his devotion until death.*

She turned off the light.

Is this OK? she asked, navigating his dead hand, leaning back.

Taking an initiative beyond his ten years, my grandfather pulled her to him, removed, with her help, her black blouse, which smelled so strongly of old age he was afraid he would never be able to smell young again, and then her skirt, her stockings (bulging under the pressure of her varicose veins), her panties, and the cotton pad she kept there in case of the now regular unexpecteds. The room was soaked with smells he had never before known together: dust, sweat, dinner, the bathroom after his mother had used it. She removed his shorts and briefs, and eased onto him backward, as if he were a wheelchair. *Oh,* she moaned, *oh.* And because my grandfather didn't know what to do, he did as she did: *Oh,* he moaned, *oh*. And when she moaned *Please*, he also moaned *Please*. And when she fluttered in small, rapid convulsions, he did the same. And when she was silent, he was silent.

Because my grandfather was only ten, it didn't seem unusual that he was able to make love—or have love made to him—for several hours without pause. But as he would later discover, it was not his pre-pubescence that gave him such coital longevity, but another physical shortcoming owing to his early malnutrition: like a wagon with no brakes, he never stopped short. This quirk was met with the profound happiness of his 132 mistresses, and with relative indifference on his part: how, after all, can one miss something one has never known? Besides, he never loved any of his lovers. He never confused anything he felt for love. (Only one would mean anything to him at all, and a problematic birth made real love impossible.) So what should he expect?

His first affair, which lasted every Sunday afternoon for four years—until the widow realized that she had taught his mother piano more than thirty years before, and couldn't bear to show him another letter—was not a love affair at all. My grandfather was an acquiescing passenger. He was happy to give his arm—the only part of his body that Rose paid any real attention to; the act itself was never anything more than a means to get closer to his arm—as a once-a-week gift, to pretend with her that it was not a canopy bed in which they were making love, but a lighthouse out on some windy jetty, that their silhouettes, shot by the powerful lamp deep out into the black waters, could serve as a blessing for the sailors, and summon her husband back to her. He was happy to let his dead arm serve as the missing limb for which the widow longed, for which she reread yellowing letters, and lived outside herself, and outside her life. For which she made love to a ten-year-old. The arm was the arm, and it was the arm—not her husband, or even herself—that she thought about seven years later, on June 18, 1941, as the first German war blasts shook her wooden house to its foundations, and her eyes rolled back in her head to view, before dying, her insides.

THE THICKNESS OF BLOOD and Drama, 1934

UNAWARE OF the nature of his errands, the Sloucher congregation paid my grandfather to visit Rose's house once a week, and came to pay him to perform similar services for widows and feeble ladies around Trachimbrod. His parents never knew the truth, but were relieved by his enthusiasm to make money and spend time with the elderly, both of which had become important personal concerns as they descended into poverty and middle age.

We were beginning to think you had Gypsy blood, his father told him, to which he only smiled, his usual response to his father.

Which means, his mother said—his mother whom he loved more than himself—*that it's good to see you doing something good with your time.* She kissed him on the cheek and mussed his hair, which upset his father, because Safran was now too old for that kind of thing.

Who's my baby? she would ask him when his father was not around.

I am, he would say, loving the question, loving the answer, and loving the kiss that came with the answer to the question. *You don't have to look any farther than me.* As if that were something he truly feared, that she *would* one day look farther. And for this reason, because he wanted her to look to him and never elsewhere, he never told his mother anything that he thought might upset her, that might make her think less of him, or make her jealous.

Likewise, perhaps, he never told a friend of his exploits, or any lover of her predecessor. He was so afraid of being discovered that even in his journal—the only written record I have of his life before he met my grandmother, in a displaced-persons camp after the war—he never mentions them once.

The day he lost his virginity to Rose: *Nothing much happened today. Father received a shipment of twine from Rovno, and yelled at me when I neglected my chores. Mother came to my defense, as usual, but he yelled at me anyway. Thought about lighthouses all night. Strange.*

The day he had sex with his first virgin: *Went to the theater today. Too bored to stay through the first act. Drank eight cups of coffee. I thought I was going to burst. Didn't burst.*

The day he made love from behind for the first time: *I've given much thought to what mother said about watchmakers. She was so persuasive, but I'm not yet sure if I agree. I heard her and father yelling in their bedroom, which kept me awake most of the night, but when I finally did sleep, I slept soundly.*

It's not that he was ashamed, or even that he thought he was doing something wrong, because he knew that what he was doing was right, more right than anything he saw anyone do, and he knew that doing right often means feeling wrong, and if you find yourself feeling wrong, you're probably doing right. But he also knew that there is an inflationary aspect to love, and that should his mother, or Rose, or any of those who loved him find out about each other, they would not be able to help but feel of lesser value. He knew that *I love you* also means *I love you more than anyone loves you, or has loved you, or will love you,* and also, *I love you in a way that no one loves you, or has loved you, or will love you,* and also, *I love you in a way that I love no one else, and never have loved anyone else, and never will love anyone else.* He knew that it is, by love's definition, impossible to love two people. (Alex, this is part of the reason I can't tell my grandmother about Augustine.)

The second was also a widow. Still ten, he was invited by a schoolmate to a play at the shtetl theater, which also served as dance hall and twice-a-year synagogue. His ticket corresponded to a seat that was already taken by Lista P, whom he recognized as the young widow of the first victim of the Double House. She was small, with wisps of thin brown hair hanging out of her tight ponytail. Her pink skirt was conspicuously smooth and clean—too smooth, too clean—as if she had washed and ironed it dozens of times. She was beautiful, it's true, beautiful for the pitiably meticulous care with which she attended to every detail. If one were to say that her husband was immortal, insofar as his cellular energy dissipated into the earth, fed and fertilized the soil, and encouraged new life to grow, then so did her love go on living, diffused among the thousands of daily things to do—such a magnitude of love that even when divided so many ways, it was still enough to sew buttons onto shirts that would never again be worn, gather fallen twigs from the bases of trees, and wash and iron skirts a dozen times between wearings.

I believe . . ., he began, showing her his ticket.

But if you look, Lista said, showing him her own, which clearly indicated the same seat, *it is mine.*

But it's also mine.

She began to mutter about the absurdity of the theater, the mediocrity of its actors, the foolishness of its playwrights, the inherent silliness of drama itself, and how it was no surprise to her that those morons should botch up something so simple as providing one seat for each patron. But then she noticed his arm, and was overcome.

It seems we have only two options, she said, sniffling. *Either I sit on your lap or we get out of here.* As it turned out, they reversed the order and did both.

Do you like coffee? she asked, moving through her immaculate kitchen, touching everything, reorganizing, not looking at him.

Sure.

A lot of younger people don't care for it.

I do, he said, although in truth he'd never had a cup of coffee.

I'm going to move back in with my mother.

Excuse me?

This house was supposed to be for when I was married, but you know what happened.

Yes. I'm sorry.

Would you like some, then? she asked, fingering a cabinet's polished handle.

Sure. If you're going to have some. Don't make some just for me.

I will. If you want some, she said, and picked up a sponge, and put the sponge down.

But not just for me.

I will.

Two years and sixty-eight lovers later, Safran understood that the tears of blood left on Lista's sheets were virginal tears. He remembered the circumstances of the death of her soon to be husband: a scaffolding collapse that took his life the morning of the wedding as he walked to kneel before the Dial, making Lista a widow only in spirit, before the marriage could be consummated, before she could bleed for him.

My grandfather was in love with the smell of women. He carried their scents around on his fingers like rings, and on the end of his tongue like words—unfamiliar combinations of familiar odors. In this way, Lista held a special place in his memory—although she was hardly unique in being a virgin, or a one-episode lover—as being the only partner to inspire him to bathe.

Went to the theater today. Too bored to stay through the first act. Drank eight cups of coffee. I thought I was going to burst. Didn't burst.

The third was not a widow but another chance theater encounter. Again he went on the invitation of a friend—the same one he had deserted for Lista—and again he left without him. This time, Safran was seated between the schoolmate and a young Gypsy girl, whom he recognized as one of the vendors from Lutsk's Sunday bazaar. He couldn't believe her audacity: to show up at a shtetl function, to risk the humiliation of being seen by the unpaid and overzealous usher Rubin B and asked to leave, to be a Gypsy among Jews. It demonstrated a quality he was sure he was lacking, and it stirred something in him.

At first glance, the long braid that hung over her shoulder and spilled onto her lap looked to my grandfather like the serpent she would make dance from one tall woven basket to the next at the Sunday bazaar, and at second glance it looked the same. As the lights went down, he used his left arm to plop the dead one onto the rest between himself and the girl. He made sure that she noticed it—observing with pleasure the transformation of loose pitying lips to tight erotic grin—and when the heavy curtains parted, he was certain he would part her thin skirt that night.

It was March 18, 1791, echoed an authoritative voice from offstage, *when Trachim B's double-axle wagon pinned him against the bottom of the Brod River. The young W twins were the first to see the curious flotsam rising to the surface...*

(The curtain opens to reveal a provincial setting: a babbling brook running from upstage left to downstage right, many trees and fallen leaves, and two girls, twins, approximately six years old, wearing wool britches with yarn ties and blouses with blue-fringed butterfly collars.)

AUTHORITATIVE VOICE

...three empty pockets, postage stamps from faraway places, pins and needles, swatches of crimson fabric, the first and only words of a last will and testament: "To my love I leave everything."

HANNAH

(Deafening wail.)
(CHANA wades into cold water, pulling up above her knees the yarn ties at the ends of her britches, sweeping TRACHIM's rising life-debris to her sides as she wades farther.)

THE DISGRACED USURER YANKEL D

(Kicking up shoreline mud as he hobbles to the girls.) I ask, what are you doing over there, fatuous girls? The water? The water? But lo, there is nothing to see! It is only a liquidy thing. Stay back! Don't be so dumb as I once was. Life is no fair payment for idiocy.

BITZL BITZL R

(Watching the commotion from his paddleboat, which is fastened with twine to one of his traps.) I say, what is going on over there? Bad Yankel, step away from the Rabbi's twin female daughters!

SAFRAN

(Into GYPSY GIRL's ear, under a blanket of muted yellow stage lighting.) Do you like music?

CHANA

(Laughing, splashing at the mass forming like a garden around her.) It's bringing forth the most whimsical objects!

GYPSY GIRL

(In the shadows cast by the two-dimensional trees, very close to SAFRAN'*s ear.)* What did you say?

SAFRAN

(Using his shoulder to push his dead arm onto the GYPSY GIRL'*s lap.)* I was curious as to whether or not you liked music.

SOFIOWKA N

(Coming out from behind a tree.) I have seen everything that happened. I was witness to it all.

GYPSY GIRL

(Squeezing SAFRAN'*s dead arm between her thighs.)* No, I do not like music. *(But what she was really trying to say was this: I like music better than anything in the world, after you.)*

THE DISGRACED USURER YANKEL D

Trachim?

SAFRAN

(With dust descending from the rafters, with lips probing to find GYPSY GIRL'*s caramel ear in the dark.)* You probably don't have time for music. *(But what he was really trying to say was: I'm not at all stupid, you know.)*

SHLOIM W

I ask, I ask, who is Trachim? Some mortal curlicue?
(The playwright smiles in the cheap seats. He tries to gauge the audience's reaction.)

THE DISGRACED USURER YANKEL D

We don't so fully fathom anything yet. Let's not be hasty.

PEANUT GALLERY

(An impossible-to-place whisper.) This is so unbelievable. Not at all like it was.

GYPSY GIRL

(Kneading SAFRAN*'s dead arm between her thighs, tracing the bend of his unfeeling elbow with her finger, pinching it.)* Don't you think it's hot in here?

SHLOIM W

(Quickly undressing himself, revealing a belly larger than most and a back matted with ringlets of thick black hair.) Cover their eyes. *(Not for them. For me. I'm ashamed.)*

SAFRAN

Very hot.

GRIEVING SHANDA

(To SHLOIM, *as he emerges from the water.)* Was he in solitude or with a wife of many years? *(But what she was really trying to say was this: After everything that's happened, I still have hope. If not for myself, then for Trachim.)*

GYPSY GIRL

(Intertwining her fingers with SAFRAN*'s dead ones.)* Can't we leave?

SAFRAN

Please.

SOFIOWKA N

Yes, it was love letters.

GYPSY GIRL

(With anticipation, with wetness between her legs.) Let's leave.

THE UPRIGHT RABBI

And allow life to go on in the face of this death.

SAFRAN

Yes.

(Musicians prepare for climax. Four violins are tuned. A harp is breathed on. The trumpeter, who is really an oboist, cracks his knuckles. The hammers of the

piano know what happens next. The baton, which is really a butter knife, is lifted like a surgical instrument.)

THE DISGRACED USURER YANKEL D

(With hands raised to the heavens, to the men who aim the spotlights.) Perhaps we should begin to harvest the remains.

SAFRAN

Yes.

(Enter music. Beautiful music. Hushed at first. Whispering. No pins are dropped. Only music. Music swelling imperceptibly. Pulling itself out of its grave of silence. The orchestra pit fills with sweat. Expectancy. Enter gentle rumble of timpani. Enter piccolo and viola. Intimations of crescendo. Ascent of adrenaline, even after so many performances. It still feels new. The music is building, blooming.)

AUTHORITATIVE VOICE

(With passion.) The twins covered their eyes with their father's tallis. (CHANA *and* HANNAH *cover eyes with tallis.)* Their father chanted a long and intelligent prayer for the baby and its parents. *(*UPRIGHT RABBI *looks at his palms, nods his head up and down, gesturing prayer.)* Yankel's face was veiled in the tears of his sobbing. *(*YANKEL *gestures sobbing.)* Unto us a child was born!

(Blackout. Curtains wed. GYPSY GIRL *spreads her thighs. Applause mingled with hushed chatting. Players prepare stage for the next scene. The music is still building.* GYPSY GIRL *leads* SAFRAN *by his dead right arm out of the theater, through a maze of muddy alleys, past the confectioners' stands by the old cemetery, under the hanging vines of the synagogue's crumbling portico, through the shtetl square — the two separated for a moment by the Dial's final casting of the day — along the Brod's loose bank, down the Jewish/Human fault line, beneath the dangling palm fronds, bravely through the shadows of the crag, across the wooden bridge —)*

GYPSY GIRL

Would you like to see something you've never seen before?

(With an honesty previously unknown to him.) I would. I would.

(— over the black- and blueberry brambles, into a petrified forest that SAFRAN
has never before seen. GYPSY GIRL *stands* SAFRAN *under the rock canopy of a
giant maple, takes his dead arm into hers, allowing the shadows cast by the stone
branches to consume her with nostalgia for everything, whispers something in
his ear [to which no one other than my grandfather is privileged], eases his dead
hand under the hem of her thin skirt, says)* Please *(bends at the knees)*, please
(lowers herself onto his dead index finger), yes *(crescendo)*, yes *(puts her caramel
hand on the top button of his dress shirt, sways at the waist)*, please *(trumpet
flourish, violin flourish, timpani flourish, cymbal flourish)*, yes *(dusk spills
across the nightscape, the night sky blots up the darkness like a sponge, heads
crane)*, yes *(eyes close)*, please *(lips part)*, yes. *(The conductor drops his baton,
his butter knife, his scalpel, his Torah pointer, the universe, blackness.)*

Dear Jonathan,

Salutations from Ukraine. I just received your letter and read it many times, notwithstanding parts that I read aloud to Little Igor. (Did I tell you that he is reading your novel as I read it? I translate it for him, and I am also your editor.) I will utter no more than that we are both anticipating the remnants. It is a thing that we can think about and converse about. It is also a thing that we can laugh about, which is something we require.

There is so much that I want to inform you, Jonathan, but I cannot fathom the manner. I want to inform you about Little Igor, and how he is such a premium brother, and also about Mother, who is very, very humble, as I remark to you often, but nonetheless a good person, and nonetheless My Mother. Perhaps I did not paint her with the colors that I should have. She is good to me, and never bad to me, and this is how you must see her. I want to inform you about Grandfather, and how he views television for many hours, and how he cannot witness my eyes anymore, but must be attentive to something behind me. I want to inform you about Father, and how I am not being a caricature when I tell you that I would remove him from my life if I was not such a coward. I want to inform you about what it is like to be me, which is a thing that you still do not possess a single whisper of. Perhaps when you read the next division of my story, you will comprehend. It was the most difficult division that I have yet composed, but I am certain not nearly so difficult as what is still to come. I have been putting on a high shelf what I know I must do, which is point a finger at Grandfather pointing at Herschel. You have without doubts observed this.

I have learned many momentous lessons from your writing, Jonathan.

One lesson is that it does not matter if you are guileless, or delicate, or modest. Just be yourself. I could not believe that your grandfather was such an inferior person, to be carnal with the sister of his wife, and on the day of his wedding, and to be carnal while standing, which is a very inferior arrangement, for reasons you should be aware of. And then he is carnal with the aged woman, who must have had a very slack box, which I will utter no more about. How can you do this to your grandfather, writing about his life in such a manner? Could you write in this manner if he was alive? And if not, what does that signify?

I have a further issue to discuss about your writing. Why do women love your grandfather because of his dead arm? Do they love it because it enables them to feel strong over him? Do they love it because they are commiserating it, and we love the things that we commiserate? Do they love it because it is a momentous symbol of death? I ask because I do not know.

I have only one remark about your remarks about my writing. With regards for how you ordered me to remove the section where you talk about your grandmother, I must tell you that this is not a possibility. I accept if because of my decision you choose not to present me any more currency, or if you command for me to post back the currency you have given me in the previous months. It would be justifying every dollar, I will inform you.

We are being very nomadic with the truth, yes? The both of us? Do you think that this is acceptable when we are writing about things that occurred? If your answer is no, then why do you write about Trachimbrod and your grandfather in the manner that you do, and why do you command me to be untruthful? If your answer is yes, then this creates another question, which is if we are to be such nomads with the truth, why do we not make the story more premium than life? It seems to me that we are making the story even inferior. We often make ourselves appear as though we are foolish people, and we make our voyage, which was an ennobled voyage, appear very normal and second rate. We could give your grandfather two arms, and could make him high-fidelity. We could give Brod what she deserves in the stead of what she gets. We could even find Augustine, Jonathan, and you could thank her, and Grandfather and I could embrace, and it could be perfect and beautiful, and

179

funny, and usefully sad, as you say. We could even write your grandmother into your story. This is what you desire, yes? Which makes me think that perhaps we could write Grandfather into the story. Perhaps, and I am only uttering this, we could have him save your grandfather. He could be Augustine. August, perhaps. Or just Alex, if that is satisfactory to you. I do not think that there are any limits to how excellent we could make life seem.

Guilelessly,
Alexander

WHAT WE SAW WHEN WE SAW TRACHIMBROD, *or* FALLING IN LOVE

"I HAVE NEVER been in one of these," said the woman we continued to think of as Augustine, even though we knew that she was not Augustine. This required Grandfather to laugh in volumes. "What's so funny?" the hero asked. "She has never been in a car." "Really?" "There is nothing to be afraid of," Grandfather said. He opened the front door of the car for her and moved his hand over the seat to show that it was not evil. It seemed like a common decency to relinquish the front seat to her, not only because she was a very old woman who had endured many terrible things, but because it was her first time in a car, and I think it is most awesome to sit in front. The hero later told me that this means to sit shotgun. Augustine sat shotgun. "You will not travel with too much speed?" she asked. "No," Grandfather said as he arranged his belly under the steering wheel. "Tell her that cars are very safe, and she shouldn't be scared." "Cars are safe things," I informed her. "Some even have airbags and crumple zones, although this one does not." I think that she was not primed for the *vrmmmm* sound that the car manufactured, because she screamed with much volume. Grandfather quieted the car. "I cannot," she said.

So what did we do? We drove the car behind Augustine, who walked. (Sammy Davis, Junior, Junior walked next to her, to be her companion, and so that we would not have to smell the bitch's farts in the car.) It was only one kilometer distance, Augustine said, so it would be possible for her to walk, and we would still arrive before it was too dark to see anything. I must say that it seemed very queer to drive behind someone who is walking, especially when the person who is walking is Augustine. She was only able to walk several tens of meters before she would become fatigued and have to make a hiatus. When she hiatused, Grandfather would stop the car, and she would sit shotgun until she was ready to walk in her strange way again.

"You have children?" she asked Grandfather while she gathered her breath. "Of course," he said. "I am his grandson," I said from the back, which made me feel like such a proud person, because I think it was the first occasion I had ever said it in the loud, and I could perceive that it also made Grandfather a proud person. She smiled very much. "I did not know this." "I have two sons and one daughter," Grandfather said. "Sasha is the son of my most aged son." "Sasha," she said, as if she desired to hear what my name sounded like when she uttered it. "And do you have any children?" she asked me. I laughed, because I thought this was a weird question. "He is still young," Grandfather said, and put his hand on my shoulder. I found it very moving to feel his touch, and to remember that hands can show also love. "What are you talking about?" the hero asked. "Does he have any children?" "She wants to know if you have any children," I told the hero, and I knew that this would make him laugh. It did not make him laugh. "I'm twenty," he said. "No," I told her, "in America it is not common to have children." I laughed, because I knew what a fool I sounded like. "Does he have parents?" she asked. "Of course," I said, "but his mother works as a professional, and it is not unusual for his father to prepare dinner." "The world is always changing," she said. "Do you have children?" I asked. Grandfather presented me a look with his face that signified, Shut up. "You do not have to answer that," he told her, "if you do not desire to." "I have a baby girl," she said, and I knew that this was the end of the conversation.

When Augustine walked she did not exclusively walk. She picked up rocks and moved them to the side of the road. If she witnessed a thing of garbage, she would also pick that up and move it to the side of the road. When there was nothing in the road, she would cast a rock several meters in front of her, and then recover it, and then cast it in front of her again. This ate a large quantity of time, and we never moved any faster than very slow. I could perceive that this frustrated Grandfather because he held the steering wheel with much strength, and also because he said, "This frustrates me. It will be dark before we arrive there."

"We are near," she said many times. "Soon. Soon." We pursued her off of the road and into a field. "It is OK?" Grandfather asked. "Who will prevent us?" she said, and with her finger showed us that there was nobody in existence for a long distance. "She says that nobody will prevent us," I told the hero. He had his camera around his neck and was anticipating many photographs. "Nothing grows here anymore," she said. "It does not even belong to anyone. It is only land. Who would want it?" Sammy Davis, Junior, Junior galloped unto the canopy of the car, where she sat like a Mercedes sign.

We persevered to pursue Augustine, and she persevered to cast her rock in front of her and then recover it again. We pursued her, and pursued her more. Like Grandfather, I also was becoming frustrated, or at least confused. "We have been here before," I said. "We have already witnessed this place." "What's going on here?" the hero asked from the back seat. "It's been an hour and we haven't gotten anywhere." "Do you think that we will arrive soon?" Grandfather asked, moving the car next to her. "Soon," she said, "soon." "But it will be dark, yes?" "I am moving as fast as I can."

So we persevered to pursue her. We pursued her through many fields and into many forests, which were difficult for the car. We pursued her over roads made of rock, and also over dirt, and also over grass. I could hear the insects were beginning to announce, and this is how I knew that we would not see Trachimbrod before night. We pursued her past three stairs, which were very broken and appeared to have once introduced houses. She put her hand on the grass in front of each. It became more dark—darker?—as we pursued her on trails, and also where there were no trails. "It is almost impossible to witness her," Grandfather uttered, and even though he is blind, I must confess that it was becoming almost impossible to witness her. It was so dark that sometimes I had to skew my eyes to view her white dress. It was like she was a ghost, moving in and out of our eyes. "Where did she go?" the hero asked. "She is still there," I said. "Look." We went past a miniature ocean—a lake?—and into a small field, which had trees on three sides and spread into a space on the fourth side, where I could hear distant water from. It was now too dark to witness almost anything.

We pursued Augustine to a place near to the middle of the field, and she stopped walking. "Get out," Grandfather said. "Another hiatus." I moved to the back seat so that Augustine could sit shotgun. "What's going on?" the hero asked. "She is making hiatus." "Another?" "She is a very aged woman." "You are tired?" Grandfather asked her. "You have done a lot of walking." "No," she said, "we are here." "She says we are here," I told the hero. "What?" "I informed you that there would be nothing," she said. "It was all destroyed." "What do you mean we're here?" the hero asked. "Tell him it is because it is so dark," Grandfather said to me, "and that we could see more if it was not dark." "It is so dark," I told him. "No," she said, "this is all that you would see. It is always like this, always dark."

I implore myself to paint Trachimbrod, so you will know why we were so overawed. There was nothing. When I utter "nothing" I do not mean there was nothing except for two houses, and some wood on the ground, and pieces of glass, and children's toys, and photographs. When I utter that there was nothing, what I intend is that there was not any of these things, or any other things. "How?" the hero asked. "How?" I asked Augustine. "How could anything have ever existed here?" "It was rapid," she said, and that would have been enough for me. I would not have made another question or said another thing, and I do not think that the hero would have. But Grandfather said, "Tell him." Augustine positioned her hands so far in the pockets of her dress that it looked like she had nothing after her bends. "Tell him what happened," he said. "I do not know everything." "Tell him what you know." It was only then that I understood that "him" was me. "No," she said. "Please," he said. "No," she said. "Please." "It was all very rapid, you must understand. You ran and you could not care about what was behind you or you would stop running." "Tanks?" "One day." "One day?" "Some departed before." "Before they came?" "Yes." "But you did not." "No." "You were lucky to endure." Silence. "No." Silence. "Yes." Silence. We could have stopped it there. We could have viewed Trachimbrod, returned to the car, and followed Augustine back to her house. The hero would have been able to say that he was in Trachimbrod, he could have even said that he met Augustine, and Grandfather and I would have been able to say that we had completed our mission. But Grandfather was not content with this. "Tell him," he said. "Tell him what happened." I was not ashamed and I was not scared. I was not anything. I just desired to know what would occur next. (I do not intend what would occur in Augustine's story, but amid Grandfather and her.) "They made us in lines," she said. "They had lists. They were logical." I translated for the hero as Augustine spoke. "They burned the synagogue." "They burned the synagogue." "That was the first thing they did." "That was first." "Then they made all of the men in lines." You cannot know how it felt to have to hear these things and then repeat them, because when I repeated them, I felt like I was making them new again. "And then?" Grandfather asked. "It was in the middle of the town. There," she said, and she pointed her finger into the darkness. "They unrolled a Torah in front of them. A terrible thing. My father would command us to kiss any book that touched the ground. Cooking books. Books for children. Mysteries. Plays. Novels. Even empty journals. The General went down the line and told each man to spit on the Torah or they would kill his family." "This is not true," Grandfather said. "It is true," Augustine said, and she was not crying, which surprised me very much, but I understand now that she had found places for her melancholy that were behind more masks than only her eyes. "The first man was Yosef, who was the shoemaker. The man with a scar on his face said spit, and he held a gun to Rebecca's head. She was his daughter, and she was a good friend of mine. We used to play cards over there," she said, and pointed into the darkness, "and we told secrets about boys who we were in love with, who we wanted to marry." "Did he spit?" Grandfather asked. "He spit. And then the General said, Step on it." "Did he?" "He did." "He stepped on it," I told the hero. "Then he went to the next person in line, who was Izzy. He taught me drawing in his house, which was there," she said, and pointed her finger into the darkness. "We would remain very late, drawing, laughing. We danced, some nights, to Father's records. He was a friend of mine, and when his wife had the baby, I would care for it like it was my own. Spit, the man with blue eyes said, and he put a gun in the mouth of Izzy's wife, just like this," she said, and put her finger in her mouth. "Did he spit?" Grandfather asked. "He spit." "He spit," I told the hero. "And then the General made him curse the Torah, and this time he put the gun in Izzy's son's mouth." "Did he?" "He did. And then the General made him rip the Torah with his hands." "Did he?" "He did." "And then the General came to my father." It was not too dark for me to see that Grandfather closed his eyes. "Spit, he said." "Did he?" "No," she said, and she said no as if it was any other word from any other story, not having the weight it had in this one. "Spit, the General with blond hair said." "And he did not spit?" She did not say no, but she rotated her head from this to that. "He put it in my mother's mouth, and he said spit or." "He put it in her mother's mouth." "No," the hero said without volume. "I will kill her here and now if you do not spit, the General said, but he would not spit." "And?" Grandfather asked. "And he killed her." I will tell you that what made this story most scary was how rapid it was moving. I do not mean what happened in the story, but how the story was told. I felt that it could not be stopped. "It is not true," Grandfather said, but only to himself. "Then the General put the gun in the mouth of my younger sister, who was four years old. She was crying very much. I remember that. Spit, he said, spit or." "Did he?" Grandfather asked. "No," she said. "He did not spit," I told the hero. "Why didn't he spit?" "And the General shot my sister. I could not look at her, but I remember the sound of when she hit the ground. I hear that sound when things hit the ground still. Anything." If I could, I would make it so nothing ever hit the ground again. "I don't want to hear any more," the hero said, so it was at this point that I ceased translating. (Jonathan, if you still do not want to know the rest, do not read this. But if you do persevere, do not do so for curiosity. That is not a good enough reason.) "They tore the dress of my older sister. She was pregnant and had a big belly. Her husband stood at the end of the line. They had made a house here." "Where?" I asked. "Where we are standing. We are in the bedroom." "How can you perceive this?" "She was very cold, I remember, even though it was the summer. They pulled down her panties, and one of the men put the end of the gun in her place, and the others laughed so hard, I remember the laughing always. Spit, the General said to my father, spit or no more baby." "Did he?" Grandfather asked. "No," she said. "He turned his head, and they shot my sister in her place." "Why would he not spit?" I asked. "But my sister did not die. So they held the gun in her mouth while she was on the ground crying and screaming, and with her hands on her place, which was making so much blood. Spit, the General said, or we will not shoot her. Please, my father said, not like this. Spit, he said, or we will let her lie here in this pain and die across time." "Did he?" "No. He did not spit." "And?" "And they did not shoot her." "Why?" I asked. "Why did he not spit? He was so religious?" "No," she said, "he did not believe in God." "He was a fool," Grandfather said. "You are wrong," she said. "You are wrong," Grandfather said. "You are wrong," she said. "And then?" I asked, and I must confess that I felt shameful about inquiring. "He put the gun against my father's head. Spit, the General said, and we will kill you." "And?" Grandfather asked. "And he spit." The hero was several meters distant, placing dirt in a plastic bag, which is called a Ziploc. After, he told me that this was for his grandmother, should he ever inform her of his voyage. "What about you?" Grandfather asked. "Where were you?" "I was there." "Where? How did you escape?" "My sister, I told you, was not dead. They left her there on the ground after they shot her in her place. She started to crawl away. She could not use her legs, but she pulled herself with her hands and arms. She left a line of blood behind her, and was afraid that they would find her with this." "Did they kill her?" Grandfather asked. "No. They stood and laughed while she crawled away. I remember exactly what the laughing sounded like. It was like"—she laughed into the darkness—"HA HA HA HA HA HA HA HA HA HA HA. All of the Gentiles were watching from their windows, and she called to each, Help me, please help me, I am dying." "Did they?" Grandfather asked. "No. They all turned away their faces and hid. I cannot blame them." "Why not?" I asked. "Because," Grandfather said, answering for Augustine, "if they had helped, they would have been killed, and so would their families." "I would still blame them," I said. "Can you forgive them?" Grandfather asked Augustine. She closed her eyes to say, No, I cannot forgive them. "I would desire someone to help me," I said. "But," Grandfather said, "you would not help somebody if it signified that you would be murdered and your family would be murdered." (I thought about this for many moments, and I understood that he was correct. I only had to think about Little Igor to be certain that I would also have turned away and hid my face.) It was so obscure now, because it was late, and because there were no artificial lights for many kilometers, that we could not see one another, but only hear the voices. "You would forgive them?" I asked. "Yes," Grandfather said. "Yes. I would try to." "You can only say that because you cannot imagine what it is like," Augustine said. "I can." "It is not a thing that you can imagine. It only is. After that, there can be no imagining."

"It is so dark," I said, which sounded queer, but sometimes it is better to say something queer than not to say anything. "Yes," Augustine said. "It is so dark," I told the hero, who had returned with his bags of dirt. "It is," he said, "very dark. I'm not used to being so far from artificial lights." "This is true," I said. "What happened to her?" Grandfather asked. "She escaped, yes?" "Yes." "Someone saved her?" "No. She knocked on one hundred doors, and not one of them opened. She pulled herself into the forest where she became asleep from spilling blood. She woke up that night, and the blood had dried, and even though she felt like she was dead, it was only the baby that was dead. The baby accepted the bullet and saved its mother. A miracle." It was now happening too rapidly for me to understand. I wanted to understand it completely, but it would have required a year for each word. "She was able to walk very slowly. So she went back to Trachimbrod, following the line of her blood." "Why did she go back?" "Because she was young and very stupid." (Is this why we went back, Jonathan?) "She was afraid of becoming killed, yes?" "She was not afraid of this at all." "And what occurred?" "It was very dark, and all of the neighbors were sleeping. The Germans were already at Kolki, so she was not afraid of them. Although she would not have been afraid even if. She went through the Jewish houses with silence, and gathered everything, all of the books, and clothing, and everything." "Why?" "So that they would not take it." "The Nazis?" "No," she said, "the neighbors." "No," Grandfather said. "Yes," Augustine said. "No." "Yes." "No." "She went to the bodies, which were in a hole in front of the synagogue, and removed the gold fillings, and cut the hairs as much as she could, even her own mother's, even her husband's, even her own." "Why? How?" "Then?" "She hid these things in the forest so that she could find them when she returned, and then she went forth."

"Where?" "Places." "Where?" "Russia. Other places." "Then?" "Then she returned." "Why?" "To gather the things she had hidden, and to discover what remained. Everyone who went back was certain that she would discover her house and her friends and even the relatives that she saw killed. It is said that the Messiah will come at the end of the world." "But it was not the end of the world," Grandfather said. "It was. He just did not come." "Why did he not come?" "This was the lesson we learned from everything that happened—there is no God. It took all of the hidden faces for Him to prove this to us." "What if it was a challenge of your faith?" I said. "I could not believe in a God that would challenge faith like this." "What if it was not in His power?" "I could not believe in a God that could not stop what happened." "What if it was man and not God that did all of this?" "I do not believe in man, either."

"What did she discover when she returned the second time?" Grandfather asked. "This," she said, and moved her finger over the mural of darkness. "Nothing. It has not altered at all since she returned. They took everything that the Germans left, and then they went to other shtetls." "Did she go forth when she saw this?" I asked. "No, she remained. She discovered the house most proximal to Trachimbrod, all of the ones that weren't destroyed were empty, and she promised herself to live there until she died. She secured all of the things that she had hidden, and she brought them to her house. It was her punishment." "For what?" "For surviving," she said.

Before we departed, Augustine guided us to the monument for Trachimbrod. It was a piece of stone, approximately of the size of the hero, placed in the middle of the field, so much in the middle that it was very impossible to find at night. The stone said in Russian, Ukrainian, Hebrew, Polish, Yiddish, English, and German:

THIS MONUMENT STANDS IN MEMORY

OF THE 1,204 TRACHIMBRODERS

KILLED AT THE HANDS OF GERMAN FASCISM

ON MARCH 18, 1942.

Dedicated March 18, 1992.
Yitzhak Shamir, Prime Minister of the State of Israel

I stood with the hero in front of this monument for many minutes while Augustine and Grandfather walked off into the darkness. We did not speak. It would have been a common indecency to speak. I looked at him once while he was writing the monument's information in his diary, and I could perceive that he looked at me once while I was viewing it. He roosted in the grass, and I roosted next to him. We roosted for several moments, and then we both laid on our backs, and the grass was like a bed. Because it was so dark, we could see many of the stars. It was as if we were under a large umbrella, or under a dress. (I am not only writing this for you, Jonathan. This is truly what it was like for me.) We talked for many minutes, about many things, but in truth I was not listening to him, and he was not listening to me, and I was not listening to myself, and he was not listening to himself. We were on the grass, under the stars, and that is what we were doing.

Finally, Grandfather and Augustine returned.

It captured us only 50 percent of the time to travel back that it captured us to travel there. I do not know why this was, but I have a notion. Augustine did not invite us into her house when we returned. "It is so late," she said. "You must be fatigued," Grandfather said. She smiled halfly. "I am not so good at making sleep." "Ask her about Augustine," the hero said. "And Augustine, the woman in the photograph, do you know anything of her or how we could find her?" "No," she said, and she looked only at me when she said this. "I know that his grandfather escaped, because I saw him once, maybe a year later, maybe two." She gave me a moment to translate. "He returned to Trachimbrod to see if the Messiah had come. We ate a meal in my house. I cooked him the little things that I had, and I gave him a bath. We were trying to make ourselves clean. He had experienced very much, I could see, but we knew not to ask each other anything." "Ask her what they talked about." "He wants to know what you talked about." "Nothing, in truth. Featherweight things. We talked about Shakespeare, I remember, a play we had both read. They had them in Yiddish, you know, and he once gave me one of them to read. I am sure I still have it here. I could find it and give it to you." "And what happened then?" I asked. "We had a fight about Ophelia. A very bad fight. He made me cry, and I made him cry. We did not talk about anything. We were too afraid." "Had he met my grand-mother yet?" "Had he met his second wife yet?" "I do not know. He did not mention it once, and I would think that he would have mentioned it. But maybe not. It was such a difficult time with talking. You were always afraid of saying the wrong thing, and usually it felt befitting not to say anything at all." "Ask her for how long he stayed in Trachimbrod." "He wants to know how long his grandfather stayed in Trachimbrod." "Only for the afternoon. Lunch and a bath and a fight," she said, "and I think that was longer than he desired. He only needed to see if the Messiah had come." "What did he look like?" "He wants to know what his grand-father looked like." She smiled and put her hands in the pockets of her dress. "He had a rough face and thick brown hairs. Tell him." "He had a rough face and thick brown hairs." "He was not very tall. Maybe as tall like you. Tell him." "He was not very tall. Maybe as tall like you." "So much had been taken from him. I saw him once and he was a boy, and in two years he had become an old man." I told this to the hero and then asked, "Does he appear like his grandfather?" "Before everything, yes. But Safran changed so much. Tell him that he should never change like that." "She says he looked like you once, but then he changed. She says that you should never change." "Ask her if there are any other survivors in the area." "He wants to know if there are any Jews in the remnants." "No," Augustine said. "There is a Jew in Kivertsy who brings me food sometimes. He says that he knew my brother from business in Lutsk, but I did not have a brother. There is another Jew from Sokeretchy who builds fires for me in the winter. It is so difficult in the winter for me, be-cause I am an old woman, and I cannot cut wood anymore." I told this to the hero. "Ask her if she thinks they might know about Augustine." "Would they know anything about Augustine?" "No," she said. "They are so old. They do not remember anything. I know that a few Jews sur-vived from Trachimbrod, but I do not know where they are. People moved so much. I knew a man from Kolki who escaped and never said another word. It was like his lips were sewn shut with a needle and string. Just like that." I told this to the hero. "Will you come back with us?" Grandfather asked. "We will take care of you, and make fires in the win-ter." "No," Augustine said. "Come with us," he said. "You cannot live like this." "I know," she said, "but." "But you." "No." "Then." "No." "Could." "Cannot." Silence. "Remain a moment," she said. "I would like to present him something." It then materialized to me that just as we did not know her name, also she did not know the name of Grandfather, or the hero. Only my name. "She is going inside to retrieve a thing for you," I told the hero. "She does not know what is good for her," Grandfather said. "She did not survive in order to be like this. If she has submitted, she should kill herself." "Perhaps she is happy on occasions," I said. "We do not know. I think that she was happy today." "She does not desire happiness," Grandfather said. "The only way she can live is if she is melancholy. She wants us to feel remorseful for her. She wants us to grieve her, not the others."

Augustine returned out of her house with a box marked IN CASE in blue pencil. "Here," she said to the hero. "She desires you to have this," I told him. "I can't," he said. "He says he cannot." "He must." "She says that you must." "I did not understand why Rivka hid her wedding ring in the jar, and why she said to me, Just in case. Just in case and then what? What?" "Just in case she was killed," I said. "Yes, and then what? Why should the ring be any different?" "I do not know," I said. "Ask him," she said. "She wants to know why her friend saved her wedding ring when she thought that she would be killed." "So there would be proof that she existed," the hero said. "What?" "Evidence. Documentation. Testimony." I told this to Augustine. "But a ring is not needed for this. People can remember without the ring. And when those people forget, or die, then no one will know about the ring." I told this to the hero. "But the ring could be a reminder," he said. "Every time you see it, you think of her." I told Augustine what the hero said. "No," she said. "I think it was in case of this. In case someone should come searching one day." I could not perceive if she was speaking to me or to the hero. "So that we would have something to find," I said. "No," she said. "The ring does not exist for you. You exist for the ring. The ring is not in case of you. You are in case of the ring." She excavated the pocket of her dress and removed a ring. She attempted to put it on the hero's finger, but it did not harmonize, so she attempted to put it on his most petite finger, but it still did not harmonize. "She had small hands," the hero said. "She had small hands," I told Augustine. "Yes," she said, "so small." She again attempted to put the ring on the hero's little finger, and she applied very rigidly, and I could perceive that this made the hero with many kinds of pain, although he did not exhibit even one of them. "It will not harmonize," she said, and when she removed the ring I could see that the ring had made a cut around the hero's most petite finger.

"We will go forth," Grandfather said. "It is time to depart." I told this to the hero. "Tell her thank you once more." "He says thank you," I said. "And I also thank you." Now she was crying again. She cried when we came, and she cried when we departed, but she never cried while we were there. "May I ask a question?" I asked. "Of course," she said. "I am Sasha, as you know, and he is Jonathan, and the bitch is Sammy Davis, Junior, Junior, and he, Grandfather, is Alex. Who are you?" She was silent for a moment. "Lista," she said. And then she said, "May I ask you a question?" "Of course." "Is the war over?" "I do not understand." "I am," she uttered, or began to utter, but then Grandfather performed something that I was not anticipating. He secured Augustine's hand into his and gave her a kiss on her lips. She rotated away from us, toward the house. "I must go in and care for my baby," she said. "It is missing me."

FaLLING in LOVe, 1934–1941

STILL EMPLOYED by the Sloucher congregation, which had become something of an unknowing escort service for the widows and elderly, my grandfather made house calls several times a week, and was able to save up enough money to begin thinking about a family of his own, or for his family to begin thinking about a family of his own.

It's so good to see your work ethic, his father told him one afternoon before he left for the widow Golda R's small brick house by the Upright Synagogue. *You're not the lazy Gypsy boy we thought you were.*

We are very proud of you, his mother said, but did not, as he had hoped, follow it with a kiss. *It's because of Father,* he thought. *If he weren't here, she would have kissed me.*

His father came close to him, patted his shoulder, said, without knowing what he was saying, *Keep it up.*

Golda covered all of the mirrors before she made love to him.

Leah H, twice widowed, to whom he would return three times a week (even after his marriage), asked nothing more than his seriousness when handling her aged body: that he should never laugh at her dropped breasts or balding genitalia, that he should be earnest with the varicose veins of her calves, that he should never shrink from her smell, which she knew was like rot on the vine.

Rina S, widow of the Wisp Kazwel L, the only Wisp of Ardisht able to kick the habit and descend from the rooftops of Rovno to a life on the ground—a victim, like the Dial, of the flour mill's disk saw—bit into Safran's dead arm while they made love, so she could be sure he wasn't feeling anything.

Elena N, widow of the undertaker Chaim N, had seen death pass through her cellar doors a thousand times, but never could have imagined the depth of the grief that she would live with after the chicken bone went sideways and stuck. She asked him to make love to her under her bed, in a shallow subnuptial grave, to take away a bit of the pain, to make things a little easier. Safran, my grandfather, my mother's father, whom I never met, obliged them all.

But before the portrait is painted too flatteringly, it should be mentioned that widows comprised only half of my young grandfather's lovers. He lived a double life: lover of not only grievers, but women untouched by grief's damp hand, those closer to their first death than their second. There were some fifty-two virgins, to whom he made love in each of the positions that he had studied from a dirty deck of cards, loaned to him by the friend whom he kept leaving at the theater: sixty-nining the one-eyed jack Tali M, with tight pigtails and folded-yarmulke eye patch; taking from behind the two of hearts Brandil W, who had only one very weak heart, which made her hobble and wear thick spectacles, and who died before the war—too early, and just early enough; spoons with the queen of diamonds Mella S, all breasts and no backside, the only daughter of the wealthiest family in Kolki (who, they say, would never use silverware more than once); mounted by the ace of spades Trema O, most diligent in the fields, whose shrieks, he was sure, would give them away. They loved him and he fucked them—ten, jack, queen, king, ace —a most straight and royal flush. And so he had two working hands: one with five fingers and one with fifty-two young girls who couldn't, and wouldn't, say no.

And, of course, he had a life above his waist as well. He went to school and studied with the other boys his age. He was quite good at arithmetic, and his teacher, the young Sloucher Yakem E, had suggested to my great-grandparents that they send Safran to a school for gifted children in Lutsk. But nothing could have bored my grandfather more than his studies. *Books are for those without real lives*, he thought. *And they are no real replacement.* The school he attended was a small one—four teachers and forty students. Each day was divided between religious studies, taught by the Fair-to-Middling Rabbi and one of his Upright congregants, and secular, or useful, studies, taught by three—sometimes two, sometimes four—Slouchers.

Every schoolboy learned the history of Trachimbrod from a book originally written by the Venerable Rabbi—*AND IF WE ARE TO STRIVE FOR A BETTER FUTURE, MUSTN'T WE BE FAMILIAR AND RECONCILED WITH OUR PAST?*—and revised regularly by a committee of Uprighters and Slouchers. *The Book of Antecedents* began as a record of major events: battles and treaties, famines, seismic occurrences, the beginnings and ends of political regimes. But it wasn't long before lesser events were included and described at great length—festivals, important marriages and deaths, records of construction in the shtetl (there was no destruction then)—and the rather small book had to be replaced with a three-volume set. Soon, upon the demand of the readership—which was everyone, Uprighter and Sloucher alike—*The Book of Antecedents* included a biennial census, with every name of every citizen and a brief chronicle of his or her life (women were included after the synagogue split), summaries of even less notable events, and commentaries on what the Venerable Rabbi had called *LIFE, AND THE LIFE OF LIFE*, which included definitions, parables, various rules and regulations for righteous living, and cute, if meaningless, sayings. The later editions, now taking up an entire shelf, became yet more detailed, as citizens contributed family records, portraits, important documents, and personal journals, until any schoolboy could easily find out what his grandfather ate for breakfast on a given Thursday fifty years before, or what his great-aunt did when the rain fell without lull for five months. *The Book of Antecedents*, once updated yearly, was now continually updated, and when there was nothing to report, the full-time committee would report its reporting, just to keep the book moving, expanding, becoming more like life: *We are writing... We are writing... We are writing...*

Even the most delinquent students read *The Book of Antecedents* without skipping a word, for they knew that they too would one day inhabit its pages, that if they could only get hold of a future edition, they would be able to read of their mistakes (and perhaps avoid them), and the mistakes of their children (and ensure that they would never happen), and the outcome of future wars (and prepare for the death of loved ones).

And I'm sure that my grandfather was no exception. He, too, must have skipped from volume to volume, page to page, searching...

YANKEL D'S SHAMEFUL BEAD

The result of certain shameful activities, the disgraced usurer Yankel D's trial took place in the year 1741 before the High Upright Court. Said usurer, after being found guilty of having committed said shameful deeds in question, was obligated by shtetl proclamation to wear the incriminating abacus bead on a white string around his neck. Let the record show that he wore it even when no one was looking, even to sleep.

TRACHIMDAY, 1796

A fly of particular pestiferousness stung on its tuches the horse that pulled the Rovno Trachimday float, causing the touchy mare to buck and toss its fieldworker effigy into the Brod. The parade of floats was delayed for some thirty minutes while strong men recovered the soggy effigy. The culpable fly was caught in the net of an unidentified schoolboy. The boy raised his hand to smash it, knowing that an example must be made, but as his fist began its descent, the fly twitched its wing without flight. The boy, the sensitive boy, was overcome by the fragility of life and released the fly. The fly, also overcome, died of gratefulness. An example was made.

UNHEALTHY BABIES

(*See* GOD)

WHEN THE RAIN FELL WITHOUT LULL FOR FIVE MONTHS

This worst of all rain spells occurred in the last two months of 1914 and first three of 1915. Cups left on sills quickly overflowed. Flowers bloomed and then drowned. Holes were cut into the ceilings above bathtubs... It should be noted that the rain without lull coincided with the period of Russian occupation,* and that no matter how much water came down, there were those who still claimed to be thirsty. (*See* GITTLE K, YAKOV L.)

*Upon hearing that it was a Jew who invented the love poem, the unrequited magistrate Rufkin S, may his name be lost between cushions, rained all fire and broken glass upon our simple shtetl. (It was not the Jew, of course, who invented the love poem, but the other way around.)

The Flour Mill

It so happened that in the eleventh year of a long-past century, the Chosen People (us) were sent forth from Egypt under the guidance of our then wise leader, Moses. There was no time for bread to rise in the haste of escape, and the Lord our God, may His name inspire buoyant thoughts, who, in seeking perfection with his every creation, would not want an imperfect bread, said unto his people (us, not them): *MAKE NOT ANY BREAD THAT WILL BE AT ALL CRUNCHY, BLAND, BAD TASTING, OR THE CAUSE OF HOPELESS CONSTIPATION.* But the Chosen People were very hungry, and we took our chances with some good yeast. What baked on our backs was less than perfect, indeed bland, crunchy, bad tasting, and the cause of many a good poop withheld, and God, may His name be always on our unchapped lips, was made very angry. It is because of this sin of our ancestors that one member of our shtetl has been killed in the flour mill every year since its founding in 1713. (For a list of those who have perished in the mill, *see* Appendix G: Untimely Deaths.)

The Existence of Gentiles

(*See* God)

The Entirety of the World as We Do and Don't Know It

(*See* God)

Jews Have Six Senses

Touch, taste, sight, smell, hearing...memory. While Gentiles experience and process the world through the traditional senses, and use memory only as a second-order means of interpreting events, for Jews memory is no less primary than the prick of a pin, or its silver glimmer, or the taste of the blood it pulls from the finger. The Jew is pricked by a pin and remembers other pins. It is only by tracing the pinprick back to other pinpricks—when his mother tried to fix his sleeve while his arm was still in it, when his grandfather's fingers fell asleep from stroking his great-grandfather's damp forehead, when Abraham tested the knife point to be sure Isaac would feel no pain — that the Jew is able to know why it hurts.

When a Jew encounters a pin, he asks: *What does it remember like?*

THE PROBLEM OF EVIL: WHY UNCONDITIONALLY BAD THINGS HAPPEN TO UNCONDITIONALLY GOOD PEOPLE
They never do.

THE TIME OF DYED HANDS
Occurring shortly after the mistaken suicides, the time of dyed hands began when the baker of rolls Herzog J observed that those rolls that were not watched with a cautious eye would sometimes disappear. He repeated this observation numerous times, placing his rolls about his bakery, even marking their placement with a coal pencil, and each time he would turn quickly away and steal a glance back, only the markings would remain.

All this stealing, he said.

At that point in our history, the Eminent Rabbi Fagel F (*see also* APPENDIX B: LISTING OF UPRIGHT RABBIS) was chief executor of legal regulation. So as to conduct a fair investigation, he saw to it that everyone in the shtetl was treated like a suspect, guilty until proven otherwise. *WE WILL DYE THE HANDS OF EACH CITIZEN WITH A DIFFERENT COLOR,* he said, *AND WILL THIS WAY DISCOVER WHO HAS BEEN PUTTING THEIRS BEHIND HERZOG'S COUNTER.*

Lippa R's were dyed blood red. Pelsa G's the light green of her eyes. Mica P's a subtle purple, like the sliver of sky above the Radziwell Forest's tree line when the sun set for the third Shabbos of that November. No hands or hues were exempt. To be fair, even Herzog J's were dyed, the pink of a particular *Troides helena* butterfly that happened to have died on the desk of Dickle D, the chemist who invented the chemical that couldn't be washed off, but would leave smears on whatever the dyed hands touched.

As it turned out, a simple mouse, may his memory live close to a stinky tuches, had been sneaking away with the rolls, and no colors ever appeared behind the counter.

But they appeared everywhere else.

Shlomo V found silver between the thighs of his wife, Chebra, may her behavior be unique in this and every other world, and said nothing about it until he'd painted her breasts green with his hands and then covered those breasts in white semen. He pulled her naked through the gray moonlit streets, from house to house, bruising his knuckles black-blue on the doors. He forced her to watch as he cut off the testicles of Samuel R, who, with raised silver fingers, pleaded for mercy and cried, ambiguously, *There has been a mistake.* Colors everywhere. The Eminent Rabbi Fagel F's indigo fingerprints on the pages of more than one ultrasecular periodical. The cold-lip blue of the grieving widow Shifrah K across her husband's gravestone in the shtetl cemetery, like the rubbings children do. Everyone was quick to accuse Irwin P of running his brown hands up and down the Dial. *He's so selfish!* they said. *He wants everything for himself!* But it was *their* hands, all of their hands, a compressed rainbow of every citizen in the shtetl who had prayed for handsome sons, a few more years of life, protection from lightning, love.

The shtetl was painted with the doings of its citizens, and since every color was used—except for that of the counter, of course—it was impossible to tell what had been touched by human hands and what was as it was because it was as it was. It was rumored that Getzel G had secretly played every fiddler's fiddle—even though he didn't play the fiddle!—for the strings were the color of his fingers. People whispered that Gesha R must have become an acrobat—how else could the Jewish/Human fault line have become as yellow as her palms? And when the blush of a schoolgirl's cheeks was mistaken for the crimson of a holy man's fingers, it was the schoolgirl who was called *hussy, tramp, slut.*

THE PROBLEM OF GOOD: WHY UNCONDITIONALLY GOOD THINGS HAPPEN TO UNCONDITIONALLY BAD PEOPLE
   (*See* GOD)

Cunnilingus and the Menstruating Woman

The burning bush must not be consumed. (For a complete listing of rules and regulations concerning you know what, *see* Appendix F-ING.)

The Novel, When Everyone Was Convinced He Had One in Him

The novel is that art form that burns most easily. It so happened that in the middle of the nineteenth century, all the citizens of our shtetl —every man, woman, and child—was convinced he had at least one novel in him. This period was likely the result of the traveling Gypsy salesman who brought a wagonload of books to the shtetl square on the third Sunday of every other month, advertising them as *Worthy would-be worlds of words, whorls of working wonder.* What else could come to the lips of a Chosen People but *I can do that?*

More than seven hundred novels were written between 1850 and 1853. One began: *How long it's been since I last thought of those windswept mornings.* Another: *They say everyone remembers her first time, but I don't.* Another: *Murder is an ugly deed, to be sure, but the murder of a brother is truly the most ghastly crime known to man.*

There were 272 thinly veiled memoirs, 66 crime novels, 97 stories of war. A man killed his brother in 107 of the novels. In all but 89 an infidelity was committed. Couples in love wondered what the future would hold in 29; 68 ended with a kiss; all but 35 used the word "shame." Those who couldn't read and write made visual novels: collages, etchings, pencil drawings, watercolors. A special room was added to the Yankel and Brod Library for the Trachimbrod novels, although only a handful were read five years after their composition.

Once, almost a century later, a young boy went browsing the aisles.

I'm looking for a book, he told the librarian, who had cared for the Trachimbrod novels since she was a girl, and was the only citizen to have read them all. *My great-grandfather wrote it.*

What was his name? the librarian asked.

Safranbrod, but I think he wrote it under a pseudonym.

What was the name of his book?

I can't remember the name. He used to talk about it all the time. He'd tell me stories from it to put me to sleep.

What's it about? she asked.

It's about love.

She laughed. *They're all about love.*

ART

Art is that thing having to do only with itself—the product of a successful attempt to make a work of art. Unfortunately, there are no examples of art, nor good reasons to think that it will ever exist. (Everything that has been made has been made with a purpose, everything with an end that exists outside that thing, i.e., *I want to sell this,* or *I want this to make me famous and loved,* or *I want this to make me whole,* or worse, *I want this to make others whole.*) And yet we continue to write, paint, sculpt, and compose. Is this foolish of us?

IFICE

Ifice is that thing with purpose, created for function's sake, and having to do with the world. Everything is, in some way, an example of ifice.

IFACT

An ifact is a past-tensed fact. For example, many believe that after the destruction of the first Temple, God's existence became an ifact.

ARTIFICE

Artifice is that thing that was art in its conception and ifice in its execution. Look around. Examples are everywhere.

ARTIFACT

An artifact is the product of a successful attempt to make a purposeless, useless, beautiful thing out of a past-tensed fact. It can never be art, and it can never be fact. Jews are artifacts of Eden.

Music is beautiful. Since the beginning of time, we (the Jews) have been looking for a new way of speaking. We often blame our treatment throughout history on terrible misunderstandings. (Words never mean what we want them to mean.) If we communicated with something like music, we would never be misunderstood, because there is nothing in music to understand. This was the origin of Torah chanting and, in all likelihood, Yiddish—the most onomatopoeic of all languages. It is also the reason that the elderly among us, particularly those who survived a pogrom, hum so often, indeed seem unable to stop humming, seem dead set on preventing any silence or linguistic meaning in. But until we find this new way of speaking, until we can find a nonapproximate vocabulary, nonsense words are the best thing we've got. Ifactifice is one such word.

The First Rape of Brod D

The first rape of Brod D occurred amid the celebrations following the thirteenth Trachimday festival, March 18, 1804. Brod was walking home from the blue-flowered float—on which she had stood in such austere beauty for so many hours on end, waving her mermaid's tail only when appropriate, throwing deep into the river of her name those heavy sacks only when the Rabbi gave her the necessary nod—when she was approached by the mad squire Sofiowka N, whose name our shtetl now uses for maps and Mormon census records.

I have seen everything, he said. *I watched the parade, don't you know, from so high, high, high above the commoners and their common festivities, in which, I must confess, of course I would have liked to partake some bit. I saw you on our float, and oh, you were so uncommon. You were, in the face of such fakery, so natural.*

Thank you, she said, and proceeded on, taking to heart Yankel's warning that Sofiowka could talk your ear off if you gave him a chance.

But where are you going? That's not all, he said, grabbing her skinny arm. *Didn't your father teach you to listen when you're being talked at, or to, or under, or around, or even in?*

I would like to go home now, Sofiowka. I promised my father that we would eat pineapple together, and I'm going to be late.

No you didn't, he said, turning Brod to face him. *Now you're lying to me.*

But I did. We agreed that after the parade I would come home and eat pineapple with him.

But you said you promised your father, and Brod, maybe you're using that term loosely, maybe you don't even know what it means, but if you're going to stand here and tell me you made a promise to your father, then I am going to stand here and call you a liar.

You're not making any sense. Brod laughed nervously and again started walking to her house. He followed close behind, stepping on the end of her tail.

Who, I wonder, is not making any sense, Brod?

He stopped her again, and turned her to face him.

My father named me after the river because —

There you go again, he said, moving his fingers up from her shoulder to the base of her hair and into her hair, pushing off the blue Float Queen tiara. *Lying is no good way for a little girl to be.*

I want to go home now, Sofiowka.

Then go.

But I can't.

Why not?

Because you're holding my hair.

Oh, you're quite right. I am. I hadn't even noticed. This is your hair, isn't it? And I am holding it, aren't I, thereby preventing you from going home, or anywhere else. You could shout, I suppose, but what would that accomplish? Everyone is doing their own shouting by the banks, shouting out of pleasure. Shout out of pleasure, Brod. Come on, you can do it. One little shout out of pleasure.

Please, she began to whimper. *Sofiowka, please. I just want to go home, and I know that my father is waiting —*

There you go again, you lying cunt! he hollered. *Haven't we had enough lying for one night already!*

What do you want? Brod cried.

He took a knife from his pocket and cut the shoulder straps of her mermaid suit.

She pulled the suit down around her ankles and off her feet, and then removed her panties. She made sure, with the arm that wasn't held behind her back, that the tail didn't get muddy.

Later that night, after she returned home and discovered Yankel's dead body, the Kolker was illuminated at her window by a wink of lightning.

Go away! she cried, covering her bare chest with her arms and turning back toward Yankel, protecting their bodies from the Kolker's gaze. But he did not leave.

Go away!

I won't go without you, he called to her through the window.

Go away! Go away!

The rain dripped from his upper lip. *Not without you.*

I'll kill myself! she hollered.

Then I'll take your body with me, he said, palms against the glass.

Go away!

I won't!

Yankel jerked in rigor mortis, knocking over the oil lamp, which blew itself out on its way to the floor, leaving the room completely dark. His cheeks pulled into a tight smile, revealing, to the banished shadows, a contentedness. Brod let her arms brush down her skin to her sides and turned to face the Kolker—the second time she'd shown her naked body in thirteen years of life.

Then you must do something for me, she said.

Sofiowka was found the next morning, swinging by the neck from the wooden bridge. His severed hands were hanging from strings tied to his feet, and across his chest was written, in Brod's red lipstick: ANIMAL.

WHAT JACOB R ATE FOR BREAKFAST ON THE MORNING OF
FEBRUARY 21, 1877

Fried potatoes with onion. Two slices of black bread.

PLAGIARISM

Cain killed his brother for plagiarizing one of his favorite little poems, which went like this:

> *Willows whiten, aspens quiver,*
> *Little breezes dusk and shiver*
> *Through the wave that runs for ever*
> *By the island in the river.*

Unable to thwart the fury of a poet scorned, unable to continue writing as long as he knew that the pirates pens-sans would reap the booty of his industry, unable to suppress the question *If iambs not for me, what will be for me?*, he, unable Cain, put an end to literary larceny forever. Or so he thought.

But much to his surprise, it was Cain who was caned, Cain who was cursed to labor the earth, Cain who was forced to wear that terrible mark, Cain who, for all of his sad and witty verse, could get laid every night, but didn't know anyone who had read a page of his magnum opus.

Why?

God loves the plagiarist. And so it is written, "God created humankind in His image, in the image of God He created them." God is the original plagiarizer. With a lack of reasonable sources from which to filch—man created in the image of what? the animals?—the creation of man was an act of reflexive plagiarizing; God looted the mirror. When we plagiarize, we are likewise creating *in the image* and participating in the completion of Creation.

Am I my brother's material?
Of course, Cain. Of course.

THE DIAL

(*See* FALSE IDOLS)

THE HUMAN WHOLE

The Pogrom of Beaten Chests (1764) was bad, but it was not the worst, and there still are, no doubt, worse to come. They moved through on horses. They raped our pregnant women and cut down our strongest men with sickles. They beat our children to death. They made us curse our most holy texts. (It was impossible to distinguish the cries of babies and adults.) Immediately after they left, the Uprighters and Slouchers joined together to lift and move the synagogue all the way into the Human Three-Quarters, making it, if for only one hour, the Human Whole. Without knowing why, we beat our own chests, as we do when seeking atonement on Yom Kippur. Were we praying, *Forgive our oppressors for what they have done?* Or, *Forgive us for what has been done to us?* Or, *Forgive You for Your inscrutability?* (*See* APPENDIX G: UNTIMELY DEATHS.)

US, THE JEWS

Jews are those things that God loves. Since roses are beautiful, we must assume that God loves them. Therefore, roses are Jewish. By the same reasoning, the stars and planets are Jewish, all children are Jewish, pretty "art" is Jewish (Shakespeare wasn't Jewish, but Hamlet was), and sex, when practiced between husband and wife in a good and suitable position, is Jewish. Is the Sistine Chapel Jewish? You'd better believe it.

THE ANIMALS

The animals are those things that God likes but doesn't love.

OBJECTS THAT EXIST

Objects that exist are those things that God doesn't even like.

OBJECTS THAT DON'T EXIST

Objects that don't exist don't exist. If we were to imagine such a thing as an object that didn't exist, it would be that thing that God hated. This is the strongest argument against the nonbeliever. If God didn't exist, he would have to hate himself, and that is obviously nonsense.

THE 120 MARRIAGES OF JOSEPH AND SARAH L

The young couple first married on August 5, 1744, when Joseph was eight, and Sarah six, and first ended their marriage six days later, when Joseph refused to believe, to Sarah's frustration, that the stars were silver nails in the sky, pinning up the black nightscape. They remarried four days later, when Joseph left a note under the door of Sarah's parents' house: *I have considered everything you told me, and I do believe that the stars are silver nails.* They ended their marriage again a year later, when Joseph was nine and Sarah seven, over a quarrel about the nature of the bottom of the Brod. A week later, they were remarried, including this time in their vows that they should love each other until death, regardless of the existence of a bottom of the Brod, the temperature of this bottom (should it exist), and the possible existence of starfish on the possibly existing riverbed. They ended their marriage thirty-seven times in the next seven years, and each time remarried with a longer list of vows. They divorced twice when Joseph was twenty-two and Sarah twenty, four times when they were twenty-five and twenty-three, respectively, and eight times, the most for one year, when they were thirty and twenty-eight. They were sixty and fifty-eight at their last marriage, only three weeks before Sarah died of heart failure and Joseph drowned himself in the bath. Their marriage contract still hangs over the door of the house they on-and-off shared—nailed to the top post and brushing against the SHALOM welcome mat:

> It is with everlasting devotion that we, Joseph and Sarah L, reunite in the indestructible union of matrimony, promising love until death, with the understanding that the stars are silver nails in the sky, regardless of the existence of a bottom of the Brod, the temperature of this bottom (should it exist), and the possible existence of starfish on the possibly existing riverbed, overlooking what may or may not have been accidental grape juice spills, agreeing to forget that Joseph played sticks and balls with his friends when he promised he would help Sarah

thread the needle for the quilt she was sewing, and that Sarah was supposed to give the quilt to Joseph, not his buddy, deeming irrelevant certain details about the story of Trachim's wagon, such as whether it was Chana or Hannah who first saw the curious flotsam, ignoring the simple fact that Joseph snores like a pig, and that Sarah is no great treat to sleep with either, letting slide certain tendencies of both parties to look too long at members of the opposite sex, not making a fuss over why Joseph is such a slob, leaving his clothes wherever he feels like taking them off, expecting Sarah to pick them up, clean them, and put them in their proper place as he should have, or why Sarah has to be such a fucking pain in the ass about the smallest things, such as which way the toilet paper unrolls, or when dinner is five minutes later than she was planning, because, let's face it, it's Joseph who's putting that paper on the roll and dinner on the table, disregarding whether the beet is a better vegetable than the cabbage, putting aside the problems of being fat-headed and chronically unreasonable, trying to erase the memory of a long since expired rose bush that a certain someone was supposed to remember to water when his wife was visiting family in Rovno, accepting the compromise of the way we have been, the way we are, and the way we will likely be...may we live together in unwavering love and good health, amen.

THE BOOK OF REVELATIONS

(For a complete listing of revelations, *see* APPENDIX Z32. For a complete listing of genesises, *see* APPENDIX Z33.)

The end of the world has come often, and continues to often come. Unforgiving, unrelenting, bringing darkness upon darkness, the end of the world is something we have become well acquainted with, habitualized, made into a ritual. It is our religion to try to forget it in its absence, make peace with it when it is undeniable, and return its embrace when it finally comes for us, as it always does.

There has yet to be a human to survive a span of history without at least one end of the world. It is the subject of extensive scholarly debate whether stillborn babies are subject to the same revelations — if we could say that they have lived without endings. This debate, of course, demands a close examination of that more profound question: *Was the world first created or ended?* When the Lord our God breathed on the universe, was that a genesis or a revelation? Should we count those seven days forward or backward? How did the apple taste, Adam? And the half a worm you discovered in that sweet and bitter pulp: was that the head or the tail?

JUST WHAT IT WAS, EXACTLY, THAT YANKEL D DID

(*See* YANKEL D'S SHAMEFUL BEAD)

THE FIVE GENERATIONS BETWEEN BROD AND SAFRAN

Brod had three sons with the Kolker, all named Yankel. The first two died in the flour mill, victims, like their father, of the disk saw. (*See* APPENDIX G: UNTIMELY DEATHS.) The third Yankel, conceived through the hole after the Kolker's exile, lived a long and productive life, which included many experiences, feelings, and small accumulations of wisdom, about which none of us will ever know. This Yankel begot Trachimkolker. Trachimkolker begot Safranbrod. Safranbrod begot Trachimyankel. Trachimyankel begot Kolkerbrod. Kolkerbrod begot Safran. For so it is written: *AND IF WE ARE TO STRIVE FOR A BETTER FUTURE, MUSTN'T WE BE FAMILIAR AND RECONCILED WITH OUR PAST?*

The following encyclopedia of sadness was found on the body of Brod D. The original 613 sadnesses, written in her diary, corresponded to the 613 commandments of our (not their) Torah. Shown below is what was salvageable after Brod was recovered. (Her diary's wet pages printed the sadnesses onto her body. Only a small fraction [55] were legible. The other 558 sadnesses are lost forever, and it is hoped that, without knowing what they are, no one will have to experience them.) The diary from which they came was never found.

SADNESSES OF THE BODY: Mirror sadness; Sadness of [looking] like or unlike one's parent; Sadness of not knowing if your body is normal; Sadness of knowing your [body is] not normal; Sadness of knowing your body is normal; Beauty sadness; Sadness of m[ak]eup; Sadness of physical pain; Pins-and-[needles sadness]; Sadness of clothes [*sic*]; Sadness of the quavering eyelid; Sadness of a missing rib; Noticeable sad[ness]; Sadness of going unnoticed; The sadness of having genitals that are not like those of your lover; The sadness of having genitals that are like those of your lover; Sadness of hands...

SADNESSES OF THE COVENANT: Sadness of God's love; Sadness of God's back [*sic*]; Favorite-child sadness; Sadness of b[ein]g sad in front of one's God; Sadness of the opposite of belief [*sic*]; What if? sadness; Sadness of God alone in heaven; Sadness of a God who would need people to pray to Him...

SADNESSES OF THE INTELLECT: Sadness of being misunderstood [*sic*]; Humor sadness; Sadness of love wit[hou]t release; Sadne[ss of be]ing smart; Sadness of not knowing enough words to [express what you mean]; Sadness of having options; Sadness of wanting sadness; Sadness of confusion; Sadness of domes[tic]ated birds; Sadness of fini[shi]ng a book; Sadness of remembering; Sadness of forgetting; Anxiety sadness...

INTERPERSONAL SADNESSES: Sadness of being sad in front of one's parent; Sa[dn]ess of false love; Sadness of love [*sic*]; Friendship sadness; Sadness of a bad convers[at]ion; Sadness of the could-have-been; Secret sadness...

SADNESSES OF SEX AND ART: Sadness of arousal being an unordinary physical state; Sadness of feeling the need to create beautiful things; Sadness of the anus; Sadness of eye contact during fellatio and cunnilingus; Kissing sadness; Sadness of moving too quickly; Sadness of not mo[vi]ng; Nude model sadness; Sadness of portraiture; Sadness of Pinchas T's only notable paper, "To the Dust: From Man You Came and to Man You Shall Return," in which he argued it would be possible, in theory, for life and art to be reversed...

We are writing...We are writing...We are writing...We are writing ...We are writing...We are writing...We are writing...We are writing...We are writing...We are writing...We are writing...We are writing...We are writing...We are writing...We are writing... We are writing...We are writing...We are writing...We are writing ...We are writing...We are writing...We are writing...We are writing...We are writing...We are writing...We are writing...We are writing...We are writing...We are writing...We are writing... We are writing...We are writing...We are writing...We are writing ...We are writing...We are writing...We are writing...We are writing...We are writing...We are writing...We are writing...We are writing...We are writing...We are writing...We are writing... We are writing...We are writing...We are writing...We are writing ...We are writing...We are writing...We are writing...We are writing...We are writing...We are writing...We are writing...We are writing...We are writing...We are writing...We are writing...

We are writing…We are writing…We are writing…We are writing …We are writing…We are writing…We are writing…We are writing…We are writing…We are writing…We are writing…We are writing…We are writing…We are writing…We are writing… We are writing…We are writing…We are writing…We are writing …We are writing…We are writing…We are writing…We are writing…We are writing…We are writing…We are writing…We are writing…We are writing…We are writing…We are writing… We are writing…We are writing…We are writing…We are writing …We are writing…We are writing…We are writing…We are writing…We are writing…We are writing…We are writing…We are writing…We are writing…We are writing…We are writing… We are writing…We are writing…We are writing…We are writing …We are writing…We are writing…We are writing…We are writing…We are writing…We are writing…We are writing…We are writing…We are writing…We are writing…We are writing… We are writing…We are writing…We are writing…We are writing …We are writing…We are writing…We are writing…We are writing…We are writing…We are writing…We are writing…We are writing…We are writing…We are writing…We are writing… We are writing…We are writing…We are writing…We are writing …We are writing…We are writing…We are writing…We are writing…We are writing…We are writing…We are writing…We are writing…We are writing…We are writing…We are writing… We are writing…We are writing…We are writing…We are writing …We are writing…We are writing…We are writing…We are writing…We are writing…We are writing…We are writing…We are writing…We are writing…We are writing…We are writing… We are writing…We are writing…We are writing…We are writing …We are writing…We are writing…We are writing…We are writing…We are writing…We are writing…We are writing…We are writing…We are writing…We are writing…We are writing…

Dear Jonathan,

Let us not mention each other's writing ever again. I will post you my story, and I beg of you (as does Little Igor) that you continue to post yours, but let us not make corrections or even observations. Let us not praise or reproach. Let us not judge at all. We are outside of that already.

We are talking now, Jonathan, together, and not apart. We are with each other, working on the same story, and I am certain that you can also feel it. Do you know that I am the Gypsy girl and you are Safran, and that I am Kolker and you are Brod, and that I am your grandmother and you are Grandfather, and that I am Alex and you are you, and that I am you and you are me? Do you not comprehend that we can bring each other safety and peace? When we were under the stars in Trachimbrod, did you not feel it then? Do not present not-truths to me. Not to me.

And here, Jonathan, is a story for you. A faithful story. I informed Father that I was to go to a famous nightclub last night. He said, "I am certain that you will return home with a comrade?" If you want to know what was on his mouth, vodka was. "I do not intend to," I said. "You will be so so carnal," he said, laughing. He touched me on the shoulder, and I will tell you that it felt like a touch from the devil. I was most ashamed of us. "No," I said. "I am only going to dance and be amid my friends." "Shapka, Shapka." "Shut up!" I told him, and I seized his wrist. I will inform you that this was the first occasion that I have ever uttered anything like this to him, and the first occasion that I have ever moved at him with violence. "I am sorry," I said, and let his wrist free. "I will make you sorry," he said. I was a lucky person because he had so much vodka in him that he did not have regard enough to punch me.

I did not go to a famous nightclub, of course. As I have mentioned, I often inform Father that I will go to a famous nightclub, but then I go to the beach. I do not go to a famous nightclub so that I can deposit my currency in the cookie box for moving to America with Little Igor. But I must inform you that it is also because I do not love famous nightclubs. They make me feel very cheerless and abandoned. Am I applying that word correctly? Abandoned?

The beach was beautiful last night, but this did not surprise me. I love sitting on the edge of the land and feeling the water verge me, and then leave me. Sometimes I remove my shoes and put my feet where I think the water will approach to. I have attempted to think about America in regard to where I am on the beach. I imagine a line, a white line, painted on the sand and on the ocean, from me to you.

I was sitting on the edge of the water, thinking about you, and us, when I heard a thing. The thing was nor water, nor wind, nor insects. I turned my head to see what it was. Someone was walking to me. This scared me very much, because I never behold another person at the beach when I am there at night. There was nothing proximal to me, nothing to be walking to but me. I put on my shoes and began to walk away from this person. Was he a police? The police will often make advantages on people who are sitting alone. Was he a criminal? I was not very scared of a criminal, because they do not have premium weapons, and cannot inflict very much. Unless the criminal is a police. I could hear that the person was still coming to me. I made a more rapid walk. The person pursued me with speed. I did not look again to attempt to witness who it was, because I did not want the person to know that I was apprised of him. It sounded to my ears like he was getting closer, that he would soon reach me, so I began to run.

Then I heard, "Sasha!" I terminated my running. "Sasha, is that you?"

I turned around. Grandfather was bended over with his hand on his stomach. I could see that he was manufacturing very large breaths. "I was looking for you," he said. I could not understand how he knew to look for me at the beach. As I informed you, nobody is aware that I go to the beach at night. "I am here," I said, which sounded queer, but I did not know what else to say. He stood up and said, "I have a question."

It was the first occasion that I could remember when Grandfather ad-

dressed me without something amid us. There was no Father, no hero, no bitch, no television, no food. Merely us. "What is it?" I asked, because I could perceive that he would not be able to ask his question unless I aided him. "I have to ask you for something, but you must comprehend that I am only asking to borrow this thing, and you also must comprehend that you can deny me and I will not be injured or think anything bad of you." "What is it?" I could not think of anything that I possessed that Grandfather would desire. I could not think of anything in the world that Grandfather would desire.

"I would like to borrow your currency," he said. In truth I felt very shamed. He did not toil his whole life in order that he should have to ask his grandson for currency. "I will," I said. And I should have uttered nothing more, and allowed my "I will" to speak for everything that I have ever had to say to Grandfather, for the "I will" to be all of my questions, and all of his answers to those questions, and all of my answers to those answers. But this was not possible. "Why?" I asked.

"Why what?"

"Why do you desire my currency?"

"Because I do not have a sufficient sum."

"For what? For what do you need currency?"

He turned his head to the water and did not say a thing. Was this his answer? He moved his foot in the sand and made a circle.

"I am unequivocal that I can find her," he said. "Four days. Perhaps five. But it could not require more than a week. We were very near."

I should have again said "I will," and again not said anything more. I should have esteemed that Grandfather is much more aged than me, and because of this he is wiser, and if not that, then he deserves to have me not question him. But instead I said, "No. We were not near."

"Yes," he said, "we were."

"No. We were not five days from finding her. We were fifty years from finding her."

"It is a thing that I must do."

"Why?"

"You would not understand."

"But I would. I do."

216

"No, you could not."

"Herschel?"

He drew another circle with his foot.

"Then take me with you," I said. I was not intending to say that.

"No," he said.

I desired to say it again, "Take me with you," but I knew that he would have answered again, "No," and I do not think I could have heard that without crying, and I know that I cannot cry in view of Grandfather.

"It is not necessary for you to decide now," he said. "I did not think that you would decide rapidly. I anticipate that you will say no."

"Why do you think I will say no?"

"Because you do not understand."

"I do."

"No, you do not."

"It is possible that I will say yes."

"I would give you any possession of mine that you desire. It can be yours until I restore the currency to you, which will be soon."

"Take me with you," I said, and again I did not intend to say it, but it released from my mouth, like the articles from Trachim's wagon.

"No," he said.

"Please," I said. "It will be less rigid with me. I could assist very much."

"I need to find her alone," he said, and at that moment I was certain that if I gave Grandfather the currency and allowed him to go, I would never see him again.

"Take Little Igor."

"No," he said. "Alone." No words. And then: "Do not inform Father."

"Of course," I said, because of course I would not inform Father.

"This must be our secret."

It is this last thing that he said that left the most permanent mark on my brain. It had not occurred to me until he uttered it, but we have a secret. We have a thing amid us that no one else in the world knows, or could know. We have a secret together, and no longer asunder.

I informed him that I would rapidly present him with my answer.

I do not know what to do, Jonathan, and would desire for you to tell me *what you think is the right thing. I know that it is not necessary that there be one right thing. There may be two right things. There may be no right things. I will consider what you deem. This is a promise. But I cannot promise that I will harmonize. There are things that you could not know. (And also, of course, I will have made my decision by the time you receive this letter. We have always communicated in this misplaced time.)*

I am not a foolish person. I know that Grandfather will never be able to restore the currency. This signifies that I will not be able to move myself and Little Igor to America. Our dreams cannot exist at the same time. I am so young, and he is so aged, and both of these facts should make us people who are deserving of their dreams, but this is not a possibility.

I am certain of what you will utter. You will utter, "Let me give you the currency." You will utter, "You can return the currency when you have it, or you can never return the currency, and it will not be mentioned again." I know you will utter this because I know that you are a good person. But this is not acceptable. For the same reason that Grandfather cannot take me with him on his voyage, I cannot take the currency from you. This is about choosing. Can you understand? Please attempt to. You are the only person who has understood even a whisper of me, and I will tell you that I am the only person who has understood even a whisper of you.

I will expect for your letter with anticipation.

> *Guilelessly,*
> *Alexander*

an overture to illumination

By THE TIME we returned to the hotel, it was very late, and almost very early. The owner was heavy with sleep at the front desk. "Vodka," Grandfather said. "We should have a drink, the three of us." "The four of us," I counseled, pointing to Sammy Davis, Junior, Junior, who had been such a benign tumor all day. So the four of us went forth to the hotel bar. "You are returned," said the waitress when she witnessed us. "Back with the Jew," she said. "Shut your mouth," Grandfather said, and he did not say it in an earsplitting voice, but quietly, as if it were a fact that she should shut her mouth. "I am apologizing," she said. "It is not a thing," I told her, because I did not want her to feel inferior for a small mistake, and also I could see her bosom when she bent forward. (For whom did I write that, Jonathan? I do not want to be disgusting any- more. And I do not want to be funny, either.) "It is a thing," Grandfather said, "and you must now ask leniency of the Jew." "What's going on?" the hero asked. "Why aren't we going in?" "Make apologies," Grandfa- ther told the waitress, who was only a girl, even more young than me. "I am apologizing for calling you a Jew," she said. "She is apologizing for calling you a Jew," I told the hero. "How did she know?" "She knows be- cause I told her before, at breakfast." "You told her I was a Jew?" "It was an appropriate fact at the time." "I was drinking mochaccino." "I must correct you. It was coffee." "What is he saying?" Grandfather asked. "Perhaps it would be best," I said, "if we acquire a table and order a large amount of drinks and also food." "What else did she say about me?" the hero asked. "Did she say anything else? You can see her tits when she leans over." (This was yours, you will remember. I did not invent this, and so cannot be blamed.)

219

We pursued the waitress to our table, which was in the corner. We could have had any table, because we were the exclusive people there. I do not know why she put us in the corner, but I have a notion. "What can I obtain for you?" she asked. "Four vodkas," Grandfather said. "One of them in a bowl. And do you have anything to eat that does not have meat?" "Peanuts," she said. "This is excellent," Grandfather responded, "but none for Sammy Davis, Junior, Junior because it makes her very ill. It is a terrible thing for even one to touch her lips." I informed this to the hero because I thought he might find it humorous. He merely smiled.

When the waitress returned with our drinks and a bowl of peanuts, we were already conversing about our day, and also our schemes for tomorrow. "He must be present at the train by 19:00 of the evening, yes?" "Yes," I said, "so we will desire to depart the hotel at lunch, to be on the side of safety." "Perhaps we will have time for more searching." "I am not so certain," I said. "And where would we search? There is nothing. There is no one to inquire. You remember what she said." The hero was not giving any attention to us, and never asked even one time what we were conversing about. He was being sociable only with the peanuts. "This would be more easy without him," Grandfather said, moving his eyes at the hero. "But it is his search," I said. "Why?" "Because it is his grandfather." "We are not looking for his grandfather. We are looking for Augustine. She is not any more his than ours." I had not thought of it in this way, but it was true. "What are you talking about?" Jonathan asked me. "And could you ask the waitress for some more of these peanuts?"

I told the waitress to retrieve us more peanuts, and she said, "I will do this, even though the owner commands that no one should ever receive more than one bowl of peanuts. I will except you because I feel so wretched about calling the Jew a Jew." "Thank you," I said, "but there is no reason to feel wretched." "And what about tomorrow, then?" Jonathan asked. "I have to be at the train at 7:00, right?" "Correct." "What will we do until then?" "I am not a certain person. We must depart very early, because you must be at the train station two hours before your train goes forth, and it is a three-hour drive, and it is likely that we will become lost people." "It sounds like we should leave now," he said, and laughed. I did not laugh, because I knew that the reason we would depart early is not in truth because of the justifications I said to him, but because there was nothing more to search for. We had failed.

"Let us investigate IN CASE," Grandfather said. "What?" I asked. "The box, let us see what is inside of it." "Is this a bad idea?" "Of course it is not," he said. "Why would it be?" "Perhaps we should allow Jonathan to investigate it confidentially, or perhaps no one should investigate it." "She presented it to him for a purpose." "I know," I said, "but perhaps that purpose had nothing to do with investigating it. Perhaps the purpose is that it should never be opened." "You are not a curious person?" he asked me. "I am a very curious person." "What are you guys talking about?" "Would you be content to investigate IN CASE?" "What do you mean?" "The box that Augustine presented you today. We could search it." "Is that a good idea?" "I am not certain. I asked the identical thing." "I don't see why it's a bad idea. I mean, she did give it to me for a reason." "This is what Grandfather uttered." "You don't think there's any good reason not to?" "I cannot forecast one." "Neither can I." "But." "But?" "But nothing," I uttered. "But what?" "But nothing. It is your decision." "And yours." "Unclose the fucking box," Grandfather said. "He says unclose the fucking box." Jonathan removed the box from under his seat and placed it on the table. IN CASE was written on the side, and from more proximal, I could perceive that the words had been written and erased many times, written, erased, and written again. "Mmmm," he said, and made gestures to a red ribbon that was fastened around the box. "It is only to keep it closed," Grandfather said. "It is only to keep it closed," I told him. "Probably," he said. "Or," I said, "to forestall us from examining it." "She didn't say anything about not examining it. She would have said something, don't you think?" "I would think so." "Your grandfather thinks we should open it?" "Yes." "And you?" "I am not certain." "What do you mean you're not certain?" "I think it would not be such a wretched thing to open it. She would have uttered something if she desired it to remain uninvestigated." "Open the fucking box," Grandfather said. "He says open the fucking box."

Jonathan dislodged the ribbon, which was wrapped many times around IN CASE, and opened it. Perhaps we were anticipating it to be a bomb, because when it did not explode, we were all flabbergasted. "That wasn't so bad," Jonathan said. "That was not so bad," I told Grandfather. "This is what I said," he told me. "I said it would not be so bad." We looked into the box. Its ingredients appeared very much similar to those in the REMAINS box, except there were perhaps more. "Of course we were supposed to open it," Jonathan said. He looked at me and laughed, and then I laughed, and then Grandfather laughed. We laughed because we knew how witless we had been when we were shitting bricks about opening the box. And we laughed because there was so much that we did not know, and we knew that there was so much we did not know.

"Let us search," Grandfather said, and he moved his hand through the box marked IN CASE like a child reaching into a box of gifts. He excavated a necklace. "Look," he said. "It's pearl, I think," Jonathan said. "Real pearl." The pearls, if they were real pearls, were very dirty, and yellow, and there were pieces of dirt stranded amid them, like food amid teeth. "It appears very aged," Grandfather said. I told this to Jonathan. "Yes," he harmonized. "And dirty. I bet it was buried." "What does it mean buried?" "Put in the ground, like a dead body." "Yes, I know this thing. It could be similar like the ring in the REMAINS box." "Right." Grandfather held the necklace to the candle on our table. The pearls, if they were real pearls, had many taints, and were no longer resplendent. He tried to clean them with his thumb, but they remained dirty. "It is a beautiful necklace," he said. "I purchased one very much similar to this for your grandmother when we first became in love. This was many years ago, but I remember what it looked like. It obligated all of my currency to purchase it, so how could I forget?" "Where is it now?" I asked. "At home?" "No," he said, "she is still wearing it. It is not a thing. Just how she desired it to be." He put the necklace on the table, and I could perceive that the necklace did not make him melancholy, as it might be anticipated, but it made him a very contented person. "Now you," he told me, and punched my back in a manner that was not intended to hurt me, but did nonetheless. "He says I should choose something," I told Jonathan, because I desired to discover how he would answer to the notion that Grandfather and I had the same privilege as he did to investigate the box. "Go ahead," he said. So I inserted my hand into IN CASE.

I felt many abnormal things, and could not tell what they were. We did not say it, but it was part of our game that you could not view in the box when you were selecting the thing to excavate. Some of the things that my hand touched were smooth, like marble or stones from the beach. Other things that my hand touched were cold, like metal, or warm, like fur. There were many pieces of paper. I could be certain of that without witnessing them. But I could not know if these papers were photographs or notes or pages from a book or magazine. I excavated what I excavated because it was the largest thing in the box. "Here," I said, and removed a piece of paper that was in a coil and fastened with white string. I removed the string and unrolled the paper on the table. Jonathan restrained one end, and I restrained the other. It was marked MAP OF THE WORLD, 1791. Even though the shapes of the land were some amount different, it remained to appear very much like the world as we currently know it. "This is a premium thing," I said. A map such as that one is worth many hundreds, and as luck will have it, thousands of dollars. But more than this, it is a remembrance of that time before our planet was so small. When this map was made, I thought, you could live without knowing where you were not living. This made me think of Trachimbrod, and how Lista, the woman we desired so much to be Augustine, had not ever heard of America. It is possible that she is the last person on earth, I reasoned, who does not know about America. Or it is so nice to think so. "I love it," I told Jonathan, and I must confess that I had no notions when I told him this. It is only that I loved it. "You can have it," he said. "This is not a true thing." "Take it. Enjoy it." "You cannot give this to me. The items must remain together," I told him. "Go on," he said. "It's yours." "Are you certain?" I asked, because I did not desire him to feel burdened to present it to me. "I'm positive. It can be a memento of our trip." "Memento?" "Something to remind you." "No," I said. "I will give it to Little Igor, if that is acceptable with you," because I knew that the map was a thing that Little Igor would love also. "Tell him to enjoy it," Jonathan said. "It can be his memento."

"You," I told Jonathan, because it was now his opportunity to excavate from IN CASE. He turned his head away from the box and inserted his hand. He did not require a long amount of time. "Here," he said, and removed a book. He placed it on the table. It appeared very old. "What is it?" he asked. I moved the dust off of the cover. I had never previous witnessed a book similar to it. The writing was on both covers, and when I unclosed it, I saw that the writing was also on the insides of both covers, and, of course, on every page. It was as if there was not sufficient room in the book for the book. Along the side was marked in Ukrainian, *The Book of Past Occurrences.* I told this to Jonathan. "Read me something from it," he said. "The beginning?" "Anywhere, it doesn't matter." I went to a page in the middle and selected a part from the middle of the page to read. It was very difficult, but I translated into English while I read. " 'The shtetl was colorful with the actions of its residents,' " I told him, " 'and because every color was used, it was impossible to perceive what had been handled by humans and what was of nature's hands. Getzel G, there were rumors, must have played everyone's fiddle — even though he did not know how to play the fiddle! — because the strings were the color like his fingers. People whispered that Gesha R was trying to be a gymnast. This is how the Jewish/Human fault line was yellow like her hands. And when the red of a schoolgirl's face was wronged for the red of a holy man's fingers, the schoolgirl was called names.' " He secured the book and examined it while I told Grandfather what I had read. "It's wonderful," Jonathan said, and I must confess that he examined it in a fashion similar to how Grandfather examined the photograph of Augustine.

(You may understand this as a gift from me to you, Jonathan. And just as I am saving you, so could you save Grandfather. We are merely two paragraphs away. Please, try to find some other option.)

"Now you," Jonathan said to Grandfather. "He says it is now you," I told him. He turned his head away from the box and inserted his hand. We were similar to three children. "There are so many things," he told me. "I do not know which thing to take." "He does not know which to take," I told Jonathan. "There's time for all of them," Jonathan said. "Perhaps this one," Grandfather said. "No, this one. It feels soft and nice. No, this one. This one has pieces that move." "There is time for all of them," I told him, because remember where we are in our story, Jonathan. We still thought we possessed time. "Here," Grandfather said, and excavated a photograph. "Ah, a simple one. Too unfortunate. I thought it felt like something different."

He placed the photograph on the table without examining it. Also I did not examine it, because why should I, I reasoned. Grandfather was correct, it appeared very simple, and ordinary. There were likely one hundred photographs of this manner in the box. The rapid view that I presented it showed me nothing abnormal. It was three men, or perhaps four. "Now you," he told me, and I turned my head and inserted my hand. Because my head was turned to not view in the box, I was witnessing Jonathan while my hand investigated. A soft thing. A rough thing. Jonathan moved the photograph to his face, not because he was an interested person, but because there was nothing else to do at the moment while I searched the box. This is what I remember. He ate a hand of peanuts, and let a handful descend to the floor for Sammy Davis, Junior, Junior. He made a petite drink from his vodka. He looked away from the photograph for a moment. I felt a feather and a bone. Then I remember this: he looked at the photograph again. I felt a smooth thing. A petite thing. He looked away from the photograph. He looked at it again. He looked away. A hard thing. A candle. A square thing. A prick from a pin.

"Oh my God," he said, and he held the photograph up to the light of the candle. Then he put it down. Then he held it again, and this time put it close to my face so that he could observe both the photograph and my face at the same time. "What is he doing?" Grandfather asked. "What are you doing?" I asked him. Jonathan placed the photograph on the table. "It's you," he said.

I removed my hand from the box.

"Who is me?" "The man in this picture. It's you." He gave me the photograph. This time I examined it with much scrutiny. "What is it?" Grandfather asked. There were four people in the photograph, two men, a woman, and a baby that the woman was holding. "The one on the left," Jonathan said, "here." He put his finger beneath the face of the man, and I must confess, there could be nothing truthful to do but admit, he looked like me. It was as if a mirror. I know that this is an idiom, but I am saying it without any meaning other than the words. It was as if a mirror. "What?" Grandfather asked. "A moment," I said, and held the photograph to the light of the candle. The man even stood in the same potent manner as I stand. His cheeks appeared like mine. His eyes appeared like mine. His hairs, lips, arms, legs, they all appeared like mine. Not even like mine. They *were* mine. "Tell me," Grandfather said, "what is it?" I presented him the photograph, and to write the rest of this story is the most impossible thing.

At first he examined it to see what it was a photograph of. Because he was looking down to view the photograph, which was on the table, I could not see what his eyes were performing. He looked up from the photograph and viewed Jonathan and me, and he smiled. He even moved his shoulders up, as a child will sometimes do. He made a small laugh and then picked up the photograph. He held it to his face with one hand and held the candle to his face with the other. It made many shadows where his skin had folds, which were many more places than I had before observed. This time I could see his eyes voyage this and that over the photograph. They stopped on each person, and witnessed each person from feet to hairs. Then he looked up again and smiled again at Jonathan and me, and he also moved his shoulders like a child again.

"It looks like me," I said.

"Yes it does," he said.

I did not look at Jonathan, because I was certain that he was looking at me. So I looked at Grandfather, who was investigating the photograph, although I am certain that he could feel that I was viewing him.

"Exactly like me," I said. "He also observed this," I said of Jonathan, because I did not want to be alone in this observation.

(Here it is almost too forbidding to continue. I have written to this point many times, and corrected the parts you would have me correct, and made more funnies, and more inventions, and written as if I were you writing this, but every time I try to persevere, my hand shakes so that I can no longer hold my pen. Do it for me. Please. It is now yours.)

Grandfather concealed his face behind the photograph.

(And this does not seem to me like such a cowardly thing to do, Jonathan. We would also conceal our faces, yes? In truth, I am certain that we would.)

"The world is the smallest thing," he said.

(He laughed at this moment, as you remember, but you cannot include that in the story.)

"It looks so much like me," I said.

(And here he put his hands under the table, you will remember, but this is a detail which will make him appear weak, and is it not enough that we are writing this at all?)

"Like a combination of your father, your mother, Brezhnev, and yourself."

(It was not wrong to make a funny here. It was the right thing to do.) I smiled.

"Who do you think it is?" I asked.

"Who do *you* think it is?" he asked.

"I do not know."

"You do not have to present not-truths to me, Sasha. I am not a child."

(But I do. That is what you always fail to understand. I present not-truths in order to protect you. That is also why I try so inflexibly to be a funny person. Everything is to protect you. I exist in case you need to be protected.)

"I do not understand," I said. (I understand.)

"You do not?" he asked. (You do.)

"Where was the photograph made?" I asked. (There must be some explanation.)

"In Kolki."

"Where you were from?" (You always said Odessa... To fall in love...)

"Yes. Before the war." (This is the way things are. This is, in truth, what it is like.)

"Jonathan's grandmother?"

"I do not know her name, and I do not want to know her name."

(I must inform you, Jonathan, that I am a very sad person. I am always sad, I think. Perhaps this signifies that I am not sad at all, because sadness is something lower than your normal disposition, and I am always the same thing. Perhaps I am the only person in the world, then, who never becomes sad. Perhaps I am lucky.)

"I am not a bad person," he said. "I am a good person who has lived in a bad time."

"I know this," I said. (Even if you were a bad person, I would still know that you are a good person.)

"You must inform all of this to him as I inform it to you," he said, and this surprised me very much, but I did not ask why, or ask anything. I only did as he commanded. Jonathan opened his diary and commenced to write. He wrote every word that was spoken. Here is what he wrote:

"Everything I did, I did because I thought it was the correct thing to do."

"Everything he did, he did because he thought it was the correct thing to do," I translated.

"I am not a hero, it is true."

"He is not a hero."

"But I am not a bad person, either."

"But he is not a bad person."

"The woman in the photograph is your grandmother. She is holding your father. The man standing next to me was our best friend, Herschel."

"The woman in the photograph is my grandmother. She is holding my father. The man standing next to Grandfather was his best friend, Herschel."

"Herschel is wearing a skullcap in the photograph because he was a Jew."

"Herschel was a Jew."

"And he was my best friend."

"He was his best friend."

"And I murdered him."

FALLING IN LOVE, 1934–1941

THE FINAL TIME they made love, seven months before she killed herself and he married someone else, the Gypsy girl asked my grandfather how he arranged his books.

She had been the only one he returned to without having to be asked. They would meet at the bazaar—he would watch, with not only anticipation but pride, as she coaxed snakes from woven baskets with the tipsy music of her recorder. They would meet at the theater or in front of her thatch-roofed shanty in the Gypsy hamlet on the other side of the Brod. (She, of course, could never be seen near his house.) They would meet on the wooden bridge, or beneath the wooden bridge, or by the small falls. But more often than not, they would end up in the petrified corner of Radziwell Forest, exchanging jokes and stories, laughing afternoons into evenings, making love—which might or might not have been love—under stone canopies.

Do you think I'm wonderful? she asked him one day as they leaned against the trunk of a petrified maple.

No, he said.

Why?

Because so many girls are wonderful. I imagine hundreds of men have called their loves wonderful today, and it's only noon. You couldn't be something that hundreds of others are.

Are you saying that I am not-wonderful?

Yes, I am.

She fingered his dead arm. *Do you think I am not-beautiful?*

You are incredibly not-beautiful. You are the farthest possible thing from beautiful.

She unbuttoned his shirt.

Am I smart?

No. Of course not. I would never call you smart.

She kneeled to unbutton his pants.

Am I sexy?

No.

Funny?

You are not-funny.

Does that feel good?

No.

Do you like it?

No.

She unbuttoned her blouse. She leaned in against him.

Should I continue?

She had been to Kiev, he learned, and Odessa, and even Warsaw. She had lived among the Wisps of Ardisht for a year when her mother became deathly ill. She told him of ship voyages she had taken to places he had never heard of, and stories he knew were all untrue, were bad nottruths, even, but he nodded and tried to convince himself to be convinced, tried to believe her, because he knew that the origin of a story is always an absence, and he wanted her to live among presences.

In Siberia, she said, *there are couples who make love from hundreds of miles apart, and in Austria there is a princess who tattooed the image of her lover's body onto her body, so that when she looked in the mirror she would see him, and and and on the other side of the Black Sea is a stone woman—I have never seen it, but my aunt has—who came to life because of her sculptor's love!*

Safran brought the Gypsy girl flowers and chocolates (all gifts from his widows) and composed poems for her, all of which she laughed at.

How stupid could you possibly be! she said.

Why am I stupid?

Because the easiest things for you to give are the hardest things for you to give. Flowers, chocolates, and poems don't mean anything to me.

You don't like them?

Not from you.

What would you like from me?

She shrugged her shoulders, not out of puzzlement but embarrassment. (He was the only person on earth who could embarrass her.)

Where do you keep your books? she asked.

In my room.

Where in your room?

On shelves.

How are your books arranged?

Why do you care?

Because I want to know.

She was a Gypsy. He was a Jew. When she held his hand in public, something he knew she knew he hated, he created a reason to need it—to comb his hair, to point at the spot where his great-great-great-grandfather spilt the gold coins onto the shore like golden vomit from the sack—and would then insert it in his pocket, ending the situation.

You know what I need right now, she said, reaching for his dead arm as they walked through the Sunday bazaar.

Tell me and it's yours. Anything.

I want a kiss.

You can have as many as you want, wherever you want them.

Here, she said, putting her index finger on her lips. *Now.*

He gestured to a nearby alley.

No, she said. *I want a kiss here*, she put her finger on her lips, *now.*

He laughed. *Here?* He put his finger on his own lips. *Now?*

Here, she said, putting her finger on her lips. *Now.*

They laughed together. Nervous laughter. Starting with small giggles. Summing. Louder laughter. Multiplying. Even louder. Squaring. Laughter between gasps. Uncontrollable laughter. Violent. Infinite.

I can't.

I know.

My grandfather and the Gypsy girl made love for seven years, at least twice every week. They had confessed every secret; explained, to the best of their abilities, the workings of their bodies, each to the other; been forceful and passive, greedy and giving, wordy and silent.

How do you arrange your books? she asked as they lay naked on a bed of pebbles and hard soil.

I told you, they're in my bedroom on shelves.

I wonder if you can imagine your life without me.

Sure I can imagine it, but I don't like to.

It's not pleasant, is it?

Why are you doing this?

It was just something I was wondering.

Not one of his friends—if it could be said that he had any other friends—knew about the Gypsy girl, and none of his other women knew about the Gypsy girl, and his parents, of course, didn't know about the Gypsy girl. She was such a tightly kept secret that sometimes he felt that not even he was privy to his relationship with her. She knew of his efforts to conceal her from the rest of his world, to keep her cloistered in a private chamber reachable only by a secret passage, to put her behind a wall. She knew that even if he thought he loved her, he did not love her.

Where do you think you'll be in ten years? she asked, raising her head from his chest to address him.

I don't know.

Where do you think I'll be? Their sweat had mingled and dried, forming a pasty film between them.

In ten years?

Yes.

I don't know, he said, playing with her hair. *Where do you think you'll be?*

I don't know.

Where do you think I'll be?

I don't know, she said.

They lay in silence, thinking their own thoughts, each trying to know the other's. They were becoming strangers on top of each other.

What made you ask?

I don't know, she said.

Well, what do we know?

Not a lot, she said, easing her head back onto his chest.

They exchanged notes, like children. My grandfather made his out of newspaper clippings and dropped them in her woven baskets, into which he knew only she would dare stick a hand. *Meet me under the wooden bridge, and I will show you things you have never, ever seen.* The "M" was taken from the army that would take his mother's life: GERMAN FRONT ADVANCES ON SOVIET BORDER; the "eet" from their approaching warships: NAZI FLEET DEFEATS FRENCH AT LESACS; the "me" from the peninsula they were blue-eyeing: GERMANS SURROUND CRIMEA; the "und" from too little, too late: AMERICAN WAR FUNDS REACH ENGLAND; the "er" from the dog of dogs: HITLER RENDERS NONAGGRESSION PACT INOPERATIVE . . . and so on, and so on, each note a collage of love that could never be, and war that could.

The Gypsy girl carved love letters into trees, filling the forest with notes for him. *Do not forsake me,* she removed from the bark of a tree in whose shade they had once fallen asleep. *Honor me,* she carved into the trunk of a petrified oak. She was composing a new list of commandments, commandments they could share, that would govern a life together, and not apart. *Do not have any other loves before me in your heart. Do not take my name in vain. Do not kill me. Observe me, and keep me holy.*

I'd like to be wherever you are in ten years, he wrote her, gluing clips of newspaper headlines to a piece of yellow paper. *Isn't that a nice idea?*

A very nice idea, he found on a tree at the fringe of the forest. *And why is it only an idea?*

Because — the print stained his hands; he read himself on himself — *ten years is a long time from now.*

We would have to run away, carved in a circle around a maple's trunk. *We would have to leave behind everything but each other.*

Which is possible, he composed with fragments of the news of imminent war. *It's a nice idea, anyway.*

My grandfather took the Gypsy girl to the Dial and related the story of his great-great-great-grandmother's tragic life, promising to ask for her help when he one day tried to write Trachimbrod's history. He told her the story of Trachim's wagon, when the young W twins were the first to see the curious flotsam rising to the surface: wandering snakes of white string, a crushed-velvet glove with outstretched fingers, barren spools, schmootzy pince-nez, rasp- and boysenberries, feces, frillwork, the shards of a shattered atomizer, the bleeding red-ink script of a resolution: *I will . . . I will . . .* She spoke honestly of her father's abuses, and showed him the bruises that not even a naked body will reveal. He explained his circumcision, the covenant, the concept of his being of the Chosen People. She told him of the time her uncle forced himself on her, and how she had been capable, for several years now, of having a baby. He told her that he masturbated with his dead hand, because that way he could convince himself that he was making love to someone else. She told him that she had contemplated suicide, as if it were a decision. He told her his darkest secret: that unlike other boys, his love for his mother had never diminished, not even the smallest bit since he was a child, and please don't laugh at me for telling you this, and please don't think any less of me, but I would rather have a kiss from her than anything in this world. The Gypsy girl cried, and when my grandfather asked her what was wrong, she did not say, *I am jealous of your mother. I want you to love me like that*, but instead said nothing, and laughed as if: how silly. She told him that she wished there were another commandment, an eleventh etched into the tablets: *Do not change.*

For all of his liaisons, for all of the women who would undress for him at the show of his dead arm, he had no other friends, and could imagine no loneliness worse than an existence without her. She was the only one who could rightly claim to know him, the only one he missed when she was not there, and missed even before she was absent. She was the only one who wanted more of him than his arm.

I don't love you, he told her one evening as they lay naked in the grass.

She kissed his brow and said, *I know that. And I'm sure you know that I don't love you.*

Of course, he said, although it came as a great surprise — not that she didn't love him, but that she would say it. In the past seven years of lovemaking he had heard the words so many times: from the mouths of widows and children, from prostitutes, family friends, travelers, and adulterous wives. Women had said *I love you* without his ever speaking. *The more you love someone*, he came to think, *the harder it is to tell them.* It surprised him that strangers didn't stop each other on the street to say *I love you.*

My parents have arranged a marriage, he said.

For you?

With a girl named Zosha. From my shtetl. I'm seventeen.

And do you love her? she asked without looking at him.

He broke his life into its smallest constituent parts, examined each, like a watchmaker, and then reassembled it.

I hardly know her. He also avoided eye contact, because like Pincher P, who lived in the streets as a charity case, having donated even his last coin to the poor, his eyes would have given away everything.

Are you going to go through with it? she asked, drawing circles in the earth with her caramel finger.

I don't have a choice, he said.

Of course.

She would not look at him.

You will have such a happy life, she said. *You will always be happy.*

Why are you doing this?

Because you are so lucky. Real and lasting happiness is within your reach.

Stop, he said. *You're not being fair.*

I would like to meet her.

No you wouldn't.

Yes I would. What's her name? Zosha? I would like very much to meet Zosha and tell her how happy she will be. What a lucky girl. She must be very beautiful.

I don't know.

You've seen her, haven't you?

Yes.

Then you know if she's beautiful. Is she beautiful?

I guess.

More beautiful than I am?

Stop.

I would like to attend the wedding, to see for myself. Well, not the wedding, of course. A Gypsy girl couldn't enter the synagogue. The reception, though. You are going to invite me, aren't you?

You know that isn't possible, he said, turning away.

I know it isn't possible, she said, knowing that she had pushed it too far, been too cruel.

It isn't possible.

I told you: I know.

But you have to believe me.

I do.

They made love for the last time, unaware that the next seven months would pass without any words between them. He would see her many times, and she him — they had come to haunt the same places, to walk the same paths, to fall asleep in the shade of the same trees — but they would never acknowledge each other's existence. They both wanted badly to go back seven years to their first encounter, at the theater, and do it all again, but this time *not* to notice each other, *not* to talk, *not* to leave the theater, she leading him by his dead right arm through a maze of muddy alleys, past the confectioners' stands by the old cemetery, down the Jewish/Human fault line, and so on and so on into the blackness. For seven months they would ignore each other at the bazaar, at the Dial, and at the fountain of the prostrate mermaid, and they were sure they could ignore each other anywhere and always, sure they could be complete strangers, but were proven wrong when he returned home one afternoon from work only to pass her on her way out of his house.

What are you doing here? he asked, more afraid that she had revealed their relationship — to his father, who would surely beat him, or his mother, who would be so disappointed — than curious as to why she was there.

Your books are arranged by the color of their spines, she said. *How stupid.*

His mother was in Lutsk, he remembered, as she was every Tuesday at this time of the afternoon, and his father was washing himself outside. Safran went to his room to make sure everything was in order. His diary was still under his mattress. His books were properly stacked, according to color. (He pulled one off the shelf, to have something to hold.) The picture of his mother was at its normal skew on the nightstand next to his bed. There was no reason to think that she had touched a thing. He searched the kitchen, the study, even the bathrooms for any trace she might have left. Nothing. No stray hairs. No fingerprints on the mirror. No notes. Everything was in good order.

He went to his parents' bedroom. The pillows were perfect rectangles. The sheets were as smooth as water, tucked in tightly. The room looked as if it hadn't been touched in years, since a death, perhaps, as if it were being preserved as it once was, a time capsule. He didn't know how many times she had come. He couldn't ask her because he never talked to her anymore, and he couldn't ask his father because he would have had to confess everything, and he couldn't ask his mother because, if she were to find out, it would kill her, and that would kill him, and no matter how unlivable his life had become, he was not yet ready to end it.

He ran to the house of Lista P, the only lover to inspire him to bathe. *Let me in*, he said with his head against the door. *It's me, Safran. Let me in.*

He could hear shuffling, someone laboring to get to the door.

Safran? It was Lista's mother.

Hello, he said. *Is Lista in?*

Lista's in her room, she said, thinking what a sweet boy he was. *Go on up.*

What's wrong? Lista asked, seeing him at the door. She looked so much older than she had only three years before, at the theater, which made him wonder whether it was she or he who had changed. *Come in. Come in. Here*, she said, *sit down. What's going on?*

I'm all alone, he said.

You're not alone, she said, taking his head to her chest.

I am.

You're not alone, she said. *You only feel alone.*

To feel alone is to be alone. That's what it is.

Let me make you something to eat.

I don't want anything to eat.

Then have something to drink.

I don't want anything to drink.

She massaged his dead hand and remembered the last time she had touched it. It was not the death that had so attracted her to it, but the un-knowability. The unattainability. He could never completely love her, not with all of himself. He could never be completely owned, and he could never own completely. Her desire had been sparked by the frustra-tion of her desire.

You're going to be married, Safran. I got the invitation this morning. Is that what's upsetting you?

Yes, he said.

Well, you've got nothing to worry about. Everybody gets nervous before being wed. I did. I know my husband did. But Zosha's such a nice girl.

I've never met her, he said.

Well, she's very nice. And beautiful, too.

Do you think I will like her?

I do.

Will I love her?

It's possible. You should never make predictions with love, but it's definitely possible.

Do you love me? he asked. *Did you ever? That night with all the coffee.*

I don't know, she said.

Do you think it's possible that you did?

He touched the side of her face with his good hand, and moved it down to her neck, and then down under the collar of her shirt.

No, she said, taking his hand out.

No?

No.

But I want to. I really do. This isn't for you.

That's why we can't, she said. *I never would have been able to do it if I had thought that you wanted to.*

He put his head in her lap and fell asleep. Before leaving that evening, he gave Lista the book that he still had with him from his house — *Hamlet*, with a purple spine — that he had taken from the shelf to have something to hold.

For keeps? she asked.

You'll give it back to me one day.

My grandfather and the Gypsy girl knew none of this as they made love for the last time, as he touched her face and fingered the soft underside of her chin, as he paid her the attention received by a sculptor's wife. *Like this?* he asked. She brushed her eyelashes against his chest. She moved her butterfly kiss across his torso and up his neck to where his left earlobe connected to his jaw. *Like this?* she asked. He pulled her blue blouse over her head, he undid her bead necklaces, he licked her smooth and sweaty armpits and ran his finger from her neck to her navel. He drew circles around her caramel areolas with his tongue. *Like this?* he asked. She nodded and craned her head back. He flicked her nipples with his tongue, and knew that it was all so completely wrong, everything, from the moment of his birth to this, everything was coming out the wrong way—not the opposite, but worse: close. She used both hands to undo his belt. He lifted his backside off the ground so she could pull down his slacks and underpants. She took his penis into her hand. She wanted so badly for him to feel good. She was convinced that he had never felt good. She wanted to be the cause of his first and only pleasure. *Like this?* He put his hand on top of hers and guided it. She removed her skirt and panties, took his dead hand, pressed it between her legs. Her thick black pubic hair was wound in loose curls, in waves. *Like this?* he asked, although she was guiding his hand, as if trying to channel a message on a Ouija board. They guided each other over each other's body. She put his dead fingers inside her and felt, for a moment, the numbness and paralysis. She felt the death in and through her. *Now?* he asked. *Now?* She rolled onto him and spread her legs around his knees. She reached behind her and used his dead hand to guide his penis into her. *Is this good?* he asked. *Is this good?*

Seven months later, June 18, 1941, as the first display of German bombing lit the Trachimbrod skies electric, as my grandfather had his first orgasm (his first and only pleasure, of which she was not the cause), she slit her wrist with a knife that had been made dull carving love letters. But then, there, his sleeping head against her beating chest, she revealed nothing. She didn't say, *You are going to marry.* And she didn't say, *I am going to kill myself.* Only: *How do you arrange your books?*

Dear Jonathan,

I promised that I would never mention writing again, because I thought that we were beyond that. But I must break my promise.

I could hate you! Why will you not permit your grandfather to be in love with the Gypsy girl, and show her his love? Who is ordering you to write in such a manner? We have such chances to do good, and yet again and again you insist on evil. I would not read this most contemporary division to Little Igor, because I did not appraise it worthy of his ears. No, this division I presented to Sammy Davis, Junior, Junior, who acted faithfully with it.

I must make a simple question, which is what is wrong with you? If your grandfather loves the Gypsy girl, and I am certain that he does, why does he not leave with her? She could make him so happy. And yet he declines happiness. This is not reasonable, Jonathan, and it is not good. If I were the writer, I would have Safran show his love to the Gypsy girl, and take her to Greenwich Shtetl in New York City. Or I would have Safran kill himself, which is the only other truthful thing to perform, although then you would not be born, which would signify that this story could not be written.

You are a coward, Jonathan, and you have disappointed me. I would never command you to write a story that is as it occurred in the actual, but I would command you to make your story faithful. You are a coward for the same explanation that Brod is a coward, and Yankel is a coward, and Safran is a coward — all of your relatives are cowards! You are all cowards because you live in a world that is "once-removed," if I may excerpt you. I do not have any homage for anyone in your family, with exceptions of your grandmother, because you are all in the proximity of love, and all disavow love. I have enclosed the currency that you most recently posted.

Of course, I understand, in some manners, what you are attempting to perform. There is such a thing as love that cannot be, for certain. If I were to inform Father, for example, about how I comprehend love, and who I desire to love, he would kill me, and this is no idiom. We all choose things, and we also all choose against things. I want to be the kind of person who chooses for more than chooses against, but like Safran, and like you, I discover myself choosing this time and the next time against what I am certain is good and correct, and against what I am certain is worthy. I choose that I will not, instead of that I will. None of this is effortless to say.

I did not give Grandfather the money, but it was for very different reasons than you suggested. He was not surprised when I told him. "I am proud of you," he said.

"But you wanted me to give it to you?" I said.

"Very much," he said. "I am sure that I could find her."

"How can you be proud, then?"

"I am proud of you, not me."

"You are not angry with me?"

"No."

"I do not want to disappoint you."

"I am not angry or disappointed," he said.

"Does it make you sad that I am not giving you the money?"

"No. You are a good person, doing the good and right thing. It makes me content."

Why, then, did I feel that it was the pathetic, cowardly action, and that I was the pathetic coward? Let me explain why I did not give Grandfather my money. It is not because I am saving it for myself to go to America. That is a dream that I have woken up from. I will never see America, and neither will Little Igor, and I understand that now. I did not give Grandfather the money because I do not believe in Augustine. No, that is not what I mean. I do not believe in the Augustine that Grandfather was searching for. The woman in the photograph is alive. I am sure she is. But I am also sure that she is not Herschel, as Grandfather wanted her to be, and she is not my grandmother, as he wanted her to be, and she is not Father, as he wanted her to be. If I gave him the money, he would have found her, and he would have seen who she really is, and this would have killed him. I am not saying this metaphorically. It would have killed him.

But it was a situation without winning. The possibilities were none, between what was possible and what we wanted. And here I have to confer you some terrible news. Grandfather died four days ago. He cut his hands. It was very late in the night and I could not sleep. There was a noise coming from the bath, so I went to investigate it. (Now that I am the man of the house, it is up to me to see that everything works.) I found Grandfather in the bath, which was full of blood. I told him to stop sleeping, because I did not yet understand what was going on. "Wake up!" Then I shook him violently, and then I punched him in the face. It hurt my hand, I punched him so hard. I punched him again. I do not know why, but I did. To tell you the truth, I had never punched anyone before, only been punched. "Wake up!" I shouted at him, and I punched him again, this time the other side of his face. But I knew that he would not wake up. "You sleep too much!" My shouting woke up my mother, and she ran to the bath. She had to forcefully pull me off of Grandfather, and she later told me that she thought I had killed him, the way I was punching so much, and the look in my eyes. We invented a story about an accident with sleeping pills. This is what we told to Little Igor, so that he would never have to know.

It had been such an evening already. Volumes had happened, just as volumes now happen, just as volumes will happen. For the first time in my life, I told my father exactly what I thought, as I will now tell you, for the first time, exactly what I think. As with him, I ask for your forgiveness.

Love,
Alex

ILLUMINATION

"HERSCHEL would care for your father when I had to make an errand, or when your grandmother was ill. She was ill all of the time, not only at the end of her life. Herschel would care for the baby, and hold it as if it were his own. He even called him son."

I told all of this to Jonathan as Grandfather told it to me, and he wrote all of it in his diary. He wrote:

"Herschel did not possess a family of his own. He was not such a social person. He loved to read very much, and also to write. He was a poet, and he exhibited me many of his poems. I remember many of them. They were silly, you could say, and about love. He was always in his room writing those things, and never with people. I used to tell him, What good is all of that love doing on paper? I said, Let love write on you for a little. But he was so stubborn. Or perhaps he was only timid."

"You were his friend?" I asked, although he had already said that he was Herschel's friend.

"We were his only friends, he once told us. Your grandmother and I. He would eat dinner with us, and on occasions remain very tardy. We even made vacations together. When your father was born, the three of us would make walks with the baby. When he needed a thing, he would come to us. When he had a problem, he would come to us. He once asked me if he could kiss your grandmother. Why, I asked him, and it made me an angry person, in truth, very angry, that he should desire to kiss her. Because I am afraid, he said, that I will never kiss a woman. Herschel, I said, it is because you do not try to kiss any."

(Was he in love with Grandmother?)

(I do not know.)

(It was a possibility?)

(It was a possibility. He would look at her, and also bring her flowers as gifts.)

(Did this upset you?)

(I loved them both.)

"Did he kiss her?"

"No," he said. (And you will remember, Jonathan, that he laughed here. It was a short, severe laugh.) "He was too timid to ever kiss anyone, even Anna. I do not think that they ever did anything."

"He was your friend," I said.

"He was my best friend. It was different then. Jews, not Jews. We were young still, and there was very much life in advance of us. Who knew?" (We did not know, is what I am attempting to say. How could we have known?)

"Knew what?" I asked.

"Who knew that we were living on such a needle?"

"A needle?"

"One day Herschel is eating dinner with us, and he is singing songs to your father in his arms."

"Songs?"

(Here he sang the song, Jonathan, and I know how you relish inserting songs in writing, but you could not require me to write this. I have tried for so long to displace the song from my brain, but it is always there. I hear myself singing it when I walk, and in my courses at university, and before sleep.)

"But we were very stupid people," he said, and he again examined the photograph and smiled. "So stupid."

"Why?"

"Because we believed in things."

"What things?" I asked, because I did not know. I was not understanding.

(Why are you asking so many questions?)

(Because you are not being clear with me.)

(I am very ashamed.)

244

(You do not have to be shamed in my closeness. Family are the people who must never make you feel ashamed.)

(You are wrong. Family are the people who must make you feel ashamed when you are deserving of shame.)

(And you are deserving of shame?)

(I am. I am trying to tell you.) "We were stupid," he said, "because we believed in things."

"Why is this stupid?"

"Because there are not things to believe in."

(Love?)

(There is no love. Only the end of love.)

(Goodness?)

(Do not be a fool.)

(God?)

(If God exists, He is not to be believed in.)

"Augustine?" I asked.

"I dreamed that this might be the thing," he said. "But I was wrong."

"Perhaps you were not wrong. We could not find her, but that does not signify anything about whether you should believe in her."

"What is the good of something that you cannot find?"

(I will tell you, Jonathan, that at this place in the conversation, it was no longer Alex and Alex, grandfather and grandson, talking. We yielded to be two different people, two people who could view one another in the eyes, and utter things that are not uttered. When I listened to him, I did not listen to Grandfather, but to someone else, someone I had never encountered before, but whom I knew better than Grandfather. And the person who was listening to this person was not me but someone else, someone I had never been before but whom I knew better than myself.)

"Tell me more," I said.

"More?"

"Herschel."

"It was as if he was in our family."

"Tell me what happened. What happened to him?"

"To him? To him and me. It happened to everybody, do not make any mistakes. Just because I was not a Jew, it does not mean that it did not happen to me."

"What is it?"

"You had to choose, and hope to choose the smaller evil."

"You had to choose," I told Jonathan, "and hope to choose the smaller evil."

"And I chose."

"And he chose."

"He chose what?"

"What did you choose?"

"When they captured our town—"

"Kolki?"

"Yes, but do not tell him. There is no reason to tell him."

"We could go in the morning."

"No."

"Perhaps it would be a good thing."

"No," he said. "My ghosts are not there."

(You have ghosts?)

(Of course I have ghosts.)

(What are your ghosts like?)

(They are on the insides of the lids of my eyes.)

(This is also where my ghosts reside.)

(You have ghosts?)

(Of course I have ghosts.)

(But you are a child.)

(I am not a child.)

(But you have not known love.)

(These are my ghosts, the spaces amid love.)

"You could reveal it to us," I said. "You could take us to where you once lived, and where his grandmother once lived."

"There is no purpose," he said. "Those people signify nothing to me."

"His grandmother."

"I do not want to know her name."

"He says that there is no purpose to return to the town that he came from," I told Jonathan. "It means nothing to him."

"Why did he leave?"

"Why did you leave?"

"Because I did not want your father to grow up so close to death. I did not want him to know of it, and live with it. This is why I never informed him of what occurred. I wanted so much for him to live a good life, without death and without choices and without shame. But I was not a good father, I must inform you. I was the worst father. I desired to remove him from everything that was bad, but instead I gave him badness upon badness. A father is always responsible for how his son is. You must understand."

"I am not understanding. I am not understanding any of this. I do not understand that you are from Kolki, and why I never knew. I do not understand why you came on this voyage if you knew how close we would be. I do not understand what are your ghosts. I do not understand how a picture of you was in Augustine's box."

(Do you remember what he did next, Jonathan? He examined the photograph again, and then placed it on the table again, and then he said, Herschel was a good person, and so was I, and because of this it is not right what happened, not anything of it. And then I asked him, What, what happened? He returned the photograph to the box, you will remember, and he told us the story. Exactly like that. He placed the photograph in the box, and he told it to us. He did not once avoid our eyes, and he did not once put his hands under the table. I murdered Herschel, he said. Or what I did was as good as murdering him. What do you mean? I asked him, because what he said was such a potent thing to say. No, this is not true. Herschel would have been murdered with or without me, but it is still as if I murdered him. What happened? I asked. They came in the most darkest time of the night. They had just come from another town, and would go to another after. They knew what they were doing, they were so logical. I remember with very much precision the feeling of my bed shaking when the tanks came. What is it? What is it? Grandmother asked. I moved from bed, and I examined out of the window. What did you see? I saw four tanks, and I can remember them in every aspect. There were four green tanks, and men walking along the sides of them. These men had guns, I will tell you, and they were pointing them at our doors and windows in case that someone should try to run. It was dark but I could still see this. Were you scared? I was scared, although I knew that I was not the one they wanted. How did you know? We knew about them. Everyone knew. Herschel knew. We did not think it would happen to us. I told you, we believed in things, we were so foolish. And then? And then I told Grandmother to get the baby, your father, and to take him into the cellar and not to manufacture any noise but also not to become overly afraid because we were not the ones that they wanted. And then? And then they stopped all of the tanks and for a moment I was so foolish to think that it was over, that they had decided to return to Germany and end the war because nobody likes war not even those who survive it, not even the winners. But? But they did not of course they had only stopped the tanks in front of the synagogue and they came out of their tanks and moved into very logical lines. The General who had blond hair put a microphone to his face and spoke in Ukrainian he said that everyone must come to the synagogue everyone with no omissions. The soldiers punched on every door with their guns and investigated the houses to be certain that everyone should be in front of the synagogue I told Grandmother to return upstairs with the baby because I feared that they would discover them in the basement and shoot them because of their hiding. Herschel I thought Herschel must escape how can he escape he must run now run into the darkness perhaps he has already run perhaps he heard the tanks and ran but when we arrived at the synagogue I saw Herschel and he saw me and we stood next to each other because that is what friends do in the presence of evil or love. What is going to happen he asked me and I told him I do not know what is going to happen and the truth is that not one of us knew what was going to happen although every one of us knew that it would be evil. It captured so long for the soldiers to finish their investigating of the houses it was very important to them to be certain that everyone was in front of the synagogue. I am so scared Herschel said I think I am going to cry. Why I asked why there is nothing to cry for there is no reason to cry but I will tell you that I too wanted to cry and I too was afraid but not for myself for Grandmother and for the baby. What did they do? What happened next? They made us stand in lines and I was next to Anna on the one side and Herschel on the other side some of the women were crying and this was because they were very afraid of the guns that the soldiers were holding and they thought that all of us were going to be killed. The General with blue eyes put the microphone to his face. You must listen carefully he said and do everything that is commanded or you will be shot. Herschel whispered to me I am very scared and I wanted to tell him run your chances are better if you run it is dark run you have no chances if you do not but I could not tell him this because I was afraid that I would be shot for speaking and I was also afraid of yielding to Herschel's death by admitting it be brave I said with as little volume as I could manufacture it is necessary that you be brave which I know now was such a stupid thing to utter the stupidest thing I have ever uttered be brave for what? Who is the rabbi the General asked and the rabbi elevated his hand. Two of the guards seized the rabbi and pushed him into the synagogue. Who is the cantor the General asked and the cantor elevated his hand but he was not so quiet about death as the rabbi he was crying and saying no to his wife no no nonono and she lifted her hand to him and two guards seized her and put her in the synagogue also. Who are the Jews the General asked into his microphone all the Jews move forward but not one person moved forward. All of the Jews must move forward he said again and this time he shouted it but again not one person moved forward and I will tell you that if I were a Jew I would also not move forward the General went to the first line and he said into his microphone you will point out a Jew or you will be considered a Jew the first person he went to was a Jew named Abraham. Who is a Jew the General asked him and Abraham trembled Who is a Jew the General asked again and he put his gun to Abraham's head Aaron is a Jew Aaron and he pointed to Aaron who was in the second row which is where we were standing. Two guards seized Aaron and he was resisting very much so they shot him in the head and this is when I felt Herschel's hand touch mine. Do as you are commanded the General with a scar on his face shouted into his microphone or. He went to the second person in the line who was a friend of mine Leo and he said who is a Jew and Leo pointed to Abraham and he said that man is a Jew I am sorry Abraham two guards secured Abraham into the synagogue a woman in the fourth row tried to run away with her baby in her arms but the General shouted something in German that most terrible horrible ugly disgusting vile monstrous language and one of the guards shot her in the back of the head and they pulled her and her baby who was still alive into the synagogue. The General went to the next man in line and the next and everyone was pointing at a Jew because nobody wanted to be killed one Jew pointed at his cousin and one pointed at himself because he would not point at another. They secured Daniel into the synagogue and also Talia and Louis and every Jew there was but for some reason that I will never know Herschel was never pointed to perhaps this is because I was his only friend and he was not so social and many people did not even know he existed I was the only one who would know to point at him or perhaps it was because it was so dark that he could not be seen anymore. It was not forever before he was the only Jew remaining outside of the synagogue the General was now in the second row and said to a man because he only asked men I do not know why who is a Jew and the man said they are all in the synagogue because he did not know Herschel or did not know that Herschel was a Jew the General shotthismaninthehead and I could feel Herschel's hand touching mine very lightly and I made certain not to look at him the General went to the next person who is a Jew he asked and this person said they are all in the synagogue you must believe me I am not lying why would I lie you can kill them all I do not care but please spare me please do not kill me please and then the General shothiminthehead and said I am becoming tired of this and he went to the next man in line and that was me who is a Jew he asked and I felt Herschel's hand again and I know that his hand was saying pleaseplease Eli please I do not want to die please do not point at me you know what is going to happen to me if you point at me do not point at me I am afraid of dying I am so afraid of dying I am soafraidofdying Iamsoafraidofdying who is a Jew the General asked me again and I felt on my other hand the hand of Grandmother and I knew that she was holding your father and that he was holding you and that you were holding your children I am so afraid of dying I am soafraidofdying Iamsoafraidofdying Iamsoafraidofdying and I said he is a Jew who is a Jew the General asked and Herschel embraced my hand with much strength and he was my friend he was my best friend I would have let him kiss Anna and even make love to her but I am I and my wife is my wife and my baby is my baby do you understand what I am telling you I pointed at Herschel and said he is a Jew this man is a Jew please Herschel said to me and he was crying tell them it is nottrue please Eli please two guards seized him and he did not resist but he did cry more and harder and he shouted tell them that there are no more Jews nomoreJews and you only said that I was a Jew so that you would not be killed I am begging you Eli youaremyfriend do not let me die I am so afraid of dying Iamsoafraid it will be OK I told him it will be OK do not do this he said do something do something dosomething dosomething it will be OK it will beOK who was I saying that to do something Eli dosomething I am soafraidofdying I am soafraid you know what they are going to do youaremyfriend I told him although I do not know why I said that at that moment and the guards put him in the synagogue with the rest of the Jews and everyone else was remaining outside to hear the cryingofthebabies and the cryingoftheadults and to see the black spark when the first match was lit by a youngman who could not have been any older than I was or Herschel was or you are it illuminated those who were not in the synagogue those who were not going to die and he cast it on the branches that were pushed against the synagogue what made it so awful was how it was soslow and how the fire made itself deadmanytimes and had to be remade I looked at Grandmother and shekissedmeontheforehead and I kissedheronthemouth and our tearsmixedonourlips and then I kissedyourfather many times I secured him from Grandmother's arms and Iheldhimwithmuchforce so much that he started crying I said I love you I love you I love you I love you I loveyou I loveyou I loveyou I loveyou Iloveyou Iloveyou Iloveyou Iloveyou Iloveyou IloveyouIloveyouIloveyouIloveyou and I knew that I had to change everything to leave everything behind and I knew that I could never allow him to learn of whoIwas or whatIdid because it was for him that I didwhatIdid it was for him that I pointed and for him that Herschel was murdered that I murdered Herschel and this is why he is how he is he is how is he because a father is always responsible for his son and I am I and Iamresponsible not for Herschel but for my son because I held him with somuchforcethathecried because I loved him so much that I madeloveimpossible and I am sorry for you and sorry for Iggy and it is you who must forgive me he said these things to us and Jonathan where do we go now what do we do with what we know Grandfather said that I am I but this could not be true the truth is that I also pointedatHerschel and I also said heisaJew and I will tell you that you also pointedatHerschel and you also said heisaJew and more than that Grandfather also pointedatme and said heisaJew and you also pointedathim and said heisaJew and your grandmother and Little Igor and we all pointedateachother so what is it he should have done hewouldhavebeenafooltodoanythingelse but is it forgivable what he did canheeverbeforgiven for his finger for whathisfingerdid for whathepointedto and didnotpointto for whathetouchedinhislife and whathedidnottouch he is stillguilty I am I am Iam IamI?)

"And now," he said, "we must make sleep."

THE WEDDING RECEPTION WAS SO EXTRAORDINARY!

or

THE END OF THE MOMENT THAT NEVER ENDS, 1941

AFTER THOROUGHLY satisfying the sister of the bride against a wall of empty wine racks—*Oh, God!* she screamed, *Oh, God!* her hands in the phantom Cabernet—and being himself so thoroughly unsatisfied, Safran pulled up his trousers, climbed the newly installed spiral staircase —brushing his hand deliberately, thoughtfully along the marble newel —and greeted the wedding guests, who were only then seating themselves after the haunting gust.

Where were you? Zosha asked, taking his dead hand into hers, something she had wanted to do since first seeing it at the announcement of their engagement more than half a year before.

Downstairs, changing.

Oh, I don't want you to change, she said, thinking she was making a good joke. *I think you're perfect.*

My clothes.

But it took you so long.

He nodded at his arm and watched her questioning lips pucker into a small peck for his cheek.

The Double House was brimming with organized pandemonium. Even up to the last minute, even past the last minute, hangings were still being hung, salads mixed, girdles clenched and tied, chandeliers dusted, throw rugs thrown...It was extraordinary.

The bride must be so happy for her mother.

I always cry at wedding receptions, but this one's gonna make me wail.

It's extraordinary. It's extraordinary.

The dark women in white uniforms were just beginning to serve bowls of chicken soup when Menachem clinked a fork against his glass and said, *I'd like to have a moment of your time.* The room quickly became silent, everyone stood—as was traditional for the toast of the father of the bride—and my grandfather recognized, out of the corner of his eye, the caramel hand that slid his bowl in front of him.

It's said that the times are changing. Borders around us shift under the pressure of the war; places we have known for as long as we can remember are called by new names; some of our own sons are absent from this joyous occasion because of their national service; and, on a brighter note, we are pleased to announce that we will have delivered to us in three months the first automobile in Trachimbrod! (This was met by a collective gasp and then raging applause.) *Well,* he said, moving behind the newlyweds to put one hand on his daughter's shoulder and one on my grandfather's, *let me keep this moment, this early afternoon, June 18, 1941.*

The Gypsy girl never said a word—because even if she hated Zosha, she didn't want to ruin her wedding—but pressed against my grandfather's left side, and took, under the table, his good hand into hers. (Did she even slide a note into it?)

Let me wear it in a locket over my heart, the proud father continued, pacing the room with his empty crystal goblet held in front of him, *and keep it forever, because I have never been so happy in my life, and will be perfectly content if I never experience half of this happiness again — until the wedding of my other daughter, of course. Indeed,* he said, hemming the laughter, *if there are to be no other moments for the rest of time, I would never once complain. Let this be the moment that never ends.*

My grandfather squeezed the Gypsy girl's fingers, as if to say, *It's not too late. There is still time. We could run, leave everything behind, never look back, save ourselves.*

She squeezed his fingers, as if to say, *You are not forgiven.*

Menachem continued, trying to hold back tears, *Please raise your empty glasses with me. To my daughter and new son, to the children they will produce, and the children of those children, to life!*

L'chaim! echoed voices down the line of tables.

But before the father of the bride had taken his seat, before the glasses had a chance to clink their reflected smiles against one another in hope, the house was again swept with a haunting gust. The place cards were again thrown into the air, and the floral centerpieces were again knocked over, this time spreading dirt over the white tablecloth and onto almost every lap. The Gypsy women rushed to clean up the mess, and my grandfather whispered into Zosha's ear, which for him was the Gypsy girl's ear: *It will be OK.*

The Gypsy girl, the *real* Gypsy girl, did slip my grandfather a note, although it fell out of his hand in the commotion and was kicked across the floor—by Libby, by Lista, by Omeler, by the nameless fishmonger —to the far end of the table, where it came to rest under an overturned wine glass, which kept it safe under its skirt until that night, when a Gypsy woman picked up the glass and swept the note (along with fallen food, dirt from the centerpieces, and piles of dust) into a large paper bag. This bag was put out in front of the house by a different Gypsy woman. The next morning, the paper bag was collected by the obsessive-compulsive garbage man Feigel B. The bag was then taken to a field on the other side of the river—the field that would, soon enough, be the site of Kovel's first mass execution—and burned with dozens of other bags, three quarters of which contained debris from the wedding. The flames reached into the sky, red and yellow fingers. The smoke spread like a canopy over the neighboring fields, making many a Wisp of Ardisht cough, because every kind of smoke is different and must be made familiar. Some of the ash that remained was incorporated into the soil. The rest was washed away by the next rain and swept into the Brod.

This is what the note said: *Change.*

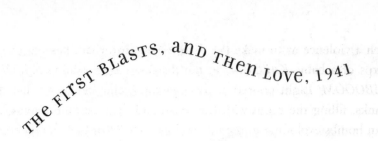

THE FIRST BLASTS, and THEN LOVE, 1941

THAT NIGHT, my grandfather made love to his new wife for the first time. He thought, as he performed the act that he had practiced to perfection, about the Gypsy girl: he reweighed the arguments for running away with her, for leaving Trachimbrod with the knowledge that he could never go back. He did love his family—his mother, anyway—but how long would it take before he stopped missing them? It sounded so terrible when articulated, but, he wondered, was there anything he couldn't leave behind? He entertained thoughts so ugly and true: everyone but the Gypsy girl and his mother could die and he would be able to go on; every aspect of his life, save his time with the Gypsy girl and his mother, was insufficient and undeserving of life. He was about to become someone who has lost half of everything he lived for.

He thought about the various widows of his past seven years: Golda R and her covered mirrors, Lista P's blood, which was not intended for him. He thought about all of the virgins that summed to nothing. He thought, easing his new wife's nervous virgin body onto the marriage bed, about Brod, author of the 613 sadnesses, and Yankel, with his abacus bead. He thought, while explaining to Zosha that it would only hurt the first time, about Zosha, whom he hardly knew, and her sister, who made him promise that their postnuptial tryst would not be a one-time occurrence. He thought about the legend of Trachim, about where his body might be, and from where it once came. He thought about Trachim's wagon: the wandering snakes of white string, the crushed-velvet glove with outstretched fingers, the resolution: *I will...I will...*

And then something extraordinary happened. The house shook with such a violence as to make the day's earlier disturbances seem like the burps of a baby. *KABOOM!* in the distance. Approaching *KABOOM! KABOOOM!* Light poured in through the cracks between cellar door planks, filling the room with the warm and dynamic radiance of German bombs exploding in the nearby hills. *KABOOOOM!* Zosha howled in fear—of physical love, of war, of emotional love, of dying—and my grandfather was filled with a coital energy of such force that when it unleashed itself—*KA-BOOOOOOOOOOOOOM! KA-BOO-BOOOOOOOOOOOOOOOOOOOOOOOOOOOOOOOOOOM! KA-KA-KA-KA-KA-KA-BOOOOOOOOOOOOOOOOOOOOOOOOOOOOM!*— when he tripped over the precipice of civilized humanity into the free fall of unadulterated animal rapture, when, in seven eternal seconds, he more than made up for the sum of what was now more than 2,700 acts without consequence, when he flooded Zosha with a deluge of what could no longer be held back, when he released into the universe a copulative light so powerful that if it could have been harnessed and utilized, rather than sent forth and wasted, the Germans wouldn't have had a chance, he wondered if one of the bombs hadn't landed on the marriage bed, wedged itself between the shuddering body of his new wife and his own, and obliterated Trachimbrod. But when he hit the rocky canyon's floor, when the seven seconds of bombing ended and his head settled into the pillow damp with Zosha's tears and drenched with his semen, he understood that he was not dead, but in love.

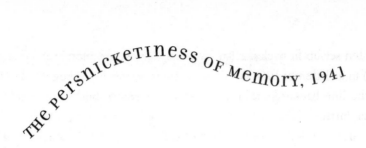

THE PERSNICKETINESS OF MEMORY, 1941

JUST AS my grandfather's first orgasm was not intended for Zosha, the bombs that inspired it were not intended for Trachimbrod but a site in the Rovno hills. It would be nine months—on Trachimday, no less—before the shtetl was the focus of direct Nazi assault. But the Brod's waters roiled onto its banks that night with the same fervor as if it had been war, the wind snapped in the explosive wake with the same resonance, and the shtetl folk trembled as if the sites were tattooed on their bodies. From that moment on—9:28 in the evening, June 18, 1941—everything was different.

The Wisps of Ardisht turned their cigarettes backward, cupping their mouths around the lit ends to prevent their being spotted from a distance.

The Gypsies in their hamlet took down their tents, dismantled their thatch shanties, and lived uncovered, clinging to the earth like human moss.

Trachimbrod itself was overcome with a strange inertness. The citizenry, which once touched so many things it was impossible to know what was natural, now sat on their hands. Activity was replaced with thought. Memory. Everything reminded everyone of something, which seemed winsome at first—when early birthdays could be recalled by the smell of an extinguished match, or the feeling of one's first kiss by sweat in the palm—but quickly became devitalizing. Memory begat memory begat memory. Villagers became embodiments of that legend they had been told so many times, of mad Sofiowka, swaddled in white string, using memory to remember memory, bound in an order of remembrance, struggling in vain to remember a beginning or end.

Men set up flow charts (which were themselves memories of family trees) in an attempt to make sense of their memories. They tried to follow the line back, like Theseus out of the labyrinth, but only went in deeper, farther.

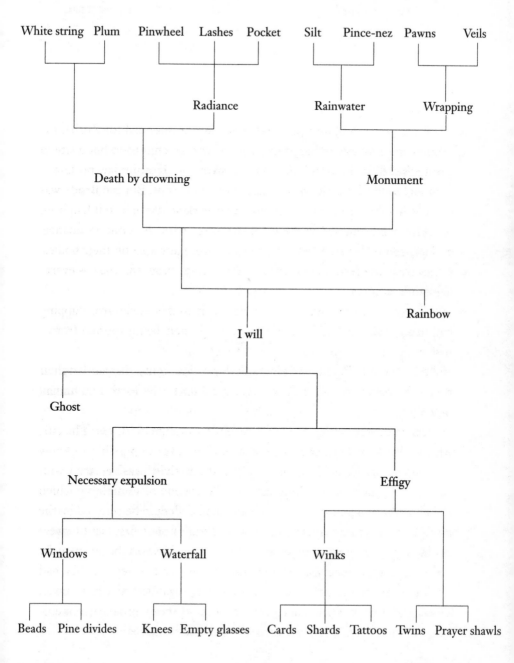

Women had it worse. Unable to share their tinglings of memory in the synagogue or at the workplace, they were forced to suffer over laundry piles and baking pans, alone. There was no help in their searches for beginnings, no one to ask what the grit of pressed raspberries might have to do with a steam burn, or why the sound of children playing in the Brod made their hearts drop out of their chests and onto the floor. Memory was supposed to fill the time, but it made time a hole to be filled. Each second was two hundred yards, to be walked, crawled. You couldn't see the next hour, it was so far in the distance. Tomorrow was over the horizon, and would take an entire day to reach.

But children had it worst of all, for although it would seem that they had fewer memories to haunt them, they still had the itch of memory as strong as the elders of the shtetl. Their strings were not even their own, but tied around them by parents and grandparents — strings not fastened to anything, but hanging loosely from the darkness.

The only thing more painful than being an active forgetter is to be an inert rememberer. Safran lay in bed trying to string the events of his seventeen years into a coherent narrative, something that he could understand, with an order of imagery, an intelligibility of symbolism. Where were the symmetries? The rifts? What was the meaning of what had happened? He had been born with teeth, and that's why his mother had stopped breastfeeding him, and that's why his arm had gone dead, and that's why women loved him, and that's why he did what he did, and that's why he was who he was. But why was he born with teeth? And why didn't his mother just express her milk into a bottle? And why did an arm go dead instead of a leg? And why would anyone love a dead limb? And why did he do what he did? Why was he who he was?

He couldn't concentrate. His love had overtaken him from the inside out, like a sickness. He became terribly constipated, nauseated, and weak. In the reflection of the new porcelain toilet's water, he saw a face he didn't recognize: sagging jowls with white whiskers, pouches under his eyes (which must, he reasoned, hold all of the tears of joy that he wasn't crying), cracking, fattening lips.

But it wasn't the same recognition as the previous morning, when he saw his face in the Dial's glass eyes. He wasn't becoming older as part of some natural process, but being made old as a victim of his love, which was itself only one day old. He was a boy still, but no longer a boy. A man, but not yet a man. He was caught somewhere between his mother's last kiss and the first kiss he would give his child, between the war that was and would be.

A shtetl meeting was held in the theater the morning after the bombs exploded—the first since the debate over electric lighting several years before—to discuss the implications of a war whose tracks seemed to be laid directly over Trachimbrod.

RAV D

(Holding a sheet of paper above his head.) I have read in a letter from my son, who is fighting bravely on the Polish front, that the Nazis are committing unspeakable atrocities and that Trachimbrod should prepare for the worst. He said we should *(looks at paper, gestures reading)* "do anything and everything immediately."

ARI F

What are you talking about! We should go to the Nazis! *(Calling out, waving a finger above his head.)* It's the Ukrainians who'll do us in! You've heard what they did in Lvov! (It reminds me of my birth [I was born on the Rabbi's floor, you know (my nose still remembers that mix of placenta and Judaica [he had the most beautiful candle holders (from Austria [if I'm not mistaken (or Germany)])])]) . . .

RAV D

(Puzzled, gesturing puzzlement.) What are you talking about?

ARI F

(Most sincerely puzzled.) I can't remember. The Ukrainians. My birth. Candles. I know there was a point. Where did I begin?

And so it was when anyone tried to speak: their minds would become tangled in remembrance. Words became floods of thought with no beginning or end, and would drown the speaker before he could reach the life raft of the point he was trying to make. It was impossible to remember what one meant, what, after all of the words, was intended.

They had been terrified at first. Shtetl meetings were held daily, news reports (NAZIS KILL 8,200 ON UKRAINIAN BORDER) examined with the care of editors, plans of action drawn up and crumpled up, large maps spread out on tables like patients waiting to be cut open. But then the meetings convened every other day, and then every other every other day, and then weekly, serving more as social minglers for singles than planning sessions. After only two months, without the impetus of any further bombing, most Trachimbroders had removed all of the splinters of the terror that had entered them that night.

They hadn't forgotten, but accommodated. Memory took the place of terror. In their efforts to remember what it was they were trying so hard to remember, they could finally think over the fear of war. The memories of birth, childhood, and adolescence resonated with greater volume than the din of exploding shells.

So nothing was done. No decisions were made. No bags packed or houses emptied. No trenches dug or buildings fortified. Nothing. They waited like fools, they sat on their hands like fools, and spoke, like fools, about the time Simon D did that hilarious thing with the plum, which all could laugh about for hours but none could quite remember. They waited to die, and we cannot blame them, because we would do the same, and we *do* do the same. They laughed and joked. They thought about birthday candles and waited to die, and we must forgive them. They wrapped Menachem's jumbo trout in newspaper (NAZIS APPROACH LUTSK) and carried beef briskets in wicker baskets to picnics under tall tree canopies by the small falls.

Bedridden since his orgasm, my grandfather was unable to attend the first shtetl meeting. Zosha handled hers with more dignity, perhaps because she didn't have one at all, or perhaps because even though she loved being a married woman, and loved to touch that dead arm, she had yet to fall in love. She changed the semen-starched sheets, made her new husband toast and coffee for breakfast, and brought him a plate of left-over wedding chicken for lunch.

What is it? she asked, seating herself on the end of the bed. *Did I do something wrong? Are you unhappy with me?* My grandfather remembered that she was only a child: fifteen, and younger than her years. She had experienced nothing compared to him. She had felt nothing.

I am happy, he said.

I can wear my hair in a ponytail if you think that would make me more pretty.

You're pretty as you are. Really.

And last night. Did I please you? I will learn. I'm sure I will.

You were wonderful, he said. *I'm just not feeling well. It's nothing with you. Everything with you is wonderful.*

She kissed him on the lips and said, *I am your wife,* as if to reaffirm her vows, or remind herself, or him.

That night, when he had recovered enough strength to wash and dress, he returned to the Dial for the second time in two days. It was quite a different scene. Stark. Empty. Without yoidle-doidling. The shtetl square was still caked with white flour, although a rain had swept it into the spaces between cobblestones, replacing the sheet with an intricate network. Most of the banners of the previous day's festivities had been taken down, but a few remained, draped from the sills of high windows.

Great-great-great-grandfather, he said, lowering himself (with great difficulty) to his knees, *I feel that I ask for so little.*

In the sense that you never come to talk to me, the Dial said (with the unmoving lips of a ventriloquist), *what you say is true. You never write, you never —*

I haven't ever wanted to burden you.

I haven't ever wanted to burden you.

But you have, great-great-great-grandfather. You have. See my face, with its sag and give. I look four times my age. I have this dead arm, this war, this problem with memory. And now I am in love.

What makes you think I have anything to do with this?

I am a dupe of chance.

The Gypsy girl. What ever became of her? She was nice.

What?

The Gypsy girl? The one you loved.

It's not her that I love. It's my girl. My girl.

Oh, the Dial said, letting his *Oh* fall to the cobblestones and settle into the flour in the cracks before continuing. *You love the baby in Zosha's belly. The others are being pulled back, and you're being pulled forward.*

In both directions! he said, seeing the wagon's refuse, the words on Brod's body, the pogroms, the weddings, the suicides, the makeshift cribs, the parades, and seeing also his possible futures: life with the Gypsy girl, life alone, life with Zosha and the child who would fulfill him, the end of life. The images of his infinite pasts and infinite futures washed over him as he waited, paralyzed, in the present. He, Safran, marked the division between what was and what would be.

And what is it that you want from me? the Dial asked.

Make her healthy. Let her be born without sickness, without blindness, weak heart, or dead limbs. Let her be perfect.

Hush, and then: Safran retched his morning's toast and midafternoon's leftovers onto the Dial's rigid feet in a chunky pool of yellows and browns.

At least I didn't step in it, the Dial said.

You see! Safran pleaded, barely able to support his kneeling body. *This is what it's like!*

What what's like?

Love.

What?

Love, Safran said. *This is what it's like.*

Do you know that after my accident your great-great-great-grandmother would enter my room at night?

What?

She would get in bed with me, God bless her soul, knowing that I would attack her. We were supposed to sleep in separate rooms, but every night she'd come to be with me.

I don't understand.

Every morning, she'd clean me of my excrement, bathe me, dress me, and see that my hair was combed like a sane man's, even when it meant an elbow to the nose or a broken rib. She polished the blade. She wore my teeth marks on her body like other wives might wear jewelry. The hole didn't matter. We paid it no attention. We shared a room. She was with me. She did all of those things and so many more, things I would never tell anyone, and she never even loved me. Now that's love.

Let me tell you a story, the Dial went on. *The house that your great-great-great-grandmother and I moved into when we first became married looked out onto the small falls, at the end of the Jewish/Human fault line. It had wood floors, long windows, and enough room for a large family. It was a handsome house. A good house.*

But the water, your great-great-great-grandmother said, I can't hear myself think.

Time, I urged her. Give it time.

And let me tell you, while the house was unreasonably humid, and the front lawn perpetual mud from all the spray, while the walls needed to be repapered every six months, and chips of paint fell from the ceiling like snow for all seasons, what they say about people who live next to waterfalls is true.

What, my grandfather asked, *do they say?*

They say that people who live next to waterfalls don't hear the water.

They say that?

They do. Of course, your great-great-great-grandmother was right. It was terrible at first. We couldn't stand to be in the house for more than a few hours at a time. The first two weeks were filled with nights of intermittent sleep and quarreling for the sake of being heard over the water. We fought so much just to remind ourselves that we were in love, and not in hate.

But the next weeks were a little better. It was possible to sleep a few good hours each night and eat in only mild discomfort. Your great-great-great-grandmother still cursed the water (whose personification had become anatomically refined), but less frequently, and with less fury. Her attacks on me also quieted. It's your fault, she would say. You wanted to live here.

Life continued, as life continues, and time passed, as time passes, and after a little more than two months: Do you hear that? I asked her on one of the rare mornings we sat at the table together. Hear it? I put down my coffee and rose from my chair. You hear that thing?

What thing? she asked.

Exactly! I said, running outside to pump my fist at the waterfall. Exactly!

We danced, throwing handfuls of water in the air, hearing nothing at all. We alternated hugs of forgiveness and shouts of human triumph at the water. Who wins the day? Who wins the day, waterfall? We do! We do!

And this is what living next to a waterfall is like, Safran. Every widow wakes one morning, perhaps after years of pure and unwavering grieving, to re-alize she slept a good night's sleep, and will be able to eat breakfast, and doesn't hear her husband's ghost all the time, but only some of the time. Her grief is re-placed with a useful sadness. Every parent who loses a child finds a way to laugh again. The timbre begins to fade. The edge dulls. The hurt lessens. Every love is carved from loss. Mine was. Yours is. Your great-great-great-grandchildren's will be. But we learn to live in that love.

My grandfather nodded his head, as if he understood.

But it's not the entire story, the Dial continued. *I realized this when I first tried to whisper a secret and couldn't, or whistle a tune without instilling fear in the hearts of those within a hundred yards, when my coworkers at the flour mill pleaded with me to lower my voice, because, Who can think with you shouting like that? To which I asked, AM I REALLY SHOUTING?*

Hush, and then: sky obscuring, the curtains of clouds parting, the hands of thunder clapping. The universe poured down in a bombing on-slaught of heavenly vomit.

Those still awake and outside ran for cover. The traveling journalist Shakel R held the *Lvov Daily Observed* (NAZIS MOVE EAST) over his head. The famous visiting playwright Bunim W, whose tragicomic ren-dition of the Trachim story—*Trachim!*—was met with popular enthusi-asm and critical indifference, jumped into the Brod to avoid being hit. The divine hurl fell from the firmament in newborn-sized chunks at first, then sheets, soaking Trachimbrod to its foundations, turning the Brod waters orange, filling the prostrate mermaid's dry fountain to its lip, filling the cracks of the synagogue's crumbling portico, glazing the poplars, drowning small insects, making drunk with pleasure the rats and vultures by the riverbank.

THE BEGINNING OF THE WORLD OFTEN comes, 1942–1791

CANOPIES OF THIN WHITE STRING spanned the narrow cobbled arteries of Trachimbrod that afternoon, March 18, 1942, as they had every Trachimday for one hundred fifty years. It had been the good gefiltefishmonger Bitzl Bitzl R's idea, to commemorate the first of the wagon's refuse to surface. One end of white string tied around the volume knob of a radio (NAZIS ENTER UKRAINE, MOVE EAST WITH SPEED) on the wobbly bookcase in Benjamin T's one-room shanty, the other around an empty silver candle holder on the dining room table of the More-or-Less-Respected Rabbi's brick house across muddy Shelister Street; thin white string like a clothesline from the light-boom stand of Trachimbrod's first and only photographer to the middle-C hammer of the darling of Zeinvel Z's piano shop on the other side of Malkner Street; white string connecting freelance journalist (GERMANS PUSH ON, SENSING IMMINENT VICTORY) to electrician over the tranquil and anticipating palm of the River Brod; white string from the monument of Pinchas T (carved, perfectly realistically, of marble) to a Trachimbrod novel (about love) to the glass case of wandering snakes of white string (kept at 56 degrees in the Museum of True Folklore), forming a scalene triangle, reflected in the Dial's glass eyes in the middle of the shtetl square.

My grandfather and his very pregnant wife watched from a picnic blanket on their lawn as the floats began the parade. First, as was traditional, went the float from Rovno: skimpy, with wilted yellow butterflies immodestly covering the splintered pine of a fieldworker effigy, which didn't look good last year and looked even worse now. (The carcasses could be seen in the spaces between the wings.) Klezmer bands preceded the float from Kolki, which hobbled on the shoulders of middle-aged men, as the young men were on the front lines, and the horses were being used in a nearby coal mine to support the war effort.

OH! Zosha giggled loudly, unable to control her voice. *IT JUST GAVE ME A KICK!*

My grandfather put his ear against her belly and received a powerful knock to the head, lifting him off the ground, landing him on his back a few feet away.

THAT CHILD IS EXTRAORDINARY!

There were fewer handsome men assembled along the shoreline than any year since that first one when everything began, when Trachim did or did not get pinned under his wagon. The handsome men were away fighting a war whose ramifications no one had yet to understand, and no one would or will understand. Most of what was left for the contest were the cripples, and cowards who crippled themselves—broke a hand, burnt an eye, feigned deafness or blindness—in order to dodge conscription. It was a contest of cripples and cowards, diving for a sack of gold that was a sack of fool's gold. They were trying to believe that life was as usual, healthy, that tradition could plug the leaks, that joy was still possible.

The floats and marchers made their way from the river's mouth to the toy and pastry stands set up by the rusting plaque commemorating where the wagon did or didn't flip and sink:

THIS PLAQUE MARKS THE SPOT
(OR A SPOT CLOSE TO THE SPOT)
WHERE THE WAGON OF ONE
TRACHIM B
(WE THINK)
WENT IN.

Shtetl Proclamation, 1791

As the first floats passed the More-or-Less-Respected Rabbi's window (from which he gave the necessary nod of approval), men in green-gray uniforms were being killed in shallow trenches.

Lutsk, Sarny, Kovel. Their floats were adorned with thousands of butterflies, and alluded to aspects of the Trachim story: the wagon, the twins, the umbrella ribs and skeleton keys, the bleeding red-ink script: *I will...I will...* In another place, their sons were killed between the barbs of their own guard wire, killed with misfired bombs while squirming in the mire like animals, killed with friendly fire, killed sometimes without knowing that they were about to die—a bullet through the head while joking with a comrade, laughing.

Lvov, Pinsk, Kivertsy. Their floats were marched along the Brod's bank, adorned in red, brown, and purple butterflies, showing their carcasses like ugly truths. (And here it is becoming harder and harder not to yell: *GO AWAY! RUN WHILE YOU CAN, FOOLS! RUN FOR YOUR LIVES!*) The bands bellowed, trumpets and violins, pocket trumpets and violas, homemade wax-paper kazoos.

ANOTHER KICK! Zosha laughed. *ANOTHER!*

And again my grandfather put his ear to her belly (having to get on his knees just to reach its crest), and again he was thumped backward.

THAT'S MY BABY! he hollered, his right eye absorbing the bruise like a sponge.

The Trachimbrod float was covered with black and blue butterflies. The daughter of the electrician Berl G sat on a raised platform in the middle of the float, wearing a blue neon tiara whose power cord reached back hundreds of yards to the outlet above her bed. (She had planned to recoil it as she traced her way back home when the parade was over.) The Float Queen was surrounded by the young float princesses of the shtetl, dressed in blue lace, waving their arms about like waves. A quartet of fiddlers played Polish national songs from a stand in the front of the float, and another played Ukrainian traditionals from the back.

On the banks, men sitting in wooden chairs reminisced about old loves, and girls never kissed, and books never read and written, and the time So-and-So did that funny thing with the what's-it-called, and injuries, and dinners, and how they would have washed the hair of women they never met, and apologies, and whether Trachim was or was not pinned under his wagon after all.

The earth turned in the sky.

Yankel turned in the earth.

The prehistoric ant on Yankel's thumb, which had lain motionless in the honey-colored stone since Brod's curious birth, turned away from the sky and hid its head between its many legs, in shame.

My grandfather and his young, tremendously pregnant wife walked up to the shore to watch the dive.

(Here it is almost impossible to go on, because we know what happens, and wonder why they don't. Or it's impossible because we fear that they do.)

When the Trachimbrod float reached the toy and pastry stands, the Float Queen was given the signal by the Rabbi to throw the sacks into the water. Mouths opened. Hands were separated—the first halves of applause. Blood flowed through bodies. It was almost like old times. This was celebration, unmitigated by imminent death. This was imminent death, unmitigated by celebration. She threw them high into the air. . . . . They stayed there . . . . They hung as if on strings . . . .

. . . .
. . . .
. . . .

. . . The Dial tiptoed across the cobblestones like a chess piece and hid himself under the breasts of the prostrate mermaid. . . . .
. . . .
. . . .
. . . .
. . . .
. . . .
. . . .
. . . .
. . . .
. . . .

. . . . There is still time. . . . . . .
. . . .
. . . .
. . . .
. . . .
. . . .
. . . .
. . . .
. . . .
. . . .
. . . .
. . . .
. . . .
. . . .
. . . .
. . . .
. . . .
. . . .
. . . .

After the bombing was over, the Nazis moved through the shtetl. They lined up everyone who didn't drown in the river. They unrolled a Torah in front of them. "Spit," they said. "Spit, or else." Then they put all of the Jews in the synagogue. (It was the same in every shtetl. It happened hundreds of times. It happened in Kovel only a few hours before, and would happen in Kolki in only a few hours.) A young soldier tossed the nine volumes of *The Book of Recurrent Dreams* onto the bonfire of Jews, not noticing, in his haste to grab and destroy more, that one of the pages fell out of one of the books and descended, coming to rest like a veil on a child's burnt face:

9:613 — *The dream of the end of the world.* bombs poured down from the sky exploding across trachimbrod in bursts of light and heat those watching the festivities hollered ran frantically they jumped into the bubbling splashing frantically dynamic water not after the sack of gold but to save themselves they stayed under as long as they could they surfaced to seize air and look for loved ones my safran picked up his wife and carried her like a newlywed into the water which seemed amid the falling trees and hackling crackling explosions the safest place hundreds of bodies poured into the brod that river with my name I embraced them with open arms come to me come I wanted to save them all to save everybody from everybody the bombs rained from the sky and it was not the explosions or scattering shrapnel that would be our death not the heckling cinders not the laughing debris but all of the bodies bodies flailing and grabbing hold of one another bodies looking for something to hold on to my safran lost sight of his wife who was carried deeper into me by the pull of the bodies

the silent shrieks were carried in bubbles to the surface where they popped
PLEASE PLEASE PLEASE PLEASE
the kicking in zosha's belly became more
and more PLEASE PLEASE the baby refused to die like this PLEASE the bombs
came down cackling smoldering and my
safran was able to break free from the
human mass and float downstream over
the small falls to clearer waters zosha was
pulled down PLEASE and the baby refus-
ing to die like this was pulled up and out
of her body turning the waters around
her red she surfaced like a bubble to the
light to oxygen to life to life WAWAWA-
WAWAWA she cried she was perfectly
healthy and she would have lived except
for the umbilical cord that pulled her back
under toward her mother who was barely
conscious but conscious of the cord and
tried to break it with her hands and then
bite it with her teeth but could not it
would not be broken and she died with
her perfectly healthy nameless baby in her
arms she held it to her chest the crowd
pulled itself into itself long after the
bombing ceased the confused the frightened the desperate mass of babies children teenagers adults elderly all pulled at
each other to survive but pulled each
other into me drowning each other killing
each other the bodies began to rise one at
a time until I couldn't be seen through all
of the bodies blue skin open white eyes I
was invisible under them I was the carcass
they were the butterflies white eyes blue
skin this is what we've done we've killed
our own babies to save them

Dear Jonathan,

    If you are reading this, it is because Sasha found it and translated it for you. It means that I am dead, and that Sasha is alive.

    I do not know if Sasha will tell you what has happened here tonight, and what is about to happen. It is important that you know what kind of man he is, so I will tell you here.

    This is what happened. He told his father that he could care for Mother and Little Igor. It took his saying it to make it true. Finally, he was ready. His father could not believe this thing. What? he asked. What? And Sasha told him again that he would take care of the family, that he would understand if his father had to leave and never return, and that it would not even make him less of a father. He told his father that he would forgive. Oh, his father became so angry, so full of wrath, and he told Sasha that he would kill him, and Sasha told his father that he would kill him, and they moved at each other with violence and his father said, Say it to my face, not to the floor, and Sasha said, You are not my father.

    His father raised himself and removed a bag from the cabinet under the sink. He filled the bag with things from the kitchen, with bread, bottles of vodka, cheese. Here, Sasha said, and he took from the cookie jar two handfuls of money. His father asked where the money was from and Sasha told him to take it and never return. His father said, I do not need your money. Sasha said, It is not a gift. It is payment for everything that you will leave behind. Take it and never return.

    Say it into my eyes and I promise you I will.

    Take it, Sasha said, and never return.

274

Mother and Iggy were so upset. Iggy told Sasha how stupid he was, how he ruined everything. He cried all night, and do you know what it is like to hear Iggy cry all night? But he is so young. I hope that he will one day be able to understand what Sasha did, and forgive him, and also thank him.

I spoke with Sasha tonight, after his father left, and I told him that I was proud of him. I told him that I had never been so proud, or so certain of who he was.

But Father is your son, he said. And he is my father.

I said, You are a good man, and you have done the good thing.

I put my hand on his cheek and remembered when my cheek was like his cheek. I said his name, Alex, which has also been my name for forty years.

I will toil at Heritage Touring, he said. I will fill Father's absence.

No, I told him.

It is a good job, he said, and I can make enough money to care for Mother and Little Igor and you.

No, I said. Make your own life. That is how you can best care for us.

I put him to bed, which I have not done for him since he was a child. I covered him in blankets, and combed his hair with my hand.

Try to live so that you can always tell the truth, I said.

I will, he said, and I believed in him, and that was enough.

Then I went to Iggy's room and he was already sleeping, but I kissed him on his forehead, and I said a blessing for him. I prayed in silence that he should be strong, and know goodness, and never know evil, and never know war.

And then I came here, to the television room, to write you this letter.

All is for Sasha and Iggy, Jonathan. Do you understand? I would give everything for them to live without violence. Peace. That is all that I would ever want for them. Not money and not even love. It is still possible. I know that now, and it is the cause of so much happiness in me. They must begin again. They must cut all of the strings, yes? With you (Sasha told me that you will not write to each other anymore), with their father (who is now gone forever), with everything they have known. Sasha has started it, and now I must finish it.

Everyone in the house is in bed but me. I am writing this in the lumi-nescence of the television, and I am so sorry if this is now difficult to read, Sasha, but my hand is shaking so much, and it is not out of weakness that I will go to the bath when I am sure that you are asleep, and it is not because I cannot endure. Do you understand? I am complete with happiness, and it is what I must do, and I will do it. Do you understand me? I will walk without noise, and I will open the door in darkness, and I will